More Praise for *The Fourteen Sisters of Emilio Montez O'Brien*

"Exuberant...Oscar Hijuelos 'gets it' all right, and he serves it up with surpassing joy."

—New York Times Book Review

"Reading *The Fourteen Sisters of Emilio Montez O'Brien* is like leafing through the pages of a treasured family album."

—Time

"A major work destined to take its rightful place in the literary world."

—Chicago Sun-Times

"Hijuelos's American baroque is joyous, ecstatic, with an indulgence in sensuality, in the pleasures of living, a densely textured, thickly detailed excursion, but with a unity of focus that carries the reader along."

—San Francisco Chronicle

"What emerges powerfully here...is the notion that happiness comes to us only in brief, unexpected moments."

—People

"Matchless, soaring prose.... Combines the exuberance of Gabriel García Márquez with the dogged genealogies of Oscar Lewis's *La Vida.*"

—Publishers Weekly

"Hijuelos's stories have such soul.... [The Montez O'Briens] hold us captive until the very last page of this generous novel.... Once in a great while a novelist emerges who is remarkable...for the precision of his gauge on the rising sensibilities of his time. Oscar Hijuelos is one of these."

—Tampa Tribune-Times

The Fourteen Sisters
of Emilio Montez O'Brien

THE FOURTEEN SISTERS OF EMILIO MONTEZ O'BRIEN

A NOVEL BY

OSCAR HIJUELOS

HarperPerennial

A Division of HarperCollins*Publishers*

The author gratefully thanks the John Simon Guggenheim Memorial Foundation for support during the writing of this novel.

This book was originally published in 1993 by Farrar, Straus and Giroux. It is here reprinted by arrangement with Farrar, Straus and Giroux. A paperback edition was published in 1994 by HarperPaperbacks, a division of HarperCollins Publishers.

HarperCollins books may be purchased for educational, business, or sales promotion use. For information please write: Special Markets Department, HarperCollins Publishers, Inc., 10 East 53rd Street, New York, NY 10022.

First HarperPerennial edition published 1996.

ISBN 0-06-097594-6

99 00 RRD 10 9 8 7 6 5 4

For Lori Carlson

Contents

The Fourteen Sisters of Emilio Montez O'Brien

NELSON O'BRIEN = MARIELA MONTEZ

MARGARITA	*b.* 1902
ISABEL	*b.* 1904
MARIA	*b.* 1906
OLGA *and*	
JACQUELINE	*b.* 1908
HELEN	*b.* 1910
IRENE	*b.* 1911
SARAH	*b.* 1912
PATRICIA	
(who lived)	*b.* 1914
VERONICA	*b.* 1916
MARTA	*b.* 1917
CARMEN	*b.* 1919
VIOLETA	*b.* 1921
GLORIA	*b.* 1923
EMILIO	*b.* 1925

A lot of people wrongly discount the quality of photographs produced by the type of camera I use, mainly because it is bulky and inconvenient to move. You have to fiddle with plates and chemicals and make sure that your subjects do not wriggle around or blink as they pose, for with this camera they must remain still. And some people don't have the patience. But that's a lazy outlook. Not to take anything away from the Kodak Brownie, mind you—it makes pictures nice enough to frame, but this apparatus, in my opinion, captures not only the superficial qualities of its subjects but also, because of the time it takes to properly collect light, their feelings, as they settle on the subjects' expressions; sadness and joy and worry, with variations therein, are collected on the plate.

—NELSON O'BRIEN *to his son,* EMILIO, *while explaining his preference for his archaic folding-bellows-type camera, with Thorton-Pickard shutter, in 1937*

The Fourteen Sisters
of Emilio Montez O'Brien

The Handsome Man from Heaven

THE HOUSE in which the fourteen sisters of Emilio Montez
O'Brien lived, radiated femininity. Men who passed by the white
picket fence—the postman, the rag seller, the iceman—were
sometimes startled by a strong scent of flowers, as if perfume
had been poured onto the floorboards and ground. And when
the door to the house—a rickety, many-roomed Victorian affair
some few miles outside the small Pennsylvania town of Cobbleton, with teetering beams and rain-soaked clapboard façade (and
with gables, rusted hinges, and a fetid outhouse on a foundation
that tended to creak during heavy rains, a roof that leaked, surfaces splintering everywhere)—when their door opened on the
world, the power of these females, even the smallest infants,
nearly molecular in its adamancy, slipped out and had its trans-
forming effect upon men. Over the years a thick maple tree,
standing out in the yard, had been the scene of numerous ac-
cidents: men were thrown from their horses or, begoggled and
yet blinded by what they may have taken as the sun, skidded
their Model Ts, their Packards, their sporty sedans off the road
into a ditch, axles bent and crankcases hissing steam.

Even their Irish father, Nelson O'Brien, photographer and
the owner of the Jewel Box Movie Theater in town, sometimes
noticed the effects of their feminine influence on himself: this

gentleman would move through the rooms of the house feeling a sense of elation and love that sometimes startled him; on other days, he had the air of a lost sailor looking out toward the edges of the sea. Struggling with his thoughts, he'd try to understand just what his pretty girls were thinking, and he, a brooding man, aware of life's troubles, did not know what to make of their gaiety. Sometimes, when his daughters were gathered in the parlor, he would walk by them slowly, as if passing through a corridor thick with silk curtains that had been warmed in the sun. And he would find himself sitting on the couch with one of his little daughters on his lap, playing a silly game like "smack-your-Poppy-on-the-nose," or easily spend a half hour trying to teach baby a single word like "apple," repeating it until he would pull from his jacket pocket a watch on a chain and, noticing the time, make his way out into the world to work, leaving his quivering, exuberant daughters behind. And they would call out to him or follow him to the door, and when he got into his Model T to drive into town or along the country roads to some job, they would gather on the porch, waving goodbye to their father, who at such moments would experience a pleasant befuddlement.

Once, around 1921, when Margarita Montez O'Brien, the oldest of the sisters, was nineteen, an aviator brought down his biplane, a Sopwith Camel, in a hayfield about a quarter of a mile west of the house, a dizziness having come over him just as his plane was passing overhead, as if caught in a sirenic beam of influence that flowed upward from the parlor, where the sisters happened to have gathered in chaotic preparation for a midday meal. He had been flying west over the fields of grazing cattle and sheep, silos, barns, and farmhouses, a banner advertising the Daredevils' Flying Circus trailing behind him, when they heard his engine sputtering, the propeller jamming in the distance, and out their window they watched him drop down through the clouds, his craft much like a falling and sometimes spinning cross. And because they hadn't seen very many airplanes in their lives, they had rushed outside to their porch, along with everybody else in that part of the countryside.

At that time of the day, some of them were sitting around

on couches, studying their schoolbooks, yawning, laughing, sewing, while others were stretched out on the rug before the fireplace, trying to contact the spirits with a Ouija board or playing rummy or Go Fish, good American card games. Still others were in the kitchen helping their mother (hers was the voice that, sighing, one heard every now and then as she would cross a room). And the twins were practicing—Olga playing the piano, Jacqueline the violin, and the third of the musical sisters, Maria, singing, everything from "I'd Rather Love What I Cannot Have Than Have What I Cannot Love" to "The Sheik of Araby" (or, as a joke, to announce the arrival of their father, "Ta-Ra-Ra-Boom-Dee-Ay"). And others were scavenging for chairs, preparing the children's table for the toddlers and pulling the long oak table, with animal feet and lion knobs with brass rings through their noses, away from the wall and setting each place with its proper utensils, plates, and glasses—all this work for a single meal, momentous.

There were thirteen sisters then—counting little Violeta, four months old, who had been born in February of that year, colicky and quite adept at waking the house up in the middle of the night, when she'd scream out for her tired Cuban mother's milk; and excluding the fourteenth sister, Gloria, who would be born in 1923. The oldest of the sisters, Margarita—or Meg, as her Irish father called her—had been born aboard a ship bound from Cuba to the United States in 1902. Then coming into the world with a scowl, Isabel had been born in 1904, in that very house, like the others, and was named after the queen who had ruled Spain at the time of Columbus. And then Maria, the third of the sisters, was born in 1906, Maria whose effortless and nearly weightless birth had filled her mother's belly with light and the candle-like warmth of grace. Marieta would name this daughter after her own mother, Maria, in Cuba, as she too was a beautiful and graceful presence who would never bring harm to others. And little Maria would be blessed with a nearly divine singing voice and with so good a disposition and such humility as to have the air of a saint or an angel culled from the choirs of the Lord. Then came the

birth (and death) of Ebe, who lived for five days and passed away
in 1907 because of a draft from the window, coming down with
a fever which she, poor thing, could not overcome. Because of
that trial, Mariela wanted to name the next daughter Dolores,
but the following year, perhaps because of a curious conjunction
of the planetary spheres, melodious with astral harmonies, the
twins Olga and Jacqueline arrived, among the sisters the two who
loved each other the most in their cribs and wailed and cooed
in harmony, banged and kicked in time, and were most aware
of the musical nature of things. Olga was named after a Russian
ballerina whose picture had once appeared in a local advertisement for a ballet company that was to perform in Philadelphia
during the weeks of her impending conception, and who was
shown pirouetting on a point of light, impressing their mother.
Jacqueline was so named simply because their mother had liked
the ring of the word, sounding Parisian and worldly and augur-
ing, to her mind, a good life. These were the mellifluously cooing
daughters whose presence, with Maria's, would inspire music in
the household, for their father, Nelson O'Brien, would one day
buy them a weighty upright piano, an accordion, and a violin
and they would learn to play and sing, their first teacher a Miss
Redbreast, for piano and violin, and the elegant and most Parisian Mrs. Vidal for voice, so that the house would fill with lieder
and popular songs—"If Money Is Friendly, It Ain't on Speaking
Terms with Me!" They would hum as babies and later sing, these
two sisters, along with Maria, one day forming the musical trio
that would be known as the Three Nightingales, the Chanteuses,
and finally, and more simply, as Olga, Maria, and Jacqueline.
The following year their mother rested, but in 1910 she brought
Helen into the world, the little female, or *"mujercita,"* as her
mother called all the babies, naming her after the glittery label
on a facial ointment, The Helen of Troy Beauty Pomade, said
to eradicate wrinkles, to soften and add a youthful glow to the
user's skin—a fortuitous choice because, of all the sisters, she
would be the most beautiful and, never growing old, would always possess the face of a winsome adolescent beauty. Then in
1911 the ever-plump, from the cradle into life, Irene was born,

and then Sarah in 1912, pensive and a little angry, the first of
the fourteen sisters to feel as though her older sisters were aunts.
She was the first of the daughters whom their mother relegated
to the care of the others, and she spoke fewer words of Spanish
than her older sisters and tended to feel lost in the house when
they started chitchatting in the parlor. Then came another girl,
who strangled on her umbilical cord, and she was called Patricia,
and that name passed on to the next girl, born in 1914, Patricia,
the ninth living sister, who because of her namesake's misfortune
came in the wake of grief and seemed terribly aware of shadows
and fleeting spirits—sometimes spying them in the hall, in the
windowpanes, and in the mirrors. She'd hope for a glimpse of
that other Patricia, who frightened and castigated her and who
would over the years bring her to the edge of an affable, spiritist
eccentricity, so that one day she would live in a nondescript house
in northern New York State, in a community of spiritists, and
hang in her window a little sign reading, "Fortunes Told." Then
in 1916 Veronica was born and she was named after the saint
who had covered Christ's bloodied face with a veil. She was the
sister who would perceive the suffering and torment of men in
this world and who would like a strong man to protect her, even
if she would confuse harshness and abruptness of action with
strength, as if it would be her destiny to wipe the bloodied face
of a husband who was to bring unnecessary pain into her life
and the lives of others. Then Marta was born in 1917, then
Carmen in 1919, and poor Violeta in 1921—pleasure-bound and
promiscuous, happy and delighted with the pleasing complexities
of her body, the sister who liked to linger the longest in the
bathtub, touching herself and pinching her breasts so much that
they grew the largest, whose nipples would become famous with
her lovers for being so cherry-red, and whose left labia had a
mole, which intensified the pleasure of love.

These were calamitous sisters, ambitious sisters, sisters who
stood by the windows at night weeping over the moon; they were
sisters who cut out advertisements from the newspapers for pretty
dresses and sat in front of an old foot-pedaled Singer sewing
machine making lace bonnets and lace-trimmed dresses. They

were sisters who had once sat dreaming about the Great War; sisters with arched eyebrows, who undressed quietly, their skirts and undergarments falling softly to the floor, whose toes turned red and breasts taut-tipped, nipples puckering when they bathed, sinking into the water; sisters who played the piano, stoically practicing their scales and daydreaming about a world in which music gushed and every blossom sang. They were small-boned or buxom sisters, sisters with moles and sisters whose infantile nakedness revealed the featureless beauty of angels, sisters whose bodies began to quiver voluptuously, some with the high and wide cheekbones of their father, those who would be tall, those with blue or hazel eyes or the dark eyes of their mother, and some who were petite and elegant, some whose eyes would suggest mischief and mirth: vibrant, sad, funny, and powerful sisters.

Their presence was so intense that, even at night, when slipping off into dreams, Margarita, the oldest, sometimes could not escape them. Not that they were always physically there, but while sleeping she'd come across them in other manifestations: as wiry ivy, entangled and dense on a wall, as a piece of rope knotted many times into itself, or as a spool of yarn being pummeled and drawn through the legs of chairs and tables by a playful cat. She sometimes found herself imagining the night sky and counting out the stars over the horizon, and two planets: Jupiter, her father, the Irishman Nelson O'Brien; and Venus, the morning star, her Cuban mother (as, in life itself, her mother had an affinity for looking up and watching for heavenly motions from the porch of their house). And she often dreamed about flocks of birds and schools of fish, and buzzing hives, herds of cattle and sheep. Weather vanes spun, porch chimes rang, flower petals fell from the clouds, a dozen (or more) moons rose. Sometimes she dreamed of roaming through a house much like the one in which they lived but with an endless number of rooms whose doors opened to another succession of rooms, each dense and crowded with the rudimentary objects of Margarita's and her sisters' lives. (Some rooms, she would remember years later, were cluttered with dolls—china dolls, bisque-headed dolls, rag dolls, Marie Antoinette dolls—and sometimes, just when she would begin to feel queasy, knowing that in fact her sisters were still all around her, the dolls simply hopped to their feet, turned into figures of flesh, bone, and blood, and, as in a fairy tale, became, quite simply, her sisters.)

Even while innocently attending to their business, the Montez O'Brien sisters were able, whether in a crib or in the bud of their troubling, alluring femininity, to produce such disturbances as to make even an experienced pilot (a veteran of the campaigns of France during the Great War) grow lachrymose and, without knowing why, lose control of his aircraft. As farmers stopped before their plows, kids climbed trees, and housewives with aprons on and plates in hand gazed up at the sky, the aircraft's shadow passed over the quilted earth, a jagged, wobbly, T-shaped phantasm breaking up and subdividing each time it passed over a fence or sloping rooftop. Then the engine stopped altogether and the Sopwith Camel dropped down in a blunt glide toward the ground, where its tires blew out from the impact and its wings clipped a haystack, the craft rolling along a field, scaring away the grazing animals and sending the crows and blackbirds out of the trees, before it tumbled over on its side.

When the sisters, among others, arrived at the wreck, the pilot had already made his way out of the plane, zigzagging like a drunkard around hay mounds and limping past the most docile cows with sad beetle-brown eyes and fly-wracking tails. He was wearing a brown, wind-worn leather jacket, a helmet, and aviator's goggles, his handsome brow smeared with engine grease. Overwhelmed by delirium and a desire to sleep, he found the sight of the sisters, who'd surrounded him, too much to resist. Soon the powerful Isabel and the rotund and ever-hungry Irene were helping him back to the house. There he collapsed on the parlor sofa and fell asleep.

Later, opening his eyes (he'd dreamed about swimming through a dense, nearly gelatinous water thick with wavery plants and blossoms), the aviator, weary and a little startled, suddenly found himself in the center of this household. Female molecules, the perfume of their bodies, the carbon dioxide of their breath, left him light-headed, and the excitement of the landing and subsequent sleep made him voraciously hungry. It did not help that Irene and Maria, two of the most natural cooks in the world, were in the kitchen preparing fattening and delicious food, inexpensive but enlarging, as these sisters were fond of using heavy cream and butter and liked to fry potatoes and onions and chicken and had become specialists when it came to making big pots of Irish-style beef stew, which was really like a Cuban concoction called *caldo gallego* with a broth base. And even though their mother had never been one to dwell on the finer details of cuisine, often daydreaming and burning the bottoms of pots, these sisters displayed great natural talents in this regard, knowing their sweets and fats and herb-spiced sauces. As a result, there was always great industry in their kitchen. They made applesauce with boiled raisins, pancakes with sugar, flour, and butter. Muffins and cookies, long loaves of the hardiest breads, all came from their oven—foods which, like the sisters' collective personalities, had a pleasant effect on those who passed into the house, so that even their father, who tended to think women "fat," especially when they were wide of hip and heavy in the chest, could not resist picking around in the kitchen cupboards and pantry boxes. The foods he ate, despite his reservations, were so flavorful that he would often astound himself by the servings he wolfed down, as if the naturalness of such consumption seemed to contradict the steely aloofness of being a man. These meals were not only delicious and fattening but they were rich in affection, as the sisters poured not only butter and sugar and blueberry and blackberry sauces over the pancakes they served, but they inculcated the very substance of this fare with such natural tenderness and love that one arose from their meals filled with a sunny optimism, a desire to laugh, and a generally cheerier outlook on life.

This the pilot felt when, swarming around him, the sisters served him a piquant lemonade and some leftover beef stew and potato salad, their eyes on each movement of his knife and fork, impressed by his knee-high leather boots, the half-moons of dust and oil on his brow, the boniness of his hands.

In something like an Arkansas accent, he remarked, "I don't

recall having eaten anythin' quite so tasty in a long, long time, ladies. I thank you."

He noticed, too, a pretty young woman across the room in an indigo dress with a red bow, and long black hair to her waist, Italian or in any case Mediterranean-looking—Margarita, with her blue Irish eyes, intently watching the pilot's handsome face. When he looked at her, she smiled and seemed aglow, as she was sitting by the window, a book in hand, she would one day recall. In the natural light, form radiant, her quite beautiful gypsy-looking face was marred only by a slightly crooked row of teeth—her father Nelson's other physical legacy to her—so that her smile was tight-lipped but pleasing just the same.

Margarita had been reading one of L. Frank Baum's *Oz* tales to two-year-old Carmen when the plane had started buzzing downward, and by then she was immersed in a dog-eared edition of Sir Walter Scott's *Ivanhoe*, which she had taken from one of the cluttered bookshelves to be found here and there around the house. This, ladies and gentlemen, was the great stash of books that Margarita and her sisters, on her behalf, had collected after a fierce storm in 1915, when the old public library roof was torn away and such books as its humble collection held were carried aloft and scattered over the countryside and left for dead, as it were, their covers buckled, pages swollen and torn or lost, ink running, and text sometimes indecipherable. The sisters headed out with a wheelbarrow and baskets, picking the books out of puddles and fields and out of treetops and down wells and off barn roofs, in the end returning the best-preserved to the library, for which they were paid a penny apiece, and coming away with those books in too bad a condition for the library to keep—a hardship for the collection, but a boon for the household, and especially for Margarita, who loved books and thought that there had never been enough in the house. Suddenly they had gone from owning a dozen books—photography manuals, two Bibles (one in English, another in Spanish), an atlas, a Catechism (wonderful with its evocation of dark little devils and luminescent angels with burning swords and souls that, as in *The Picture of Dorian Gray*, turned black with sin), and a few other books in

Spanish which their mother brought with her in 1902 on her journey from Cuba, one of them entitled *La vida en el planeta marte*, or *Life on the Planet Mars*—to possessing several hundred warped, water-stained, mildewed volumes unsavory in appearance but whose presence, despite their flaws, had made Margarita quite happy in her youth. And there were also the books she would pick out from a barrel in front of Collins' General Store in town, which sold for five cents apiece, obscure stories for the most part, written by retired schoolteachers and New England high-society matrons, with titles like *The President of Quex: A Woman's Club Story* or *The Life of Mary Zenith Hill, Explorer of the Heart*, books in whose pages she would often find pressed flowers and old valentines—"*For my love, thou art the dearest blessing, dearer than the sun*"—and sometimes more well-known books inscribed by their famous authors—"*With best wishes for a jolly Christmas, Rudy Kipling, London 1906.*"

Perhaps the docile way Margarita wiped his face with a lemon-scented handkerchief and looked him deep in the eyes, doting upon him, inspired the aviator to call her "kid," as in "Thank you much, kid." And while she, being the oldest of the sisters, felt complimented, at the same time it made her feel a little angry—a second-classness anger, a skin-darker-than-what-people-were-used-to-in-these-parts anger, a female-wanting-to-be-taken-seriously anger. And yet, because she liked him so, she thought of his daring exploits and how he had nice full lips, a hard jaw, a curly head of hair, all manly, like in those old army recruitment posters in the town hall, and she blushed.

That was when the twins, Olga and Jacqueline, hoping to impress the handsome young man, stood by the upright piano performing "Come, Josephine, in My Flying Machine."

The Parlor

IN THOSE DAYS, the parlor reflected the creative longings of their mother, Mariela Montez, and the artistic bent prevalent among certain of her daughters. (In fact, without knowing so, the pilot had stumbled into the household in the middle of what would be known as their painted-glass years.) This creativity was expressed at times in song and in the cookery of the household, in the sewing of quilts and gay embroidery—farm scenes in general, but also, to honor the Catholic Church, scenes out of the lives of the Apostles and saints—and in other ways, for the sisters were forever trying to make the household a more pleasant place in which to live.

When, for example, it had become second-oldest Isabel's idea that more color would greatly benefit the ambience of the parlor, some years before, she had traded a week's labor in the biggest general store in town for a thick roll of a flowery paper that turned that room, with its dark wood walls, into a cheery paradise of violet and marigold patterns. And with that wallpaper soon came a host of potted houseplants—spider plants and wandering Jews—which thrived in the morning and early-afternoon sun. And it had been third-oldest Maria's idea to decorate those walls with prints of birds (beside the fireplace, one could find our willowy friends the bobolink, noble goldfinch, and hermit thrush), which had cost ten cents each at a church sale and which she had put in frames herself on a rainy afternoon, those birds sharing the walls with crucifixes, shadowy mirrors, images of St. Francis, the Holy Mother, and a few photographs—the professional work of their father, Nelson O'Brien, taken during his years in Cuba, around the turn of the century, alongside photographs of his daughters, one by one and in group shots, as they came, year by year, into the world.

The sisters also sewed bright peacock curtains with florid trim, blooming with sunlight, and they had decorated the fireplace mantel with the bisque-headed dolls of their childhood. There was a clock with a reverse mirror painting of an idyllic Japanese scene, chiming on the hour—it was three when he'd heard it—and kerosene lamps and candelabra set here and there. Then a great cabinet piled high with plates and silverware, and beside that, an RCA horn-speaker phonograph machine, next to a stack of unsleeved metal and acetate recording discs. And there were hand-painted glass jars and vases which the younger sisters, such as Veronica or Marta, five and four at the time, would fill with wildflowers from the yard. The making of these glass objects had started a few years before his visit to the house, when Mariela Montez, bored and wishing for a diversion from the daily chores and trials of child-rearing, took an ordinary pickle jar and, sitting down in the kitchen with some mail-order paints, began to decorate it, producing with her inspired fingers crude but winning scenes of the tropics—green hills and overwhelming palm trees, with a backdrop of sea and sun. For the second, she made a design of flowers, like those she remembered growing out of the stone walls in Cuba, big bougainvillea and light blue roses, and this success led her to a third jar, which was a simple portrait of a house with a wrought-iron balcony, with some friendly people standing on its porch, perhaps a house such as she would see on the streets of her neighborhood in Santiago de Cuba. Each subsequent piece turned out better than its predecessor, and these objets d'art soon began to fill the house.

That simple performance had inspired a craze among the sisters, and they soon took up the painting of jars. And once they covered all the jars in the house with birds and trees and suns and scenes of night, they went a little mad, climbing on chairs and bringing down the ball lamps and covering them with paint, so that the light in the household was diffuse with lime greens and cerises and pale blues. By the time they had nearly exhausted this proclivity, their father, Nelson, started to complain of headaches from the somewhat obscured lights, and so they had to undo the work with turpentine, returning to the painting of jars, selling the leftovers for a few pennies each at the fair.

And there were bassinets and cribs everywhere, ironing boards and laundry baskets piled high with dampened underdrawers and diapers, menstrual "rags," as they were called at that time, camisoles and flannel gowns, simple cotton dresses and dresses made of crinoline and muslin and lace. Bonnets and stockings which Helen or the plump Irene were stoically ironing as the pilot opened his eyes.

He saw that the furniture was old.

Although they were not poor, their father had always tried to conserve his funds, and while he had prospered during his years of life and marital bliss with his Cuban wife in America, he did not have much faith in the certainty of the financial future. Hence the fact that they owned very little new furniture, much of it having been acquired with the house at the time of its purchase many years before, in 1897, when their Poppy had first arrived from Ireland to seek his fame as a photographer, or bought cheaply at barn and church sales. Even discarded furniture was not beyond them, as the older sisters were constantly finding ways to beautify the most faded and cracked surfaces: chairs that had looked as if they would fall apart were fortified with wires and glue, and if the finish was drab, the sisters would paint them white or black and then, cutting out nature scenes from magazines, transfer those pretty pictures before applying a final coat of varnish. (At times, they turned out so well that the sisters would sell these pieces at the Sunday markets or at the big county fairs for a few dollars, enough perhaps to buy a slightly better class of shattered chair, which they would also transform and sell or keep in the household for their enjoyment, rockers with plump straw cushions and animal-footed love seats being especially welcome.)

That afternoon Margarita, sighing, put aside her book and lost herself in speculation about the man; she knew that he was a "daredevil" with a flying circus, and that in his injured state he most certainly needed the attention and affection of a young woman like herself, and he seemed magnificent, stretched out on the couch, lanky and strong. He was wearing a pair of leather trousers, all gnarly and ridged in certain places, his maleness provoking in Margarita a strong curiosity as to what might happen if, alone in the house, she knelt beside him and gave him a tender kiss. She was, after all, at an age when she felt most curious about love and, if truth be told, a little bored with the mundanity of her life in that household. Mainly, however, she slipped back into her reading and did her best to keep the little ones such as Veronica and Marta from playing too noisily around the man. With great patience, and thinking that she and the aviator might become friends, she awaited his recovery.

Nelson O'Brien and His Beloved Wife,
Mariela Montez

LATER THAT afternoon Mariela and Nelson returned from an excursion to a nearby town. Their father, Nelson O'Brien, on that sunny day, had decided to take his wife, Mariela, along with him on one of his photography jobs. Hired to photograph a wedding, they had gotten into his Model T, loaded up with his tripod, his bellows-type camera with the Thorton-Pickard roller-blind shutter, his black trunk of chemicals and portraitist plates, and made their way down the road at nine in the morning, as it happened, their automobile disappearing in a cloud of monarch butterflies swirling around the apple blossoms. Their mother, who rarely had much of an opportunity to leave the house, and who was always concerned about her public appearance—she hated to go out without being elegantly dressed—made a very good impression at the wedding, comporting herself like a lady (in silence, for she did not much like to speak English). A small but voluptuous woman with beautiful eyes, an oval face serene and intelligent in its definition, a great head of dark hair and olive skin that gave her the air of a gypsy, she had worn an ankle-length bell-shaped dress with puff sleeves and a ruffled silk belt of her own design and a leghorn hat in whose brim she had stuffed artificial flowers. By the time they got home, the parlor was swarming with female giddiness and energy and Mariela was in a state of elation, for she had danced with her husband, Nelson, something else that was rare in those days.

Furthermore, Nelson O'Brien had gone through the entire day in a state of unusually good cheer—no sadness or moodiness about him—and had remained completely sober, thanks in part to the Volstead Act of 1919, but also because he, in order to please her, had refrained from imbibing his usual substitute, a medicinal concoction called Dr. Arnold's Relaxation Heightener which helped this kindhearted but sometimes doubting and frightened man through many a hard day of spiritual torpor and bone-aching depression.

He was not enormous, perhaps five ten in height, tending toward a slight paunch, but big-boned; and with his ruddy face, reddish-blond hair, handlebar mustache, and Celtic eyes, he sometimes resembled those engravings of country folks from tales about old England or Ireland—the looks of a blacksmith or a carpenter whom one might find working, ever cordial, ever friendly, in a village square. The sisters would remember that he'd walk with a stoop to his shoulders, that he favored brown derbies, top coats and jackets, dark green Argyle stockings, button-fly trousers, pinstriped shirts with detachable collars, and plaid-patterned Teck-brand cravats, and that he would wear these outfits until the threading wore thin, long after they had gone out of fashion. (Years later they would laugh among themselves, Margarita remembering how on some mornings she would look out of her upstairs bedroom window to the yard, where, weather permitting, her father, Nelson, would perform his calisthenic exercises, a practice he had taken up after he'd read an article about prolonging life and good health that had run in the Cobbleton *Chronicle* sometime in the spring of 1920. Though he worked hard, his body had nothing of the stringiness one observed as a generality among men of the working class, gaunt and sinewy fellows whose arms rippled with taut muscle and bone, their forearms and wrists gnarly like the roots of great trees. Because of this he was often chagrined by the profile of his unclothed anatomy, due, he figured, to the inactivity of sitting upright in the warm seat of his Model T during his travels over the countryside, and perhaps to the soul-sweetening and gut-expanding ingredients of his occasional tonic—and while he had kept himself in good trim for much of his youth, age and his dietary habits added to Mr. O'Brien's girth. So it happened that in his spare moments, most usually during the early-morning hours, when the fields started to burn with light, the sisters would behold their father going through the paces of a rigorous exercise routine: arm stretches and leg bends, push-ups and sit-ups, and much that involved the expansion of the chest and the sucking in of the stomach. These he performed in a sleeveless jersey and form-fitting black tights which gave him the appearance of an acrobat or a circus strongman: with his hair parted in the middle and his curly-tipped mustache, ends pointing straight toward heaven, he would go through this regimen with manly grunts, great heaves of breath, and so much exertion that he would sometimes frighten the birds, alarm the dogs, and cause much consternation in the household. His fair head would turn blood-red, his cheeks would puff out, his red-blond locks would dangle, beaded with sweat, and the sisters would swear that he was on the verge of a heart attack. And yet he always managed to survive this ordeal and with time acquired the somewhat puzzling physique of an oak door, and his footsteps seemed suddenly weighted with steel. Chairs and tables toppled over, china trembled in his wake, delicate flowers crumbled in his grip. And though he was not given to vanity, going about the task of sponging himself down in the cool bathroom as efficiently and quickly as possible, he was spotted, at certain moments when he thought himself alone, making a muscle in front of the mirror.) He spoke a slightly brogued English, his construction clipped as in " 'Twas a lovely day," or " 'Tis a pity," and a passable but sometimes forgetful Spanish (in the middle of the night) which he had learned down in Cuba around the turn of the century during the four years he had lived there, and which he came to use reluctantly, for he often made mistakes.

That day, for the wedding, Nelson, splendid in a brown $12 suit with red cravat and suspenders, rode hatless, for he enjoyed the rush of the wind against his full head of reddish-blond hair, and in the pleasant sunlight as they drove along in his automobile, derby by his side, his cheeks and fair face had gotten some color. As Nelson entered the household, he carried a great box of hard candies and caramels left over from the celebration—and emptying his pockets, he withdrew not only some rice and a few cigars but two crisp bills, a ten and a fiver, as he liked to call them, his payment, excluding the cost of prints, for the

day. Sober, he would regard his wife with *amor*—the kind of
amor the oldest sisters, Margarita and Isabel, knew took place
at the end of the evening, when they were all supposed to be
asleep and not listening for bedroom noises, agitated springs,
gasping, rocking movements, moans of pleasure, or any other
such unparental sounds, drifting down the halls, as if they were
wall-less and not a single cicada nor a rushing wind existed in
all the world.

Before such occasions, their father's eyes became mischievous with desire—well, there were thirteen of his offspring in the
world by then, weren't there? Margarita would tell herself, the
existence of all half-Cuban, half-Irish females much indebted to
their mother and father's bedroom conviviality and the fact that,
for all their conservatism, practiced in many other areas of their
life, they delighted in and felt enlivened by the act of love. They
were in such good spirits that afternoon, laughing and speaking
affectionately—he in English and she in the music of her Cuban
Spanish—that, were it not for the pilot's presence in their parlor,
Nelson and Mariela might have escaped upstairs immediately to
the canopy bed of their room (with its door that often squeaked
open at the most inopportune times) for a "nap."

But the pilot was still there when they arrived, and Nelson,
responsible and friendly, decided, after hearing of his accident,
that it would be best for the young man to spend the night with
them.

"Then tomorrow you'll feel rested before you take care of
your business."

So later, cleaned up and wearing a fresh shirt which Nelson
had lent him, the pilot, whose name was Curtis, joined the family
for dinner. He sat beside Nelson at one end of the long table,
and the two men, like old companions, spoke of "manly things,"
their conversation turning to talk of war, the pilot having been
shot down in France by the Germans, and Nelson having witnessed firsthand the war in Cuba between the Spanish and the
Americans, when, a young man, he had gone down there as a
civilian volunteer—company photographer—with the 1st New
York infantry brigade.

" 'Twas ruination and death, I recall," her father told him.

"A pure despair such as the Lord should never allow in this world, tell you that."

It would be hard for Margarita to remember everything the two men discussed—only that they often nodded in mutual respect—for that had been so long ago and she, while recalling that day, was a very old woman. But she remembered that Isabel, Maria, and the twins were curious about her behavior, that while cuddling little Violeta, she would take a quick look into the pilot's eyes and swear to herself that he was like a character out of a Sir Walter Scott novel, noble, pure and, in memory, bathed in a saintly light, and that she had wanted him to hold her, to take her off to some distant and beautiful place.

"Well, sir, I work for this outfit, an aviation company based in Camden, New Jersey, the Daredevils' Flying Circus. Most of us learned to fly during the war, and that's mainly what we like to do. We stage shows here and there, mostly at state fairs and Fourth of July celebrations and such. I'm just a pilot, I can do loops and spirals, stuff like that. But we've got some fellows who walk out on the wings, and that always excites the crowd."

"And can you earn a good living that way?" Nelson asked him.

"It's okay, nothing special, but better than being out of work. If you can do three or four shows a week, you can make some money. The worst part is that we're always traveling; it gets a little lonesome going from town to town and pitching a tent out in some field or living out of hotel rooms."

What else was there? Violeta threw up all over Patricia; Isabel washed her. Their mother, Mariela, listening in silence and smiling from time to time when the pilot looked over at her, had excused herself from the table, so that she could attend to the little ones. Their father yawned, and the pilot, speculating as to the cause of his engine failure, decided that some of the fuel lines had gotten jammed, or maybe his mechanic had forgotten about the oil, but listening, Margarita disagreed: the pilot had been lured down by the femininity of the household.

A Spring Night's Idyll

AROUND NINE O'CLOCK that evening, when most of the electric lights and kerosene lamps had been dimmed in the house, Margarita, in a nightgown, left her room and went downstairs to the parlor. The pilot was sitting on the couch, looking through some old magazines, and seemed most preoccupied. The next day, he'd have to hire a truck to haul the airplane back to Camden and he would have to pay for it out of his own pocket. He had a *Saturday Evening Post* open before him and a clump of one-dollar bills spread out on the floor. He was worried about money, she about romance. Her breasts were very beautiful then, and though she would wear a corset and a slip, cleavage hidden, it was a time when the very suggestion of lingerie seemed outrageous and provocative to men. Before heading downstairs, she'd opened the top three buttons of her flannel gown. She stood in the hallway wetting her palm with saliva, and stuck her hand in her gown, rubbing herself so that her nipples stiffened like buttons through the material. She had gone downstairs to look for a book and, after finding her copy of *Ivanhoe*, sat across from the young and distraught man and, sighing, said, "It's such a lovely night, but I just can't sleep. Sometimes I like to take a walk in the field outside the house." Then: "Would you like to join me?"

And he did, following her out into the field and walking with her toward a fence at the edge of their property, where she asked the pilot if he would like to sit down on a pile of stones to watch the stars. And just as he sat beside her, the sky, as if cooperating, sent two streaks of light shooting across the horizon.

"Did you see them?" she asked, and he nodded. "Yes, miss."

"Oh, but call me Meggy, if you like." Then: "My, but I love this place! Do you know that when I was very little, before many of my sisters were born, my mother used to bring me out on warm nights to watch the sky. I was a kid when Halley's comet came around, do you remember that? It was bright as anything and low in the sky and each night we would watch it until our eyes became heavy with its light. I didn't know much about anything scientific in those days, but I used to believe that it came out of heaven. Do you remember that?"

"A little. I remember walking with my father—he was a fireman—along the streets of our little town, and standing on a street corner and noticing that comet, bright as a Fourth of July sparkler, coming up over the roof of a house, and thinking, When will wonders end?"

They sat for a long time, quietly, her hand settled just next to his, her hand waiting for his hand to touch hers, but that did not happen. And when he, yawning abruptly, got up and announced, "Guess we should be getting back," she followed after him and asked, "Curtis, do you think I'm pretty?"

"Yeah, I pretty much do."

Then she said, "And are you sure you want to go back to the house? Wouldn't you like to sit out here longer?"

"I'd like to, but I can't. I've got a lot on my mind."

That was all, until they made their way into the house and Margarita, fancying him and thinking that they'd entered the preliminary stage of a romance, bid him good night in their parlor—for he was to sleep on the couch, under some quilted blankets—her lips pecking at his right, stubbly cheek, her eyes closed, as she wished for more.

Later, in the bedroom that she shared with the twins, Margarita settled in bed, and by dim lamplight started to read *Ivanhoe* again, until, having fallen asleep, she began to feel her nipples pinch the sheets through her gown and a quite pleasant sensation in her female center, so that, without knowing it, she passed the night grinding her hips into the bed and sighing—until her sister Isabel, hearing her, peered into the room briefly, for she thought that poor Margarita (with the crooked teeth that never allowed her to smile) was having a bad dream—in the same way that the sisters would sometimes hear their father, in his own bad dreams, moaning at night. She had gone in to dim the gaslight beside the bed, Isabel bending to pick up from the floor the copy of *Ivanhoe* that had slipped from her older sister's

fingers. And when she heard Margarita sighing again, she decided to waken her.

"Are you all right?" Isabel asked her. "*¿Todo está bien?*"
repeating the question in Spanish, the language she used when
wanting to be more emphatic, or affectionate.

"Yes! And now please leave me alone!"

With that, poor Isabel felt her fair Irish face flush. (It was
the big-boned, wide-shouldered, tall Isabel who had been born
with the most Irish appearance and the old-fashioned Cuban
morality and a tendency to get herself involved in everyone else's
business.) She left the bedroom as if a bee had stung the tip of
her tongue, and feeling, as she would much of her life, a little
unappreciated by her older sister, whom she considered too im-
mature to make her own decisions. She had no idea that Margarita had gone to bed that night in a revelry of fabrications
about the pilot, that in the name of self-amusement, and because
she had perhaps become a little bored with Sir Walter Scott's
tales of knightly daring, she had invented or allowed herself to
drift into a most pleasant and unladylike dream—the pleasurable
memory of which would come to her even years later, when she,
a much older woman, would turn to look at the glowing aqua-
blue dial of an electric clock and then into a mirror, remembering.

Margarita's Dream, 1921

SHE WAS WEARING a diaphanous wedding gown and a veil
that gave her the mysterious air of a harem girl, a Salome, her
hair coiffed into a great wisp of curls, blossoms such as she had
once worn at a May festival, sunk into the crepe of that veil. Her
skin, olive-colored like that of her Cuban mother, had miracu-
lously lightened, and her teeth had straightened. Her breasts,
which she'd always considered much too large, took on the proportions of the breasts she had once seen on a statue of Aphrodite
in an art book. In the dream, she and the pilot were joined in a

long, impassioned kiss, prelude to their honeymoon—for, apparently, they were married—which would begin with a flight in his airplane. (She heard the musical twins at the tinny upright piano playing "Come, Josephine . . .") He took her up through the clouds into the chilly heights, in loops toward the sun, and in bed Margarita was so convinced she was flying that her breath shortened, she gasped and had the sensation of falling headlong, piercing the atmosphere, like a pebble through water.

Landing in a field, they found their honeymoon abode, a simple cottage. A private place, for not one of her sisters, nor her mother or father, nor the passersby on the road, nor guardian angels, nor the eyes of God were upon them. They could do whatever they liked: he carried her over the threshold of a bedroom, and through the window she could see cows and sheep grazing in the distance. At first they simply sat on opposite sides of the bed. And he started to speak softly, his voice quavery and uncertain: he began by making a confession. He had deceived her. He was not the good man that she had imagined. He wasn't a virgin. He had been with other women, sophisticated women, tramps, who knew their way around a bedroom. In France, during the war, he had seduced the women of Paris and learned the secrets of love, and while he was telling her this, he could not help but run his fingers down the front of her lacy dress; and soon enough he was standing behind her, holding her breasts in his hands and pressing against her. That was when Margarita, exercising some restraint, broke away from him and cried out, "Let's go running in the fields."

Soon they were out amid the dung piles and flies, and the cows sidled toward them with great interest. She would recall feeling a need for distraction, even though her loins ached for release (she was grinding into her bed), and so passed part of the dream picking flies off the cows' heavy lids. He sat down on a bundle of hay and watched her. He told her, in his Arkansas twang, "I love you, doll."

From a hilltop they could see far into the distance—toward farms and a winding river, the fields covered with dandelions and daisies. He undid her dress and was soon suckling her, in the way she imagined a man would, his head to one side of her, so he could hold and suckle her at the same time, his neck muscles stretching. And soon she was feeling the long, slender bolt of flesh—his male appendage—which he'd let out from his trousers. (She imagined its appearance, deciding it would look like a six-week-old river trout, having seen different versions of that anatomy on hounds and country animals—her mother sometimes covering her eyes when, in the wagon, they would pass by two horses coupling in the field. She remembered many things in a simple moment: how she had once watched a quite proper lady in town turn purple and then faint at the sight of a Clydesdale horse spontaneously mounting another—and on the main street of town, not far from the church! And recalled the afternoon, some years before, when she had been naughty and gone off by herself to follow the river that crossed under the bridge near Tucker's Pond; book and a little bag of fruit in hand, she passed some good and earnest young men—Tom Sawyer types, she had thought—fishing with crayfish lures; and moving along the mossy bank, she came to a place where the whitewater flowed and bubbled against the rocks. She could rest there, eat an apple, and read in peace without anyone to disturb her, for she had come to love her privacy and there was little of that in her household. When she reached her spot, she'd found that it had been commandeered by some schoolboys who had slung a rope up over the thick branch of an oak and were swinging naked in a long, sweeping arc over the water, their pink snout-hooded privates flying with them through the air. And there had been the time when she and Isabel, taking a shortcut through the town cemetery—where they liked to play "ghost" among the blackened and wind-weathered, half-toppled tombstones centuries old—made their way past the seventeenth-, eighteenth-, and nineteenth-century dead and were near the gate on a gray and dreary day when the groundskeeper, slightly addlepated, approached them, his demeanor normal except for the fact that he wore neither trousers nor breeches and allowed them—out of senility? mischief? insanity?—a good look at his lackadaisically hanging lantern of flesh, for that was what it seemed in that moment, the two sisters covering their mouths as if to suppress their cries of grief or laughter or surprise as they hurried off toward a path that would eventually lead them to the main road out of town and home. Those few incidents passed through her mind in this particular moment of fabrication.) But he never stopped kissing her breast and she never stopped touching him with her soft and elegant fingers and then he started to touch her, and not just her breasts but down below her navel, and she began to squirm, a sensation that warmed honey had been poured between her thighs overwhelming her.

Then she was back in the airplane: from up high, aloft in the clouds and looking down, as she had years before when as a little girl she'd once dreamed of being transported by angels, she saw that the countryside, with its patches of brown, green, and clay red, the irrigation ditches and streams and rivers, farmhouses and silos and cross-hatchery of roads, resembled a wavery quilt or a great flag. As the plane continued to arch upward through the clouds as if to break through the roof of life itself (to arrive in some heaven of pleasant sensations), he turned to look at her, smiling and gallantly nodding his head. A long, silk scarf flowed behind him in the wind and he laughed, telling her, "Let me show you something, sweetheart," and he pulled up on the throttle so that the plane rose steeply into the sky and then he brought it abruptly down, countering gravity and telling her, "Hang on," and just then she sensed gravity dissipating. A book, Scott's *Ivanhoe*, which had accompanied her into the dream, and a silver chatelaine purse with beaded fringe began to float off her lap during the dive; her hair also began to float and she had similar sensations throughout her body, her interior organs, her breasts, and every strand of her hair stretching upward as if to float free of all concern.

In bed, she pressed her legs together so tight an insane rushing pleasure filled the length of her womb. She squirmed, she shook, she moaned, her bones slipping out through her skin and clattering about the room, and she felt herself falling backward as if she had stepped off a cloud. Then she opened her eyes, the mattress damp beneath her, and realized that when the shuddering had rushed through her, she had kicked off the merry-looking quilt and had almost rolled off the bed: she had given the sheets such a tug that she had wrapped herself in them like a Greek goddess, and because it was still so dark—the dawn would come in a few hours and there would be the cock's crows and the neighing of horses, roused from their stalls, the sunlight edging slowly along the field—the moon through the window appeared in her half-sleep vision like a burning shield and she sighed, unable to rest any more that night.

*

Making her way along the hall (and hearing through the doorway nearest the stairs the whispering voices of her mother and father, who sometimes spoke fitfully throughout the morning hours—about what, no one would ever know), she went down the rickety stairs to the kitchen, where she lit a kerosene lamp, and, sitting at a table, passed the rest of the night sipping buttermilk, eating apple slices and pieces of pan-fried, sugar-coated bread, and reading Sir Walter Scott.

That fried bread's aroma, a lilting thread of nearly crystalline or carmelized air rising to the upper floors (smoke curling in cat's-cradle configurations up the stairs and under the doors of the rooms where her sisters were sleeping), roused the ever-plump and food-loving Irene from her slumbers, and this sister, in a great flannel gown and with red ribbons in her pigtails, soon had made her way into the kitchen. And although she was half asleep, her eyes nearly shut, she, like a somnambulist chef or a spirit nostalgic for the earthly happiness of tasting a sweet upon its tongue, also sliced up some bread, fried it in butter and sugar, and sat beside Margarita, happily devouring this pre-morning snack, though without saying a word to her older sister. For her part, Margarita was used to this, having spent many an hour with Irene in the same sort of situation—that is, Margarita diapering, ironing, sewing, washing dishes, sweeping the floor, or intently reading a book or a magazine, while Irene assumed the posture of someone whose vocation in life was the savoring, mastication, and digestion of all pleasurable foods. That night, she remained

beside her oldest sister, filling her belly, and then as abruptly—
and as sleepily—as she had appeared, she took (as Walter Scott
might have described it) "her lady's leave."

Then Margarita sat alone, occasionally looking out the window for dawn, and happy when the morning star, Venus, that
brilliant pearl of light shrouded by the morning mists and milk-
white in its solitude, began to rise over some distant willows, a
greenish water-stained luminescence burning around them ever
so briefly, and she listened carefully for the puttering of a bi-
wing aircraft engine, for she was at the age when she sometimes
thought that her dreams, no matter how frightening or naughty,
were premonitions, that over the aureoletically splendid horizon
would appear the gallant and handsome pilot, up from the sofa
and in the air, his heart enthralled by the prospect of seeing her
again, his knees weak with desire, and his head filled with the
promise and hope of love.

*

The next morning, when her father drove the pilot into town
(they had waved at him as he made his way, limping, out to the
automobile), Margarita, feeling most interested in the man, insisted on coming along and she luxuriated, sitting behind him
in the back seat, inhaling deeply of his adventurer's leather and
the sweet Brilliantine hair tonic that he had scrubbed into the
dense head of curly hair as he dallied before the washstand
earlier.

When they reached Main Street and the pilot climbed down,
Margarita, extending her hand delicately covered in a white doe-
skin glove, bid him farewell again and told him, in a whisper:
"Please come back and see us." Then: "Or at least come back
and see me."

"I surely will," he told her.

Another Saturd

TWO MONTHS had passed, it was a Saturday, O'Brien sisters had more or less forgotten about the is, all but Margarita, who felt a little slighted that the ga aviator never returned. That morning the sisters were out in the yard under the shade of the spreading chestnut tree, parasols in hand or sun hats on their heads, the littlest ones playing tag out by the barn and running in circles or jumping from the rear of their old cabriolet, that elegant, high-wheeled wagon which their father, Nelson O'Brien, used as transport in the days before his purchase of an automobile. To the south, a grand view of hills and other houses, prosperity in the air and felicity communicated by the sunlight, feminine in its giving nature. Nine years old, Sarah was up on a stepladder filling the bird feeders, like lanterns off the lower limbs of the trees, with seed, for, during those months, tawny sparrows, blue- and yellow-rumped warblers, goldfinches and meadowlarks and blue jays, among so many others, would in memory come flying across every spring morning of her youth—crowding the branches and swooping around the delighted, spinning child, as if she had the powers of a female St. Francis, whose image hung on the kitchen wall, titmice and petite chickadees scampering and hopping on the lawn below, pecking after the fallen bits of nut and grain.

These were beautiful bird feeders, some dating back to when the house had been built many years before; others, resembling pagodas and little churches, gifts to the family from their mother's good friend, Herman García, a most un-British Puerto Rican butler who, working for one of the richer estates of their town, represented exactly one half of the rest of the Spanish-speaking population of Cobbleton, the other half (excluding the Romance-language teacher, Miss Covington) being a certain baker, Mr. Roig, a tall, pock-faced Spaniard who resembled Abraham Lincoln, and his wife, famous in the town for their many-tiered wedding cakes, their puff pastries, strudels, and pretzels. ("One adapt," Mr. Roig, with his deep Basque voice, used to say. hen in Rome, do as the Romans do.") And while these asques were friendly with the family—whenever Mariela and her daughters went into his shop, he would always chat with her—it was García who had over the years become a regular visitor to the household, dining with them every so often on Sundays, when he would show up with his two sons and his young wife, his arms filled with gifts for the house. Over time, he would bring them cribs, rocking horses, children's chairs, a hat rack, wooden puppets, even a domino set that he made for Nelson O'Brien on his birthday (he rarely played with them, preferring the game of checkers), all of the aforementioned items constructed in a little workshop behind the cottage of the estate where he was a butler and sometime chauffeur, and where his wife also worked as a maid. Many years before—it must have been around 1909 or 1910—their mother and Mr. García had met in the town post office, he waiting for a letter from San Juan, she for one from Cuba. He was "new" in those parts then, as he had arrived to work from New York, on the recommendation of a former employer ("You don't have to pay him much, you know"), on the estate of a prominent banker. With his dark-whorled eyes, his great crooked nose and gaunt frame, he had an ascetic, nearly monkish bearing. But that was not his way: a man in his late thirties at the time, he had been married to a woman fifteen years younger than himself. And despite his appearance, he was ebullient and friendly. He, too, had felt the loneliness of being one of the other foreigners in town, but had the advantage of having relatives who lived in a place called Harlem, New York, and so now and then, on his free Sundays, when he was not visiting the house, he would take the train into that city, return late at night, and the next day, usually in the mid-afternoon, appear at the door of the house where the sisters lived, holding a bag filled with plantains, *yuca*, mangoes, *malangas*, and other foods that would not appear on the shelves of any store in Cobbleton for another sixty years or so. (Years later, a large Shop-Rite would take up half of Farmer Dietrich's field. And its manager would notice those items listed on an inventory

order sheet and check them off, for he had heard that there were
inhabitants whose peculiar tastes had brought these foods into
demand.)

Their mother was seated before a picnic table in the yard,
with little Violeta, healthy and brimming with life, on her lap,
enjoying the breeze and looking forward to that moment later in
the day when García would invariably show up to discuss the
next afternoon's menu: would they cook a suckling pig? or a big
pot of chicken to go with their other dishes? They still had some
green plantains left over from the week before, and half a sack
of black beans—a happy prospect, in terms of the stomach and
heart, for whenever García visited the family, Mariela Montez
would feel elated, as she considered him both a friend and an
artistic confidant, to whom she allowed access to her most inward
thoughts.

Trusting him in a way she had trusted few others, Mariela
was reminded by García of a poet named José Luna, who for
the years of her childhood had been a close friend of her father
in Cuba and a frequent visitor to their house on Victoriana de
Avila Street in the city of Santiago. This Luna had been a chaste
and impoverished, elderly Don Quixote-like fellow, whose poetry
(who could say if it was good or bad?) had been an inspiration
to her own young life. So much an inspiration that now, these
years later, whenever she sat down to write her own poems, or
"*versitos*," as she would call them, she always felt that in some
way they were written for this man—and the life she had once
lived. And because she saw something of José Luna in García,
he was about the only person to whom she ever showed them.
Even though she sometimes read these verses, often religious
and contemplative musings, to the older sisters, like Margarita,
who understood much of what she had written, she never took
their opinions seriously, as, in her view, their comprehension and
use of Spanish, in the main conversational and gossipy, could
not begin to grasp her poetic intentions. At some point during
his visits, Mariela would take García aside—out to the yard or
for a walk in the field around the house—and recite these poems
to him, the man walking quietly and perhaps stoically beside her,

hands in pockets and head nodding, as she would go on with her orations of poems that she would not read to her own husband. Sometimes they would walk for an hour through the fields. There was a path that cut downhill from their property to another farm where there was a great meadow of wildflowers, a favorite place for the sisters to collect bouquets of convolvulus, heartsease, and snapdragons, and there they would find a place to sit while Mariela recited. Found in a cigar box in 1972, a fragment of a poem, circa June 1920, scribbled on the back of a calendar page, entitled "Lamentation of the Crow":

> *Poor Crows, dark and heavy-winged,*
> *with their ugly beaks and horrid caw-caw.*
> *They, too, would like to fly to heaven*
> *and live among the pure doves*
> *and the flamboyance of the peacocks . . .*
> *[Breaks off]*

They would sit there for so long, sometimes until it began to get dark, when the farthest ridges of the hill disappeared gradually in the shadows and the last pink radiances of the sun were swallowed by the sky. And although no one would say it, there would remain for Margarita and the sisters the impression that something might have been going on between their mother and García—the unthinkable, perhaps, the two of them walking in one of those fields after she had bared her soul with those verses that she kept a virtual secret from the others, stopping behind a tree for a quick kiss, was that a possibility? the two embracing at that time of the day when the meadows were liquid and mist-ridden and the wind tousled the grass and chilled the fingers, so that they would hold hands, up along the serpentine path, ever so quietly breaking their hold at the first sight of the house or the barn in the distance.

*

These walks brought her much satisfaction. But they confused the sisters, because, despite her initial elation—she would

come back to the house laughing and ever so happy—later, washing dishes, breast-feeding her little one in a corner, their mother
would seem suddenly so overcome with sadness that she could
not open her eyes and her hands would begin to shake. And then
their father, who sometimes noticed this and ascribed it not to
melancholy or soulful longing for a different life or homesickness
but to what in that epoch was known as "feminine weakness,"
would take from the kitchen a bottle of Dr. Arnold's Relaxation
Heightener and pour three tablespoons of this curative potion
into a tin cup for his wife. Then he would tell her, "Drink it
down. Now, that'll do the trick."

Margarita's Bath

THAT SATURDAY MORNING, while her father was out in the
yard among his daughters, the horses, the birds, and his wife,
performing his exercises, Margarita was locked up in the bathroom, just off the back porch, taking one of her twice-weekly
baths. Much work was involved in this simple act in those days,
the water heated on the kitchen stove or on a burner in the
bathroom and poured from buckets into the metal, gondola-
shaped tub to keep it warm, always aiming the hot water in a
certain direction—that is, between her legs—its lick of heat slipping down over the matted, sea-orchid-like opening of her pubis,
the young woman luxuriating in the flow, the sensation of bodily
pleasure, a way of getting outside herself. The room was one of
the few private places in that house where she could remain
alone, to read, to hum, to do whatever she liked, without anyone
seeing her, tranquilly floating in the bathwater.

(Someone's eyes were always on you, a small hand tugging
at your skirt, a voice calling from another room: Margarita! No
privacy unless you locked yourself in the bathroom or in the
recently installed toilet, which was off a hall from the kitchen.
On cold winter nights, she would lift her nightgown hem to her
knees, pulling down her underdrawers, her buttocks touching
the weathered wood of the commode seat, a shocking feeling—

and it was fly-ridden and sometimes unbearable in the summers—but there she would sit, just to be alone and pass the time, until someone—and there was always someone—would bang on the door and demand, "Margarita! Please let me in.")

Being the oldest and always surrounded by younger sisters whom she had to look after, Margarita spent much of her youth, in that crowded household, busy, sometimes reluctantly, with chores and the upbringing of the others. She had also been the first to experience many things: the first to attend Miss Peterson's grammar school in Cobbleton; the first to contend with the taunts of her fellow students, who had confused her initial shyness with stupidity; the first to experience shame whenever her mother, who did not speak very much English, met with her teachers; the first to be ridiculed because she possessed that Cuban's dark spirit and skin in a town filled with Swedes and Finns and Norwegians and Germans; and the first to daydream about running away. But she had also been the first to experience the simple pleasures of this life: the first to inhale deeply from the garden's aromatic blooms; the first to run, turning in circles, under a heaven of falling snow; to watch with sweet interest the swallows exercising in the clouds; and the first to rest in a bed beside her mother, listening as her mother read to her from the books she had brought with her from Cuba, one about the planet Mars and the other about the creation of the earth, the travels of chosen people and the salvation of men's souls. And she had been the first to look at the maps of Cuba and Ireland which their mother had cut out from some old book and put in frames in the hall so the children would at least know the cartographic appearance of those distant lands in which their parents were born. And the first to hear her mother singing a zarzuela in Spanish and to hear her father, corny as he could be, moving through the rooms of that house on one of his good days, whistling an Irish air; and the first to navigate through the two flowing rivers of language in that house, to sense the music and the voluptuousness of each and yet to feel them sometimes warring inside her, when she was not sure if she was a bit more of a Montez or of an O'Brien. And she was the first—or would be the first—to wake up one morning and, looking back, sigh wistfully and with affection for that time when her life had been filled with many moments of earthly happiness.

*

Year by year, she had watched the rooms of their house fill with cribs and basins and mounds of diapers and with new sisters, who ran, charged the sunlight on the walls, danced and squealed, cried, shouted, plucked flowers, sucked sugar cubes, smeared jelly into their hair, pounded the floors with their little feet, turned in circles, sang in and out of key, rested in her arms, yanked on her apron, napped in corners, piled on top of one another, and, filling the house with exuberant femininity, made like Spanish- and English-speaking sprites.

Attentive to her duties in the household, she had, as a little girl, always felt "saintly" and humble in the manner of a good, demure, and obedient daughter. She had been the kind of young girl who, in the days when she knew mainly work, was rarely seen in the house without a laundry basket, an iron, a broom in hand. She was obedient then and lived in a good tremulous fear of failing her mother, wiped chins, wiped bottoms, learned to cook, to sew, to spend an hour turning the crank-driven mech- anism of a pot-shaped laundry machine, later diligently appear- ing in the yard with bundles of sheets and dresses, stockings, underdrawers, and linens and sheets, which she would pin to lines, doing all such work cheerfully and without a thought for herself.

But as she got older she happily discovered the benefits of her seniority and was not at all reticent to play the mistress of the house when Isabel and the other older sisters (Maria, Olga and Jacqueline, Helen and Irene) reached the age when she could give them work. They, in turn, did the same with their younger sisters, to whom the oldest were like aunts. And while she had never truly been freed from housework and always enjoyed the simple pleasure of bouncing a newly arrived Montez O'Brien sister on her knee (yes, and sniffing the sweet scent of unspoiled, talcum-powdered skin and curly locks, and feeling the touch of soft, grasping fingers, the tip of their digits damp from sucking, nails marked by a swirling white moon, on her nose and chin and cheeks), she had by now, and with great delight, experienced something of the outside world. She could look back to those times when she went to work for her father, sometimes accompanying him on his photography excursions and business trips, and helped to run the movie house, where she had been doing odd jobs for the past seven years—back to 1914, when the theater first opened. (She did everything in the Jewel Box Movie House. Sometimes she was the projectionist, the ticket taker, the usher, the lobby manager, the distributor of promotional items by the entrance; that is, she would oversee the distribution of such items—certain of the younger sisters, "cute as all-get-out," as they used to say, standing inside the doors in their ruffle-skirt pink and yellow dresses, their knee stockings, and with ribbons in their hair, giving away decorative and entertaining items whose purpose was publicity for the theater and for silent movies in general. They'd distribute "Hoot Gibson" and "Buck Jones" glasses, Abraham Lincoln spoons, lead doughboy and lasso-twirling bowlegged cowpoke figurines, Spanish fans that opened to the words "The Jewel Box Movie House," and "For the Best and Latest in Biograph and Kinescopic Entertainments!"; and Kewpie and Raggedy Ann dolls, and, later, during the King Tut craze of 1923, Pharaoh whistle rings and jigsaw puzzles of the Great Pyramids. Cap pistols, too, and on the last Sunday of the month, "Hollywood Star of the Month" plates, featuring such prominent screen idols as Rudolph Valentino, Theda Bara, Mae Marsh, Douglas Fairbanks, and Julia Opp.)

Still, she valued her privacy and loved the bathroom, as it was in some sense a historic place. It was in that room, during that very same act of bathing, one autumn day in 1915—she had already passed into her fourteenth year—that Margarita Montez O'Brien moved from the physical oblivion of childhood into the sudden awareness that she had acquired the body of a woman. That day she had removed her dress, stripped down to her underbodice and camisole, slipped those off, and then climbed out of her cotton underdrawers and, looking into the large speckled

mirror on the wall, with its oak cherub frame, first realized that
the thick womanly shock of black pubic hair between her legs
and the plump breasts that she was observing had just burst forth,
as if overnight, overtaking the child that she had once been. There
she stood, curvaceous, sweaty, with mangly body hair which
erupted not only below, its highest reaches a thin delicate line
of hair rising to her navel, but under her arms and all over her
legs—which young women in that epoch never shaved (unless
they were "professional ladies"). Once she had gotten over this
change, fascinated (and sometimes repulsed) by the sight of her
own body, she got into the unbookish habit of parading about
naked in the upstairs bedroom and posing before the dresser
mirror, where she would examine herself carefully, her hands
touching her breasts, as if to measure their daily change in size
and weight. She would do this even when the room was chilled
and goosebumps covered her skin and her nipples puckered, her
body stretching in all angles, as if to accentuate the natural grace
of her form, or to transform some unpleasant feature. This physical onslaught seemed to have come over her suddenly and without anyone, not her mother or her father (certainly not him!), to
explain what was going on.

(And she never knew that the mailman, Mr. Smith, once
saw her standing naked before her bedroom window and every
day for months afterwards would dally by their mailbox, looking
up at that window on the chance of seeing her again, that for
many nights, when the mailman would go home and sit down
to dinner, he could hardly bear to look at the affectionate and
matronly corpulence of his wife, and that on some evenings the
mailman would tell her that he was going out for a walk and,
putting on his boots and coat and hunter's cap, make his way
into the rawness of the season by lantern light, trudging along
the back lots and streets of Cobbleton and down the mile or so
of road to the house where the sisters lived. He would stand in
the darkness, observing their silhouettes through the yellow-lit
windows, unable to understand what he, a man of forty or so
and married for eighteen years, with three children of his own,
was doing there. One night, snowflakes like porch moths fluttered

down around him and still he remained another hour, until every one of the lights in the house dimmed and the winds had risen and a chill had entered his bones, and he sadly made his way homeward, back to the comfort of his own household.)

In those days she became so self-involved, spending long hours in the bathroom and bedroom, that Isabel, who'd always had the disposition of a matronly aunt, would bang on the door to rouse her from her reveries, or, if she happened to be passing by and saw her older sister in a natural state, would throw her a robe, a sheet, a blanket, and ask, "What's wrong with you, anyway, that you suddenly detest clothing?" And reluctantly Margarita, who tended to defer to her younger, more authoritative sister on the practical matters of life, would get dressed, that matter of exhibitionistic glee or vanity resolving itself over the coming months and gradually giving way to other, more humble pursuits, such as crocheting, embroidery, dressmaking, and the playing of parlor games with her younger sisters, and to other diversions which in that epoch were deemed proper to the upbringing of a young lady (and boringly so, because Margarita in the midst of a card game, in the process of choosing between a queen of hearts and a seven of clubs to discard, sometimes yawned or let out a sigh, the sigh of a young woman from whose life the excitement of adventure and love was absent).

Although she kept much of what had taken place in her body a secret—or tried to—it was the bloodied evidence of her sheets and the complaints of the twins about her moodiness that made her mother, Mariela Montez, realize what was happening to her daughter. Feminine and suddenly voluptuous, Margarita not only began to attract the solicitous smiles and glances of shopkeepers and male passersby in town, but during a certain time of the month she began to experience pains so severe (as if her kidneys had been punched, her rump were stuffed with broken glass, her belly filled with stones, and her intestines with prickly worms, as if a thorny rope had been wrapped around her internal organs and had been pulled taut by a powerful and unrelenting wheel to the point of breaking—that's what it was like) that she would take to her bed for days at a time, feeling both disgraced and powerless. And while the severity of those pains would pass with the years, the humiliation would not: she always hated wearing a strip of cotton from a torn sheet pinned like a diaper over her vagina to absorb the flow of her monthly cycle's blood, and found that the cloth made her feel self-conscious as she walked, especially when she accompanied her mother or father to town or was hurrying along the streets with her younger sister to shop, convinced that people somehow knew about her condition, that she was marked or smelled bad or was leaving a trail of blood behind her. And because Mariela, who'd never bothered to explain the biology of the occurrence, always reminded her to put on the *trapo*, or "rag," as it was indelicately called, Margarita despised the term and its implication, finding it an offense to the haughtier part of her female disposition.

And yet she got accustomed to all that and used her experience to make things easier for her younger sisters, Isabel being the first beneficiary of her sister's knowledge and research (for Margarita had studied the symptoms and biophysiology in a book that she'd borrowed from Dr. Schultz, the family physician, who had delivered each of the sisters with the exception of herself, Isabel navigating the sometimes turbulent waters of that condition with cantankerous piety. And she had advised Maria as to what to expect—Maria would stoically sit out on the porch, rocking in a wicker chair, discomfort teeming through her body, bones, belly, and head painful with the "female malady"—and had recently introduced her to the concept of "hygienic dressing" and the safety pins to her two playful and elegant sisters, the musical twins, who, sharing the experience so closely—Olga's menses would begin a few hours before Jacqueline's—always endured its discomforts together. (Margarita could tell, for during those times Jacqueline's violin playing, celestial and melodious, would begin to screech and shriek as if to call out to all the other mournful violins in the world, and Olga's piano playing became more halting and she tended to lose her patience with lovely chords like the E-flat major of a Mozart sonata and would, for no apparent reason, begin to hate every note on the piano, abruptly slamming her palms down at random on the keys and

crashing the fall board so hard that on two occasions the cher-
rywood cover loosened from its hinges—and then, frustrated, she
would head up the stairs, forlorn and lost to music, throwing
herself on the bed to cry.)

*

In the early afternoon Margarita bathed and put on a sweet
pink dress and sun hat, a pair of low-heeled lace-tied shoes, and
decided that she would go for a walk along the country roads to
the field near Farmer Tucker's pond where she would often sit
under a tree with a book and read for a while before heading off
to town to work in the movie house, for in those days she was
already known as the sister who liked books and it was a normal
thing for her to seek solitude. She'd always liked to read—books
taking her out of herself and the "little shames" Margarita would
feel in her young life, beginning with the image of her ever-
pregnant mother, Mariela Montez, whom she loved very much
but whose dogged "foreignness" and absolute determination to
remain Cuban in an all-American town, the other Spanish-
speaking inhabitants of which could be counted on the fingers
of one hand, prevented her from caring in the slightest about the
way she spoke English, which she did only in snippets with her
youngest daughters, from Helen on, and with her husband, even
then saying little—"I'm coming," and "Yes," in response to a
question or an order, at dinner instructing her daughters, amid
the slurping of soup and the chomping of buttered slices of bread,
to pass their father another bowl of stew, and saving her gossip
or her most rarefied opinions for her older, Spanish-speaking
daughters. She had not bothered to teach the babies Spanish;
like a grandmother, she'd delegate that work to the oldest daughters, if they so liked. She regarded the youngest girls, following
her in packs about the house, their heads filled with English,
with both pity ("The poor things are too distracted to learn proper
Spanish") and contempt ("They don't really want to learn!"),
forming her strongest alliance with the oldest sisters, like Margarita and Isabel, who of course had their own opinions on the
subject. For Margarita, the oldest, the soft and beautiful vowels

of the language were one with the tint of her skin—she'd once gone to the rail station to see her father off on a trip to New York and some wise-guy kid, a soldier, had leaned over the caboose railing and called out to her: "So long, gypsy!"—words that had somehow stuck in her gut and sent her home in a sad mood, up to her room, where she sat before the mirror plucking the barely perceptible bridge of black hairs over her nose and scouring her chin for facial hairs—what gypsies had . . . This in itself did not make Margarita ashamed, for she much enjoyed the music of her mother's voice, her mother reading to her as a young girl from a Spanish Bible or from *La vida en el planeta marte*, or singing in some heaven of old Cuban danzons, lines of which Margarita would be able to remember into old age. All that was good, and warming to her heart, but there was also her mother's absolute terror of the world outside their house, which had always made Margarita unhappy.

When Margarita Was Alone

SHE DID NOT MIND the solitude of her walks, when she'd experience the odd sensation that she could go on forever in one direction and never escape the household. She'd carry a straw basket filled with books—some of which she had read a dozen times—and a copy of one of the Philadelphia newspapers, the Philadelphia *Times*, and the local, the Cobbleton *Chronicle*, which were usually two or three days old. Sometimes as she left the yard and watched her younger sisters at play—Marta, Veronica, and Patricia, running in circles, each properly attired in lady-like fashion, in dresses that reached down past their knees, and high stockings and beribboned hats—she had the impression that she could have been observing herself; and she'd think about what she had been like as a little girl, in those days before she'd started to appreciate and deplore her maturity and awareness (fledgling) of the way the world worked.

*

She loved the open air, the sight of a sparrow alighting on
the ground, a breeze through her curly black hair, and the scent
of the wildflowers all around her, what an old Mennonite farmer
used to call the work of the Lord. (He was gone now, as she
made her way along the country roads, but she'd remember how,
when she was a little girl, this captainly-looking fellow with his
great white beard and in a black top coat and bent-up hat would
come by in his wagon and at the sight of her suddenly command
his heavy-hoofed Clydesdale horses "Whoa," these animals coming to a halt, their reins jingling. And the farmer, tipping his hat,
saying to her, "Isn't it a nice day, yes? And do you know why,
because it's the work of the Lord"—that's what he would say,
his hand spread out toward the fields and the vivid life around
them, God brilliant everywhere. Then he would reach into his
pocket and, with his immense frame towering over her, his hands
thickly calloused, would give her a little cube of sugar or a hard
candy, telling her: "Now you be a good little girl and always pay
heed to your parents.") Sometimes, in a "naughty" mood, she
would open the top buttons of her dress so the sun could warm
her breasts under the slip and camisoles she'd wear. (She also
daydreamed about swimming naked where the willows bent low
over their own maudlin shadows in the waters of Tucker's
Pond—how she had been tempted to do so, especially on unbearably hot summer days.) A bluebird flew overhead and disappeared in the treetops, then darted out of the branches,
followed by another bluebird, the two singing merrily.

She sighed and remembered the handsome pilot and her
dream of love. She read the Cobbleton *Chronicle*, full of local
farmers' news, and news about the more provocative events taking place in the outside world—an announcement, for example,
that a new contest called the Miss America Pageant would be
held that coming September at Keith's Theatre on the Garden
Pier in Atlantic City, New Jersey, or, sadly, that Mr. Enrico
Caruso, the great Italian tenor (whom she had once heard sing),
had been called forth from this life. Also an item about the

lynching by a mob of Ku Klux Klansmen of "two negro males, suspected of thievery" in Alabama. What else did she read? On the society pages: "Mr. and Mrs. Pendergast of Chestnut Hill will be arriving in New York from their extended tour of the Orient aboard the steamship *Crescent* out of Southampton, England, on June 17"—the words "Orient" and "Southampton" enchanting her. ("The name is Dame Margaret," she fancied herself haughtily instructing a ship porter. "Please do be careful about moving my trunk into the stateroom.") She twitched: there was a photograph of Suzanne Lengleng, Wimbledon tennis champion, in a scandalously short tennis outfit, leaning over a net and shaking the hand of a vanquished opponent. For a while she stared straight up into the blue of the sky, experiencing nothing but its blueness for many minutes—no leaf, bird, cloud, or aviator in sight . . .

Then her eyes fell on an advertisement whose illustration showed a young woman crying hysterically in a dark room, stretched across a divan that seemed to be floating in the air, imagining that rugged pilot's fingers touching her, his lips on her neck, and she noted the headline over the ad: "Often the Bridesmaid but Never the Bride." And that was true in her own case. Over the past few years, she had watched three of her high-school friends get married, but that did not really bother her, though the girl in the purgatorial shadows of solitude, pictured in the advertisement that read: "The Diary of a Lonesome Girl," wandering aimlessly in a many-roomed, lightless house, seemed reminiscent of herself on those days when she felt that love would never come into her life.

*

Of course, she knew all about love—feeling so much for the family and affection for movie stars like Valentino and Ramon Novarro and for literary creations like David Copperfield or Captain Blood, and for those avuncular types who slipped in and out of her life such as the milkman and the postmaster and the stable owner and the ice-house man. But little else, as life in their town, she thought, was a bore, and left her with much time to read, to

cultivate herself as a lady and pursue her impure thoughts, as
the handsome Catholic priest might have put it. On many a day
she sorrowfully regretted that her family lived in Cobbleton, as
quiet and orderly a town as one might ever find but with little
promise of romance, unless one counted the society balls, to
which the sisters were never invited. In her habits, she seemed
restless, and because she was naturally pensive, there had been
talk of sending her to secretarial school or to a women's college,
where she might apply herself to education courses or household
management; but, most of all, her mother and father simply
wanted her to get married—the proper destiny of a young lady
of that epoch.

But there were no men in that town who appealed to her,
not the men who would sometimes come with their haughty dates
to films at the movie house, or farm boys, or the sons of railroad
workers; nor was she interested in Rafael Garcia, the butler's
oldest son. Ever attentive and courteous, and a few years older
than herself, he'd follow Margarita about the house, treating her
with so much respect and reverence as to turn her stomach. This
young Rafael, as darkly serious but not as handsome as his butler
father, was a studious and quiet fellow. During the few moments
when he would say anything at all, he tended to speak about his
life as a college student in Philadelphia—"the only Puerto Rican
in that school," he would say in his low voice—where he studied
law. For Margarita, whose head sometimes floated in the clouds,
he was so practical, sincere, and "good" that she found him a
bore, her own preferences tending toward the more adventurous
type of man such as she perceived her father, Nelson O'Brien,
to be, or the likes of that pilot.

While away at school, he'd write Margarita long, evasive,
and finally (that is, obliquely) confessional letters, which she
would never finish and would tuck away in a lacquer box, and
while she would write him back appreciative notes, she did not
give him much thought. Then something new began to appear
in the bundles of mail that would come to the house: little envelopes, smelling of violet perfume and love poetry, addressed
to Margaret from an "anonymous admirer"—Rafael himself, of

course—poems which he may have styled after the ditties that
appeared in little "love booklets" such as could be found in the
local pharmacist's, which cost ten cents and came nicely bound
in pocket-size editions and had, with their flowery designs, something of an air of Japanese art, much in vogue then. His own
poems were carefully written out, in as fine a script as he could
manage (the *g*'s and *h*'s shaky, the *w*'s bending to one side, the
j's often not dotted), and surrounded by a border of hand-drawn
cherubs and blossoms—why, the man must have spent hours on
those notes. The poems, as Margarita would recall them years
later, could have been composed by an adolescent boy. One ditty
called "Dreams of You" went as follows:

> *In Spring my dreams of you*
> *come joyously welling*
> *up like the waters of brooks*
> *bubbling clear in the sun.*
> *What a joy in the telling,*
> *for to my heart you will*
> *remain forever dear.*
> *Come the roses of May*
> *or the snows of December,*
> *my love for you I will*
> *always remember.*
> *Gray be the skies or like azure*
> *the blue, far be the day*
> *I slumber without my dreams of you.*

These and others arrived from time to time, and she knew
the poor fellow's reserve would dissolve just by looking at her—
he had always looked at her in a certain way, even when she was
a little girl—his expression conveying to her, as male expressions
would, the simple wish that he might connect with so pleasing
a being, as if she were an angel with the power to remake a man's
life, his sense of the past and of himself, as if a woman was
something in which a man and his history, his pains, his failings,
could reside.

Sometimes she would accompany him out to a dance or a movie, though not without misgivings: Rafael had inherited the Negro blood of a grandmother, and although she did not care about it herself and liked the "boy," as she'd call him, thinking him far from a man, it made Margarita uncomfortable, as she did not like the feeling that people might find new ways to look down on her. She did like him and sometimes thought that, were he a few shades lighter and more handsome, she might entertain the idea of a romance with him. But it would not happen, and whenever he tried to hold her hand as they walked down the street, she would pull it away.

*

That was during the time when Margarita believed that all men could fall in love with her, and she had acquired an alarming tendency to flirt—when she would come to town, knowing (or wishing it so) that the men were looking at her. If she went into Mr. Roig's bakery, as she did that day before making her way to the movie house, and there was a handsome man waiting about beside his wife, or one of the hicky farm boys with his mother, she would have fun dallying with loaves of bread, pouty as she appraised them, nose whiffing the grain, eye darting to see if she was being watched, and, while doing so, sometimes imagining the most lurid conversations with men, for she was aware, coming from so fecund a household, of the laws and bawdiness of nature. (How many times had she looked on a tree branch in the spring at a configuration of blossoms and realized that it was one butterfly mounted on another?) As she and her vivacious younger sisters walked in a group, the unspoken rule among them was to relate by posture and general giddiness a contempt for men —to parade in a startling procession, on their way to church or to the movie house, aware of how men tipped their hats and young boys whistled, while they comported themselves with the mischievous authority of European countesses.

She believed that all her sisters were lovely, save Isabel, with her matronly wide, hard-boned face, freckly, she thought, like an apple, her moody disposition and propensity for plain dresses—but she had always enjoyed the attention they attracted when she and her sisters went to town together and marched as a chatty, clamorous group down Main Street to a dance or a silent picture at their father's movie house, or while hearing Sunday Mass at Father Mancuso's church, a casual and capricious flirtation prevailing whenever they saw men and (consciously or unconsciously) exerted their female influence. In those days she wanted to be like the women in those engravings of famous goddesses that she saw in the old history books—Demeter, Aphrodite, Venus—or like a Gibson Girl from old magazines like *The Saturday Evening Post*, which their mother, to practice reading English, kept in the house. All these had in common the same serenely lilting foreheads, genteel and somehow transcendent—what medieval physiognomists would define as "noble." She wanted to be as beautiful as the lady depicted in a Grecian tunic, reclining on a couch, who was on the label of the Helen of Troy Beauty Pomade jar, which, at thirty-five cents a jar, often found its way into the house—and wished, while posing one afternoon, her hair pinned up in a great mangled coif above her head, that she could resemble the beautiful Florentine lady, Beatrice, pictured on the wall of the Cobbleton Library, crossing the Ponte Vecchio to meet, as the caption confided, the poet Dante. She saw images of herself, or suggestions of her own hopeful feminine beauty, so often repeated—on coins, stamps, magazine ads, movie posters.

Spring Photograph

THE SPRING, ice beds breaking up and the trees budding, she remembered, was her favorite season in adolescence, the world fertile, the sunlight contagious, her head filled with nothing but the future. Their father, Nelson O'Brien, sleeves rolled to his elbows, would stand behind the tripod of his folding-bellows-type camera, posing the sisters out under an elm tree in their yard, blanket spread out underneath them as if they were having

a picnic, butterflies fluttering about, and the Pennsylvania countryside radiant as far as one could see; or he would have them
climb on a wagon, the littlest ones squirming and carrying on,
while their mother, Mariela Montez, ever serious and moody in
an introspective way, seemed unable to smile. She would stare
intently ahead, her expression passive, the very same expression
she would maintain for cameras for the rest of her days. A great
silence would ensue as Nelson, with artistic and fatherly pride,
head disappearing under a black velvet cloth and hand on a
pneumatic bulb, recorded for posterity the feminine progress of
his daughters. Photograph taken, life would come swirling back
into motion—Margarita and Isabel tending to the household
chores and the care of the little ones, diapers everywhere, while
their mother would make her way through the house, her stride
often weighed down with the emergence of life, for it seemed
she was always pregnant.

There was something else in regard to the photographs. Even
though Margarita had always seemed outwardly humble, bowing
her head and averting her eyes when a man or a woman would
pay her a compliment—"My, but aren't you the prettiest
thing"—she, having her moments of vanity, secretly believed that
it was so. ("If you look too long," she can hear her mother saying
in Spanish, "your reflection will swallow you.") Years later, when
regarding those photographs, cracked and tinted by age, she
would take a good hard look at herself and find that she had
had, more or less, pleasant but ordinary looks as a young
woman—she would blossom with age—and that while she certainly had something of a foreign air about her, which would
always seem to intrigue men, she was not beautiful, though her
father, Nelson, would tell her differently.

"You have classical features like a Venus," he would say
while posing this daughter, alone in his studio (crack of light,
chemical flash, the child brilliantly smiling). "You know that,
yes?"

The funny thing was that he'd tell each of his daughters, be
they plain or beautiful, that they were equally "generous to the
eyes."

*

Margarita would remember that in the earliest days of her life, before her father would buy himself the Model T, they would go to town in a cabriolet, the simple carriage pulled along by their serene horse Hercules, who liked to eat apples and who inhabited the barn along with the swallows. They would ride the few miles of tranquil country road to Cobbleton, her mother holding her younger sister, Isabel, born in 1904, the plainest-looking baby in the world, with a broad, sunken-featured face, but with pretty eyes, wailing away, Mariela ever pregnant, with Maria or the musical twins, Olga and Jacqueline, perhaps, cuddling her daughter and looking off into the woods around them and saying, "Hmmm," when asked by Margarita's father, "Are you comfortable?"—the Irishman tugging on the reins and giving out a click of his tongue to encourage their horse, with its cocking ears, forward, the man hunkered over and brooding, a derby atop his head, his blue eyes straight on the road, his clothing smelling of a cherry blend of pipe tobacco and burned firewood.

They'd make their way down past Farmer Tucker's pond, where in the winters the girls and the other children of the town would learn to skate (and where poor Sarita, born in 1912, would fall into the frozen water through a crack in the sun-softened ice and develop the infection that almost took her from the family), and the roads known as Farmers' Crossing, where, if you made a turn in either direction, you could ride past miles and miles of dairy and wheat and corn farms, before coming to the gentle glen, glorious in the spring (and she can't help imposing this), where years later her first husband, then a new gentleman acquaintance, would nearly succeed in seducing her. Everywhere she looked along that road, there were farmhouses and silos, farmers working their fields, and dogs to bark protectively, and little stands and tables on which there were unattended baskets of apples and pears and fresh corn, each costing ten cents, which one would put in a tin cup: cows and horses grazing, the fields running in bands toward the horizon, and flocks of wild geese and wrens and crows spiraling in loops toward the sun.

They'd come to Cobbleton, whose streets were lined with thick oaks, hickories, maples, butternuts, and locust willows, trees that in the summers provided much shade. Her Cuban mother never knew the names of those trees. To her, Margarita imagined, they were simply trees, great decorative and flower-boughed ornaments that sprouted out of the ground, shedding leaves in the autumn, covered with snow and knobby tubes of ice in the winter, and returning in the spring—elms (*olmos*), oaks (*robles*), and white-barked birch trees (*abeduls*), among others that she simply thought of as *árboles*, as in "Look at that pretty tree," her mother, if she knew them, keeping the Spanish equivalents of their names to herself. And she was the same way about the names of flowers, happy when there was an equivalent, *rosa* for "rose," but moving through their yard that would grow thick with *claveles, violetas, azucenas, flamenquillas, hibiscos*, and *botones de oro*, without knowing that in English they were called carnations, violets, lilies, marigolds, hibiscus, and buttercups. Literate in Spanish, she simply could not relate the English names of things to her daughters; intelligent and secretly erudite, she, in her linguistic solitude, moved through this world tentatively: "Oh, look at that! "*¿Cómo se llama eso en inglés?*" to Margarita. "*¿Cómo se llama un granero aquí?*" And Margarita would tell her, curtly at times: "It's called a barn here, Mama." She would be happy to inform her mother of such things, but at the same time she would feel annoyed at having to relay such "common" information again and again, tired of being the teacher of her own mother.

When they'd arrive in town, people, lining benches, were fanning themselves, gents moving in and out of the shadows, and the world, as in a film of that time, filled with a kind of oscillating light. Her father, or Poppy as she liked to call him, would head off to the Farmers' Market to buy some chickens, which they would later carry home squawking in a wire cage and defeather over a bloody tub in the yard, and great bags of rice and potatoes and carrots or whatever they might need. In the post office, they would ask if any letters from Cuba had arrived, by way of Havana and Tampa, and every few months one would, Mariela tearing open the envelope, always scented with the tropics and the perfume of blossoms, to receive the family news. Thus Mariela had learned about her father's ailing health—he'd broken his hip a few years before while hoisting a Chinese lantern onto the eave of the porch—the birth of nieces and nephews, and the political situation, Cuba now being a republic, all summed up in her mother's arthritic script; her own responses, meticulously written, conveying an ever-cheerful tone, for Mariela could never allow her parents to sense her own self-doubts about her new life.

It was rare that anything came posted from Ireland, sometimes a note from Nelson's old parish priest, with its little prayer pamphlets and news of life in the town, where nothing much seemed to happen (and he would shrug), and at Christmas the occasional greeting from an old friend who'd been informed of his whereabouts. Very little else from that distant place.

They would stroll along Main Street, among the good citizens of the town, who by that time had gotten more or less used to the ever-pregnant Spanish lady whose aristocratic demeanor and tendency to silence in their presence set her apart. There was something else: though she was a beautiful woman who liked to dress well—she favored great plumed hats, which with vibrant creativity she would further adorn with beads, artificial birds, and flowers, and wear white gloves and carry a parasol to avoid direct contact with the sun ("It will turn your skin to parchment, children")—her coloring, "Mediterranean," "swarthy," or "Mex," as it was sometimes referred to in the yellow press of the day, made some people distrust her. And she displayed her religious inclination on her breast, wearing a large silver crucifix with a sullen Christ on a chain around her neck, an heirloom, which may have seemed ostentatious, for in that town religion was concealed within the heart and displayed only during evening prayers and in the pews of the Protestant churches.

There was also a Catholic church in that town, with a handsome and youthful priest named Father Mancuso. Like a circuit judge of the Old West, on Sundays and Wednesdays he would travel from town to town, saying Mass and hearing confession. In the days when they had first arrived in Cobbleton, Nelson had taken her to this simple church, St. Anthony's, tucked away some few blocks behind the Jewel Box Movie House on Main Street, where she heard an eleven o'clock Sunday Mass. And although she did not know enough English to pursue a confession, she returned on a Wednesday at four, joining a line of penitents and awaiting nervously to see if God would hear her confession in Spanish.

"*Padre, quiero confesarme, pero no hablo inglés muy bien.*" Then she added: "I want confess, but my English is no so good."

"Well then," he asked, "*parla italiano?*"

"*¿Italiano?*" and she thought about it and said: "*Quizás un poquito.*"

"*Allora, possiamo fare la confessione in italiano e espagnolo, si?*"

"*Bien, padre.*" And she began her confession and then asked, "*¿Pero usted me entiende?*"

"*Così così, un poco.*" And when he laughed, it was the first time she'd heard laughter from such dark seclusion.

"*Ma, debemos provare tutto nel nome del Signore.*"

Absolution for her sins, the cleanliness of her soul, and much happiness that she had someone new to talk with, even if she did not understand everything he had been saying.

Those walks to town, to market, were mainly conducted in silence. Margarita could barely recall any conversations between her mother and father—just intimations: "Shall we go in here?" Or: "I have to go to the bank," her father would say. Or her mother, attention caught by the sight of an item of interest, would happily point it out to the children: "What a beautiful hat that woman has on!" Or: "Look there at that little bird on the fence." Or: "That horse over there is smiling at us!" But they would always greet passersby, men tipping their bowler hats and der-bies, the ladies with their parasols and ripple-layered, out-of-fashion Empress Eugénie hairdos, nodding and occasionally smiling.

Still, her mother was a fragile, changeable being. Whenever she and the children attended to a chore, and Nelson was else-where, and they entered one of the shops, like Collins' General Store, their mother would become timid. The shopkeeper's wife,

addled by problems of health—people whispered that she suffered from a terrible rheumatism—was sometimes so severe that
Margarita would think the thin-lipped porcelain cups, with their
little Cupids adorning the sides, were shaking and the air would
have (in memory) a singed smell, as if an electrical wire had
been smoldering inside a wall. Quiet and sullen, Mariela might
say, "Good afternoon," but that was all. And she would begin
to get nervous, standing in a corner of the shop and wanting to
touch, but refusing, the things around her. Suddenly she would
become tentative and the very thought of examining one of those
delicate cups was enough to bring down the entire rack of tureens,
bowls, and pitchers above them.

Needing an intermediary, she would then begin to ask
questions:

"Margarita, ask the lady how much for that sack of flour."

"Yes, Mama."

"And, Margarita, would you please explain to her that last
time we were here she did not give us the correct change."

"Yes, Mama."

Once she was out on the street again and free from nerve-
racking scrutiny, either her gaiety would return or she would
take on the air of an offended aristocrat—"Who does that woman
think she is, looking at us in such a way!" Those looks—those
expressions of opinion with a glance of the eyes—seemed terribly
important to her. "That woman, the poor thing," her mother
would say, "is pure envy. *¿Sabes que es una envidiosa?*"

The daughters would nod.

"She's jealous of us because we are so pretty to look at? Yes?
And because we are a happy family, while that woman suffers
from a terrible solitude, and a state of solitude makes a person
envy everyone else in the world."

"But, Mama," Margarita would feel like asking her, "why
are you so afraid?"

"Whatever these people do, children, don't forget the family
is all that matters, that even though you have the name of
O'Brien, my family name, Montez, is just as good as any other.
Do you understand me?"

(And she did, Margarita and her sisters regarding themselves not just as O'Briens but as Montez O'Briens, their mother's family name slipping away from the more traditional Spanish order and going before their father's: the utterance Montez O'Brien falling quite simply on their ears as more "American.")

Strolling, they'd pass the three-story red-brick building near the town square, Miss Peterson's elementary school, which all the sisters and their brother would attend, with its proud forty-eight-star American flag on the front lawn, and then come to the ordinary white clapboard house, with its Georgian porch, where one could find the offices of both the Morality League and the Good Citizens' Club. Sometimes they would make their way to the hotel and its dining room, where Nelson would treat the family to heaping bowls of ice cream, Mariela always ordering vanilla and Nelson, not prone to appetite, contenting himself in the days before Prohibition with a glass of whiskey or a schnapps. And she would remember that when she was older and at liberty to roam along the main street with her younger sisters, she liked to sit on the high front steps of the town hall, where President McKinley had once given a speech, and they'd be sucking on hard candies or eating ice-cream cones, ever careful not to stain their pretty dresses and content to watch the wagons and trucks and automobiles moving along the street. Those steps were especially good for watching parades on the Fourth of July, circus processions and the great displays that the drum-banging Democrats and Republicans would put on at election time. (And she would remember that on the Fourth of July her father would walk around with an American flag pin on the lapel of his jacket, samples of which he sold with other patriotic buttons outside his photography shop for a dime, the buttons stuck to a board on which he had placed velvet mounting. He'd hoist an American flag over the doorway of his shop and, climbing a high ladder, tack a flag to the porch rim of the house, so that people could see this flag from the road, this great symbol of patriotism covering the east view windows of their parlor and kitchen and leaving that part of the house in a kind of perpetual shade. Proudly—for passersby always noticed it—he watched as a troop of soldiers in full uniform marched past the house, turned their heads, and gave the flag a salute. He saluted them back, his eyes squinting, as if caught by the light—the soldiers' brilliance, their heroism, their manly virtues rising in a cloud of dust around them.) Sitting for hours sometimes, Margarita would never suspect or even begin to imagine that some years later she would be walking up those very same steps to a reception, blushing and laughing as she passed through a storm of tossed blossoms, a wedding bouquet in one hand and the skirt of a long, flower-embroidered bridal gown hoisted high in the other, her heart in love.

The Photography Studio

OFTEN, they would accompany Nelson to his photography studio, where he would sit waiting for customers or he'd go see if someone had dropped off a note, requesting his services, through the mail slot of his door. He would sometimes find customers waiting inside—for this was an honest town, where few would steal—and he would go about his work methodically and with good cheer, removing his jacket and working in a vest, his shirt-sleeves rolled up to his elbow. He'd light the room with a chemical flash (a flint spark igniting the magnesium and potassium chlorate), and with a press of a pneumatic bulb take the shot. Margarita, observing this from the bench he kept before the window, would notice on the faces of his subjects, male or female, expressions of timidity, arrogance, vanity, jealousy, love, anger, envy. And remembering now, it makes her smile, proud of how the years give validity to youthful insights, to feel that her opinions of certain of her father's subjects seemed to be true.

Mr. Henderson, a banker, natty in a tuxedo, after the fashion of the President, whose mouth seemed weak and quivering when he posed beside his gargantuan wife, or Dame Henderson, as she referred to herself, with her belly, wide as the doorway, sucked in and countless necklaces, shimmery and opaque, tinkling on her breast each time she took a breath to sit still—"And,

Mr. O'Brien, or should I say Señor O'Brien, pleeeease do capture
me in a flattering light"—this Mr. Henderson, whose eyes
seemed so frightened, would, years later, try to drown his wife
in their bathtub and suffer in the process, hitting his head against
the rim, a concussion of such force that he would spend his last
days on the porch of their house in a wheelchair, a bald man in
pajamas, tended by a nurse, his lips quivering and his eyes welling
up with tears, as he watched the life around him. There, too,
against the backdrop of velvet, pleat-centered curtains, she had
seen impossibly dim-minded husbands ordering their wives
around, and always with a scowl, shaped like the coil of a light
bulb, across their brows, growing more intense and cruel over
the years, the young brides' ankles, arms, and jowls thickening,
and their once-innocent faces growing heavy with accumulated
grief. One such couple, a certain Mr. and Mrs. Dietrich, farmers,
seemed so chatty when they'd first come to her father's studio
in 1912 or 1913. He, with his proper suit, hair parted in the
middle, and huge farmer's hands, would say to her, "Now you
sit here, my dear," while she, a vision of happiness and feminine
allure in a puff-shouldered dress, racy for those days, that she
had sewn for herself, seemed delighted, squealing and making
jokes about the prospect of having children—"Soon enough we'll
be filling the room, Mr. O'Brien, with kids." Yet this same lady,
over the years, gradually retreated into silence, her cheeriness
and vervosity disappearing. (On the other hand, Margarita thinks,
there were very happy couples who, year after year, returned to
pose at the studio, their loving expressions unchanged, becoming
ancient and quietly dramatic, like those very couples whom, in
later life, she would see browsing through the library, the man
never letting go of the woman's hand.)

Her father kept a lot of props around: a large Grecian-shaped
vase in which he would stick ostrich plumes, a head of Venus,
another of Julius Caesar, both on pedestals, which he had purchased in Philadelphia, and he had a number of backdrops, the
most popular being a scene from "classical Arcadia" with cen-
taurs and forest sylphs dancing about rolling hills, depicted after
the fashion of romantic British landscapists of the nineteenth
century, this canvas ordered from a scenario parlor on the Lower

East Side of New York. Sometimes he used the daughters as
models, posing them for fanciful shots in the spring, their hair
garlanded with flowers, and in little tunics, tossing petals out of
a basket as they danced about a Maypole—this for a calendar
which he would print. On another occasion, he had posed them
with umbrellas against an Oriental landscape, trees in the distance laden with snow, again for a calendar, and for aesthetic
interests, the daughters supposed. He also took them to some
pretty spots high in the countryside, looking west over the Susquehanna, and to isolated waterfalls that sent up rainbowed
mists, his daughters in their proper lace dresses spread out on
rocks, parasols open behind them, the white water flowing
around them, as if this was the most natural thing in the world.
Or they would go to a lake, where the girls could pull up their
skirts and go wading in their bloomers in the water. So many
other shots, his daughters growing, as it were, before his eyes:
for example, the first time she could recall seeing snow, when
the sisters huddled in a sleigh, whiteness everywhere, and he
had taken their photograph in what seemed like the North Pole;
and there had been the time, speaking of winter, when he had
bought them ice skates and taken them over to Farmer Tucker's
pond, where she and Isabel and Maria tried to navigate the blue
sheen of ice, the snow falling around them like blossoms, all of
them slipping, their bottoms aching, shouting out in fun. And
what about the Christmas season during her childhood, when
life seemed so sweet—the way life was conveyed in certain books
and in love poems and gooey valentines—the shops on Main
Street brilliant with decorations and a big tree put up in the
square, strung with candles and antique-looking ornaments.
Photographs, too, of the kids mounted on horses or on drome-
daries at the traveling circus, or eating blueberry pie at a county-
fair pie-eating contest, lips blue, teeth dotted with blueberry
seeds, breath sweet with sugar, stomachs processing pie into good
American waste; or posed in the field, the sisters pigtailed and
alert, watching the autumnal migration of birds heading south
(to Cuba?), or watching the sunset, the moon later glowing over
a blue-tinged field.

(He'd even traveled to the site of a great coal-mine disaster—was it the Darr Mine disaster, Margarita wonders. There in 1909 he gave away medicine and blankets and set up his camera, returning to Cobbleton desolate but vaguely elated, with dozens of photographs of sad-souled, twisted-spine, begrieved men with lantern caps—shadows swirling like moths around them—laid out in the mud and on planks and stretchers, expressions gnarled, faces blackened, limbs slack, hands hanging down into the dark; and he'd spent a day developing the plates, appraised them for their humanity, and then put them into boxes that he'd store in a shed.)

In fact, Nelson O'Brien not only made photographs of his daughters, but from time to time, when the fancy struck him, he would rent a moving-picture camera and for the hell of it, and because he was a lover of gadgets (in the closets in his house, in his photography studio, and in the theater, there were piles of camera, machine, and movie-equipment catalogues) and, as always, had artistic pretensions, fancying himself a director, make home movies of his daughters at play, which he would show, projecting the developed film against the side of the house on late summer evenings—the sisters moving through the world in an almost mannequin-like fashion as if their limbs were joined by screws and hinges. And horsing around, director O'Brien had filmed a few short, five-minute dramas, scenes of which he had taken out of a book of plays about early Pilgrim life in America (all these films gone now forever).

On sunny days, her father, Nelson O'Brien, would sometimes pose his subjects across the street in the town square, where there was an equestrian statue of a Revolutionary hero: he with colonial flag raised and the horse's bronze hoofs high in the air. Or he would look for a garden-like spot, sometimes taking his subjects to a farmer's field where the light fell kindly through the trees and where flowers seemed to be everywhere.

*

Now: the saloon, a pianola's ragtime melody floating out through its doors into the world, and she would sense that establishment's tug on her father, who would sometimes slip inside

for a quick mug of beer. On one of those days, after a tormented
night of sleep when he had his sad dreams about Ireland and he
had dallied in the saloon too long, Mariela, impatient about
waiting outside in the summer heat, marched in with the children, passed the "No Ladies Please" sign with its curly script on
the wall, and demanded in quickly flashing Spanish that he reas-
sume his paternal responsibilities. He reacted by wiping some
froth from his mouth, and, his face turned all red, told her, in a
Spanish that he now rarely used (except, Margarita supposed,
during moments of intimacy, for sometimes she would hear his
deep-timbred and slightly brogued Spanish cutting through the
silence of a country night, as he would tell his wife, gasping,
breathing heavily, "*Ay, siempre eres linda*," and "*Ay, mujer, mi
mujer*"), to please mind her business and not embarrass him in
front of the men.

During such incidents, when he would feel humiliated—
there would be others—he'd walk quickly ahead, leaving
them all behind, and, mounting the carriage, or later his
automobile, he'd ride away, disappearing along one of the country roads, only to turn up an hour or so later, having regained
his composure, to collect his family and bring them back to the
house.

*

She'd also remember the presence of spittoons and chamber
pots in the corners of the rooms, the annual spring visits by a
crew of men who would arrive with shovels and kerchiefs over
their faces to dig out the murky content of the outhouse and cart
it away for use in the fields. She would remember the grand day
in 1916 when the plumbers came and installed a modern water
closet and faucet-run bathtub in the room off the kitchen. Then
another day when the electrical lines were run out from town
and single plug sockets were set in the walls, and the appearance
of spiral-corded lamps—light filling the rooms and an atmosphere of modernity entering their lives. What else?

That and many things, and then the late afternoon, when
she would hear about the aviator again.

The Jewel Box Movie House and
Nelson's Commercial Trade

ALTHOUGH SHE'D often been her father's companion on his
treks about the county, she felt a special connection to the Jewel
Box Movie House, as she considered herself part of its history
and had been ten years old when the idea of opening that
theater—back in 1912—had first occurred to him. Up to that
time, their Poppy had been supporting the family through his
on-and-off photography trade, with which he could make a
living—his wages supplemented by some savings from the old
Irish inheritance which had brought him to America in the first
place (that and a wish for adventure), and from the occasional
odd jobs he would take here and there. In those days, when he
was not going about in the Model T with his new celluloid camera
with drop-leaf shutter, taking portraits (or, as he preferred, with
his reliable camera of old), he depended on the commissions he
earned as a traveling peddler of goods for the great Hemmings
Co. of Chicago, a position he had acquired after reading a recruitment ad in a Philadelphia newspaper, dated November 12,
1908: "Wanted: Men of Vision! Men with Unstoppable Goals!
Men with Unbreachable Ambitions! Men with a Love of Commerce and Unstinting Determination! To SELL the GREATEST
and UNCONTESTABLY durable goods AVAILABLE to the common
CONSUMER in AMERICA!"

He had written a letter ("Dear Sirs, I am the sole supporter
of a growing household, of Irish inclination, who, having a sound
profession in the photography trade, wishes to supplement his
income. I have no experience selling goods, man to man, but I
come from a family of merchants in Ireland, and I am certain
that, whatever your needs might be, I can fulfill them"). And
when they had not responded, he had left his wife and five daughters (Margarita, Isabel, Maria, and the twins, Olga and Jacqueline) and taken a train out to Chicago to the offices of the

company, where he obtained a brief interview with an officer, securing, with his earnestness and gentlemanly courtesy, an appointment to be the regional sales representative in the districts surrounding Cobbleton, where he earned ten and a half cents on every dollar's worth of sales. He was destined, it seemed, to a connection with black trunks, for in a trunk similar to the one in which he carted about his photography equipment he carried samples of his company's goods in the back of a wagon or in his Model T, traveling from town to town and farm to farm, trying to persuade hard-pressed customers—farmers and torpid factory and mill workers—to buy everything from animal-footed stoves to Spanish fans, all of which could be ordered from a fabulous ten-thousand-items catalogue whose proud cover was emblazoned with an American eagle and American flags, stars spiraling everywhere. Back then, he also sold all kinds of potions and pills: kidney and liver pills, pills to ease constipation and pills for troubled hearts, nerve pills intended to strengthen men afflicted by "femininely inclined emotions"; remedies for diarrhea, colic, malaria, bronchitis, asthma, croup, mumps and pleurisy; a liniment called Angel Oil that was composed of "vegetable oils and electricity," and another item named Death to Microbes. Most popular was a medicinal called Larson's Vegetable Cure for Female Weakness, which was purported to do away with ailments specific to women: inflammation, ulceration and falling of the womb, languor, nausea and deeply felt feminine fear; it also did away with hysterics, sparks before the eyes, dread of impending evil, shortened sleep, dizziness, palpitation of the heart, depressed spirits, and countless other ailments associated in those days with the monthly cycle, which tended to make women weep.

She had to give her Poppy credit, for he was always hatching schemes to make money. (One of his more practical and profitable ideas came to him in 1908, when there were forty-six states in the Union. That year he had bought some stock in the American Flag Company, so that when two states were added in 1910, he quadrupled his original investment.)

But it had been in 1912 that her father decided one day to open a movie house, the idea coming to him during a visit with an old friend from his days in Cuba. There had been a rare trip to New York City that year, a high-class outing during which Nelson tried to provide his wife with opportunities to take in culture. Nelson had initiated the journey because of Mariela's low spirits—she would sometimes pass days in silence—and Margarita and Isabel had accompanied them. On that visit they had gone to the Metropolitan Opera House and heard Enrico Caruso singing the role of the Duke in *Rigoletto*, and in the ballroom of the Waldorf they had watched the Russian dancer Pavlova perform. On other days they passed their time in the penny arcades of Times Square, where, with a derby tipped over his brow, Nelson O'Brien peered through the eyepiece of nickelodeon machines. They walked, the females lifting the hems of their dresses when crossing the dung-splattered streets, Nelson with his trouser cuffs rolled up and his tripod and folding-bellows-type camera in his arms (Margarita and Isabel playing with an Eastman Brownie camera, whose existence Nelson accepted—now everyone could take a photograph, even children—but secretly feared). They saw automobiles on Fifth Avenue, mainly Model Ts, and an endless succession of horse-drawn coal, ice, milk, fruit, and pots-and-pans wagons. Calliopes on the street corners, organ-grinders and their monkeys ("Be careful," their Poppy would say. "Them little beasts'll pick your pockets clean"). Uptown at the Metropolitan Museum of Art, they saw such things as they had never seen before: mummies and ancient sarcophagi. They saw Roman statuary and Winslow Homer's *Prisoners from the Front*. They saw paintings by the artists of the Flemish school, by the American naturalists, by Spaniards like Madrazo and Alvarez. They saw Delaroche's *Napoleon*. Down at Coney Island, Nelson blushed at the sight of a belly dancer named Abdullah's Loveliest Daughter, and they rode on carousels and Ferris wheels. They also witnessed an aviation display—three bi-wing planes flying in formation, making loops over the clouds—the first such display any of them had ever seen. (Ah, the aviator!) For the sake of promotion, three pianists, lined up in a row, were playing popular tunes. Back in Manhattan, they were among the crowds as a suffragette parade,

proud ranks of women in flower-brimmed bonnets, marched up
Fifth Avenue with arms joined, one of these ladies handing little
Margarita a feminist rose. Then they went to a movie house where
they saw some cowboy films, Mariela leaning over and asking
Nelson to verify her own translation of titles like "The Posse
advanced upon the desperadoes."

They stayed with a man in the movie business named Harrington, a tall cowboy-like fellow whom Nelson had befriended
years before during the Spanish-American War in Cuba. His
residence was on Gramercy Park, a many-roomed flat with a
view of the private green, his long hallway filled with the souvenirs and mementos of his travels. Harrington, resplendent in
pajamas and a fur-collar robe, was the head of a film outfit in
New Jersey and lived in the company of a young, pretty girl, who,
appearing in a navy-blue dress, cut high at the knees, seemed
very anxious to please him—Margarita remembered that.

The two men hadn't seen each other for years, and reunited,
they had embraced and were soon drinking champagne, the children served glasses of chocolate and soda by a gloomy manser-
vant. Mariela sipped, taking in their conversation and trying to
understand it, while Harrington, forwarding his ideas, regarded
Mariela with a gallant and patronizing attitude, the men speaking
in English.

"My friend," Harrington had said to Margarita's father, "it's
a pleasure to see you again, both of you!" (Toast.) "And I hope,"
he added, nodding to Nelson, "that you will take my advice this
evening: I'm telling you, my boy, there's money to be made in
the movie-exhibition business."

That evening, they dined in a German restaurant on Fourteenth Street where Mariela found the food too saucy and the
waiters brazen. But she enjoyed the playing of the Viennese
waltzes and the pom-pom rhythms of the orchestra. Out on the
dance floor and under the light of an ornate chandelier they
danced and for the first time she learned, in the arms of the
immense and towering Harrington, some American steps—first
the turkey trot, and another called the grizzly bear.

It was after that journey that Nelson decided he would one

day buy or rent the old Jewel Box Theater, which opened its doors only when traveling theatrical companies came to town. (It was at the Jewel Box that Nelson and Mariela saw a production of John Millington Synge's *Playboy of the Western World*, put on by the Dublin Dramatists Society, then on a tour of the country. Margarita could remember her father's pleasure in hearing the Irish actors performing, their rolling *r*'s, the clipped cut of their sentences, their melodies unfolding.)

But it took him nearly two years to realize this ambition. Gutting that theater and refitting it with new seats—that is, new secondhand seats—and with carpeting, he officially opened the Jewel Box Movie House in 1914, the year that the Patricia who lived was born. A special room was outfitted above the balcony with a slot window, and a great canvas screen raised above the stage, on which played the first feature film ever shown anywhere in that town—a four-reeler called *From the Manger to the Cross*, a New Testament epic that had been "made in Palestine" by a certain R. Henderson Bland, the posters for said film featuring, for all the world to see, a triumphant Christ rising into heaven. Charging ten cents a head, with Margarita selling tickets and Isabel as usher, Nelson O'Brien, dandy in a black long-tailed suit with top hat and striped cravat, had made a speech that night, thanking the people of Cobbleton for attending: "You know me as the fellow who takes photographs of your babies, and as the official photographer of certain civic events and other affairs—I thank you heartily for allowing me that privilege—but tonight I am here to welcome you to this silent-film exhibition. What you are about to see is a very special picture, famous all over the world, I've been told." He cleared his throat. "Well, I just want to say that I hope all of you enjoy the evening." And as a spontaneous reflex he called upon Mariela, waving her up onto the stage from her seat in the front row.

She had only two words, *"Gracias, gracias,"* before sitting again.

As the film played, the family and the audience much enjoyed themselves. Christ, whom they'd always known as the hanging figure on a Cross, or suffering in an altar panel (or as a statue, the object of a prayer), was shown at his birth, and then, after some time (after walking on the Sea of Galilee, after being tempted in the desert for forty days by the Devil, and after his triumphant arrival in Jerusalem), carrying his Cross up to Golgotha, the hill where He would be crucified. Then Christ in a great robe and in a halo of light, a spirit to his disciples, as real as the Christ who had appeared to them in their dreams, all so beautiful.

During the first months of exhibition, Nelson was also to show the films of Mary Pickford and Lillian Gish, William Faversham and Charlie Chaplin. He brought in some local musicians, a pianist and violinist to accompany the films, and a minstrel troupe to entertain the audience before the movies started. (They would sing "Fido Is a Hot Dog Now," "Down in Jungle Town," and "The Man Who Broke the Bank at Monte Carlo.") He showed *The Vixen*, with Theda Bara, *The Wharf Rat*, with Mae Marsh; and sometimes a film by his old friend Harrington.

A Saturday Night, 1921

MOVIE TICKETS cost fifteen cents, the program that day being a number of short one- and two-reel Laurel and Hardy films, one Chaplin, two Keatons, and a romantic melodrama starring John Barrymore. She would get there around four o'clock to begin selling tickets for the five o'clock show—a stack of magazines under the counter inside, *Colliers Weekly*, *The Saturday Evening Post*, and *Romance*, a cigar box (Havanas) where she would keep her change, the dollar bills going into her pocket, and the family making money. Her father would arrive later to greet the audience officially, as he did every weekend night, and with him would come his wife if she felt up to it, and certain of the sisters, walking to town if the weather was nice, for it could be a pleasant, chatty, lantern-lit stroll along the country road on a balmy night—and exciting when a truly popular film was playing, an actor like Rudolph Valentino (whose picture their father kept in the window of his photography shop, among those other photographs of local subjects) attracting crowds who'd come in automobiles and wagons from towns around, everyone waving hello and with wagonloads of school kids singing: a festive atmosphere, the sky cheery with stars—eyelets in the deep blue, as one of those old-time crooners might sing. Margarita would be waiting for the patrons: men in bowlers and derbies, wearing waistcoats, while their ladies wore taffeta and cotton dresses, the more fashionably young, razor-cut Romeos in camel's-hair coats and pleated trousers, fellows from the "good" side of town showing up with their dates in their knee-length tassel-hemmed dresses, hair bobbed (as she would have liked to have bobbed her hair, instead of keeping it long), with multi-looped fake-pearl necklaces and silver lamé or cloche hats, pulled down snug over the eyebrows for what they called the helmet effect.

And yet Margarita, with her large, expressive blue eyes and exotic looks, exerting the female influence, attracted much of her own attention, certain of these young men giving her a wink or later slipping out during the show for a smoke and approaching her to see if she'd like to take a spin in one of their sportsters— "You know, maybe head out for a picnic next Sunday down by the riverside where there's a pretty nice view, huh?" And she would smile, shrug, and say in an accent slightly touched by both her father's Irish brogue and the trilling r's of her mother's Cuban Spanish, "I must think about it, but do come back," since she distrusted those whom she'd seen with their dates. She'd sigh, selling those tickets, "Good evening, ma'am," "Thank you, sir," and smiling at some of the things she heard coming from the boys—"Ah, you're fulla balloon juice," and "Don't rubber me now"—phrases her mother would never know.

*

She was passing the time in this way and greeting her father's usual customers—one by one they came, the Fitzgeralds, the Dietrichs, the Emersons, the Dunbar family. Along, too, came Miss Covington, the Romance-language teacher from town, and one of her mother's few friends, the one town lady who was a frequent visitor to the house and who had, in the days when her mother first arrived, gone out of her way to befriend her, and the handsome priest, Father Mancuso, to whom, from time to time, Margarita, in a spirit of mischief, would make bawdy confessions ("I don't know, Father, but last night I dreamed of running naked through a house"), his presence stirring within her good Catholic soul a bit of naughty sinfulness. And then would come Mr. Roig and his family, and of course, driving up in his employer's touring car, Mr. García and wife, whom Margarita always let in for free.

Then the family would turn up, her father leading them, the littlest ones remaining at home with one of the older sisters, or with their mother—though she loved those silent movies about romance with titles like *A Woman Betrayed* and *Love's Lost Hope*, love stories, often tragic, set against the backdrop of glamorous New York salons and mansions, beautiful, virtuous, and ambitious women—good girls from poor backgrounds marrying handsome society gents, as would happen to Margarita. The sisters would take their places behind the candy counter, selling honey-roasted peanuts in paper cones and sourball candies to the customers, the others filling up a row near the front of the theater, where the family customarily sat, so that between films, if they so liked, the musical twins could get up and perform a duet at the organ, their sister Maria singing along with them, the family happy.

Usually, Margarita would remain in the ticket booth until about six, and then, closing up, join the family inside. But that evening, as the sun had started to set, a great clamor had arisen on the street—the horses in the stables bolting and neighing, kids running along and banging pots, automobiles honking horns—for, buzzing over the buildings of the town, was the Sopwith Camel, pulling along a brightly colored banner, an advertisement: "Come See the Daredevils' Flying Circus at The Pennsylvania State Fair! June 7–June 14, 1921." Drawing crowds into the street and out of the theater, the airplane circled overhead and then made its way west, the buzz diminishing and the plane shortly out of sight.

And Margarita, recognizing the craft, for a moment relived

her initial hopes about the pilot, heart racing and, if truth be told, a certain desire for release aching in her bones. But when the biplane left town, she resumed her ordinary expectations of life, finishing in the booth a magazine story recounting a chance love affair between an Italian noble posing as a peasant sheep-herder and an American society girl on vacation on the island of Capri, and just as the text described to her how, while they were standing together on a terrace of Tiberius' villa, the count, "in a magnificent, soulful whisper, told his new love: "*Ti voglio bene*"—which in Italian means "I love you"—and took the woman into his arms . . . Isabel came walking down the street and, approaching her older sister in the booth, said: "The aviator, did you see him, sister?"

"Yes."

"Well, did you know that not an hour ago he came to the house to visit?"

"Yes?"

"And he's invited us all to go flying with him one day at the state fair."

"All of us?"

"All who want to. Mama is not too happy—she lives in ancient times, sister—but he told us that when the county fair comes to Monroe we are to be his guests."

And, looking at her sister's expression, Margarita realized that she, too, must have daydreamed about the pilot.

"It'll be fun, won't it?"

"Oh, sister, I think so . . ."

Later, as she sat listening to the pipe organ, watching the ghostly figures of an elegant Manhattan couple dancing across the floor on the Jewel Box movie screen, she imagined the Mediterranean, the silvery rippling sea and the olive trees growing around Tiberius' villa in Capri, tried to imagine what it would all look like from the vantage point of the bi-wing craft. Around ten that evening, while walking back along the road, the air so fresh, the way lit by a lantern, she had looked up and watched a series of meteors breaking through the atmosphere—it was a time when the night skies were so clear, before they would be

diluted by too many earthly lights—and in the streak of falling
stars, she saw the pilot's face.

Her Flight into the Clouds

SHE CAME TO THINK of him as the handsome man from
heaven, not as Curtis, and the day the family went to the fair, a
few weeks later, she had awakened feeling wet between her legs
and not from her monthlies but from a sweet sensation, as if a
ball of candle wax had coiled and expanded inside her; she'd
touched herself until the ball was released and then, a little
saddened, for the experience would always make her feel that
way, even in old age, she sat appraising herself before a mirror
and became quite glum, because she was nowhere near as beautiful in reality as she was in her own mind, nothing like the ever-
elegant ladies of the magazines nor as pretty as certain of her
own sisters, particularly Helen, who was a natural beauty. She
derided her crooked teeth—they'd grown in after the manner of
her father's, twisted about by the introduction of too-large rear
wisdom teeth—and she wished she didn't look so much like her
mother (a part of her glorying in it, for on good days she fancied
in herself a resemblance to the courtesans of a Queen of Spain
or of a flamenco dancer, such as she had seen in the movies—
enchanting vamps with Syrian princess eyes and Pharaoh's
daughter's lips—while on other days she sometimes wished she
could close her eyes and look like Clara Bow or Theda Bara or
Gloria Swanson or Lillian Gish). Dallying before the mirror, she
had tried on different dresses before settling on a navy-motif
smock with stripes about the sleeves and neckline and white felt-
covered buttons down the front—nearly frumpish, save for the
fact that this dress was sleeveless and therefore inviting to men,
who could catch a glimpse of her curvy breasts, even if covered
by a camisole. And wanting to make herself truly sexy by wearing
a bit of ox-blood lipstick, which good girls avoided, she com-

pensated, biting down on her lips until they took a darker
coloration.

At the fair itself, they stood in a crowd eating cotton candy
and applauding, first a rodeo, a contest for best cows and bulls,
and then turned their attention to the sky above the hippodrome
tent, where the aviator's bi-wing craft flew in a formation of
similar planes—flying in loop-the-loops and tumbling in free fall,
flying upside down and then nearly atop one another, daring
acrobats hopping from the wings of one plane onto another.
When the air show ended, the sisters made their way to the
makeshift landing field, where the pilots, standing before their
planes, signed autographs for the crowds of children around
them. Waiting patiently, the oldest sisters—Margarita, Isabel,
Maria, the twins, Helen, and even ten-year-old Irene—finally
got a chance to greet the aviator who had spent some few hours
at their house, and he thanked them again, and offered to take
each up for a ride. The other pilots were doing the same, but for
a charge—a buck a head—the seats behind the pilot filling with
giggling adolescent girls and stoic and manly show-off boys. One
by one, the aviator took the sisters into the air and Margarita,
thinking that she would be the last to go up, watched each of
her sisters lifting off from the ground and being carried up
through the clouds (each climbing out of the plane happy and
exhilarated, even Isabel, who could not keep from laughing, and
each remembering that afternoon many years later, the kind of
event that would crop up in the midst of a holiday evening, during
a reunion when Maria might mention, while sipping a bit of
brandy and throwing her head back in reflection, "Do you remember that handsome aviator who took us all up into the air?
My God, what a day!"), until it was her turn. "Are you ready,
Miss Margarita?" the pilot had asked her. And she had blushed,
saying yes, and, remembering her dreams of elation and flight,
followed his instructions and put on a helmet and goggles as her
sisters had done, strapped on her belt and, waiting for the lift
upward to heaven, closed her eyes.

Before lowering his goggles, he winked at her and shouted
over the engine's loud hum, "Won't be able to say much, once
we're up, but just relax," and she had convinced herself that the

actual flight would follow her dream, that they would soar over the countryside and he would land in a quiet place, but what actually happened was this: the craft lifted off the ground and did indeed climb up toward the sun, but the slightest indication of the plane looping or tilting on its wing began to affect her balance, as if a bead of mercury were shifting in her ear and over the softest organs in her abdomen; through her stomach and large intestines seemed to flow a glutinous matter, which, shifting about inside her, induced in her such a feeling of nausea that all she could do was swallow, hoping that she would not lose the contents of her stomach and her wishes for love. A few times he had looked back and she had grown so teary-eyed that he had asked, "Are you okay? Miss?" And when, after climbing some five hundred feet higher, so she could see how the earth began to curve in the distance, how Cobbleton and the patches of farm property and the railroad tracks and rivers flowed in obvious and simple patterns—as in the dream—she started to call out to him, "Curtis, I think I want to land now," he told her, "Okay, miss," and slowly brought the plane back down, gliding in, nose up, to a proper stop, the pilot hopping to the ground and helping the quivery-legged Margarita onto the field.

It was all for the best: she went off to one of the fair outhouses to vomit, the prospect of romance and kisses behind her, and the aviator, surprising all, introduced the sisters, who were grateful for his generosity, to his fiancée, a little blonde, a sweet farm girl whom he'd met some time ago at another fair.

Two Sisters:
Maria in Photographs,
Irene on a Bike

THE EARLIEST known photograph of Maria Montez O'Brien, the third-oldest sister, was taken sometime in 1908, when she was two years old, posed by her father in the lap of her mother in the studio of his shop, the tot resplendent in a baby bonnet and lace dress, her lovely brow revealing in that moment a wary appraisal of the world around her—her father, as it happened (Margarita would remember), shaking a rattle to make sure that she looked at the camera and to prevent her from kicking about, her eyes intense and in fact focused not upon her father but through the shop window, watching a man, sleeves rolled up, fiddling with the engine of his milk truck. At the age of three, the short-cropped hair had grown out and her little hands were clutching her mother's hand, and while she had not yet suffered any trauma in her life and had begun the discovery of music, the ongoing business with the delicate etiquette of toilet training gave to her sweet mouth something of a twist, nearly anguished, for out of the Arcadian bliss of her daily routine, playing with dolls, entangling her fingers in her mother's and older sisters' hair, kissing her father, came a new discipline which, on the evidence of her disenchanted expression, did not make her happy. On the other hand, at the ages of four, five, and six, Maria, posing now alone and with her other sisters who were joining the family, especially the twins, Olga and Jacqueline, with whom she would always remain the closest, began to resemble the "mature" Maria, as she had now started to enjoy all the tasks at hand, especially when it came to teaching the littler ones about the daily necessities of life, her expression saying, "Though I am petite, I already know how to take care of things." By eight, her face started to suggest the splendid refinement of the elegant woman she would become, her hair having grown long and kept in a ponytail behind her, the slope of her high and serene forehead suggesting the virtuous nature of her future personality, angelic. And pride, too, because Mrs. Vidal, her music teacher, had already singled her out from the dozens of potential music students in Miss Peterson's grammar school in Cobbleton for her "special" talent—the woman hitting a middle C on the piano and having Maria hold that note for a long time, and, taking her through a scale of ascending half steps, making the discovery that she had the voice of a nightingale. At ten, she had given her first recital for the Ladies' Society, singing an engaging "Ave

Maria" at Christmas during a pageant, this young diva, no longer posed on anyone's lap, not on her mother's nor alongside Isabel or Margarita, but standing by the piano, an expression of accomplishment and separateness and a beaming smile on her face, for she already knew that she was going to bring pleasure to the lives of people. At that time she, the most devout of the sisters, truly believing in God, and having made her First Communion in Father Mancuso's church, would take on the air of someone unafraid of death (for death would take her into the mansions of heaven). By age thirteen, the onset of puberty rendered her face drawn, implying a terrible moodiness. Other photographs from those days show her in the company of the twins, who had already begun to blossom musically under her encouragement, their poses, standing side by side, predicting the careers that would keep them together for much of the rest of their lives. But at sixteen, in 1922, there registered on her face a recognition of her own limitations: it was in the autumn of that year that Nelson O'Brien, on the recommendation of Mrs. Vidal, had taken Maria to the Philadelphia Institute of Music to audition for a special operatic program, where it was determined that she, the poor thing, while having a pleasant mezzo-soprano voice, good for the works of Massenet and Gounod among others, did not have enough of a voice to consider that life professionally, so that the photographs of that year conveyed a terrible disappointment, eyes squinting, face downcast. She would recover, taking solace in the pure enjoyment of bringing along the twins, who, despite their operatic-quality voices, would never consider outdistancing their older sister's accomplishments. Early on, they had decided that their fates would be intertwined—and they would be, as the Three Nightingales, the Chanteuses, queens of Philadelphia and New York and small-town cabarets and musical reviews, eventually enjoying a fair livelihood that would take them often to the ports of Europe on cruise ships.

Then the mature Maria, aged nineteen and in love, for one of the two times in her life, with a plump tenor from a nearby town who would come to Cobbleton to sing duets with her in the parlor of Mrs. Vidal's house, this fellow—what was his name?

Henry Maine—a true talent, a year older than she and able to sing everything from German lieder to Italian bel canto with breathtaking finesse, the two twilling away amorously like songbirds and stealing (when left alone for a moment while Mrs. Vidal would answer the doorbell) little ennobled kisses, nothing with the tongue, that would drive Maria to the confessional in Father Mancuso's church. Going through her days in a state of complete idyllic distraction, she would wait for Mrs. Vidal to inform her that he was back in town. The two of them fell deliciously in love and remained so, even though he was not a particularly handsome man—but a very good one. Like her, a Catholic and devout, he would sometimes walk Maria home along the country road to the house where the sisters lived, the two of them singing so beautifully that birds would follow them on the road. Later, under the supervision and watchful eyes of Isabel, they'd sit on the porch and quietly speculate about a future together, the prospect both exhilarating and troubling Maria, because to remain with Henry would take her away not only from the household but from Olga and Jacqueline, to whom she felt pledged. At night she would pray, asking God what she should do. She felt many doubts, even if he had conveyed to her the beautiful promise of pursuing an artistic life by his side. And although she knew he was being kind, as her voice was not as good as his, they made plans to marry one day and commemorated this by posing for a photograph in Mrs. Vidal's studio. With a simple Kodak Brownie camera, circa 1926, Mrs. Vidal herself, loving to keep photographs of her students and always having a soft spot for Maria and her musical sisters, took the shot—a photograph that found the twenty-year-old Maria possessing the serenity and apparent happiness of a young and pretty woman who in those moments dwelled in Paradise, light brilliant around her, the crystal flower-filled vases of Mrs. Vidal's parlor aglow, a scene of earthly joy. A year of felicity for Maria, of too much hope and distraction, and then another of disappointment when Henry, sitting with her on the porch of the house on Abel-myer Road, told her that he would be journeying on scholarship to study voice in Berlin and that at the end of the year he would return to join her. Six months of heartsickness and longing passed, until, as such stories go, the bad news arrived: not that Henry had fallen in love with someone else but that Henry, whom the birds followed, had fallen into the depths of Lake Constance, in southern Germany, and drowned. Photographs of Maria from that time on show the very same expression she had in early youth, when the logic of the world was not clear and her eyes, gazing out timidly, seemed wary.

*

Better to consider the love of Irene, the seventh of the sisters, with her most elegant name. Cherubic, good-natured, and chubby as an infant and as an adolescent (how she loved it when the butler García would show up with those bags of plantains that they could fry to crispiness in a large cast-iron pan), she had always been lavished with many sweets and foods and with sisterly affection. As she became a young woman, those beautiful features were swallowed by the moonlike roundness of her excessively fleshed-out face, and she lived for meals and was most happy to sit in her room eating one-cent sweets and spoonfuls of sugar or of honey, the idea of falling in love with a man never occurring to her except when she read magazines and would envy those young women whose boyfriends and husbands brought them chocolates. She would daydream about love, not so much for the sweet kisses and embraces of a man, or the roses that romance was said to bring, but for the boxes of dome-shaped, swirl-topped Belgian chocolates with maraschino-cherry centers, marzipan delights, chocolates with coconut centers, chocolates stuffed with citron and nuts.

Still, by the time she reached her early twenties and, plump as a sultan, she decided to find herself a man and, to do so, aspired to a more lithe form, subsisting on paltry meals and becoming, for the first time in her life, foul-tempered and unhappy. That was when her father, Nelson O'Brien, took pity on her and bought her a bicycle, an Atlas "strong enough to support the world," and it was on this vehicle that she began to ride along the country roads for the sake of exercise (these roads during the bad times of the Depression, with their bands of the hungry and poor, often making her sad). She'd worked in those days in the movie house, often behind the candy counter, and afterward would take a long route home, and although she did so for a year, weather permitting, this exercise had very little effect, save for the thickening of certain muscles— in her thighs and legs. She was on the brink of despair when one day, crossing the bridge near Tucker's farm, she happened to collide with another bicyclist, this bicycle, also an Atlas, conveying on its bending frame a young man as immense and porcine as herself, a fellow in a black top coat and schoolboy's beanie cap, whose pockets, as it would turn out, were stuffed with sugar cubes and candies. Tumbling over—as in tandem they were too wide to pass each other—they had landed side by side. And while she had escaped with only a few bruises on her rump, coccyx aching for days, the fellow's trousers were badly torn and his thick knees were bleeding.

Beside herself at having hurt the young man, Irene attended to him like a nurse, tearing from her slip two pieces of cloth, and there, kneeling before him, ministered to his wounds—and most happily so, in an idyll heightened by the clamor of the birds and the sweet springtime breeze and the smell of flowers in the air. In the sunlight (all such speculations about love—love that could only be guessed at, toyed with, enjoyed from a distance of time—were drenched with light, for love, as their mother always said, filled the heart with light) he seemed noble, and because he was so good-natured that he did not complain but thanked her instead, when they had lifted up their bent bikes, they sat for a time under a tree, more or less pleased by each other's corpulence, as in this circumstance neither felt shame. They talked. His name was Pokapoulos, a Greek fellow, and he lived in a nearby town, some ten miles away from Cobbleton, and was the son of a butcher, and he, too, confessed that he loved to eat, though that spring afternoon he admitted to an interest in the veterinary arts and wished that, instead of chopping up animals, he could cure them. She felt touched by his tender, heavy-jowled face and by the way he looked at her. He had told her,

"You're a swell gal for not being angry at me, when it was really my fault—I shoulda stopped and let you pass"—and just then he pulled from his pockets some hard candies, which they both happily devoured, beginning the introduction to their love.

He started to visit with the family, always sidling in through the door and bringing parcels of meat with him, to her father's delight—for Nelson O'Brien loved his steaks thick and juicy—and when he would stroll with her, or keep her company in the kitchen while she helped cook the evening's meal, he was always attentive and complimentary to her. "My, but you look pretty today," he would tell her, and, as in a fairy tale, made her feel so happy that she began to forget about the troubles of the world—that beggars would come to the house asking for food, their mailbox marked with a white painted X, signifying "This family will give." When he ate with the family, tasting her cookery, his eyes would water with delight and he would look on her with nothing less than complete adoration. And though it would be hard for any of the sisters to think that Irene and this fellow were acquainted with the romance of heated embraces, they, when alone, would engage in long bouts of succulent, tongue-swallowing kisses, tongues tasting of sweets and nut breads and steak, entwined and thick with the blood of appetite and the promise of an all-devouring consummation. That would take place after three years of mealtime conviviality, during a honeymoon which they would spend in a country inn near Lake George, New York, a Swiss-style chalet known for its view of the Adirondacks and attendant waterway and for its quail-stuffed pastries and all-you-can-eat dessert buffet.

The romance, of course, was more complex than what a sister like Margarita might ascertain. It was filled with its pains and, as well, with its moment of sexual passion, hard to imagine but inevitable, the two generously layered bodies blissfully joined and moving through the thickest field of sensations, with hungry bites and long appraisals of tasty bodily morsels, with the promise of a happy future and many satisfying meals.

Nothing Was Sweeter:
How the Other Side Lived

NOTHING WAS SWEETER, Margarita would recall on her days alone, than to be a young girl in the spring, nothing more pleasant than to rush down the stairs into the arms of her father when he'd come home at the end of his day's work, or, when she was very little, to be carried along a country road on his shoulders, the work of the Lord all around them, or to sit and watch with great curiosity as he went about his business, fiddling with the accordion-like camera as he posed her and the family for a portrait or as he took photographs here and there in the countryside, certain of those jobs giving him access to the houses of the wealthy, who seemed to live in another world, with their great lawns and tennis courts and chauffeurs and wardrobe rooms and dolphin-mouthed waterspouts in the bathrooms and flush toilets! And Carrara marble statues of Apollo, English paintings on the walls, and floor-to-ceiling libraries (most impressive, a sweet papery smell of the past thick in the air)—that general atmosphere of pure and uncompromised gentility reminiscent, to her mind, of the aristocratic lives she'd read about in books. (She thought this even though she had once heard García, on a night when he was angry about not getting a raise and after having had one too many glasses of wine during a visit to the family, say crudely, "These people behave as if they don't have assholes!") Nelson used to take Margarita and Isabel and a few of the others along for company, and later, when she was older, he'd take Margarita along as his assistant—work that she much enjoyed, as she would then see how other people lived, from the poorest farmers, who paid her father with hens and baskets of fruit and sacks of corn and potatoes, to those of much greater means, whose hired help oftentimes let them in through the pantry and service entrance. But that was not so bad—how many times did it happen that the help, seeing the children, would call them into the kitchen and serve them feasts of pastries and sandwiches. Years later, she had to laugh remembering one occasion when she was sixteen and the plump Irene, then seven, was left alone in a kitchen on an afternoon when the pastry chefs and cooks were preparing for a banquet, the head cook or chef having made the terrible mistake of telling Irene, "Now, you can eat whatever you like, dearie." Within an hour, Irene had managed to eat much of a leg of lamb, delicately prepared with rosemary, garlic, and a basting of honey and wine, as well as a dozen puff pastries—chocolate éclairs and cream-filled napoleons, the cook astonished and shouting: "My God, no wonder you're such a fat leetle gurl!" and Irene confused but happily sated. On such occasions, Margarita'd get a chance to see how the other half lived, loved to sit outside on the grounds while her father prepared for his work, watching tennis games, badminton, croquet being played. Looking about, she'd love the feeling the high wrought-iron gates gave her, the long shadows of their tipped spires racing across the sloping lawns, the bursts of intermittent sunlight pouring through the private forests of the high, high trees, whose birds, it seemed to her, were especially elegant. (And through those corridors of shade she would see furtive does peeking.) Fountains such as the bell-cup Russian-style fountain that she once saw on a desolate estate near Quarryville made her feel as if she were in a dream or in another world (say, the planet Mars), for the fountain had been designed with fine-timbred bell cups which resonated in different glass-like tones—a water-driven glockenspiel, though she did not know the phrase at that time—and seemed to play without end. And she saw estates with their own private chapels and in one instance a genuine medieval garden with peacocks, who moved tranquilly, as did their masters, oblivious to the more mundane sufferings of life. But there were also occasions when death somehow lingered in the halls and she would know that in one of the myriad bedchambers, up one of the stairs and just beyond the landing, off one of the marble atriums, there would be a room with a tubercular or polio-racked child to whom no amount of money made a difference.

And there were occasions before the First World War when

her father was hired for debutante parties held in grand houses with many-chandeliered rooms and he would set up his equipment in a room off the dance floor. Using floral arrangements placed on a pedestal or a table, with velvet curtains as a backdrop, he would photograph young couples, the inheritors of the earth, carefree and well-coiffed, the ladies beautiful in their silk gowns and Belle Epoque, many-layered ballroom dresses, the gents in tails, enchanted with one another's company and the fact that their lives were so good.

There was always much food to eat and most of the time those employers were gracious and accommodating toward the photographer and his daughters; more rarely, there might be a twitty son or spoiled daughter to start an argument with Margarita or to point out that she and her father or whichever of her sisters had come along were not proper guests—however, that was more the exception.

Still, parties were parties, and her favorite, at least in memory, were the harvest balls held in Cobbleton—about that time of the year, with the trees turning and the first chills that made sleep so blessed (sisters' rumps pressed together in their beds, wrapped in flannel gowns, feather mattresses warmed by bricks heated on the stove, for it would get very cold in the evenings), and the special clarity of the night sky with the stars shifting in position (and perhaps because it was on an autumn night when she was very little that her mother had pointed out the brilliance of the planet Saturn)—and the hayrides, organized by the Chamber of Commerce and by the Protestant churches. The sisters, on equal footing with the other girls of town, would wait their turn to take the ride from the square two miles up the road to Mayor Heinrich's farm, where, in his barn festooned with hanging lanterns and decorated with crepe paper and cloth banners, they would have doughnuts and milk and soda pop and feast on pumpkin pies before riding back to the town hall, where a dance would take place. As usual, the timid farmboys and the sons of railroad and factory workers, hair slicked down with spit and Brilliantine and a smell of wheat sticking to their clothes, stood on one side, and on the other, the young ladies of town, seated in rows and seeming a little bored (within them, family groupings of sisters, some families having five, some twenty, as was the case with the Schneiders, with their Goldilocks hairdos and unfortunate apple-shaped faces, stout derrieres, manly gaits, and sour demeanors, the poor things), until the string band started to play and so began a program of square dancing and traditional country waltzes, the Montez O'Brien sisters, even the littlest ones, ever anxious to partake of the festivities, and waiting, waiting until they would grow impatient with the timidity of the boys and break ranks with the other girls, who already considered them too different for their own tastes, marching across the floor to initiate the proceedings—so that soon just about everybody would be dancing. And on those autumn nights, in those years before he had his success with the movie house, their father also worked at the harvest balls, taking photographs (some of them trick shots with witches brooming across the pock-faced moon in the background), and his pictures would appear in the local newspapers, and prints would be sold to the community through the offices of the Good Citizens' Club.

By the time Margarita was approaching womanhood and the movie house had opened, her father had gotten into the habit of seeking a kind of solitude at night, saying little to the sisters —of course showing them affection, and always having the strength for the rituals of love with his wife—but as the years passed, he seemed to need more and more time alone. The evenings would often find him sitting before the fireplace with a tin mug in hand, watching the embers (clustered, feathery, snowy-gray, and crumbling like wings) of the birch and elm logs dim and glow, as if they were softly breathing, his shadow thrown immense and wavery against the walls behind him, his mind moving through clouds of manly pensiveness, and muttering to himself about the passage of time and the world amounting to as much as those ashes, everything, every living creature, turning to smoke. Although he would read the *Chronicle*, full of its farmers' news and the doings of society, and from time to time give out some order, or lord over the organization of yet another nightly ritual, the pushing together of tables and the collection

of chairs so that the family could dine together, he was in many
ways an absent being, almost a ghost in his indifference to household affairs, which, from his point of view, always seemed the
same: the daughters assisting his wife, their chitchat, and some
of it in his wife's tongue, Spanish, sounding to his ears like the
forest twitter of birds in the trees, noisy, lively, melodious, and
territorial.

*

Margarita could remember the sweet endearments whispered in Spanish coming from her mother and father's bedroom
at night, and that her Poppy had long ago made a decision about
the language of Spanish in the household—it wasn't that hearing
it annoyed him, just that he thought the daughters would be
better speaking his proper kind of English. But he was not a bully
and often said nothing when their mother spoke with them. Once,
when Margarita was six or seven, he had called out to her, a little
sadly (or drunkenly): "You, come 'ere, won't ya?" And when she
did, nervously sitting beside him on a wicker chair on the porch,
he told her, touching her face and brushing aside her bangs of
thick black hair, "I'd been noticin' lately that you're always talking in Spanish, a fine language, and that's all right with me, but
so as you don't get confused, I want you to know that I expect
you to address me always in my tongue, and that's English, you
understan'? And that's for your own good, 'cause in this country
it's been my observation that Spanish will be of little use to you,
certainly useless as far as gainful employment and one day finding yourself a husband. I won't snap your head off if I hear you
speaking it, but just remember it might hurt my feelings to think
that you aren't respecting my wishes. And one more thing, darlin', I've heard you chatting away in Spanish with Isabel and
Maria, which is your business and fine with me, but don't you
ever think that you'll be pulling a fast one in terms of secrecy
around me, because I spent four years down in Cuba way learning
to speak that language, and even though it hasn't any value to
me now, in this country, and except to talk with your mother
sometimes when she doesn't understand some things in English,

I promise you that I can understand every single little word you say—so remember that."

She Rarely Came Across Anything
from Cuba

IN THAT HOUSE, with its many cluttered rooms, they could sometimes sense that there was a great difference between their mother and their father, as if two atmospheres, one Irish and one Cuban, emanated from them. In that little upstairs room where their mother would sit and sew and think, there was a box, near a basket filled with spools of yarn and fabric bunting, in which she would keep letters from Cuba, and another box in which she kept a stereoscopic viewer and a cache of stereoscopic plates of nineteenth-century scenes from Cuba, which she had found for sale in a Philadelphia antique shop on a day when, in the spirit of imbuing a sense of patriotism and national history into the sisters, Nelson had taken the family to Independence Hall for a look at the cracked Liberty Bell (where, if the truth be told, after the day's tour their Poppy had slipped out at night from their hotel suite, heading off to one of the three hundred or so speakeasies in the city). Later Mariela was enchanted with her discovery, for the stereoscopic viewer and slides, when held up to the window light, made those images—"A typical Cuban wagon, called a *volante*," "Statue of Carlos III at the entrance to the Paseo de Carlos III, Havana, Cuba," "Bridge spanning Canímar River," "Slave posing in stocks," "Sugarcane Harvest" "Row of Royal Palms," among many others—seem three-dimensional. Sometimes she would gaze through the viewer and with her eyes closed imagine, for example, that she was standing on the stone roman-arched bridge that crossed the Canímar River, birds chirping about her, lianas and trumpet flowers and bent palms, lovely and woolly-headed, reflecting in its water. And although she had access to the cartons of her husband's photo-

graphs of her family taken in Cuba (among many subjects), there
had been something beguiling about the discovery of such photographs in Philadelphia. During her days in Cobbleton, she
rarely came across anything about Cuba: cigar ads in the windows
of the tobacco shops; a photograph of Teddy Roosevelt posed in
jodhpurs and his Rough Rider uniform, tassel-handled sabre in
hand, a "Bully for me," expression staring out into the world,
nicely framed in the post office; a few paragraphs in the school
textbooks that her daughters would bring home, with references
to the Spanish-American War, which from curiosity she would
examine, the pen-and-ink drawing that had appeared on the
front page of the New York *Herald* in 1898 of the battleship
Maine exploding at night, as if struck by an immense comet; and
in the geography book, Cuba grouped with all the other countries
south of the border, its description warranting seventy-two
words—she'd counted them one afternoon. And there were, of
course, advertisements, especially after the First World War, that
concentrated on the American tourist trade: "COME TO HAVANA
AND YOU CAN BET ON A CUBAN-STYLE GOOD TIME!" And after
1919: "Forget about the Volstead Act in Cuba!" and on those
same pages, usually in the Philadelphia papers, cruise schedules
to Cuba out of Boston, New York, Baltimore, and Miami, the
Great White Line being most prominent. Its ads used an illustration of a towering, many-porthole steamship in New York
Harbor, chimneys wafting perfectly circular smoke rings, and
crowds below thronging to get aboard. And on the business pages,
if she had looked, as did her husband, who owned some shares
of Cuban–American Sugar, she would have found numerous
stocks, the word Cuba in their listings: Cuban–British Rail Cor-
poration, First National City Bank of Cuba, Cuban Electrical
Inc., etc. When it came to music, she would hear a ragtime piece
out the saloon doors, the "Cubanola Glide," and never know
that it was about Cuba, as it sounded like so many other rinky-
dinky piano rags of that time, and in the days when Nelson had
the house wired for electricity and purchased, like half of the
country, their very own Atwater Kent superheterodyne crystal-
radio set, she might cruise the stations and come across a per-

formance of the Havana Symphony conducted by the composer
Ernesto Lecuona, his splendid melodies borne on a spectrally
guided wavelength, the music fading in and out, the voice of an
announcer commenting from radio station CMCQ in Havana in
a storm of staticky convolutions and atmospheric pops, as if spirits, capricious and loud, were gushing, whistling, and shuddering
like the winds—the voice announcing the words *"de la Habana,
Cuba,"* sounding as if it were coming from far away, as far away
as the planet Mars.

But that was all, for the most part, of Cuba for many years.
She tried to keep the notion of it alive in her daughters, especially
the oldest, describing to her with true sweetness the substance
of her family's life there before the war in 1895 had disrupted
it, a serene petit-bourgeois life, her father Emilio Montez—after
whom her only son, Emilio Montez O'Brien, would be named
—being a farmer and merchant of sufficient means. He owned
two farms and a stable in the city of Santiago, the farms razed
to the ground during the war, the horses butchered for their meat
by the Spaniards, the carriages "militarized" for use as transport,
and the man and his family, who had once known a more or less
comfortable existence, reduced in status and wealth. Her stories
of her life in that household before the war, with her maids and
laundresses and liveried carriages, and cooks in the kitchen,
among so many other amenities (the pilfered furniture, the con-
fiscated jewelry), sometimes lingered in the minds of the sisters,
so that at night, when thinking about their mother and her past
life, the life she had lived before any of them was born ("From
the Darkness you had come, and to the Darkness you will go,"
Margarita would think years later), they would feel certain
changes taking place in the household. Even though they were
living just off a road called Abelmyer, some few miles outside of
a small Pennsylvania town, the notion of Cuba, like their own
femininity, exerted a powerful pull. Sometimes at night they
would think about their mother's Cuba and they would have the
sensation that the rooms of the house had been turned into a
rain forest, that orchids were budding out of the walls, that lianas
were hanging off the ceiling beams, that one could hear in the

distance the ocean and smell the sea foam—all coming on waves
of unconscious speculation, thoughts buzzing in the halls and
floating through the doors and from mind to mind of each sleeping sister, arms wrapped about one another, the sisters flinching
and breathing loudly—a sigh in the middle of the night—Cuba
in the air, the atmosphere of a house in the tropics, sunlight
glaring through the windows though it was the dead of darkness.

There was also, at the same time, the Irish influence of their
father, which certain of the sisters, most particularly the younger
ones, more closely identified with. It was a more understandable
mystery, as they had very few ideas what Ireland was like. Though
their father was not a talkative man, at least the nature of his
language, English—they knew nothing of the Gaelic tongue—
did not mystify them the way the Spanish spoken by the older
sisters with their mother did, falling upon their ears like the
nearly Babylonian chitchat of songbirds. The name O'Brien had
been their main legacy, that and fair complexions and the freckles
that burst over their faces in the spring and the blue eyes and
the feeling that far away, in a distant land—not Cuba, however—there were others like themselves. It was a world far beyond, about which they knew nothing, the principles of its history,
as with Cuba, reduced to a few names from schoolbooks, the
most prominent being that of Parnell, and the lore of the place
remembered by the shamrock and the talk of "the little people"
and notes out of the books which would say things like "And it
is said that if one kisses the Blarney Stone, then that person will
be blessed by luck." And they had those few visual clues as to
what their father had left behind in Ireland—no photographs
save for one, of a beautiful young woman, life brimming within
her, kept on the wall in a gold-leaf oval frame, their Aunt Kate,
Nelson's sister, they'd been told, with whom their father had first
traveled to America in 1896, and then there was that print, of a
lovely house in an emerald meadow in the early-morning mist,
the print captioned, "A house, Shannon, Ireland," which the
daughters had presented their Poppy for Christmas one year,
1922. Yes, the most glorious of Christmases in memory, more
glorious than any of them would ever know as adults, the pine

tree which their father cut down from the forest nearly a living, breathing creature, with magical powers, annually garlanded with colored beads and handmade ornaments and store-bought crystal angels and tulip-bulb candlelights—the tree, the fireplace, the table covered with pastries and other treats, a dream.

Sometimes His Spirits Were Low

EVEN DURING the days of his greatest success, when he'd come home with bags of caramels and teddy bears, his spirits some-times sank so low that he would fade from view, as if he were willing himself away. He could sit in a room swarming with life—her sisters by the piano, or dancing before the Victrola to the scratchy recordings of Bix Beiderbecke and his Wolverine orchestra, or sewing dresses or making quilts and having the time of their lives gossiping, or at the center of the clamor of their meals—even amid the bustle of such activity, her Poppy managed to convey such loneliness that he often seemed a ghost who had happened by, to observe, from an unimaginable distance, the doings of life and earthly happiness beyond him. He'd always have to battle against his own worst instincts—as he truly did love this world, for all its flaws—and he would seek diversion, losing himself in his various hobbies. Having become a great appreciator of science, he had over the years accumulated, for his own amusement and the family's, all kinds of projecting devices, magic lanterns and kinescopes, music boxes, Edison & Co. cylinder players, then wind-up phonographs, and then a number of electrically run devices, the most impressive being a simple house fan which helped to cool them off in the summers. He simply needed to remain busy: when he was not fiddling around in the shed that he had set up with his photography supplies behind the house, developing prints or simply sitting about reading manuals, he was out on the road looking for work, or else making his way to Philadelphia, where he would pick up some of the latest films from a distributor. And when he was not doing that, he dallied in bed upstairs with his wife, either snoring away or making love, for year by year the babies came into the world; and when he was not doing that, he would pass the time before the fireplace, contemplating the colorless, music-less world in which he sometimes lived.

Publicly cheerful and exuberant, he was the kind of fellow to slap a man on the back with a greeting, or to commiserate sorrowfully at some bit of bad news. Many a customer and friend in the region where he traveled selling his goods or taking photographs was gladdened by the sight of this man, with his gallant manners and his colorful mode of dress, and he would often be seen in a brown derby whose brim he would decorate with pins of a patriotic nature: the Statue of Liberty, a wavering American flag, a World War I doughboy, bayonet raised and ready for action. Known in town for his cheerfulness, his happy "Good mornin' to ya" and "Isn't it a nice day," and for his thick head of reddish-blond hair, his bristly and regal handlebar mustache, which he'd grown to help conceal a row of misaligned teeth, he moved through that world concealing not only the teeth but the true and private nature of his being, which the sisters knew. His personality, if it could be called that, was more of a construction based on the memories of a few kindly men he had known, cheery sorts, who, he'd noticed, attracted friends easily. And in his youth, despite his awkwardness—he could not dance, he would bump into chairs, and could not tell jokes well—he had decided that with strangers he would present himself as the most guileless, humble, and friendly man in the world. Such cheerfulness—the strain of digging down deep for the kind of sunniness that would endear him to others—often left him exhausted, and when he'd come home, a dog could mangle his trousers cuff and he would end up petting "the darlin' little thing," changing, it would seem to the fourteen sisters, the very nature of his face. By day, his face seemed wide open, accessible, jolly emotion in his blue eyes, his cheeks puffy with optimism; but when he opened the gate on the white picket fence and passed through the fanlighted entrance to his house, he seemed to become a severe-featured man, shadows forming under his eyes and the general drooping of his spirit tightening his jaw. Wrapped suddenly in a wiry anxiety, and never wanting to argue with or shout at his playful daughters, he would take refuge in silence, and as he had on many such evenings over the passing years, he would ask himself about the progression of his life, thick with emotions, doubts, and love. That he had so many daughters both delighted and troubled him, for he had always wanted a son, and although he bounced his youngest girls on his knee, he could never, for the life of him, look them in the eyes with a glance or expression that said "Everything will be all right," or that he was completely content with their sometimes overwhelming femininity.

Dr. Arnold's Relaxation Heightener

OBLIVIOUS to the cause of his suffering, he would take a sip of his evening tonic, the curative potion called Dr. Arnold's Relaxation Heightener, a dark, syrupy liquid which came in a curvaceous amber bottle and whose ingredients were listed on the label in a diminutive curlicue script as "sugar, Persian tar, honey, Arabian and Persian opiates and other miracle tonics." Two tin cups of this drink had been his nightly companions, "his little friend in time of need," since 1912, when, on a chilled and disheartening afternoon, he had first sampled its health-restoring and cheering properties. On that day, while driving his Model T Ford along a country road, its trunk filled with the household goods and medicines that, as a sideline, he peddled to farmers, torpid factory workers, and townspeople, he came down with a shortness of breath, a fierce burning pain in the back of his neck, and a severe case of spiritual dropsy that left him feeling a terrible sadness about life. Later the sight of a crippled sparrow struggling along the side of the road, its beaked head gasping for air, startled him and he pulled over to the side and, in the drizzly gray of the day, tried to revive the bird in the warm palms of his hands. When the bird continued to shake and then stopped, because it had died or was too frightened to move, he tossed the poor bird aside and threw open the heavy copper-hinged trunk that he kept on the back seat, and began to search for something to lift his flagging spirits. That day he pulled out an amber-colored bottle of Dr. Arnold's Relaxation Heightener, cautiously swallowing three mouthfuls and feeling skeptical as he did so. But soon this skepticism faded, as the medicine did indeed begin to lift his troubled male spirit, and soon he was back on the road, impressed by the potion. As the label claimed, his aches had faded and his feeling of "life fatigue" lifted away, turning into an appreciation for the vastness and diversity of God's good universe. The cold drizzle seemed suddenly to fall in sanctified sheets of wavery angel hair, and the plump-bottomed clouds, which had seemed thready with darkness, were now livid with veins of silver light. Suddenly the prospect of knocking on a poor farmer's door with the intent of selling him an item he might not necessarily need did not trouble him. In fact, that afternoon he was the grandest salesman who had ever lived. Friendly, open-eyed, and with his Irish brogue charmingly garrulous, he sold a set of silverware, a mandolin, a pair of boots, and much, much medicine. In a celebratory mood, he later took a few more swallows of that potion and decided to buy himself a twenty-four-bottle case of the relaxation heightener, and did so every six months or so, continuing to enjoy its salubrious effects, until 1938, when the manufacturer went out of business and those magic bottles were never seen again.

*

And she remembered the winter day during the Great War when her Poppy told her about the circumstances that had brought him, many years before, to Cuba, and the commencement of his love with her mother. That had been on a day when a storm had moved westward across the Delaware River and swept over their county, bringing much snow. It had first appeared as a bottom-heavy mist of clouds against the sylvan skies, and within a few hours the temperature had so dropped that a bluish ice had started to form on the pond at the edge of their

property, tree branches sprouted tubes and nodules of ice, and
the inside of the windowpanes became so frosted over that one
could write a name on them with a finger. Cold enough that the
sisters wore mufflers and gloves inside the house and they
thanked God that in the corner of the toilet room there sat a
potbellied wood-burning stove.

A chill, damp and heavy, such as their mother had never
known in Cuba, went to their very bones.

That morning, they brought more wood in from the porch
and built a great fire; they had covered their two horses, Hercules
and Tinto, with extra blankets in their stalls in the barn, their
poor ears cocking against the wind. And their mother stood by
the window, pregnant for the thirteenth time in her young life
—it was 1918 and she was not yet thirty-five—watching the road
for the approach of their father. The previous afternoon, he had
driven the Model T to Philadelphia to pick up tin canisters of
film from a distributor, and she wondered just where along his
route he might be—Ward, Unionville, Kirkwood? And as her
mother waited by the window watching the snow falling in fierce
swirls, carried by winds that twisted the house's timbers, which
creaked like a wooden ship, there came over her an expression
of pallid fear—it was as if anxiety had pulled back the skin of
her lovely face, so that one could make out the outlines of her
skull. But they all felt a tightening in their limbs, for after such
storms the papers listed who had been found in a field, in an
underheated house, in a pond, "overcome by the elements."
What could they do but attend to those duties which most pleasantly produced more heat—a stew of vegetables and beef under
way in the kitchen, candles and kerosene lamps lit to help warm
the parlor, where they had gathered on the couches, covered in
blankets, yawning and asking, "Where is he?" A few hours
passed and still no motion on the road—no sleigh carriages or
milk truck or automobile, or animals grazing in the fields or birds
in flight; just old cocoons and desolate birds' nests and snow,
while in the barn, in the upper rafters, the mute gray pouchy-
looking creatures called *murciélagos* in Cuba (bats) hung upside
down, asleep. Time slowed to a tedium of worry. Then at two

o'clock in the afternoon they saw him, their Poppy, Nelson O'Brien, a great shadowy mass struggling against the winds up the incline some twenty yards from the road toward the house, flushed with exhaustion and pulled along by Margarita and Isabel, who had gone out to fetch him.

His clothing drenched, he warmed himself by the fire, rubbing and blowing warm breath into his hands and calling out for a cup of whiskey—justifiably so—and their mother, her arms wrapped tenderly around him, saying to him in Spanish, as was her habit in moments of emotional agitation: "I thank God that you're here, my husband, but, my God, where was your common sense?"

"Oh, my dear wife," he said in English, pulling her close, "I couldn't get past the drifts by Tucker's Pond and I thought it best that I leave the Model T, so please calm yourself, woman, and pass out some of the candies I've brought along—over there in my pocket, caramels and hardballs. And don't be angry with me."

Warmed by the fire, he sat there with two of the littlest ones in his arms, holding them proudly, while his wife mopped up the floor. He had stretched and yawned, feeling the dampness through his thick flannel union suit; he had pulled off his stockings, which lay in crumpled balls, sending up steam by the fire. Margarita had knelt down before him, rubbing his frozen feet with a cloth dipped in kettle-warmed water. And then she brought him a bowl of stew.

"*¿Quieres algo más?*" she had asked.

"No, no," he'd told her.

Then, watching and listening to the storm as it continued, he announced, "My God, but I think it's time for a nap."

When he got to his feet, the fatigue of his trek through the snow made his knees quake. Yawning again, he made his way up the stairs to their bedroom, where he managed to put on some dry clothing, and then he collapsed on their canopied bed, sleeping until the following afternoon. Late the next day, the family still snowbound, he sat fortified by whiskey and his nightly tonic before the fire.

He was worried, he'd told his daughters, about getting out to the automobile with a shovel so that he might retrieve for his business's sake the films he had brought back from Philadelphia, and hoped that it would stop snowing soon, as he was very much concerned that the tins he'd left behind, and the silver-nitrate films they contained, might freeze to brittleness and crumble if the storm's cold persisted.

And yet it was that afternoon, and on into the night, that her Poppy spoke to his daughters about his past. Margarita listened and years later she imagined. Later in life, she would wrap that minor incident around the circumstances that first brought him to Cuba in 1898—seeing him as a man battling the storm of his own powerful emotions.

THEIR POPPY

AND THE STORY

OF HOW

HE CAME

TO AMERICA

A Mist-ridden Place

SHE'D IMAGINE that the Ireland of her father's youth was a sad, mist-ridden place where it was always four o'clock on a late January afternoon in 1895. An endless drizzle fell, with stronger winds in wavery sheets like sea gales over the green countryside, and the chimneys of houses hundreds of years old sent up puffs of peat smoke. Men would appear on the horizon, guiding their carts and horses out of the muddy bogs and through the fields of clover, breath steaming from their lips, their bones rheumatic from the dampness, cheeks flushed from drink or the wind.

He might have lived in Drogheda, Dundalk, Glandore, Glengarriff, Youghal, Kinsale, Wexford, for all the sisters knew, for their father never mentioned the name of the town where he was born and he burned all his letters. Perhaps it had been a magical place with fairy mounds where the spirits of old poets —*Ollam fili*, they were called—and of Celtic warriors awaiting entry into the Mag Mell, the Plain of Pleasures, went roving about in clouds of mist over hills and creeks, water draining into the river that their father called the River of Sorrows.

Like a snare drum tapped by a child's fingers, the rainwater leaking from the ceiling of the inn where the O'Briens operated a pub and dry-goods store, and settling into a porcelain bowl placed on the floor to catch it. Elsewhere in the room, on the wall behind the bar, the dripping water had buckled the matted

picture of Germanus of Auxerre handing the bishop's scepter to
the young St. Patrick, bathed in the light and glory of God, a
picture which his dead mother, a woman who had come from
Belfast, had put up for the Catholics of that town—and they were
mainly that, Catholics. There was an oak counter, and behind
its whiskey-stained surface were kegs of ale in a row and Nelson
O'Brien, not yet eighteen years old, schooled by priests and good
with numbers, working over a black ledger, taking inventory of
the sundry provisions that his father and uncle would sell to the
people of the town. It was a hard job, because his uncle was
always pilfering goods, selling whiskey and ale on the side, and
slipping money out of the till, so that at the week's end Nelson,
head lowered close to the columns in the ledger, and trying to
protect his uncle by rigging the numbers, trembled.

The inn's business a "tethered weight" on his shoulders,
Nelson's father would take it out on him, beating him with a
strap, until his son's arms and legs were covered with welts. That's
when he'd daydream about leaving that town for a place filled
with light and peace.

Or perhaps he simply had a young man's craving for adventure: all he knew was that he wanted to go away.

In those days, he and his older sister, Kate, would make their
way along the meadows and picnic under the leafy boughs of a
great spreading tree. Kate was eighteen then, in 1895, and quite
beautiful, a buxom and comely woman with a head of red hair,
a widow's peak, and soft blue eyes like his own. But, like his
mother, she was not always in the best of health. On one of those
afternoons, when they had napped under the tree, she had sat
up and said to her brother, waking him, "I was just thinking that
it would be a most pleasant thing to have a farm, away from the
troubles that people make. Do you think so, Nelson?"

"Yes, I can see that. But how?"

She shrugged and said, "I don't know, but it's a thought I
relish."

On those strolls, he'd carry a satchel with him filled with
books—a photography manual, the gift of a fellow named
MacPhearson, for whom he sometimes worked, and penny novels

that caught his fancy, about cowboys and Indians and the likes of Wild Bill Hickock and Jesse James, which, with their diverting tales, helped to lift him out of himself.

"Now, Kate, listen to this," he would say, flipping the pages of the book and coming to a chapter called "The day that Jesse James got his Revenge": *"As Jesse, sorely wounded, hid, lying low behind a horse trough and still bleedin', he watched the bushwhackers riding sinisterly into town. Although they outnumbered him eight to one, they was eight varmints against one real man: drunk on their mounts, and reeling about in circles, they fired their pistols into the air. That's when Jesse saw his chance. Springing up with both his six-guns loaded, he took aim and one by one brought them down off their horses; five he hit squarely in the head, got two right through the heart, and the last he clipped in the knees so that he crawled on his belly like a snake. Jesse, blowing smoke out of the barrels, stood over the fallen craven cur, grinning coolly. . . ."*

"Ah," he said to his sister, "isn't that a rousing tale?"

And she laughed, remembering this younger brother's flights of fancy, and sadly, too, thinking of how, when things weren't good in the household, he would sometimes sink down in the corner of a barely lit storage room to read his little books by the faint window light. He would turn over a bucket and sit on it, pulling his jacket closed and holding its lapels together in one shivering hand, while lifting the book up toward the glow, his posture, as he tried to fold his limbs into himself, intended to diminish his presence in the world and therefore, as happens with little creatures, his potential to be harmed.

"A good tale," she said to her brother. "My, but you love those troublesome folk."

Nelson O'Brien nodded. For a moment, the meadow before them filled with whooping Indians and desperadoes and buffalo herds, and he imagined himself and Kate on one of the American Great Plains, he positioned behind a tripod-and-bellows camera, the kind that MacPhearson owned, his hand ready to press the pneumatic bulb, the camera and the promise of adventure one of the daydreams of his young life.

To that end, since the time he was about twelve years old, he would try to escape his duties at the inn and, often getting into trouble, spend two hours walking along the roads to the town where MacPhearson ran a photography studio and pass the day there working for the man—firing off chemical flashes and preparing, according to MacPhearson's instruction, silver-nitrate plates, and offering whatever assistance he might need. (Nelson setting off the chemical flash, and in the parlor of MacPhearson's studio bursting with light; the subjects, a fashionably dressed newlywed couple, who had likely dropped down from heaven, posing proudly against the backdrop of a mythological scene— golden Arcadia, perhaps. Her hair, blond and curly, rises above her ears; she is wearing a great beribboned bonnet and a high-busted, hip-padded velvet dress with puff sleeves that trails to the floor, and a five-foot-long ostrich-feather boa. She purses her lips like a Gibson Girl, while her husband, more simply attired, in a topcoat and vest and button-fastened pinstripe trousers, sits posed with his top hat on his lap and a silver-tipped cane in hand. MacPhearson, lost under a black cloth, mutters to her father, "Now then, lad, on the count of three!") Liking that work—the modernity of the photographic art—and always touched by the way MacPhearson treated him, with generous pay, reassurances, and talks about life such as he never heard in his household, he did not care that his father—jealous, possessive—sought to punish him on his return.

That afternoon, as on many other afternoons, feeling as if he would never escape from their household to enjoy the pleasures of this life, Nelson lost his vision of cowboys and Indians, and suddenly, as if carried in the wind that traveled over the glens, a great sadness overcame him. Looking out over the fields, he saw in the distant mists a conglomeration of colors welling up on themselves: the hazel trees, the thready cloud-ridden sky, the rushing hues, squirrelly and liquid, flowing toward him, like a piling of stones, shimmering in the darkness, and rising still higher. The mid-afternoon light of day darkened—and when he looked about, he saw that a high, unclimbable wall, as one would imagine God might make, had shot up around him.

"Come, let's go back," Kate would say. "Let's go see if the swans are on the river and give them bread."

But he could not move.

"Nelson, what's troubling you, let's come along, won't you? We'll get back and I'll go into the kitchen and make you something nice to eat! Come on!"

Then she pulled him up, and this goddess of love, losing her temper, said to him, "Oh, come along now," straightening his jacket and tugging on his sleeves. "Don't know why you're like that at all."

Sometimes, in those moods, he would be barely aware of the world around him and go walking about with his hands dug deep in his pockets, between his lips a sprig of rosemary or thyme that he'd chew on with his slightly uneven, crooked teeth, a good lad with a cap pulled low on his brow, and yet with a tormented posture. Perhaps he resembled those earnest Cockney boys from the Rank Organization film versions of Dickens's novels. He was a handsome youth and may have been alluring to the young ladies of their town, as he seemed industrious (though troubled), working in the inn and for the photographer MacPhearson—putting his wages carefully away, a shilling here, a pound there; and he was careful in his habits, ever courteous and capable of cheer with certain of these females, but at the same time a little removed. And while he'd tip his hat and always smiled in greeting, a certain gloominess registered on his features when they were at rest and he was not playing the good-hearted Irish lad.

While making his way along the road behind the sheepherds with his friend, the gregarious and good-natured Jim O'Nolan, whom he'd known since boyhood, he'd listen to Jim boast about his carnal dalliances at the local brothel, and nod. But he could not understand why the sight of a woman with a nice bosom hidden under layers of dress and coat would make Jim whistle and blush, or why he was rambunctious in pursuit of a pretty girl whom he fancied, picking flowers for her and doffing his hat and bowing in a sweeping gesture when she passed by; or, for that matter, why he would eventually marry her and seem the happiest man in the world.

Even back then, Nelson supposed that he might have felt differently if he'd been closer to his mother while growing up. Her name was Margaret, and she was a woman from the Protestant North. He remembered that her life could not have been very happy, for people were not kind to her. He could barely visualize her, because she had been called from this world when he was but five—something about the redness of her hands and the stringiness of her hair, the smell of coal and grease about her, and sometimes of heavy lager; and eyes clear and blue-gray like his own, catching the light, pupils expanding as she'd smile, and then those eyes getting red and her hands shaking a little at a certain time of day when she would gasp for air and clutch at her breast; and when she pinched his cheeks and called him "my little Nelson," the pinch was a bit too hard, as if her fingers were made of wood; and when she called out to him, crying, "Now, give your mum a hug," he'd press close to a body warm under a spotted dress, but also almost wooden. One day he had been sitting in the corner of their kitchen watching her chopping an apple, and the next he was moving through a crowd of strangers, and his father, who went crazy when she died, took him by the hand into a room thick with candle wax and incense that smelled like an altar, and led him to his mother, dressed in a dark dress better than she had ever owned and asleep in a box of dark wood, saying, "Now you pay your respects, son," and he knelt and pressed his hands tight around hers and later threw up and cried, and when it was all over, his father sat before a stove in the chill of an Irish winter without moving.

Thinking about his mother's death, Nelson O'Brien would feel a deflation of the heart, a miasmic ebbing in that part of his soul that had to do with love, a slothfulness of character, a sapping of ambition, a "life fatigue" which he always had to fight and which seemed to come over him at the sight of certain everyday objects. He would feel afflicted by hand mirrors, of Celtic or French design, with seashell- or gemstone-topped finials, ovular in their shapeliness; by broken morning rolls, soft silken purses, or "pursies," as he sometimes called them in his sleep, when he'd snore deeply and mumble conversations with the citizens of his past; by goldfish and slithery minnows, spiders descending through their empires of web on the porch, curling leaves in a puddle, orange and fiery-red leaves blowing through the street in the fall; by gnarled-hair brushes, soap dishes, tureens, beetles, broken eggs, walnuts and chestnuts, fur hats and muffs, ocarinas, bells, clarinets, flutes, trumpets and kettledrums, the endocarp of apples, grapes and pears, serving spoons and ladles and butter tubs; hammocks swaying in the breeze, washbasins, urinals, drains, sewers: these bothered him.

This queasiness, having to do with women, accompanied him everywhere: to work in his father's failing dry-goods store; in and out of the classroom of the good Christian Brothers' school; to the pubs at night; to the stone-floor church where, neither believing nor disbelieving, he knelt before a statue of the Virgin, whose gaze spoke of unbounded kindness and compassion, lighting candles for the soul of his long-departed mother so that she might sooner escape the fires of Purgatory. It followed him to the gate house of the cemetery, and there, amid many wind-toppled, soot-black stones, he would stand before the grave of his mother.

His emotions would get the best of him, a rush of feelings. The Celtic crosses, marking the passage of the dead, mocked him. He would listen carefully—ghosts in the ground, breathing ever so softly, a rattle of bones. Because he'd once heard, told by the fire in the inn one night, the undertaker's description of certain phenomena, he became convinced that his mother's hair and fingernails were still growing, imagined that her hair had turned white and was a dense coil against the coffin lid, trying to ease its way out; and he believed that indeed the fingers twitched and the lips sometimes trembled. And just like that, he'd blink his eyes, and though years had passed, he'd have the sensation that she was nearby—invisible, to be sure—making her way, in the agony and solitude of the dead, toward the Land of Promise.

*

But his luck was to change, though his life had continued much as it always had, with aggravations, daydreams, and days lost to torpor. He came, with some sadness, into a stroke of good fortune: MacPhearson, who'd always appreciated the young man's courteous and forthright ways—he had been a polite and quiet worker—had died of old age and left the young man his large gloomy house, the contents of his photography shop, and the considerable fortune of £800. (Margarita never really knew the source of his sudden wealth—"I had the luck to come into some money in those days," she'd heard him say—but it happened that in 1896 her father, a young man who already had accumulated savings, suddenly found himself with a large sum of money.)

He decided to go beyond the Irish sunset and the violence and confusion of his home to America and to take his sister, Kate, with him.

To America, 1896

NOW NELSON and his sister, carpetbags packed, make their way onto a weatherworn ship in Cork Harbor. Holding his sister's hand as the ship clears the port, he takes a glance back, tinged with sadness and satisfaction. On departure, his head fills with memories of the beauty of that place—the "other" Ireland—and thinking that their troubles are over, he tells her, "You'll have your little farm." Despite the inclement weather, he's happy to pose his sister on the deck of the ship. She's wearing a long coat with a fur muff and a bonnet, and as he looks through the shutter, he captures her for posterity, smiling—the crisscross of ship's masts and the bustle of the piers, busy with commerce, beyond her. Then he poses beside her, and by means of a long, pneumatic cable, he takes another photograph. He is eighteen and a somewhat handsome young man, thin and of moderate height, a tuft of longish blond hair under his derby hat, with an earnest face, his head filled with hopeful speculations. In the pocket of his coat, he has one of those tattered, much-fingered cowboy novels, and in another his passport; and he has a money belt—he trusts no one—wrapped around his waist, containing several thousand dollars in American gold pieces, which he'd acquired from the Bank of Dublin a few days before, when they had also gone sightseeing along the river Liffey and made a short visit to Trinity College and peeked at the Book of Kells. Now greeting their fellow passengers, many poorly off and destined for the third-class compartments down below, they embark; a sea whistle sounds and the ship makes its way on the waters.

*

Originally he had thought that he and his sister would travel across the United States from coast to coast on a splendid tour, visiting such legendary sights as the Grand Canyon and the prairies of the American West. He thought they would travel to the Pacific and see San Francisco, and that along the way he would compile photographs of such grandeur as to make him famous. But the ocean voyage had not been good for Kate's constitution. An especially bitter wind had blown an infection into her right ear, and the offending chill had entered her bones, whistling and wheezing out of her lungs. They stayed in New York City for a few months so that she might recover, in a Hell's Kitchen rooming house in a neighborhood where many of the Irish then lived. The city, noisy, stench-ridden, and rife with hooligan activity, and monumental with its great buildings, seemed threatening and bleak.

Nelson holed up in a small room with Kate, waiting the winter out—sitting by the window watching great banks of snow piling up on the street, and concerned; and because he was always frugal with his money, he took a job as a waiter in a beer hall.

With the coming of spring, 1896, they left that city, deciding, because of Kate's flagging health, to find another more pleasant place. Their search ended when they found the picturesque and beautiful town of Cobbleton in Pennsylvania. That's when Nelson, wishing to please his sister and feeling quite wealthy, rented and later decided to buy the house in which his daughters would live.

Because she had always spoken about farming and, despite her suffering, would become bright-eyed at the mention of it, he got a horse and paid visits to neighboring farms, inquiring about the difficulties of that life, as he knew nothing about the land; he'd ask if it was better to raise sheep or cows, or if horses were better. And if he wanted to be an agricultural man, which crops, native to the terrain—wheat or corn or soy or barley—to plant. He had about an acre of land at that time and considered buying more: he had the money, but also his uncertainties and doubts. Was he not a photographer?

Still, he speculated. Traveling from town to town daydreaming, he considered other professions. What if he worked for the railroad, which had a yard in the town, the ground rumbling at night under the weight of many-car trains loaded with ore and coal; or became a barber, set up on the main street with a shop, sociable lather-faced customers, and a red-striped pole? When he dallied outside the workhouses, watching in their cool recesses carpenters at their benches, the smell of wood and industry lingering around them as they constructed cabinets and troughs, he considered that, too—and then dismissed it all, with a vague and unproven artistic pride. Wool mills, dentistry?

No.

Their days were happy, spent tranquilly, brother and sister looking forward to the vague but promising future.

One morning in the spring he got his equipment out from a copper-hinged trunk—his camera, bottles of potassium and silver-nitrate developing solutions, tripod and light-swallowing gelatin plates—and called his sister into the yard for a portrait. Although the cough that had started at sea had not left her and she hadn't been feeling well of late, she got herself ready for the shot, putting on a ladylike felt-buttoned dress, the buttons rising on an embroidered collar to just below her chin. She sat on a chair in the yard, cheeks rouged, her widow's peak high, and her brother, Nelson, disappearing under a black cloth, holding on to a pneumatic bulb, asked her to be still.

The sad thing was that, during the coming winter, on one of the harsher days of December, she would remain still, forever—history, as it happened to his own mother, repeating.

Cuba, 1898

IN EARLY SPRING of 1898, Nelson planted a garden of flowers which he hoped would grow eternally, filled with star grass, nodding azaleas, morning glories, gaywings, geraniums, forget-me-nots, and daisies. He would walk about the yard, following the looping frittilaries and monarch butterflies as they made their rounds like otherworldly angels. He would sit on the porch stunned as swallows circled the barn, and would watch, almost studiously, as the sun's light moved from one side of the yard to the other. He put up bird feeders and stuffed them with seed, delighted when the robins and cardinals filled their bellies and flew happily away to their kingdoms in the upper branches of trees. Sometimes he would remain on the porch, sitting in a cedar rocking chair, with only the occasional wagon passing by on the road, sitting alone until the morning star, Venus, would rise, and he would note with a grand appreciation the spiral motion of the constellations. On such a night he happened to notice some black-widow spiders hanging off the eave of his porch, and, laughing, discovered the stars of the constellation Arachnid glinting through those webs. Later, when they'd moved across the horizon, he thought that all things went forward, why couldn't he?

In April of that year, he packed up his equipment and, mounted on a horse, rode to the town of Quarryville some ten miles west and made some interesting photographs of the excavations there—lunar-looking gray man-made cliffs, workers with steam-powered pile drivers, and a train of rivet-weld transport railroad cars lugging their loads slowly away; he made photographs of barges serenely meandering up the Susquehanna River, clouds like bells breaking up on the horizon. He had moments when he felt like getting on a barge and riding it until he arrived at the end of the world. Still, he had wanted to work. An advertisement that he put in the local newspaper, the Cobbleton *Chronicle*, yielded him a few jobs: he recorded for posterity the

weddings of several couples, took a group shot of the Cobbleton
City Council, those very serious fellows, which would years later
be one of those old, frayed photographs in the Council's gloomy
halls. And he had photographed newborn babies—his favorite
subjects—hair soft and willowy, eyes filled with dollops of the
sea, or chestnut gems open wide and anxious for life.

Returning from a job one late afternoon, he dallied at the
saloon, in no rush to go back home, for when he entered the
house he would often sit in the kitchen and read and reread
the obituary notice that he had clipped some months before from
the paper: "Katherine Anne O'Brien, a recent immigrant from
Ireland, and sister of Nelson O'Brien, succumbed on the afternoon of December 12, 1897, to pneumonia, after a prolonged
bout with that illness." It would make him think about his letters
to Ireland, one posted to his parish priest, the second to his father
and his uncle. Perhaps because so little had been said about his
sister, the notice consisting of a few lines, he had written those
letters with the hand of a madly contrite brother, placing much
of the blame on himself, but ever careful to note that she was
happy to the end. (So many sleepless nights then, when he would
cover her with blankets and his own coat, pile wood into the
fireplace and the wood-burning stove; he would dread leaving
her alone, hurrying off, his hands frozen to the reins, to fetch the
doctor, who wore a black frock and had muttonchops and preacher's eyes, examining her each time and leaving them with yet
another bottle of expurgative syrup, whose alcohol base seemed
to relieve her suffering. Now and then a farmer's wife would
come along, a Mrs. Kelley or a Mrs. Neustadt, with a pot of soup,
which he would feed her spoon by spoon; and yet she still shiv-
ered.) Only the priest responded, enclosing a sympathetic note
and a pamphlet of prayers, good for the reduction of purgatorial
suffering. And so, thinking that there had been a mix-up in the
mail, he had written his father and his uncle twice again. Hearing
nothing, he had come to the conclusion that he had no family
in Ireland. (What had he done to them, he must have wondered
on his nights alone. Taken his father's beatings, helped his uncle
along as he wobbled on intoxicated legs?)

These thoughts sometimes troubled him, and he would go to the saloon and have a few shots of whiskey, and for the sake of manly intercourse smoke a Havana cigar, biting off the tip and expelling it into a murky spittoon. The whiskey and the pianola would induce in him a relaxed state of mind, and as was his habit, he would start to make plans for travel—perhaps out to the American West, or down to Mexico or South America, where a man of heavyhearted temperament might lose himself in adventure. But there was something else going on, an opportunity, it might be said, staring him in the face. As he sat drinking one afternoon, in no rush to go home, a crowd had gathered on the street outside the saloon. They were waving flags and handkerchiefs, and a pom-pom band appeared, marching in place; across the way, on the balcony of the hotel, was strung a banner reading "War with Spain!" and above it stood a handsome army officer in a creaseless uniform, making a speech.

Stepping out of the saloon's door into the sunlight, hand over hat brim, eyes squinting, he listened intently to an impassioned call to patriotism, the speech titled "Reasons for an Intervention in Cuba!" The officer read with great oratorical calm and resonance: "Greed and Sedition in the Courts of Spain," "Commander Roosevelt and His Wise Words to the Spanish," "American Interests Must Be Protected from the Spanish Pirateers"—ending by asking, "The Poor Cubans—Will They Survive Without Us?"

Back in the saloon and thinking about the word "Cuba" and the war, it occurred to him that he knew nothing about the country, except that Cuban cigars—the word "Havanas" common in tobacco shops—were said to get their flavorful aromas from young girls rolling the cover leaf on their thighs. And yet, as he thought about it, he realized that he had come across the word again and again while surveying advertisements for steamers on their way to South America, the cities of Havana and Santiago being ports of call. He knew little else. For all the recent ballyhoo in the local paper, with its muckraking articles on the impending war (excerpted from newspapers like the New York *Herald* and the *World*), he had hardly paid attention to the situation. For the

most part, since the time of his sister's death, he had been moving
through the world oblivious to its occurrences: and while all this
business with the war had interested him, he did not at first give
it much serious thought, until a few days later, when he resolved
to go.

Another Journey

THERE HAD BEEN parades in New York, and near-lynchings
of opponents to intervention in Cuba, and church bells had rung
and beautiful women in great plumed hats and velvet dresses
and stiff corsets had packed the platforms of Union Station,
across the river in New Jersey, flinging bouquets of flowers at
the troops and civilians boarding the trains to Tampa. And
there had been that camp, overcrowded, filthy, disorganized,
and jammed with loons and mercenaries and professionals
who had passed the weeks before the invasion drilling,
gambling, playing baseball, and engaging in bare-knuckle
boxing matches in its muddy fields. Despite his grief, he could
not help feeling overjoyed, because here he was at last among
the wild cowboys!

Nelson O'Brien had gotten himself a berth on one of the
press boats, having signed on as a freelance photographer with
the New York offices of *Le Figaro*, which, among other European
newspapers, tended to buy photographs from a pool; they hired
Nelson, and dozens of others, to record the grand and glorious
proceedings of the war, as well as to make photographs of the
"local color," anxious for their readers to benefit from the recent
invention of the half-tone process. With his camera equipment
in a black hinged trunk and a provisions pack on his shoulders,
he, a boy of twenty, had joined a cynical and worldly contingent
of the press, who liked to drink, and in their company aboard a
chartered steamship he sailed with the flotilla south along the
mountainous and verdant southern coast of Cuba.

There he had witnessed the bombardment of the beaches of
Daiquirí and Siboney, the landing of 14,000 shouting, gun-firing,
whistle-blowing troops, the dash of stallions and cattle, romping

behind herders through the surf, the swagger of commanders, sabers and pistols raised, shouting out orders. The cavalry had charged into the brush and forests, the infantry hacking through the dense foliage with their bayonets. They encountered swamps and ponds of stagnant water, torrents of black flies and pestiferous mosquitoes. There wasn't enough quinine, or enough good canned meat, or cattle to slaughter, or pure water to drink. As the troops marched to commandeer the main roads to the city of Santiago, the Spanish capital of the island at the time, the roads were muddy from rain. Antiquated wagons, their axles snapped in two, turned over on the road. Troops opened up cans of beef from New York and found festering insect larvae. Men crouched down low in ditches beside the road, pouring their guts out under them; men staggered like drunks in their blue army jackets, a yellow pallor on their skins. And they had seen the plantations burned to the ground, spires of smoke everywhere. Troops raided towns for food, clashing with the regulars of the ragged Cuban army, demanding food and supplies. Those Cubans, the troops of the great Calixto García, exhausted from three years of war against the Spaniards, had no food; they had been living off boiled grass and snake flesh, and they told the Americans to go to hell. Many of them were there already.

Then they had arrived at a hill overlooking the river of Las Guásimas, and while Nelson set up his tripod and camera, one of the journalists, a cowboy-like fellow, Harrington, had climbed up some rocks and was taking "moving pictures" of the battle with an odd-looking device, a box-shaped camera with a crank in its side that he called a vitascope. Spotting something in the distance, he handed Nelson a pair of binoculars and shouted, "Just look at that!"

At first Nelson did not know what he was looking for, but then he saw what appeared to be a hot-air balloon with an ornate gondola, serenely drifting above the melee below—the muddy river jammed with troops in waist-high water, caught in the cross fire of smokeless Spanish Mausers and being picked off, their own guns firing blindly into the brush and barricades around them, their smoke dense as a winter fog. When the balloon got close enough, he focused on its commander, in a woolly trimmed admiral's cap, a certain Major Derby, peering out over the brush and forest around the river through a nautical telescope. It was inevitable that some Spaniard sharpshooter would have a little fun when it came within range, and just like that, the great vehicle, something out of a state fair, its canvas husk punctured, began to float slowly down toward the river, where it toppled on its side, the balloon crumpling under itself like a great wilted flower. Around it, a furious cloud of butterflies rose up out of the bushes, like angels floating upward in spirals toward God, happily oblivious as the rush of panicking, confused men continued, men in Civil War caps and cowboy hats and in tan-and-blue uniforms, screaming when hit in the kneecap, or in the shoulder, or in the neck, and crying "Mother" where they fell—clouds of black-and-white smoke rising everywhere from rifles, some men lying down in the mud, weapons cast aside, in a chaos of noise, men vomiting, some saying prayers.

Roosevelt would bring up the rear with his Rough Riders, a cavalry brigade, and then, by sheer force of numbers, a kind of mad courage prevailing, the troops forded the river, and, charging ahead across the grassy meadows before the Spanish battlements, would shortly overrun the barbed-wire defenses of Kettle Hill.

On His Way to Santiago

NELSON AND HARRINGTON rode by horse and carriage to a camp on one of the routes to Santiago. Funeral pyres were burning on the sides of the road and in fields, lofting a bad smell into the air. It had started to rain.

The night was cool and damp. Tents, stretching into the distance, were lit by lanterns, men shivering under blankets from malaria, yellow fever, and typhoid.

"A drink?" asked Harrington.

"I thank you, my friend."

As they sat sipping whiskey, Harrington, speaking in his

slangy way, cussed the situation: "It's just deplorable to be here, ain't it? And for what, the goddanged mislaid plans of a bunch of loons, scallywags, carpetbaggers, half-baked politicians, and crazy, addle-brained generals?"

Harrington spit some chewing tobacco into the fire, and flame spewed up. He leaned back on the bedding, pulled a blanket up around his neck, his boots, still spurred, cutting into the muddy ground as he spoke: "Now that son of a bitch Roosevelt, now he and McKinley and them bankers . . ." As Harrington continued his denunciations, the words "hellhole" and "cravenly muckrakers" shot out, occasionally penetrating Nelson's own distracted thoughts. The moon had peeked through a break in the clouds, a swirling face, sad and solitary, playing hide-and-seek, as would a child, and so chilled up there in the sky, features wrapped in the thready tips and swirls of dark cloud matter.

A single star appeared, faint in the heaviness of the inclement sky. He watched it cover over with clouds, then got up, a little wobbly from the whiskey, and sat dispirited on his black trunk, his stomach bothering him. He looked south, where the ridges of the mountains, covered by columns of billowing smoke, resembled, in that cluttered atmosphere, an immense altar above which vultures circled; and those vultures seemed to be everywhere, like seraphim, and it started to thunder and lightning cracked everywhere, and it looked as if the vultures were being turned into slits of fiery silver or tongues of fire above the altar of the mountains of Cuba, lightning cracking again and again everywhere.

"Oh, God Almighty in Heaven, why have you made this world so?" he asked that night long ago.

Santiago

RISING ON HILLS on a sea of pink- and blue- and yellow-walled houses and surrounded by mountains, the city that Nelson had entered in the summer of 1898 had been beautiful but devastated and rife with malaria. Before the American victory, the Spaniards had looted many of the better houses and public halls, stripping whatever valuables they could carry away. They had pulled down street lamps, destroyed or blocked the sewers, and smashed pipes so that even the more prominent citizens who had English water closets were reduced to the indignity of removing their bodily waste in carts and dumping it in great mounds in the alleys and streets—some impassable, there was sometimes so much debris. The poor state of sanitation had brought the American Red Cross, led by one Clara Barton, who had organized a headquarters down by the harbor and would appear, with a contingent of matronly New England ladies, twice daily by one of the food wagons in the Marine Park, in a Dolley Madison bonnet, soup ladle in hand, dispensing rice and stew to the poor. Hospitals had to be set up, for there were many sick Cubans. He saw them, poor souls, lingering emaciated and jaundiced by their windows, bone-thin ghosts, hands outstretched, begging for food, and whenever a horse and carriage passed by, swarms of children followed, searching the muck of the street for the grains that had dropped from the feed buckets. Some were so hungry and ill that the pyres, so disheartening in the countryside, burned nightly in that city for months, as people were dying from disease at the rate of some two thousand a week.

He had first stayed in the city to rest, taking a room over-looking a courtyard in the Grand Hotel, by the Cathedral Plaza, but the desolation and hunger around him had moved his heart. Able-bodied men were needed everywhere, and so he went to work, joining the sanitation crews as they cleaned up the streets. He dug public latrines and helped to clear away the three hundred cubic meters of refuse, dumped there by the Spaniards, out of the cavernous interior of the harborside customs house. He wrapped a bandanna over his mouth and nose and wore a helmet with mesh netting that went down to his knees. Much of this was backbreaking—his friend Harrington, with whom he would have an occasional drink at the Venus Café, thought him mad—but he found his labor and the serenity of a selfless routine comforting.

And there was something else. He must have been caught up in the promise of the future there, or perhaps he had simply enjoyed the initial bustle, the madness of troops packed in saloons and brothels, the enterprise of the ship-glutted harbor, the throngs of foreign journalists, and the energizing life of distraction. His daughters would imagine him making his way through that city—naughtily accompanying his friend Harrington, grandiose with schemes and ideas, to the brothels where the Celestinas did a rousing trade, Poppy, they were certain, abstaining. They'd see him in the Cathedral, in candlelight, listening intently to the Angelus, and afterward sitting in a café, while the heavy bronze Cathedral bells rang. Or a dove alighted on a railing, above one of the steep stairways, and he'd look out over the harbor, placing his hands on a stone head of Ceres—for that city was bursting with ornament—and watching the sun, like another dove, swooping into the sea and out, and the sky suddenly radiant, the air so clear and blue and the sea below riddled with sapphire waves and the elongated shadows of eastward-bound ships, all so beautiful.

He'd go walking up and down the same cobblestone street, over and over again, a thick scent of roses and hibiscus and jasmine in the air, Nelson saying, "Hello," or perhaps "¡*Hola!*" to one of the older dueñas peering out from behind the curlicued gate. He'd walk up and down the street, enchanted, unable to bring himself to leave, as if waiting for one of those ladies to come out and offer him a room to rent, *una habitación de alquilar.*

He moved into one of those houses, with a family whose ancestors had come from the province of Asturias; they liked his gentle and quiet nature. At first the kindly Irishman, who could not speak Spanish, tried in his friendly way to get to know them, tipping his hat, patting the head of a child, ever courteous. Dining with the family, drinking in the cafés, he would end his nights by lamplight, sitting up in bed with a Spanish–English phrase book, memorizing salutations, learning verbs and the names of common things in Spanish, until slowly he began to discern something of the grammar. It was everywhere around him, and became a buzz of voices in his sleep, so that in the middle of the

night he would sometimes think he was on a street corner eaves-
dropping on the conversations of two Cuban fellows:

"¿Sabes una cosa?"

"¿Qué?"

"¡Eres un chivón, un come-basura, un come-bola, un bobo
tremendo, un zángano, un pajuato, un chusma sin nada de valor!"

"¡Sí, ay, no me jodas!"

He did not always know or understand what he had heard,
insults to be sure, delivered with a wry smile. He'd recall the
conversations of servant women in the markets haggling over the
price of a hen with a vender—¡Noventa y cinco centavos por una
gallina! ¡Dios mío!"

And then there were conversations about the politics of the
day, the names of General Brooke, American military governor
of the island; of José Martí, the dead Cuban hero-poet; Antonio
Maceo, the great black general, killed in 1897; Calixto García,
another general; Roosevelt and McKinley—floating in swirls of
suspicion.

Thinking that Nelson could understand no more than a few
phrases of Spanish, the family spoke freely, and the young Irishman began to deduce that the Cubans were at odds about the
intervention—appreciating the assistance but disliking the med-
dling of Washington in their affairs. "So the Americans came in
on the tail end of things and helped our army to drive out the
Spaniards. And now they're telling us just who we should elect
as president. Why, that would have been as if the French had
told the American Revolutionaries whom they should have as
their president." Arguments of this nature, which he slowly began
to understand, had Nelson, who at that time felt as if he really
had no country, sympathizing with the Cubans, though he never
said a word.

He'd twist and turn under the covers, listening to the voices
in his head, each day understanding a little more, and yet always
behaving as if he did not really know what was being said—
something of an amiable spy in their midst.

*

Or perhaps he stayed simply for the work, photographers
being much in demand. Wherever speeches were made, wherever
military balls took place, or bargaining sessions between the
Spaniards and the new American military government, or between the representatives of the independence-minded Cubans
and the Americans, Nelson was on hand with his equipment. He
photographed them all: Teddy Roosevelt, perhaps his most famous American subject (in full battle regalia), the great man,
burly and high-booted, seated beside the military governor, a
long saber by his side and impatiently tapping the polished
wooden floors as the nervous photographer peered out at them
from the darkness of his black cloth, his assistant igniting the
chemical flash. He would get jobs up at the Governor's Mansion,
photographing the guests at afternoon tea parties and banquets,
at gatherings of medical professionals, social workers, businessmen, military and local politicians and their wives. Sometimes
he hired a horse and wagon to take him to that part of the city,
or they would send someone to bring him, but most often he
would carry his own equipment, cumbersome and difficult at
times, his legs growing muscular from climbing the steep hills.

*

Going about his business, he had begun to find enough work
as a photographer to consider opening a shop. Things were so
inexpensive that Nelson, who had brought five hundred American dollars to Cuba and earned occasional wages, had spent very
little of his own money. In no hurry to leave, he came to rent the
shop on Bolívar Street with its small apartment in the back, his
name stenciled on the window—a fifteen-minute walk up from
the Santiago harbor. He was twenty-two years old and wore a
linen suit and a flat-topped black-brimmed hat. As he sat in the
shade of an awning, smoking a pipe, he felt very much a citizen
of the city and would cordially tip his hat to passersby. He had
a good business, many of his customers coming by way of the
flyers, written in Spanish and English, that he had posted around.
Most of them were American businessmen or bankers in Santiago to attend to their investments or to take over a new post.

When they'd arrive at his studio to sit for a portrait with their wives and children, he was ever polite, leading them back into a sunny courtyard where he kept a canvas screen on which had been painted a view of Santiago Bay.

Many of the businessmen, it struck Nelson, were a little depressed, the necessities of business having condemned them to a new life in some godforsaken, backwater country. They were nervous about disease—he would reassure them that it had been all but wiped out—and about the occasional story about rebels in the countryside. In the sunny courtyard, they would often ask him, "And why are you here?"

To which he would calmly answer: "I like the Cubans very much."

As they posed, they felt comforted by the name O'Brien, and were charmed by his Irish brogue: he attracted their business because they trusted his name, choosing his shop even though there were others operated by Cubans here and there in the city, some also with Irish names. One of these was operated by a certain Diego O'Reilly, who did not speak a word of English, let alone have an Irish brogue, but was as Cuban as Cuban could be. And there was a street called O'Farrill and in another shop he had seen the name Guillermo Haley stenciled on the window.

Off they would go to take control of a shipping line, to set up a telephone system, to manage a sugar mill: some would remain in Santiago, living in mansions with four and five servants, jobs being scarce and labor cheap. He had seen them making their way north through the jungle and on the dirt roads, their New York suits caked with dust, and the ladies coughing delicately as their carriages went lurching and rocking forward. If they seemed quite distressed, he would urge them to enjoy the country, "beautiful as a dream," he would say. Sometimes he would show them his photographs of the Cuban countryside, taken during occasional excursions out of the city with his assistant, a Cuban boy whom Nelson had found homeless—two- or three-day journeys to the big sugar mills, where he would photograph baptisms, weddings, birthday celebrations, and other family gatherings. Among those shots: a mist of clouds over the mountains; a weeping willow caught in a shaft of sunlight; a deer sipping from a stream; a cave with the siren cry of winds, its entranceway wreathed with vines and orchids; dense forests dropping into ravines; and his favorite, a simple meadow of wildflowers over which fluttered a storm of butterflies. He would tell them, "For the naturalist there is much pleasure in this country," a phrase he had lifted from a British lord, a gentle soul in a pith helmet with a butterfly net and thick ledger books by his side, whom he had met one night by the harbor and with whom he had discussed the splendors of the island.

"Physically speaking, my dear friend," the Englishman had told him, "the countryside is paradise."

How Nelson Met Mariela

IT WAS MIDSUMMER of 1900, the war over for nearly two years, and Mariela Montez, sixteen years old, sat in the back patio of the family's house on Victoriana de Avila Street in Santiago, mending with needle and thread the loosened buttons of her father's shirt. Amid palms and scented flowers, she rocked in a wicker chair. She was a pretty woman with long black hair that fell over her shoulders, an oval face serene and intelligent in its definition, high cheekbones, a sleek nose, but with such pain or stoicism in the darkness of her eyes that people sometimes had the impression that she could read minds. She was wearing a simple white dress with pleated skirt, tied with a yellow bow around the waist, and underneath that, a long camisole and a loose-fitting corset—she'd refused to lace all the eyeholes and hooks which, crisscrossing much of her wardrobe, seemed to inform her life.

She had furrowed her lovely brow, enjoying, as she made repair, the birdsong in the trees: now and then, an iguana would peek out from under a jasmine plant, chameleons roamed over the stone walls and turned to a viny green where the ground had burst, sending up its blossoms, its thorns curling up into the arbor surrounding her.

That day she felt herself idle, each stitch a marking of time. It annoyed her, for there were so many things she had never done in her young life, and there she was, slipping a length of thread through the third hole of a button. There was much that she wanted to know about the world, a curiosity buried under layers of dress and the formalities of the strictly run household to which she had returned; she had never been anywhere—save for Santiago, their two farms, and a retreat in the Sierra Mountains where the family had lived during the last year of the war. She had not even been allowed much schooling, except for what the good sisters had taught her in Catechism, but she did have a little shelf of books: one of them, much thumbed, was a book about a pilgrimage to Rome by a Jesuit priest, called *En Roma, la ciudad de Dios*, a lively mix of pagan and Church lore that was of much interest to her. Then, too, she kept other books on a subject that had fascinated her as a child, when in the evenings out on the farms she tended to daydream about the stars, a turgid, dense, three-volume encyclopedia on the stars and planetary motion that she had spotted in a bookstall in the market, with its listing of then known stars and its speculations about the planets. Another book, of a more frivolous and frankly enjoyable nature, was a capricious volume, a gift from her father, that had been published in Spain in 1895: *La vida en el planeta marte*, or *Life on the Planet Mars*, which had been written by a certain professor Severo Fuentes of the Astronomical Society of Barcelona. He had based this exemplary work on a sixteenth-century treatise in Latin by a monk named Theocratus, who had claimed through a vision to have visited that planet, where, according to Professor Fuentes, the advanced inhabitants of this world concealed their presence with great machines that sent up plumes of red vapor into the atmosphere. Visiting that planet, he came upon "cities so majestic and serene, with hanging gardens like those of Babylon, and rivers on which its inhabitants journeyed in diamond gondolas." There the good monk heard an eternal music, the music of the spheres, and encountered a people so wise that they had never known war or illness. "It was as if I had a vision of heaven," the monk had written. "The men and women of this world, who went naked as babies and had Oriental expressions, could, by an act of will and great mental exertion, sprout wings like butterflies. This they did on their day of worship, swarming in circles over the towers of a magnificent crystal cathedral through whose diaphanous walls flowed a brilliant light, brighter than the sun. And these people were ruled by a queen so beautiful that when I beheld her from afar I trembled."

It was Professor Fuentes's opinion that all this was plausible and much of the text was a rebuke of what modern science—circa 1897—held to be true about Mars, then considered unsuitable for life. Mariela, entertained by the imagination of the professor—did a monk named Theocratus ever exist?—thought the book a pleasant invention, diverting and strangely meaningful to her. And its chapters about the possibilities that these beings had once journeyed to this world, settling on the island of Atlantis, which they later destroyed, intrigued her. Over the years the Martians had returned to this world to plant the seeds of advancement among us. It claimed, for example, that "the spirit of the Martians may have guided the ambition of one Cristobal de Colón."

Her father, Emilio Montez, had been a great supporter of the Cuban independence movement, but mainly, in his private moments, he had poetic aspirations; what notebooks he could find he filled with his lyric observations about the world and the cruelty and sanctity of men. He was not famous like the poet José Martí, but he had an elegant respect for the art of the language and often daydreamed, during those few moments of peaceful reflection after the war, about making himself a name, if not a livelihood, through the practice of that craft. Affection for the world and the small wonders of his life had poured from his pen, and his influence on his daughter Mariela, as thick as the sadness of that night, had inspired her own poetic aspirations.

Back then, she never wrote anything down, but had the distracted presence of a woman in the process of remembrance: she tended, in these continual and spontaneous but unrecorded compositions, to think in terms of flowery and avian images, as in: *The saddest hummingbird laughs dancing upon a blossom, light as the air, but carrying the world in its heart*, and so many others, so many that she confused them with the ordinary thoughts of life.

In those days, she could not walk unescorted from her house, so, during a trip perhaps with her maid Florida to the market, she would sidetrack the poor woman, leading her along the most circuitous routes around the city. From time to time in the marketplace she would purchase some magazines from the United States, coming away with copies of *The Saturday Evening Post* and *Colliers Weekly*, old, outdated issues which she could not read but much enjoyed examining. And she went to church on Sundays with her father and mother, who, as she yawned, kneeling on the stone floors, were always quick to remind her that religious devotion was in her blood. (After all, she was said to resemble her maternal great-aunt Benedicta, a saintly woman whose good deeds and exemplary life in Spain in the first part of the nineteenth century were of such merit that she had been elevated by the Pope into the hagiographic enclave in 1870, that aunt coming from a family line whose sons and daughters had often sacrificed themselves to holy vocations. She slept on planks, survived on roots and brook water, and traveled through the arid provinces of Spain preaching that faith in God was a question not of proof but of personal discipline. Miracles were attributed to her, and she'd also experienced, during a time of great good acts, a visitation by the Holy Mother, who'd advised her as to the day and hour of her death, when she would join the Lord in heaven. When that day arrived, Benedicta, suffering much, was relieved of worldly pain and lifted up to Paradise. "You have much to look forward to," her mother, María, would tell Mariela.)

Sometimes the family would take long strolls, sit in the plaza listening to political speeches, or simply to hear music or watch passersby. She had never been allowed to speak to young men, though for a time she was party to something of an arranged betrothal to a young man who was later killed during the war.

There were the occasional trips out to the farms—one managed by her brother Pablo, the other by her sister Teresa and her husband (her other sister, Vivian, living with them)—where she would spend part of her days, so happy to be away. But those trips were infrequent, her father, Don Emilio, not trusting the peace of the times.

She was forced to accept the serene monotony of those days, beside her mother and in the company of the maid. Her father was not much for speaking to her, except to give her orders, exerting his manly control. He was a good man, but a little apprehensive about life. The flight into the mountains in 1897, when fires were burning everywhere and guns sounded in the fields, had left him unnerved. They had lived in crude conditions, in one large room in a mountainside house: there was no privacy and sanitary needs were met in the brush, water fetched from a stream. She had enjoyed the rigors, and the beauty of nature at night, but her father, concerned about his properties, dreaded losing everything; he did lose his livestock and horses and had the gloom of a man who'd watched from afar his life's work turn to air. He had "retired," turning over the rebuilding of the farms to his daughter and son but, since the days of their return to the city, had suffered in spirit. Instead of managing the farms and his workers, he managed his wife and daughter Mariela, the house his kingdom. He would watch her anytime she was in a room, his eyes following her as if exerting control over her. If she moved from the parlor into the tiled hallway that led to the patio, he would never fail to ask, "Where are you going, my daughter?"

As a result, she was famous in the household for refusing to answer her father, and sometimes went for days without saying so much as a word to anyone. He regarded her as obedient but "contrary."

Still, he adored her, and being a proud father and a little sentimental, he noticed that she had matured into a young beauty, and one day, as she was sitting on the patio, he called out to her, saying, "Mariela, I want to have a photograph made of you."

So she accompanied her father to the Irishman's photography shop on Bolívar Street.

That afternoon, Don Emilio, with his wheezy anatomy, entered the Irish photographer's shop, his daughter behind him, just some few streets down the hill from Victoriana de Avila. When they entered the studio, the Irishman had just finished drinking a cup of coffee and the room itself, that long, front parlor with its mirrored wall, carried the cheery fragrance of pipe tobacco and of potassium and silver nitrate. Nelson O'Brien, in his affable way, welcomed his new subject and her father. Mariela had come in, moody and indifferent, and, barely willing to lift up her head, was averting her eyes. Nelson, coming close, appraised her. As he did so, a queasiness began to come over him, as he had caught a glimpse of her clever eyes, and he had the sensation, far more momentous than anything he had felt during his four years in Cuba, of falling through the air.

For the sake of relaxing his "subject," he tried to amuse her, launching, in his unsteady Spanish, into an explanation of the photographic process.

Light, he told her, had a physical property which allowed it to infiltrate certain chemical surfaces. He said that light to a silver-nitrate plate was what the perfume of a flower was to the nose, that she, in that very moment, was giving off her own kind of light (really, in those moments, she was giving off molecules of her own stubborn feminine allure, and these molecules were floating through the Irish photographer's studio, slipping up his nose, drifting into his eyes, seeping into his skin).

He mentioned many great photographers of the past—Daguerre, Hauron Du Cros, Ives—and hoped, as he moved close to her, that she would give some appreciative notice of his presence.

He had thought to himself, This is a woman who never smiles, and found himself intrigued.

Perhaps he had not been able to communicate his explanation in Spanish well, for after a time Mariela looked up and asked, "What are you talking about?"

Perhaps it was her indifferent beauty that moved him, but he found himself feeling a little drunk, as if he had run into Harrington again on one of his swings through Santiago and they sat in a waterfront café drinking *aguardiente* until the moon

hummed in their ears and every passing woman seemed queenly
and breathtakingly beautiful. He felt a pang of passionate interest
in Mariela—his face turned red and the palms of his hands
sweated.

Leading her out to the sunny courtyard where he would pose
his subjects, he ordered his assistant to position a mirror to reflect
light on her face. She sat on a stool, her body bent forward, her
face remote and so uncooperative that after a few minutes her
father, Don Emilio, losing patience, said to her, "Mariela, please
sit up."

She remained in that posture for a long time and then suddenly raised her head, as if awakening from a dream-ridden
sleep, and then Nelson saw a tear roll out of her eye. She was
in pain, and the sight of it nearly unraveled his businesslike
demeanor. From his vest pocket, he pulled a clean handkerchief
and wiped her cheek. Then he offered her and her father a glass
of brandy. Having sipped delicately from the glass, she seemed
in better spirits and settled into a pose, smiling and appreciative
of the Irishman's concern. He disappeared under his black cloth
but had to collect himself before proceeding to take the picture.

That night, thinking about her, he found himself unable to
sleep. It was not so much the way she looked—many beautiful
young Cuban women would come to the studio with their in-
tendeds to pose—but she seemed to possess some inward quality,
compassion perhaps, and a certain demureness that much appealed to him.

*

After dallying before the mirror, brushing his hair and parting it in the middle, clipping his whiskers and cleaning his teeth
with dental powder, he had wandered about his parlor, trying on
different waistcoats, and looping and relooping the Mississippi-
gambler bow tie that he wore around his shirt collar, and slapping
some sweet-smelling cologne on his face.

Making his way up the cobblestone streets, he was whistling
in imitation of the birds, when he heard the church bells of San
Lázaro ringing loud. Its doors were open and, from within, a

choir was singing "Ave Maria," and when he peered inside he
saw row after row of the pious, many of them war widows, kneeling, rosaries and prayer books in hand. He moved on uphill
toward Victoriana de Avila Street, where he was to deliver some
photographic plates that he had taken of the young Montez
woman a few days before.

At around 11:30 on that Sunday morning in 1900, Nelson
pulled the cord of the house bell posted by the curlicue gate of
the entrance of Avila number 17. As he stood waiting under an
orange tree, its fruit long ago picked off by passersby, his palms
were sweaty and his stomach in knots. He rang again and a voice
called out and at the entrance appeared the maid, Florida, who
led him down a tiled hallway to their parlor with its high, glassless
windows facing the street—a bodega across the way, and a shoe
repair shop. Señor Montez had been napping in a room at the
far end of the house and grunted when Florida awakened him.
Shortly, eyes still bleariéd with sleep, he shuffled in slippers and
a long robe into the parlor, where they sat.

As Montez examined the photographs, Nelson noticed beyond the parlor and dining room a set of double French doors
that opened to a patio and garden. There Montez's daughter was
sitting by a table sewing. Nelson stared at her, hoping to attract
her attention.

"Now, thank you very much, Mr. O'Brien," Montez said just
then.

"I would like to know, sir," Nelson said to Montez, "your
daughter's opinion of them."

Shortly, the two men stepped out into the light of the patio
and Mariela examined the prints. She saw herself as perhaps she
had always wished she could be, a startlingly beautiful young
woman, surrounded by an aureole of light, the surface of the
photograph dappled with what she imagined were flushes of
affection and pain. And as she held the print, lacquered and
mounted on a board (and destined to sit one day in a frame on
a dresser in a faraway place), she felt honored somehow. But,
although she wanted to smile, she set the print aside, did not
look up at Nelson, and resumed darning her father's shirts.

*

From that day on, Nelson O'Brien returned often to that house. At first, he would arrive on the pretense of taking another photograph, free of charge, of Mariela on their back patio. Then he would turn up to play checkers with her father. Finally, on a rainy Sunday afternoon, he confessed to Don Emilio that he wanted permission to see his daughter, and her father, liking the Irishman, allowed him to do so.

It was an entirely different thing for him to win her over. Because his Spanish was far from perfect, he was often tongue-tied and awkward. His hands would shake, his teeth sometimes chattered as he spoke to her, but he always comported himself with respect and courtesy—and he was ever attentive: if she walked across the patio to pet her dog, he seemed genuinely pleased; if she picked a gnat or a flower petal out of the tresses of her hair, he'd smile. If she walked into the parlor, ignoring everything around her, his eyes followed her—such good and clear and earnest eyes—the "eyes of a saint," her mother would say.

Slowly, Mariela had come to look forward to the young Irishman's visits, and she took his presence as a blessing, even when she knew that in time she might find a more handsome Cuban man, less rigid in his demeanor. He came to visit her for twenty-seven Sundays in a row, and in that time she began to discern the weight of tragedy on his heart, and slowly, though she was aloof and a bit arrogant in her own way, came to feel compassion and the beginnings of love for him.

*

In September of 1901, Nelson O'Brien asked Señor Montez for formal permission to marry Mariela. That had been on a Wednesday afternoon, when he encountered the man making his way along the market arcades. The following Sunday, when Nelson came to visit the family, the couple were left alone on the patio. There Nelson knelt on the tile floor to propose. She lowered her head, closed her eyes, nodded her consent.

By then, she had gotten used to his angular Celtic face, his good and honest though confused nature. His sincerity and inner pain had touched her. She thought, in those moments, that they would one day have a household in which they could raise children of intelligence. There would be books, and music; there would be an atmosphere in which children could be helped to take their proper place in the world.

She watched his face, befuddled by a momentary wave of thought.

He told her about his house in a distant place called Pennsylvania, deep in the heart of America, where people could do as they pleased and there was no war. She thought that they, as people of class, could travel and live a good life.

She told him, "Yes."

For his part, he was a happy man. In dreams such as one might have dreamed in a mist-ridden meadow in Ireland, he saw them in Cobbleton, restoring felicity to that house. A recent note from a banker in Cobbleton who'd hired someone to look after O'Brien's property mentioned that a storm had damaged the roof. In his happiness, this did not bother him.

They were wed in the Church of San Lázaro, the bridegroom elegant and queasy during the ceremony. Among the well-wishers was his friend Harrington, who'd stopped by on his travels, and, winking, presented Nelson with a bawdy volume of forbidden lore, *A Gentleman's Guide to Love.* They received other gifts, and that afternoon the bride and groom repaired to a hall to attend the festivities. Afterward the Irishman, ever polite, was perplexed as to how he would undertake the seduction of his wife.

Retiring with much apprehension and gaiety to a bedroom in her parents' house, they undertook the new ritual of being man and wife. She had worn a complicated white dress with flowery embroidered sleeves that her mother had made for her and she had shocked Nelson during the first moments, when they were sitting in prolonged silence on opposite sides of the canopied bed, by asking him to undo the cross-hatched laces down her back. Then she had disappeared into an adjoining room, where she took an infinite amount of time removing the dress. She was humming a melody, something like what a young girl taking a stroll with a paramour in the spring might hum, the melody of a young girl taking a walk in a field and defining, through the mellifluousness of her voice, her sovereignty. An indecipherable but distinctly female, Spanish, Arab-tinged melody. That first night together, they did not talk about the wedding, but she had called him "my husband" and did not turn her head away when, for the first time, he began to kiss her on the mouth and chin and behind her ears. She did not turn away when he timidly advanced his hands over the upper portions of her nightgown, finding (for it must have been so with a woman who would bear so many children) the firm breasts and taut nipples. She allowed his hands to roam and he touched her skin, smooth and warm as if it had been covered in heated oil, and then he attempted to lift up the hem of her gown, but she turned away, and when he tried again to lift the gown and move his hand toward the angelic heart below her navel, she abruptly turned on her side and said, "Let us wait until tomorrow."

During their honeymoon—their *luna de miel*—spent in a simple house by the sea, they made love thirty-two times in one week. The days were beautiful and grand, eternal in memory. By day they would go bathing, he in a striped outfit that reached to his knees, romping about in the surf like a nineteenth-century muscleman; she with a parasol, examining the marine fossils, in a bathing dress that hung down to her ankles, the uplifted hem of her skirt splashed and damp from the water. Ever timid, he would come in from the porch and find her naked body serrated by the shuttered sunlight. He would rest his body against hers and mumble, and she would float and shake and her womb would become packed with damp blossoms. Pressed against her, he would daydream that he was with an angel from heaven with soft and florid wings. She would twist and churn as if trying to squeeze out a ball of sugar and honey. She would think about his Celtic skin, fair and defined by many bones, pressing against hers, and that his sperm smelled of grain and the meadows of Ireland. (In his cries during orgasm, *"Oh my,"* the bleating of sheep, the murmur of bulls, the howl of wolves. Wind through the treetops, a man's breathlessness at the end of a fierce fight or a long run.)

She'd talk and talk. "People always say that we must do things in a certain way," she'd tell him in Spanish. "But we can do whatever we like, isn't that so?"

It did not matter; they were both surprised by their intimacy.

Over the Ocean, the Stars at Night

AND ON ONE of those nights Nelson handed her a wedding gift, which he had ordered from the States. It was a Newton telescope from Holland, its tube lacquered black like a Chinese trunk and covered with bronze spirals, inlaid with mother-of-pearl stars and quarter-moons. It had arrived in a slender pine case with three latches and a soft felt lining that was a pleasure, like many things of this world, to touch. It also came with a celestial map, good for the latitudes of Cuba. When Mariela unwrapped this present, her eyes grew dreamy and she stood on the porch—perhaps thinking about *La vida en el planeta marte*—trying to understand its operation. Pointing it upward, she found the stars difficult to locate, but over the following nights, she eventually glimpsed, in that age before electricity overpowered the sky, the fabled planet Saturn. Excited, she called her new husband from the house and he came out, drowsy-eyed. In her young hand, the long tube of science was revealing the singular magnificence of the planet.

"Please look," she had said to him and he had yawned, and focusing his eyes, he saw through the eyepiece Saturn, bone-white and tilted on its side. It had a polished rim that resembled an easily chipped porcelain ring that floated in the darkness, its surface reflecting the starlight.

It hung there with the weight of a cow.

"It's beautiful," he had cried those years ago. "Beautiful."

An

Unexpected

Love

A 1923 Romance

TWO YEARS HAD PASSED since Margarita had made the short-lived acquaintance of the aviator, and she was walking along the main street of Cobbleton toward the movie house one day when she noticed that a new store, something big like a five-and-dime but which would sell fancier items, was moving into town, taking over the space that had once been Collier's stable, a store so large that its windows were brought in on logger's trucks and a crane had to be rigged to lift them out and lower them into place. For weeks, trucks had brought in all manner of fancy and mysterious-looking merchandise. Shiny new counters were set up, and in short order "Help for Hire" notices were posted and soon the young ladies of the town were lining up for sales-clerk positions.

By that time, the last of the fourteen sisters, frail Gloria, had been born, and Margarita had grown a little wary of crying infants. So many years of being around them, most of her life, and too many hours of reading travel brochures and romantic magazine stories as well as all her favorite books, including her mother's more difficult one about life on the planet Mars, had brought her to the point where she wanted a change. In the last several years, she had become something of a flapper, and although she was a little too heavy for that fashion, her alluring voluptuousness, quivery in the silver-sequined skirts that worried her parents, attracted enough attention from young men that she thought herself quite successful. At the same time, she had started to confuse a certain bearing, a cultivated air, with haughtiness. She believed that if a young woman like herself was to find happiness, it would be through the cultivation of what charm schools would call a ladylike perfection. She was quite attractive in her own way, despite the liability of her Cuban looks, but she fretted about her appearance. Some days, she would detest the tint of her skin, the curliness of her hair, and spend hours before the mirror searching out the little moles that were the evidence of her imperfection. Wishing that she could cut away those little slips of nature, she would become so moody that not even the invigorating prose of a good book would remind her there was much more to her than what men might find winsome and enchanting.

Like any young woman with an interest in joining the world, she had sought to improve herself and one day began to read *The Ladies' Home Companion*, coming across a most persuasive advertisement for a book entitled *Lady Esther de Beauville's Encyclopedia of Etiquette*. It cost one dollar and the day it arrived, some two weeks later, she focused her energies anew, studying the book as if it contained a remedy for her feelings of feminine and immigrant inferiority. With great eagerness she read about the proper posture, how to hold one's head, and, to her shock, she learned that it was no longer improper for a young lady to shave her legs—hers bristled with matted black hair and that very afternoon she hid herself in their bathroom, covered her legs with her father's lathery shaving cream and, with his straight razor, a bottle of disinfectant, tincture of arnica at the ready, carefully shaved herself from ankle to upper thigh. Then she plucked a few stray hairs from between her eyebrows, covered her face with a cold-cream treatment, and hid in her bedroom for hours, waiting for beautification.

There was also an unrevised section in that book about the pursuit of romance, which seemed, in Margarita's opinion, to hark back to more innocent days of courtship, the 1880s, when the first edition had been written. She had laughed, reading that the way a young lady might properly make the acquaintance of a man was to signal her interest by dropping a handkerchief behind her, a handkerchief that had been doused with a few drops of a fragrant *eau de toilette*; or one could signal a prospective suitor with a fan, clapping the fan open before one's face and then closing it slowly, smiling. As to clothing, she read: "A lady should be reminded that the less one reveals, the more alluring she becomes."

This, as a young woman, she did not agree with, as she wanted, despite her bookishness, to become fashionable like the modern youth of the day and sometimes lamented that her own female splendor—the roundness of her hips and fullness of her bosom—excluded her from many of the tomboyish, sleeveless, tassel-hemmed dresses that the flappers in magazines and silent films wore. And though these models, thin and wiry, seemed the opposite of herself, she decided to make her own fashionable dresses, taking the patterns from magazines. She got herself a cloche hat, and shocked the household one day when she marched into a beauty salon and had the beautician pare away the lovely mane of black curly hair that for many years had reached down past her shoulders, affecting what was then called a bob hairdo, with bangs that fell to just below her brows, that cut continuing along the contours of her head, so that its shape resembled a helmet. It was a long time before the family liked it. Her mother, Mariela, whose own hair was long and curly (except when she tied it in back in a bun, her homage to her Cuban mother, whom letters always described in terms of ailments), lamented her oldest daughter's decision, as one of her great pleasures was occasionally to shampoo Margarita's hair with an egg and soap, afterward resting Margarita's head on her lap to brush it out. She had gasped at what she considered a mutilation of her daughter's hair. While their father, Nelson O'Brien, did not mind it, Isabel and Maria were exasperated (perhaps they had wanted a similar hairdo and were jealous), and the others, from Helen down to the oblivious Violeta, then two years old, did not care.

As the first to cut her hair in a fashionable way—and destined to be the first in so many other things—Margarita had set a precedent for herself. She'd even left the movie house for a

time, had stopped working with her father in his photography
business, and had gone off to live for six months in Philadelphia,
boarding with an elderly woman and attending a secretarial
school, where she learned to take shorthand, do basic accounting,
and type. She had gotten a job in downtown Philadelphia with
a dress manufacturer, but found herself depressed by the darkness of the office and the poor conditions of the factory, which
mostly employed Italian immigrants (with whom she would chat
happily in Spanish, one of the reasons she had been hired). Confused and a little homesick (before her eyes, the very same woeful
scenarios she had seen during her years at the Jewel Box had
been played out in the factory: good, hapless girls drawn by
necessity and hard times into the arms of their immoral employers and everybody knowing it but unable to change things
or not caring, women weeping, women getting sick from pregnancies, sicker from greasy, back-alley abortions, and fired if
they complained), she had quit when one of the girls in the sewing
department, pregnant by one of the floor managers, got thrown
out onto the street. She soon returned home.

Standing in line among the other girls, she had learned with
them that the new store was going to sell electrical appliances,
the town having been slowly wired for electricity over the last
twenty years. There were racks of electric lamps, fans, toasters,
blenders, electrical massage machines, electric washing machines, and even refrigerators, which few but the very rich seemed
to own. That day, out of curiosity and boredom, she went to
interview for a job and learned that the store was owned by the
Thompsons of Belvedere Estates, Pennsylvania—a railroad-
fortune family, which had branched out from the transport business into commercial trade. A portrait of the visionary elder Mr.
Thompson was set upon a wall above one of the counters, and
a gold-lettered slogan printed on a shiny cherry-red banner
across the wall reading, "Electricity: The Way of the Future!"

She had not gotten a job that day—the few positions having
been filled before she'd even had a chance to interview—and she
returned to the mundanity of her life without giving the grandeur
of the shop or the implications of electricity much thought; but

a few weeks later, she and her sisters were walking through town
to meet their Poppy at the photography shop, when they found
him in front of Thompson's Electrical Appliance Department
Store, head lost under his black cloth as he photographed the
manager of the store, the younger Mr. Thompson, who had
moved into town and had taken a house on one of the better
streets of Cobbleton. Posed in front of the store, impeccable in
a worsted English suit and hand-made shoes from New York,
he seemed perfectly tailored and elegant, and stood there with
a *chapeau claque*, or collapsible top hat, in hand, grinning for
the camera. And the young women who saw him were stricken
with joy because he was as handsome as Douglas Fairbanks and
had that actor's well-tanned jauntiness. He was a tall, dark-eyed,
quiet man, perhaps thirty, and had about him an air of sophistication and prosperity—a charming fellow who smiled and
waved at the crowd of curious passersby who had gathered to
watch. But he'd also seemed impatient as Nelson O'Brien (a little
soused, if the truth be told) fumbled with the camera and plates.

The picture appeared in that week's edition of the Cobbleton
Chronicle, in an article that celebrated the arrival of Mr. Thompson and the store, in whose back room Nelson had taken a second
photograph—of Mr. Thompson in his cramped, lamp-lit office,
pensively sitting at a paper-covered desk in a vest and striped
shirt with sleeves rolled up, the caption reading: "Mr. Thompson,
an all-around good fellow with personal qualities and attributes
that all young American men should aspire to." Beyond that,
Margarita knew little else about him, no more than what the
other women knew: that he seemed to possess an almost lordly
self-assurance, as if he were a European count or an Oxford don.
Mr. Thompson walked from his house nearly every morning
around eight to open the store—arriving there before his clerks
and the salesgirls—and later slipped out to have his lunch at the
hotel (the waiter there reporting to friends that he liked the same
meal every day, a thick New York sirloin steak, rare, and two
baked potatoes, sauerkraut, and a bottle of sugar-sweetened
seltzer, no dessert). He would sit inside, reading the New York
and Philadelphia newspapers that had been brought in on the

train, dining from twelve noon to one, and then make his way back to the store, congenially tipping his hat to passersby and, most alluringly, sometimes nodding (but ever so respectfully) to the prettier unmarried young women of town.

For Margarita's part, she never paid him much attention. She had been, like everyone else, a little curious about his private life. She knew that he was always receiving invitations to dine in the houses of the better families, and that from time to time he would take a train into New York, where he had business dealings. And she had seen him coming to the movie house— where, as usual, she worked in the evenings and on the busy weekends, the direction of her life baffling her—with one or another society girl on his arm. Dressed in a freshly pressed suit, he would wait in line, impassive and cool even in the summers, among the ladies with their rose-colored fans and the men wiping their brows with kerchiefs, his skin giving off the scent of lemon cologne. She thought him older, and though she sometimes cried at night, she was not that lonely for a man, as she had her books and her sisters and the love of the family, exasperating as they could sometimes be (as when the littlest ones would run charging through the movie house screaming, or push open the bathroom door while she was sitting on the toilet, gingerly going about her business with the demeanor of a bawdy angel squeezing out an excess of light).

The Movie Shows

DURING THE MOVIE SHOWS, when she sometimes worked in the projectionist's booth, she would laugh at the theatricality of the vaudeville performers who came in to sing a few songs before the movies began—jugglers, a magician, a tap dancer in blackface, baggy-pantsed comedians, many of them in the style of Chaplin. Her sisters Maria, Olga, and Jacqueline would perform a few popular songs of the day when the mood struck them, piano, accordion, violin, and voice their sonorous instruments,

always successful with the crowds. And on nights when their
regular pianist failed to come in, Maria took to the piano and
worked from sheet music, playing in accompaniment to the films
(tunes like "My Little Mountain Maid," "Hitchy Koo," "Oh,
Baby Mine," "Dublin Daisies," "The Peek-a-Boo Rag," among
others). On those nights, she sometimes noticed which young
couples were happy, and those who were just keeping one another
company. She put Mr. Thompson and his dates into this class,
for he seemed bored with them, and sometimes her own daydreams would begin (those late-at-night daydreams, she would
remember years later, of a man touching her body, and no one
in the world knowing it, her own fingers would touch herself,
out of boredom and desire).

He had attended perhaps two dozen programs before she
realized that whenever she worked the lobby he tended to glance
over at her. The night they had shown Elmo Lincoln in *Tarzan
of the Apes*, she had been behind the candy counter when he had
gone back to buy some sweets, and it was there, as she went
about the business of scooping out a cup of caramel-coated peanuts, that Mr. Thompson, watching her, broke into so broad a
grin that she could not keep herself from asking, "Is something
wrong?"

"Nothing at all," he told her. "You simply remind me of
someone I once knew. In France."

"In France? I've always wanted to go there."

"Then perhaps you will." And he looked at her with such
earnest longing that she blushed.

And when she had given him the cup, she said, "Well, monsieur, will that be all?"

He laughed. "Yes, I suppose so."

Then, pausing: "What's your name?"

"Margaret."

"Ah, Margaret. Mine's Lester."

And that was all that had happened at the counter. He
slipped back into the theater and she had watched him, thinking
many things—that she liked his voice and the clarity of his eyes
and, even if he was a little old, his handsomeness, and above all

the air of self-assurance he had about him, the idea that he had
ever been to France—perhaps as a soldier during the war—
intriguing her. That's what she was thinking about when the
crowd began to leave the theater and she saw him again, turning
from his companion, one of the Willis sisters, a banking family,
giving her a quick, discreet nod and smile. That had been all.
Margarita joined Isabel and the other sisters, who had attended
the show and were closing down the theater. Then the following
week she arrived to find waiting for her a carefully penned note
in an envelope in which was also enclosed a business card, the
note asking to see her.

> *Dear Margaret,*
>
>   *I hope you will forgive the liberty I'm taking in addressing
> you so informally, but ever since I've come to this town, I've
> often been gladdened by the sight of you. If you are asking
> yourself why, allow me the privilege of a few hours of your
> company to explain. Would supper at the hotel on Main Street
> this coming Sunday evening, say seven, be convenient? In any
> case, hoping for the best, I will be waiting.*
>   *Yours faithfully,*
>   *Lester L. Thompson*

She'd keep that note with her, among other items, until she
was very old, and it would amaze her, those years later, how such
a simple note—a few sentences written in a courteous and gentlemanly tone, could so change her life. She'd remember that for
days she hoarded that note, reading it over and over again, a
kind of nervousness coming over her. While reading his quite
elegant and refined script, she could hardly believe that so prosperous, handsome, and apparently erudite a man had taken an
interest in her. What did he want and what, she had asked herself,
did she have to offer him? That week, before their first "date,"
she slept fitfully, for she was at the age when proper young ladies
begin to think about marriage. Dallying in the bathtub, she would
lean her head back, touch herself, and imagine a man's lips
kissing her body—a man cupping her breasts in his hands and

biting her nipples until they were sore. Then she saw Lester, no one else, and decided that she would go.

Their First Date

TWENTY-ONE YEARS OLD, she had gone, with nervous apprehension, to meet Lester, her father driving her into town. Her father had been pleased—for he always worried about the future of his daughters, and having photographed Mr. Thompson, had judged him a "gentleman."

"Have a good time" was the sentiment in the household, and that had given her confidence. Yet, when her father had driven her to the hotel and she had gotten out of the car, giving her Poppy a kiss goodbye and promising to be home by ten, and made her way to the entrance of the hotel, she felt as if she were walking a long, long distance—toward her future.

She was wearing a pink tassel-fringed dress that night. She'd dispensed with a corset, noticing that when she lifted her arms in that sleeveless dress, a good portion of her breasts became evident. She wore a slip underneath instead, having decided that if he found her "charming" it was because of her feminine attributes. Mr. Thompson, sitting in the corner of the dining room, was elegant in a blue-serge suit; he smelled of cologne, and his cleanly manicured hands enchanted her. He had risen to greet her and had surprised Margarita by taking her right hand and giving her a little kiss on her knuckles, bowing. Then they sat in silence while the waiter brought them water, soda pop, and two plates of salad and a potato soup. Margarita, ever cognizant of Lady Esther de Beauville's advice on the proper way to eat meals (how properly to sip soup, for example, the soup spoon always tipping toward the opposite rim of the soup bowl, away from one's self, so that if a splash should occur it would not stain one's dress), did her best to comport herself like a lady, and struggling through her own initial silence, she simply sat smiling at Mr. Thompson, her hands shaking slightly. He'd only seemed to no-

tice her eyes, however, watching them intently, and smiling back
every so often as he'd dab the corners of his lips with a napkin.

"Well, now," he'd finally said to her. "If you're feeling as
awkward as I am right now, one part of you wants to run out of
the door."

"Oh no, it's just that I'm so surprised that you've asked me
out," she said. "Really, I'm enchanted. This is the most exciting
thing that's happened to me in ages."

She picked at her food.

"It's the same for me: you know one gets tired of a certain
kind of girl, and by that I mean the kind of girl whose values are
a little twisted, I mean girls who've had everything and are a
little bored with life."

Shyly she asked him, "And are you?"

"Bored, here and now? Why, no! But if you're asking me
do I find certain kinds of companions dull, yes." Then: "Really,
when I first noticed you in the movie house and on the street, I
looked into your eyes and told myself, 'Now, there's a girl who
would appreciate things.' I suppose you know that you have beautiful eyes. They're blue, aren't they?"

"I inherited them from my father."

Then the waiter came over with the menu, each of them
choosing steak with Brussels sprouts, and while they dined, Mr.
Thompson related, in his rather guarded manner, some of the
circumstances of his life: good and proper breeding, college at
Princeton, a year in business school, and before the war a year
spent on a Grand Tour of Europe—the "good life." (In those
days he'd never mention the aloofness of his family.)

"And who is it that I remind you of?" she had asked him
that night.

"Oh, just someone I knew in France, a girl named Jeannette."

And he looked off, absorbed in a sweet memory.

"She was dark-featured and very pretty like yourself, and
with a lively spirit. Have I told you enough?" Then: "But that
was long ago, in another life."

And she told him about her circumstances, that she came

from a large family, that she had thirteen sisters, and about her greatest love, books. He, in turn, mentioned that his father owned quite a large private library, containing over two thousand books, some very old; he himself had received for his sixteenth birthday an edition of Suetonius' *Twelve Caesars* that had been printed in London in 1638, a fine edition made when "paper was really paper."

"I have it back at my house and, if you like, I'll lend it to you sometime." Then: "And in fact, if you like books so much, I can take you into Philadelphia one day and we can go browsing in the rare-book shops there. I'm not much for collecting, but I've always liked the works of Dickens, and anything, absolutely anything, containing the illustrations of Gustave Doré."

"How wonderful."

"Not really—just a little sideline. Mainly I like to look around for French publications—like to keep my French up, and so, now and then, I make trips out to New York, where you can find anything." He sighed. "Of course, the best thing would be to go to France, but these days I've seemed to come into a bit of responsibility. And that can get dreary. In any case," he said to her cheerfully, hoisting a glass of root beer, "I toast you, my dear. And wish that we could sip on good French wine instead of this rot."

And they clinked glasses.

*

That first night, Mr. Thompson did not kiss her, did not attempt as much as a touch of her legs. He had driven her back to her house, and in those brief moments as they sat before the white picket fence, she decided that she liked him very much, and was suddenly overcome with the impulse to embrace him: she did, nestling her head against his neck and kissing him. She had blushed and he had moved away from her, saying, "Well now, I suppose it's best that you get on home." He got out and opened the passenger door to his Packard and stood watching her as she made her way toward the house, turning every so often to wave goodbye to him. And then, through the screen door, she watched that considerate and dapper gentleman drive off.

A Drive in the Country

THE SISTERS got to know Lester Thompson as a more or less formal fellow who'd show up at the house on Sundays in his Packard so that he could take Margarita out for a drive. Not much was said about their "dates," although there was a rumor in town that the only reason a man like Thompson would consort with someone like Margarita was to take her to bed—of course—and even though this was not the case, her father, Nelson O'Brien, had a hard time bringing himself around to the idea of having this man visiting the house so often, though Mariela had concluded that this quiet and private fellow was decent enough. And he was gracious, even while immersing himself in the persistent clamor of the household and subjecting himself to a certain dizziness that a man might feel around too much female influence. Wondering how the family could deal with the crowded nature of their existence, he had asked, "Where do you sleep?" and Margarita had shown him the rooms with three or four beds and he nodded with sympathy, doing the same when reviewing the outhouse and toilet, his nostrils assailed by the pungencies of the air. Joining them at their breakfast table, he would partake of waffles and eggs, with some bacon thrown in, chewing his food carefully, never parting his lips too wide or making the loud mastication noises of the lower class. (Their meals were chaotic sometimes, the littlest sisters stabbing, flinging, dripping food, while at the main table the older sisters, having hearty appetites, devoured turkey, chicken, pork, platters of steaks, of plantains, pots of stew, with disorderly impetuosity, the worst offender being Irene, who, despite her graceful name, would sometimes eat so much that she would lose her ability to move.) And then they would retire to the garden, where the younger ones would play and the blossoms and insects prolif-

erated. On those visits, Mr. Thompson, who was not the most
spontaneous man in the world, found time to play with the children. He would bring them candies, and they came to like him:
he was rich, his trousers pockets thick with bills, so rich that he
had an odd, almost metallic smell about him, his skin saturated
with the smell of money. Although at first he seemed strictly
business, Margarita must have had a liberating effect on him
because he had started to dress more cheerfully, taking to bright
bow ties and boater hats.

He always looked her straight in the eyes, and although he
never so much as held her hand, she had the impression that he
wanted to but restrained himself because he had so gentlemanly
a nature.

On Sundays they'd go driving around the countryside, along
the winding roads, Lester behind the wheel and Margarita always
impressed, even though she knew how to drive. But one day
Lester got it into his head to give her a driving lesson, and to
please him, she pretended that she didn't know a thing about
the business of automobiles.

As he drove along, he told her to pay attention as he explained the workings of the clutch, the choke, the accelerator
and brakes, and then pulled over and told her to try sitting behind
the wheel. And for reasons that she would never quite understand, she initiated a number of jolting, disharmonious starts and
stalls. His face turned red and he began to lose patience, and
then effortlessly, having taken in his instructions again, she
guided the automobile down the road, and when he encouraged
her to increase her speed, she pressed the accelerator down and
began to fly through the world at fifteen miles per hour. With
that, she began to laugh like a child, and kept turning to see if
Mr. Thompson was pleased, and he was, his face the epitome of
happiness and pride. They drove through arching shadows of
bending willow and oak trees and must have been out on that
particular road for half an hour when Mr. Thompson suggested
they turn off onto a road that cut through a dairy farm, which
would eventually lead them back to Cobbleton. But they came
on a team of horses dragging a harvester as wide as the road,

and when he told her to stop and pull over, she accelerated, jerking the wheel to the side of the road and then braking. The car rolled into a shallow ditch, the elegant bumpers of the machine grazing the trunk of a moss-covered tree.

It could have been a bad situation, but the farmer helped Lester to haul the automobile out of the ditch, and afterward Mr. Thompson decided that they should rest for a bit and led Margarita into the field, where they found a nice tree to sit under. After a while Mr. Thompson told her, "The truth is, honey, I'm glad we came out here—even if you nearly wrecked the jalopy. The truth is, honey, I want to kiss you."

And with that he pulled her close and, as they used to say in those days, planted a long, lingering kiss on her mouth, the coarseness of his upper lips on her, the pearly hardness of his teeth against hers, and though she had never kissed a man before, it seemed perfectly natural that she open her mouth to let his tongue in. "You know how to kiss, I see, in the French style," he had told her, the lewdness of the act, the fleshiness of his tongue, making her face turn red. He closed his hand on hers.

That afternoon he was wearing a blue blazer and gray trousers, a straw hat, and spats, and she had worn a sleeveless pink dress, this being mentioned to help describe the movement of Mr. Thompson's hand, which slid down from the back of her neck to rest on her right breast, without further movement, until he judged it appropriate to press his middle finger against her nipple, which under her camisole and brassiere grew to the size of a sewing thimble, which much pleased him and made him shift his position. When he finished caressing her, he drew a breath of air and shifted her clothes so that he could suckle her breast, which he did for a long time.

Sitting with his arm around her and peering down, as if to contemplate a squirrel which, cheerfully feeding on a chestnut, had scampered into view, he attempted to lift her skirt, and when she pulled away, he stretched out and seemed to be dreaming. Despite her reluctance to comply with all his wishes, she perceived within his creaseless trousers the quill-shaped outline of his erect penis, roughly the length of her smallish hand. Later, when he stood up and helped her to her feet, the quill was still evident, and when they were sitting in the automobile and he was again explaining the mechanical workings of the engine and its gears, she noticed that his ardor had not subsided, and though it was not anywhere as spectacular as what she had seen on bulls and horses in the fields, she felt flattered.

That night, her body burned with a desire that had precipitated in her breasts and was a constant blush between her legs. It was so bothersome that at three in the morning she got out of bed and made her way to the toilet, where she pulled her underdrawers down to her ankles and then proceeded to work her fingers through the denseness of her pubic hair, plucking and pressing, until her body, in a quite un-Catholic and unladylike way, began to double up on itself and expanded, wept, and then burst. It had not been the first time she experienced such bodily pleasures while thinking about a man (there was the aviator, and Rudolph Valentino in *The Four Horsemen of the Apocalypse*), but it was the first time she had done so because of a man she knew.

Lester Keeps His Promises

TO THAT TIME, she remembered years later, Lester had kept his promises to her. He did take her to rare-book shops and always seemed happy when she liked a particular book, its cost sometimes beyond her means, and he would delight in buying that book for her. And when Margarita, flustered, would try to refuse, he was blunt in his answer: "Really, I'm rich and a few dollars are nothing to me." She had learned in those days, despite her strong urge for independence, simply to nod and thank the man. And on days when she felt particularly grateful and wanted to please him, she would find some quiet spot, usually along a country road, where they would stand against a tree, kissing, her hands touching him in the manner that she had once read about in one of her father's books (not a photography manual) entitled *A Gentleman's Guide to Love*, rubbing him until this earnest gentleman's face would crumple up with exertion and he would moan with pleasure. Sometimes, when they were together, he would tell her, "I'm a dull man whose passions are aroused by you." On some of those days she was very nearly tempted to remove her dress and to rest back on the ground waiting for him, but her sense of propriety (and the occasional sensation that her mother and her sisters were somehow watching her) kept her from doing so.

After a year, even though he was kindly and always spoke of her good "heart," her intelligence and lively spirit, she still did not understand why he had started, in his own words, to "feel a strong attraction and affection" toward her, and yet she had also come to believe that in his eyes she was beautiful. She had long become accustomed to the fact that he was often aroused in her presence (though rarely in the house), and to the way he doted on her. There were times, however, when she noticed his "darker" side, when, suddenly displeased with his life, he would go for weeks without seeing her—his activities unknown to her —only to change again. He would then come to the house or find her in the movie theater, a bouquet of flowers and a gift of chocolates or a book in hand, Lester saying, "If you only knew how much I've missed you, my enchantress."

On some of those days, he would return from spending a weekend with his family, whom she had never met, and in speaking about them, he would always seem bitter. His eyes would screw up; he'd turn away and get crazy, his hands shaking. He'd become a spoiled child. And sometimes he would seem a little drunk, a slight odor of whiskey on his breath, as if, while driving down from their estate, he had guzzled booze from a flask. He would speak differently, the careful, measured cadences of his speech giving way to a surprisingly mundane slang. "You know what the scoop is, my dear. My folks drive me nuts, that's what. To hell with 'em, I say!"

And that's when, if they were not in public or standing in the lobby of the movie house or in the back office of his store, she would pull him close and, with great feelings of love and an almost maternal concern, she'd hold him and, caressing his head, say, "Forget all of that, my love. I'm here, your Margarita. And I will take care of you."

In such a mood one day, and perhaps feeling that Margarita Montez O'Brien was the kind of woman he needed in his life, he proposed marriage.

With thoughts of European trips, many rare books, a grand house, the companionship of a sometimes moody man who would, however, offer her a chance for a gloriously fulfilled life, she told him yes. She had been confident in her decision. A girl had to look out for herself and seize opportunity. And yet she was anxious about leaving her family. In a dream one night, in the days after Lester proposed marriage, Margarita found herself in a dentist's chair (much like the chair in Dr. MacIntyre's office on the main street of town, with the great tooth hanging outside his doorway). Looking over her mouth (that's how she perceived men, always looking at one part of her or the other), the dentist said, "I have to pull this one out," and she started to cry. Afterward, when she looked at her remaining teeth in a mirror glazed by a pinkish light, she saw that her teeth were gold, copper, bronze, silver, tin, iron, glass, seashell, porcelain, stone, and wood, and awoke with the sensation that her sisters were vaporous sprites who were forever destined to play tricks on her, and to whom she would always be drawn.

The Gentleman's Guide to Love

THE NIGHT BEFORE Margarita's wedding in 1925, the fourteen sisters were gathered in the house for dinner. Two long tables had been pushed together for the older girls, a few smaller tables set out for the children. Although it was late spring, their father, Nelson O'Brien, prosperous and happy and a little tipsy, and having always liked a fire "for the hearth of the home," had thrown some logs into the fireplace, as he claimed to feel a slight chill. They'd dined on turkey with potatoes and gravy and a good dessert of perfectly baked apple and blueberry pie, compliments of Irene, and he, a little wavery but content, proposed a toast, his hand touching Margarita's face and a glass of bootleg beer raised to the glory of his daughters, to the impending marriage, and to the fact that his wife, Mariela, was once again, for the sixteenth time in her life, pregnant.

Nearly twenty-three years had passed since his first daughter, Margarita, was born, and Nelson O'Brien had been a good father, making babies, one after the other, and loving them. But each time he was blessed with a new daughter instead of a son, he would brood, as if his inability to produce a man like himself was a curse. When Mariela became pregnant—which was often—his evenings home would find him sitting before the fireplace, his prized Dutch pipe in hand, floating regally through a cloud of manly speculation about the condition of his wife, whom he much loved, and the sex of the baby, who he hoped, as everyone else knew, might be a boy. Year after year, with this wish in mind, and in the middle of the night, usually in the autumn, when the winds were blowing and the shutters banging, he would undertake the act of love with the efficiency, he imagined, of a great and virile man, always in the same way, for he remembered the rules of coitus that he had once read in *A Gentleman's Guide to Love*, published in London in 1900, the joke wedding gift of his friend Harrington. This manual instructed the male first to indicate his interest with a few playful caresses, then to admonish the female with the lines of a love poem—a sonnet by Shakespeare that begins "So are you to my thoughts as food to life" coming most highly recommended—and then perhaps to break into a song so that the "nervous, delicate, and extremely changeable disposition of the female might be more receptive to the demands of male ardor." His wife, Mariela Montez, loving affection and bored with the dry mundanities of her life, always responded, without fear and with an enthusiasm that often astounded him. After completing the preliminaries of what had become a ritual in their canopied bed, he would reach over and part the folds of his wife's nightgown, seeking out with his tobacco-stained fingers the mat-haired opening of her femininity, which without much effort on his part would grow plump and moist with his touch, and she, his little Spanish darling, that petite and pensive dark-eyed woman whom he had met many years before in Cuba, would become a transformed being, almost greedy with desire, yanking at that part of him that he sometimes considered a nuisance, and fondling him nearly to the point of anger, as it was his considered opinion that only the man should initiate and control the act of love.

Even when the manual explained that a "man should never be surprised by or show disapproval at the sudden appearance of unbecoming unladylike behavior," he would sometimes turn away, stonily silent and unmoving, until his marital rigidity gave way to his desire and he would cover her face and body with kisses. Then, with quivery aim and for the sake of continuing the family line, Nelson O'Brien would descend again and again into his wife's mysterious and fertile depths.

Yes, and Margarita, saintly and mischievous, had discovered the book one day, long ago while searching through her parents' closet for a sun hat, and she'd smuggled it out of the house and, sitting under a willow, had read about "The Precepts of Sexual Intercourse," as one of its chapters was called. It began:

Inasmuch as many a young married couple have much affection for one another and a natural instinct for the procreational act, the authors of this manual feel that many young couples, ignorant of anatomy and the biophysiology of coitus, will much benefit from a thoroughly scientific step-by-step explanation of the act. We have thus divided this book into five sections: physiology, the psychology of love, seductions, consummation, and variations of coital position.

She shook, she blushed, she laughed.

In a state of arousal the man's penis, henceforth called 'member,' engorges with blood and expands many times in size, its membranes, once aroused, taking on a hectic, raspberry coloration and the aspect of a mushroom or a helmet; most sensitive to the touch, it hardens into the consistency of wood, an ivory horn, or, if you like, a bone, this latter term being a misconception, since the member is at all times pliable. Brimming with the heat of arousal, much veined and at times oddly shaped—hooked, arrow-like, oddly curved, or snout-like—it can seem repugnant to the female. In this instance she should be gently coached as to the naturalness of this condition.

During the act the female should be caressed upon the breasts and the contours of her body and, finally and above all, gently massaged upon her vagina, which is Latin for sheath. This is most important and it should be pointed out that many sources, among them our own esteemed Sir Richard Burton, have written extensively about the advantageous manipulation of that fleshly bulb, which, as per diagram 1a, is located just below the arch of the mons veneris labia minora and is called the clitoris or hood. The gentle manipulation of this sensory nodule can be aided with the use of a tepidly warmed vegetable oil or by the application of salivic moisture of the mouth, which is left to the judgment of the male and the prurient disposition of the female. Once properly manipulated, this sensory organ sends through the female body an effusion of pleasurable sensations much akin to what the male feels in those moments before ejaculation, and this prepares the female for the coitus by inducing a dilation of the vaginal canal which can then adjust itself to the introduction and comfortable accommodation of the erect penile member.

Margarita had read this for an hour, her face getting very warm, and while for a moment she had been incensed that her father, the most respectable, hardworking, and generally straitlaced Nelson O'Brien, had this in his possession, she had found its contents illuminating and thought that she might share this with her sisters, like the twins, Olga and Jacqueline, who would surely have a good laugh later; in her room, lying down on her belly and thinking about the book, she felt pleasant sensations rushing through her body—her breasts, pressed flat but sensitive through her soft flannel nightgown, pinching at the sheets, and a tightness, warm and dense in her center, making her curl up and churn her hips. This was in 1918.

Each year, during the autumnal sessions of love, performed with vigor, the house would fill with a scent of altar wax and butter, and soon enough rivulets of Irish sperm would join a Cuban ovum (continents of blood and memory—from Saracen to Celtic, Scythian to Phoenician, Roman to pagan Iberian, African to Dane, a thousand female and male ancestors, their histories of sorrow and joy, of devastated suffering and paradisiacal pleasures linked by the progression of the blood) and a new Montez O'Brien sister would come into the world. And on each of these occasions their father, Nelson O'Brien, looming over the cradle and ever unable to look at their unclad fannies, the peach of their sexes, blunt, raw, juicy in their cribs, would feel an odd sensation—a kind of spiritual torpor as if he were a tourist in a very strange country. The femininity of the household (what would one day be called the psychology of women, perhaps) sometimes made him feel very much alone, though that solitude lifted away when he'd find himself feeling "manly" among men. In a saloon, he'd listen to their tales of conquest and struggle, beer froth on his lips, the man clicking open his cameo pocket watch with its ornamental engraving on the case and Roman numerals on the face (figures getting nice and wobbly like Tunisian dancing girls, like Abdullah's beautiful daughter). Trying to dispense with certain of his truest feelings (of horror, of pity), he'd tell these chaps, all pals listening to the rinky-dink piano, and expectorating tadpoles of chewing tobacco into the beautiful spittoons, about those "glory days" in Cuba and how it had started with the impulse to prove to himself and the family that he was a man, ambitious (though cautious), brave (often frightened), and stoic (often sickened to his guts). The fellows had their own stories, too, some of the oldest gents going back to the days of the Civil War. And though he would tell his tales, in his heart there was always a great sadness, despite the love he felt from each of his vibrant daughters, a sadness that sometimes overwhelmed him at four in the afternoon on a November day while he was driving his automobile along a country road, leafless forest around him. He'd feel convinced that he had not measured up as a man; because he'd not had a son, the good and humble photographer and movie-house operator who was Nelson O'Brien stepping aside and allowing the maudlin, self-pitying, angry Nelson O'Brien to take his place. Time to get lost in the world and have a few drinks, either a tin cup of whiskey or a mug of beer in a speakeasy or a tin cup of some medicinal tonic or other (like the dark syrupy Dr. Arnold's Relaxation Heightener). He'd sip these drinks until the grayest day took on the heavenly colorations of spring and he would grow optimistic again, certain that one day he would indeed prove himself by bringing a son into this world.

Generally speaking, he played the cheerful and respectful father—not one to dote on his daughters, he nonetheless had bounced them on his knees and always treated them with the kindness of a hotelier inviting new guests into his establishment. Each year he would gather the daughters in the yard for new family photographs. He became more and more the sentimentalist (with each passing year)—for new life was always beautiful—crying happily as he'd hold each new daughter in his arms (ever afraid of dropping the delicate little thing). He'd even gotten into the habit of collecting certain of their effects in one of his trunks, turning this into a museum of his daughters' lives, the trunk stuffed with envelopes and lockets that contained strands of their hair, baptismal cards (each, with the exception of Margarita—who had been baptized in New York City in 1902—brought into Christendom by Father Mancuso), their baby teeth, shoes, toys, their first drawings, and so many of the countless photographs he had taken of them engaged in just about every variation of female childhood activity, even photographing the little ones hiding like water sylphs in a tin tub in the yard. Sometimes he'd pass the evenings adding color highlights to the photographs with diluted opaque paints, haloesque golds for the blondes, the blue of the sea for the blue-eyed, and the reddest of cheeks for all, even his darker daughters, who tended, in those touch-ups, to appear (in the estimation of the oldest sister, Margarita, years later as she looked through a box of said photographs) like those brightly Europeanized versions of harem girls, with their luscious peach-tinted cheeks, that one would find in books. There was no reason to think he did not love his daughters, but even in 1925, when he had already fathered so many children, the progression of his life both delighted and troubled him.

Still, Nelson was pleased for Margarita, and that night, although he was not a big man, he loomed with benevolent enormity, his eyes tearful and happy, his Celtic face bump-cheeked and brilliant as he lifted his head and balanced its weight on the outstretched fingers of his hands on the table, shoulders hunched. At forty-six, his hair had just started to show the slightest touches of gray, and fell over his brow straight and fleecy, and though he sometimes jerked his head stupidly—beyond the bounds of sobriety—his daughters focused on him with love. (For a moment, their love was so strong he felt himself lifting off the floor, and then he settled down again.) He felt good: after all, he was a reasonably successful man who'd come from humble beginnings to America and had been a good provider. By his side was their mother, Mariela Montez, her eyes half closed, for she was tired, but she paid attention when he began to address his daughters. "We are blessed tonight," he said in his brogue, "blessed to be here on the eve of Meg's happiness." His arms spread wide. "May God bless us all." His head swayed.

"Ah, if you knew, Meg, what all this means to me!"

Their Wedding

ALL LIKE A DREAM, the hail of rice down the church steps after the ceremony—the chilly (as she was "common") and rich family of Lester Thompson behind them, her father and her mother, ever pregnant (this time with Emilio), and all her sisters cheerfully following: and their friends—the García family, Miss Covington, Mrs. Vidal, the Basque bakers, and the many casual friends whom the family had made over the years.

For the reception Nelson had rented the ballroom of the town hall, rafters decorated with garlands of crepe and paper lanterns, and they had brought in "refreshments" and even a little champagne for the bridal table. Inside the hall, a string-and-brass band performed popular tunes, the Charleston being the latest dance craze, and later his musical daughters performed

for the crowd, things going well even if the bridegroom's family
were disapproving, Lester and Margarita dancing close on the
dance floor. Everybody was happy, with the exception perhaps
of García's son, who, back from college, had still harbored a hope
of loving Margarita. As he made his way over to the bridal table,
he felt a little annoyed because Margarita had written him a
casual letter saying, "There's something I haven't told you. I'm
getting married in May, to a wonderful man named Lester
Thompson." He congratulated her, but as he did so, he had a
look of deep contempt on his face. He sat with Isabel, speaking
in Spanish, and tapping his fingers on the table, and as Margarita
danced with her new husband, he watched their every move.
Continually shifting in his seat, he smiled, but bitterly, so bitterly
that Nelson walked over and, putting his arms around the young
man, said, "I don't know what happened between you and my
daughter. This fellow Thompson seems all right, but, to be honest
with you, I would have been happy if things had turned out all
right with you."

"Thank you, Mr. O'Brien," García's son said.

"*Llámame* Nelson. We're friends."

*

It was after Maria, Olga, and Jacqueline's performance that
their mother began to feel the exhaustion of the day. With her
limbs aching to the bone and her belly filled with seawater, and
with an unruly creature kicking inside her, she nearly fainted
from the effort of crossing the floor to embrace her lovely
daughter.

They had posed for some formal photographs of the occasion. Earlier, Nelson had photographed the bride and groom
separately in his studio, she holding a bouquet of roses and he,
the new husband, with his lean face, hair parted in the middle
à la Rudy Vallee, foreheads nearly touching, an aura of bliss
around them. Now the parties gathered before another camera,
the Thompson family posed beside the expansive O'Briens, the
bride and groom at the center, all giving a display of cheeriness,
even when it was obvious that his family could not rationalize

this union ("She's so dark"). Years later, the black-and-white photograph would show nothing of the sweet springtime colors of the dresses and only a little of the glitter of rings and pins and brooches, and yet the feeling of that day, with its thick-hemmed and voluminous skirts nearly carried aloft by the drafts in the hall, and Margarita's elation—and some of her weariness— would be captured on a sheet of heavy paper, chemically treated, that would one day endow the lovely colors and soft emotions, all washed out, with the gravity of stone.

*

Later—and this startled the crowd—some mischievous kids opened the back door of the hall and a great ruckus was heard, a clip-clop of hoofs, and some screaming and laughter, tables knocked over, and into the hall bounded a muscular, soot-colored horse, a wreath around its enormous neck, the horse panicking and, as if presaging the marriage itself, galloping through a row of tables, scattering the orchestra and happy celebrants, rampaging until it was subdued.

Their Honeymoon

THE MORNING they had reached their hotel, the Outlook Lodge on the American side of Niagara Falls, with windows overlooking the great white cascades and its furious currents, the foam like an exploding heaven, she stood by their window gazing out into the mist-cooled breeze. He watched her for some time and lay back in bed, waiting for her to join him. She was thinking about breakfast—the dining room was said to serve wonderful pastries—but he said, "We'll eat later." She said that it would have been nice for her mother and father—and for her sisters— to see this grand American sight.

Soon he was standing behind her, pulling her so close that she could feel the stiffness of his beastly sexuality against the softness of her gown, and although she trembled, he pressed closer, a bolt of thick and exquisite heat against her buttocks. And then, just like that, she began to feel his hands moving over her—

He loved to suckle her breasts, and when he finished with her breasts, he moved her onto the bed and undressed her: her plump nakedness pleased him, and soon he was delighting in the hairiness of her center, and wedging her legs apart, his head disappearing between them, his tongue jostling the quivery tissue of her femininity, and he lifted her up, tracing the dark pubic hair that rose from the yawning opening of her vagina to her belly button, and then he slid his tongue into the crater of her bottom, where there was a thick sheet of gleaming black hair. For all her fantasies about love, she had a hard time forgetting that she was the oldest of fourteen sisters and that, just a few days before, she had been living in a household in which most activities were public. She did not know how to react, for all she had read, and as he began to move over her, she had to laugh, because what she really wanted to think about was breakfast, and she said, "Don't you think we should go downstairs," which did not stop him.

He deflowered her and she felt a vague disappointment. The thought of making love to him had been more monumental than the act itself. He made love to her three times, each session ending quickly, and she had daydreamed, in those moments, as much as she had tried to concentrate on her own pleasure, about the way things had been back in the house in Cobbleton, when it had been much easier, despite the tactile splendor and shocking nature of his penis—for it seemed strangely formed, like a sea creature—to touch herself. And she grew nostalgic.

She had also wondered about what he meant when he'd said that she reminded him of someone else. He certainly loved her gypsy darkness, for that's what he'd call her in moments of ecstasy—my little Pennsylvania gypsy girl—and, coming, repeat, "Oh, my God. Oh, my God." She wouldn't find it out for a long time, but her husband was thinking about the wondrous Jeannette, with whom the erudite and sophisticated Lester Thompson had spent many a day in bed during the happiest time of his life, when he had been traveling in Europe—Jeannette, who, as it turned out, had been a beautiful Parisian whore.

Their Marital Bliss

AT FIRST, she had enjoyed the comforts of living in his house; they owned a radio, electric fans, a large quilted bed, curtains of French lace, and their kitchen and dining room were filled with the most elegant utensils, ceramic bowls, and glistening trays and ladles. A maid cleaned and kept things in order for them. And Margarita? As his wife, as Mrs. Thompson, her main responsibility was to look after her husband; that is, to wait for him at the end of his day, when, like a good wife, she was to attend to his bodily pleasures.

She remembered that before their love sessions he would ensconce himself in their bathroom and sit on a chair reading through rumpled, water-stained copies of a magazine called *The French Gazette*. This featured can-can girls with skirts hoisted just high enough that one could discern the shapely loveliness of their uplifted thighs, sometimes, too, revealing shadowy patches that looked like traces of pubic hair or, in any case, bursting femininity, which agitated him. He'd also read the *Gazette* (and other "European" magazines) in his office. He would daydream about love, the sight of a French gartered leg, ornamented with a rose, so exciting him that when Margarita happened by the store he would take her by the hand, lead her into his office, lift her skirt, pull off her undergarments (she much favored white buttoned panties edged with hand-crocheted lace) so that they dangled at her knees, and, looking over her legs, which were always gartered—garters he'd buy for her on his trips to New York and Philadelphia or order from the back pages of *The French Gazette*—proceed to exercise his matrimonial rights.

At that time, she remembered, she had begun to think that the matrimonial bond had somehow made her more soft and malleable, indecisive and accommodating. Lester had started to

treat her differently. He would call her "my pet," and his gentlemanly behavior had been overtaken by the attitude that he, whenever he so wished, could tell her to unbutton his trousers and
"kiss me there and put me in your mouth." She'd watch him
moving over her and worry about what she thought were un-
sightly ridges of compressing flesh across her belly. She was so
preoccupied with her physical beauty, and with pleasing him,
that in those moments when she appeared suddenly fat, she
would compensate, grinding her hips further into him, as if to
distract him. For all that sex—three, four times a day, for months,
during the initial period of their love—she had not once felt the
inward quivering of her loins, the promise of release that sometimes precipitated like a warming dew or heated sugar on her
center. Then her simple Catholic guilt, the wondering about
sins—about what she had done with her mouth, with her hips,
the way she had almost cried, stretching herself open, only to
watch the collapse of his ardor, the man quickly dressing and
making his way back out into the world.

Every night seemed to go the same way: with her husband,
Lester, elegant in his British silk smoking jacket, suave and so
debonair while pouring out from a decanter a measure of good
Napoleon brandy which he had gotten through connections in
New York, or from his family's own labyrinthine wine cellars.
(Oh, yes, the exquisiteness of wealth—of dining with his family
in their many-roomed house in Philadelphia, servants waiting
on them, butlers to open the door, the plates before them thick
with creamy French truffle-flavored dishes, ever so delicately
chewed and properly swallowed and later, not an hour later
sometimes, elegantly expelled through the rear seam of Mother
Thompson's silk gown, in the form of a slow, creeping wind, ever
redolent of the swine-haunted grounds of Provence.) Eyebrows
high, hair slicked back and parted in the middle, with a smartly
raised crescent in the manner of *Esquire* fellows, he would sip
from his little snifter, an expression across his face of sublime
satisfaction, such as he had when Margarita straddled him on
the bed. He was always wanting more and was rarely satisfied
with her efforts to please him. He wanted to hear her scream

and to rock on him as if he were a wild horse, and to sing out
the praises of his slightly bent, hook-headed armature, and to
swirl, hips wriggling, as if she had been caught by a whirlpool,
and to wince and shake her head and—he liked this especially
—to scream out *"Dios mío! Dios mío!"* in Spanish, even if she
was not having the vivid orgasms he imagined: "Yes, yes, my
darling!" He got just about as much satisfaction from those little
sniftersful of 1898 Napoleon brandy as from her, and on many
a night when he was away and she did not sit waiting for him
as instructed, he would, to his later regret, punch her in the higher
reaches of her thighs, leaving marks that no one could see. Then,
instead of just sitting there in her silk robe, her body rubbed with
oil and a French perfume, awaiting his pleasure, she would sometimes feel tempted to empty his bottle of brandy into the sink.
Or else she might sit reading books, *Madame Bovary* and *Anna
Karenina* being two of her favorites, and keep her head filled
with thoughts of her husband's magnificent, penetrating, sperm-
rich, gargantuan, life-giving, woman-splitting, spine-pounding
member. (She had always been able to reach a climax by herself,
through the manipulation of one of her sinful parts—in the toilet,
her clitoris agitated from the heat of the day or a horse ride
through the country, her body writhing from the touch of a single
finger, or unwillingly, during the sweetest dreams, when she
seemed to flow to that one point of her body and she would grind
into the mattress until Isabel awakened and, shaking her in the
darkness, would ask, "Girl, what are you doing, what's wrong,
are you in pain?" Or else Isabel, hearing her and knowing what
was going on, would ignore her, and she would squirm until her
body splintered into a hundred and twenty-two pieces, digits,
bones, loins, tendons, muscles, organs, veins, and body parts
exploding out of her in a warm gush of light and imploding back
in—what dreams those were, because, while having them, she
became the lover of her own body; men were shadows.)

   And though she could reach a climax with her husband, she
did so despite him, and not because of him: she would suspend
judgment and think of only one thing, to get it over with, to
concentrate and concentrate on the fleshly tube which at a certain

angle seemed hooked and brushed ever so pleasantly against her. But she wouldn't open her eyes, or, seeing his face, she would have to start all over again.

Miss Covington

THE SUBJECT OF Miss Covington would make all the sisters —particularly Margarita—laugh. By the standards of the day, Miss Zelinda, as her mother sometimes called her, was an unusual woman, a pesky-nosed troublemaker as far as men were concerned, for she had long been a devotee of the women's rights movement. Their mother's old friend, she was one of the first and only American ladies Mariela had befriended in that town back in the days when she first arrived in Cobbleton. An occasional and welcome visitor in the house, she had met Mariela in the General Store in 1904 while waiting out a particularly fierce rainstorm. Curious about the pregnant and beautiful young woman with the slight look of apprehension about her, Miss Covington had asked her in Spanish: "Aren't you the photographer's wife? The one from Cuba?"—and since that day, their friendship had flowered, Miss Covington becoming Mariela's most distinguished American friend and a sometime confidante: "Do you think that it's worthwhile for my daughter Margarita to go off to a finishing school?" "I want to buy my husband a special case in which he might keep his photographs. Have you any idea where I might find one?" "Zelinda," for that was her given name, "yesterday little Marta woke up with the croup, but she doesn't improve with the lemon and honey. What else can I give her?" In memory, her face was shaped like an onion bulb, her head was widow-peaked, with a large hooked nose, intense eyes, jutting chin. An unimaginably homely but elegant lady of middle age in a veiled hat and fur-collar coat, she was very much a nineteenth-century apparition, breaking into pieces and jutting movements, as if she were a character in a silent movie. She lived in a big white clapboard house and would visit the family at least once a week to practice her Spanish, a language she had studied formally at Vassar (along with French, Italian, and the banjo, as she was a member of Adella Prentiss's banjo club) and had honed during occasional journeys to Madrid and Salamanca over the years. In the spring and in good weather, she would sit with Mariela on the porch, sipping lemonade, and, with a newspaper in hand, read and translate articles for her, and the ladies would converse in Spanish, the older woman teaching Mariela snippets of French and touching on many things, from dietary habits— she was an advocate of what today would be called a holistic approach to medicine and diet—to learned talk about astronomy, enchanting to Mariela's poetic heart and a natural subject to the worldly Miss Covington, whose father, a wealthy firearms man-ufacturer, had been a member of the New York Astronomical Society. 1910 had been one of the best years for such musings, for Halley's comet had lingered for months in the upper reaches of the atmosphere, inspiring in Mariela much secret poetry and affecting with its electrodynamic impulses the inner workings not only of the heart and imagination but of clocks and most me-chanical devices. And Zelinda would often talk about how women were denied too much in this life and how she could not understand why a woman of Mariela's intelligence put up with the drudgery of child-rearing and housework, and why didn't Mariela make use of her many talents—say, becoming a painter, a portraitist, or a landscape artist, instead of painting jars—or why was she not passing her days before a desk, writing poetry in earnest. (From time to time Mariela, bursting with pride over the mellifluousness of a line, would be tempted to share it with Miss Covington.) It would have been an odd relationship to pre-dict, as Miss Covington, at first sight, seemed a stuffy, pretentious, cold, and off-putting woman, typical of the high-rumped ladies who had their own exclusive club in town—except that she did not have much use for their snobbery and was at heart, like most of those ladies, a kindly person.

Despite the chilliness of her outward demeanor, Miss Cov-ington, in fact, had become something of a great-aunt to the family, and a fine example of womanly behavior to the sisters. She had never married or been in the throes of a romance (at least, that's what their mother said), yet she was, all the same, happy. A cultivated woman, she highly advocated female independence; Margarita would remember those cheery afternoons when Miss Covington would startle the members of the Ladies' Society by bringing Mariela and the older sisters to tea and crumpets and strudel, the ladies a little put off by the family's sometimes exuberant behavior. A woman of extremes, Mariela could carry herself with a quiet dignity, while at other times, feeling nervous, she would speak rapidly in a loud voice, the stolid, carpeted quiet of the room—the tick and snap of popping firewood aside—shattered by her and her daughters' laughter. Certain women in the club would look up from their sewing, magazine reading, darning, silhouette-making, and glare at them, or clear their throats or shake their heads, as if Mariela had been a hillbilly or a savage dancing to a jig or war song atop a table.

To help prepare the family for the vicissitudes of female experience, Miss Covington would drift into recollections of her encounters with great women and stories about the challenges they had had to overcome during their lives. Women like the eminent physician Mary Corinna Putnam Jacobi, whom she knew from the New York Consumers' League, a suffragette society of which Miss Covington had been a member. "Though she was an ordinary-looking woman," Miss Covington would one day be quoted in a newspaper obituary, "Dr. Putnam Jacobi was a powerful human being who changed by dint of will the preconception most prevalent in her time, that a female doctor could never be more than a glorified midwife."

And: "Have I told you about the opera singer Louise Homer? The first time I saw her, she was singing the role of Maddalena in *Rigoletto* with the Metropolitan Opera during Caruso's debut. And I have seen her in many roles since." And she would recount to them, the musical sisters particularly enraptured: "Dalila in *Samson et Dalila*, Amneris in *Aïda*, Venus in *Tannhäuser*, Fricka in *Das Rheingold*, and Orfeo in *Orfeo ed Euridice*," and on and on. Her stories told of social reformers—"Have you ever heard of Emma Goldman?" their heads shaking no. "Well, you will now." Breaking into Spanish from time to time, she'd explain Emma Goldman's opinions on the notion of parity in romantic love between a man and a woman, or "free love," as it was called in the press. And she'd state her opinions that women were not simple "sex commodities" destined to a life in the kitchen and in the bedroom, and she spoke about birth control, among many other ideas, for the subject of women's rights was far-reaching. And she'd try to explain concepts of individuality, rights, and empowerment, and how there were many women—journalists, writers, painters and musicians, inventors, scientists—ready to take their rightful places in society. They would listen politely, trying to understand, their mother judging her talk as the rantings of a kindly but lonely old maid, passing her time on a sunny afternoon having tea with friends in a ladies' club and speaking about a world in which Mariela believed she would never live.

All that, many years ago.

Visits

DURING THE EARLY DAYS of Margarita's marriage, Miss Covington would make it a point of visiting the young bride in her grand new house once or twice a week, to have tea and talk, so that Margarita would not forget her. They'd sit, and fidgeting, Margarita would feel a little nervous in Miss Covington's presence, as her husband, Lester, in those days gave her everything and she was wary of seeming spoiled. She no longer had to work and, if she so liked, could spend her free time reading books, as long as Lester was not around; she could pass her days becoming "educated" and informed, and yet, when Miss Covington came to see her, she felt vaguely embarrassed—as if, finding happiness with a man, she had violated one of Miss Covington's rules about being a woman.

Setting teacup upon saucer, Miss Covington would look

around and tell Margarita: "Well, it all seems very nice. You've done quite well for yourself. Your husband—I've met him a few times—seems a very good man. But don't be deceived, for courtesy in a man is not everything."

On one of those afternoons, she, dry and unromantic, confided a story to Margarita about a past love.

"I once had a man in my life—a decent fellow who used to come to our college dances. A formal chap, quite educated, a law student, and handsome. What he saw in me, I don't know. I was homely as a young girl, but very alive, and at this dance he had been looking around for someone pretty: I had so many sorority sisters who were beautiful, I can't tell you, but for some reason he came up to me, and soon enough we were out on the dance floor, and I can tell you that when he pressed his handsome face against mine I was elated. But I did not believe that he liked me for myself. My family was wealthy, and so I thought that he was interested in me because of our standing. We danced all night and I made nothing of it, but at the end of that night he asked me out; the next week we went rowboating, listened to music from some distant pavilion, and I had the impression that he wanted to kiss me. I was not pretty, but I used to have a good figure, and I can remember that he caressed my hand. But, when he leaned forward to kiss me, his eyes would be closed. Not just when he was kissing me, but as he was coming toward me, as if he didn't really want to look at my face. What does that matter. Well, I'd never had a man touch me before, and frankly I liked it. We were boating on a little lake, and there was a small island where he took me, and one night, lulled by the stars and the teary-eyed moon and every dream I'd ever had about love, I gave myself to him."

"Gave yourself?"

"Yes, gave myself, and in 1888. I would be lying to you if I told you he wasn't splendid. I lost myself in him. I became a quivering young girl, and in time I became pregnant. Do you know what happened?"

"No."

"Well, I'm leading to the dirt. He was engaged to someone

else, and when I told him that I was carrying his child, he denied
it. Heartbroken, I resolved myself to bring the child to term. My
family was not happy. My father, straitlaced and proper, had
suggested the intervention of a doctor, but I refused. My parents
would not allow me to leave the house by day and forced me to
wear a wedding ring, though I wasn't engaged. Rumors circu-
lated, I lost a lot of friends, and yet, when I was carrying that
baby, I felt good. I was happy for a long time. And then I
miscarried."

"I'm sorry."

"Well, I've told you this—and even your mother doesn't
know—because I know what it's like to be in love." Then: "You
are in love, aren't you?"

"Oh, yes."

"Then I think you shouldn't look so unhappy."

On the Veranda

HE'D TAKEN CARE of her, she'd remember. Each month Lester gave Margarita a fifty-dollar allowance for clothing (for hours
she would sit looking through the fashion magazines). He'd
praise her ("You look quite nice in that little thing, my darling"),
and from time to time, returning from a business trip to New
York, he would present her with a string of pearls or a fancy silk
scarf that he'd bought at one of the nicer shops in that city. And
although on some days she felt like a heroine of a silent film,
moving through the shadows and demurely and sometimes cyn-
ically contemplating before the mirror her "new life" as Mrs.
Thompson, she took a squeamish pride in pleasing him. Whenever they'd drive to another town for a night out in some smoky
speakeasy where he could be anonymous, she'd put on the dog
for him—trampy and loose, in tight, tassel-hemmed skirts and
sleeveless, nearly transparent blouses sans brassiere or camisole
or corset, so that when she danced the Charleston she resembled
one of those flappers that ministers carried on about in church.

They would find a little corner table and sit drinking together till all hours of the night, listening to Dixieland jazz improvisations. (My God, but in those days the lushness of the music and the ease with which the musicians played, their prolonged, screaming notes cutting through her, made her envious of their creativity. Some lean black fellow would stand in front of the little orchestra, moving his fingers swiftly along the valve board of his instrument, playing notes that seemed to go all over the place, working pleasingly upon the ear, fitting in around the chords that the other musicians were playing, compositions with names like "The Cakewalk Blues" and "The Late June Shuffle.") Admiring this music, feeling a kind of pleasure in her brow— she slipping her fingers under the brim of her cloche cap to rub her scalp—Margarita would swear that she herself was playing, much in the same way she imagined herself singing with a celestial voice whenever one of her musical sisters would get up before a crowd, or felt she had a poetic bent of mind whenever her mother, in the middle of the day, would stop to scribble down a verse, or when she would imagine being as beautiful as her most beautiful sister, Helen. Or as saintly as Father Mancuso, or as strong as Miss Covington, or as delighted by life as that old farmer who used to call to her from his horse and carriage on the road and declare nature the good work of the Lord. She would listen, wondering about her own abilities, for, during her life with her husband, her own bookishness had slowly begun to fade, the pleasures of her introspection giving way to the notion of being a good and courtly wife.

She'd wear lots of jewelry, some real, some costume—even a jingly ankle bracelet, which was a craze among the college girls of the day, though she wasn't one, a bracelet that he'd given her while they were sitting at one of those tables: "This is so that I can hear you when you walk toward me." She'd sit beside him, his hand under her skirt, playing around with the snap of her garters, enjoying the music and the fact that she was now out in the world, a grown woman with her own husband. And yet she'd wish that her sisters could see her, take in some of the exotic atmosphere, sometimes shuddering from their absence, and as nice as things seemed to be—with Lester, feeling bawdy, putting her hand on his trousers pocket and asking her, "What do you think I've got in there?"—looking over at the door and wishing she did not feel, despite his presence, so alone.

Sometimes, groggy from bootleg gin, she would allow her head to fall back, so that in the midst of a slow dance Lester, with his hands braced behind her, would ask "Are you okay?" And she would dream about falling back, not on the coarseness of a dance floor, but back into the confounding, promising, yet more blissful state of the innocence of her youth.

(Having these thoughts many, many years later, she could not help but laugh, thinking about the days when the notion of a man placing his hands on her body seemed scandalously sinful, when she would pray at night to God, as her mother had taught her, her knees aching on the floor, for forgiveness for having such thoughts, and yet always fantasizing about love and how glorious the idea of love had seemed, with its promise of eternal happiness.)

For their society outings, she'd dress more elegantly, in a formal gown and in a pearl-beaded cloche cap with a plume on the brim, her hair cut fashionably short, to enter rooms thick with prideful, advantaged people—those dames and gentlemen she'd read about in the newspapers coming back to her again (Mr. & Mrs. Edward Simpson, Mr. & Mrs. Commingworth, Mr. & Mrs. Downing).

These were formal evenings, with waiters and butlers and rushing housemaids with platters of hors d'oeuvres and, despite Prohibition, glasses of champagne and wine from the family's cellar. She would carry a Spanish fan, a gift from her mother, and on the arm of her husband, train behind her, make her way through the celebrants, nodding, smiling, and, when the moment arose, lifting fan before face to peer coquettishly, humbly, deferentially out into the world. Sometimes, when a photographer would turn up, she would linger about, sitting on a couch, and quite contentedly puff on a cigarette in a long holder, watching him at work. She might walk over, offering assistance, but because she was a "high-society girl" and married to a man of importance, the photographer would do his best to keep her away. Once, she would remember, a photographer, fumbling through his equipment searching for a lens, had asked her to help; and with the joy that came when she thought about her father, she had done so.

Her husband, Lester Thompson, would get through those evenings by drinking large quantities of wine, so that by the time they would sit for the meal he would have loosened his cravat and a general disdain would creep into his expression. Sometimes, at the table, there would be a member of European royalty who'd happened to have made the acquaintance of one of the Thompsons in Europe, or there might be some old man's mistress, a little too tipsy from the champagne, or "bubbly," as Lester would call it, throwing a fit, or becoming too intimate and planting kisses on the ear of a red-faced dignitary, or, as it happened in 1926, they would be graced by the presence of a truly remarkable personage, the movie actor Buster Keaton, a shy, gnarly-faced man with soulful eyes, measured and pensive, who was on a promotional tour of the Middle American cities and had been invited to the dinner by the big-time owner of a Philadelphia movie-house chain. She would remember that he was wearing a tuxedo with bow tie and that she sat exactly four people across from Mr. Keaton and that from time to time he would take a black olive from a bowl before him and, when he thought no one was looking, pop it discreetly into his mouth. When he chewed, his face was a stoic mask, but his ears wriggled. He was so famous that her skin tingled at the thought of him, and although she had tried to concentrate on the meal itself, she could not resist a fantasy about bringing Mr. Keaton to visit her own family (her father, Nelson O'Brien, who often showed Mr. Keaton's films, stricken with joy at his presence, and everybody much impressed with her progress in the world).

Slipping off to the veranda, she and Lester would talk.

"You look at me, Meggie"—that's what he called her—"and you'd think that everything is okay, but the truth is, they're all sons of bitches."

"Oh, but you shouldn't say that about your own mother and her friends."

"No, I'm telling you, they're like octopuses gobbling everything up around them, and what they want is to be amused and told that they're really living on top of the world. But see"—and he would hold out his glass and Margarita, assigned the bottle of wine, would pour—"they don't know about the purity and happiness of us pure souls. See, they have all this money. What's money, I ask you, but an intermediary? Yes, intermediary. What they want with this money is to buy themselves . . ."

"But, Lester—"

". . . something like substance. You know that little bronze vase in the other room? Cost my mother five thousand dollars in Paris, enough for most people to live well on for a year or two, and, oh, my God, it's this Frenchy Napoleonic thing. I mean, it belonged to Napoleon, which is very interesting, but what does it have to do with this big mortuary of a house? So my mother feels she's as good as Napoleon? Probably the guy didn't even notice the goddamned thing, let alone hold it in his hands. What does it have to do with her? Nothing, doesn't that stand to reason? And it's as if—more, please, *s'il vous plaît*—by having this thing she's somehow better, when it means nothing at all."

Moody, he would carry on about the trappings of his life, unhappily so, as if he had been raised in the worst kind of slum and impoverished—not from want of things, but from want of simple affection. And though people at these gatherings seemed civil enough, on balance, general courtesies observed and the details of travel and business dealings conveyed, these evenings were marked by such a chilliness of emotion that when Margarita would sometimes dream about the expansiveness of the Thompson mansion with its marble staircases and Tiffany windows and enormous chandeliers and tables lit by so many candelabra the heat would seem oppressive, she envisioned a lifeless and dark house, its halls, through which she would wander, melancholic and sad, speaking of the terrible desolation of Lester's past. And his face would contort with bitterness—"I don't like them very much," he would say about his own parents—but she always found herself defending them, though she did not know them well, and when she did, he'd become angry. "You don't know what it was like," he'd tell her. "If you'd been raised ever so

properly by tutors who'd rapped your knuckles for failing to properly conjugate a Latin verb, if you'd had a father who was a
former collegiate boxing champion who would force you to put
on a pair of gloves and go a few rounds so that you would be
toughened up, if you'd spent many an afternoon locked up in a
closet by a governess who did not like to hear you crying . . ."

"But, Lester . . ."

"Then you'd be a little bitter, too. I could go on. Maybe you
think I'm crazy, my love. Maybe you look at me and figure that
because I've had everything that I'm a happy man. Have I ever
told you that I haven't a single memory of my mother hugging
me? Or that, when we were in Venice with my rich family when
I was a little boy and we were floating along the canals, I would
see some Italian mother holding her little baby at a window and
I would want to jump off the goddamned gondola, I was so starved
for love . . ."

"But, Lester . . ."

"And you don't know a thing about my love in France. For
once in my life I was a happy man. I'd hang around this little
restaurant with a chum on the rue de Seine, a cozy little joint
where you could sit among the Parisians and have the feast of
your life, and some good wine, too, for pennies. Well, there were
always street minstrels around, musicians who would barge in,
gypsy-looking people, the women among them in their ruffled
dresses and pushed-up busts, singing and dancing for us and
playing music, and the next thing you'd know, you'd be up on
your feet dancing, all of us, drunk and happy and having fun.
That's where I met Jeannette and, my God, she was one of the
sweetest ladies I'd ever known in my life. I spent nearly every
night with her for two months, and I fell so in love with her I
can't stand what happened, which was that one night I got a little
too drunk and felt some bad spirit entering me, and to let her
know just what I had felt most of my life I began to slap her
around, this delicate and beautiful woman, dark like you
and . . ."

"Lester, please . . ."

"I know that maybe you don't want to hear this, but I'm

telling you so there won't be secrets between us. I don't know
what came over me—it was like being caught in a nightmare
when you look in a mirror and find out that all your teeth are
rotted—but after that, I never saw her again, as much as I walked
the streets of Paris looking for her."

"Oh, Lester, you're a good man, but very drunk."

And she embraced him, patting his back and saying, "Don't
be worried, my love. You now have me."

*

They'd drive back to Cobbleton late at night, her knees trembling, Lester drunk, the Packard swerving along the roads. She
would thank God when they'd made it back to their house. Then
she would go through the business of putting him to bed, the
man sometimes falling asleep as soon as his head rested on the
pillows, or else, his manliness aroused, he'd pull her onto
the bed. When he was a little too far gone, even though Margarita
by that time had worked out a system, knowing his body well,
which squeezes, tugs, licks would bring him around most quickly,
the woman working hard to facilitate his release, their lovemaking would seem endless, the man sometimes going at her for
hours. She would want to give up but never did, always showing
him more affection than he perhaps deserved—for he would
hardly ever remember it—and always believing that she in her
kindness to him would somehow help to ease his sadness. In the
spirit of her own mother, she attended to him without complaint,
feeling that, as his wife, she could do no less.

And yet in the middle of those acts of love a profound sadness
would twist through her body—she would first feel overcome
with pity for the man and take much solace in his moans of
pleasure, and then a kind of nostalgia would come over her and
she would feel truly amazed that, just a few years before, she
had felt mischievous but innocent and much interested in the
possibilities of life, which had seemed endless. She would close
her eyes and remember the afternoon when the handsome aviator
had rested in their house, and that even though she had gotten
sick from that journey through the air, for a few moments the

anticipation of that flight had made her giddy with happiness. And she would think, more sadly, that she had taken much for granted in the days when she lived in that house. What a pleasure it would be to sit again with her mother on the porch of the house at night to see if by chance a falling meteor might streak through the sky, or to hear her father's footsteps in the hall or even to put up again with all the laundry and the business of looking after her sisters, to be mad for a few moments of peace when she might sit by herself with one of those books, to be further driven insane by the happy chaos of the meals, when she would swear to herself that, even though she was one of many, she was her own person—confusing such familial love with some kind of perpetual confinement.

First Reunion: A Son Is Born

ON A SUNDAY MORNING in the late summer of 1925, the fourteen sisters gathered in the parlor of their crowded house to get a look at the boy who had finally been born into the family, the Montez O'Briens: a bright, happy, pink-cheeked, wailing young Hercules whom their mother would name Emilio after her father—or Poppy—in Cuba. He had descended out of the heaven of his mother's womb, through clouds of Cuban and Irish humors, slipping into this feminine universe at half past ten in an upstairs bedroom brilliant with sunlight, surrounded by the chatting, nervous, delighted, and overwhelming female presences that were his sisters. The room itself had smelled like eucalyptus, mothballs, and the wildflowers that his youngest sister, Gloria, two years old, and the one Emilio would love the most, had collected. Running through nearby yards she'd found merrybells and woolly blue violets, and, coming back into the house with bunches of flowers, she'd stuffed them into a fluted pink vase beside their mother's bed (she, immersed under the sheets and lost in the pillows, breathing softly) and then run out again (screaming) and returned with gaywings, geraniums, forget-me-nots, star grass, and daisies ("She'll end up opening a florist shop," someone had said), and these flowers opened, crying out like the baby who would be carried in his sisters' arms.

*

It had been at half-past eight the night before that their mother, Mariela Montez, her belly large as the moon, began to feel the bending of her bones, the squeezing of her heart, and a blood-red queasiness inside her. That was when a sputtering force first began to move Emilio, who'd weighed as much as a bronze altar bell, from the peace of his mother's womb into the feminine universe of that house. Having brought so many daughters into the world, she knew that it was her time and that the creature inside her belly was going to turn out to be a male (praise be to God, because that's what her husband had always wanted, a big, burly, and, with hope, handsome son). She knew this, because once the baby had sprouted bone and muscle, he carried on within her in a way that her daughters had not; he had thumped and kicked, jumped up and down, and would spend hours restlessly turning inside her, whereas the sisters had been quieter and smaller-boned and given over, she would think, to the study of the life awaiting them, delicate baby girls who slept sweetly inside her, as if on a bed of flowers.

She was forty-one years old then and had nearly exhausted her maternal proclivities, as, for the last twenty-three years, she had been trying to accommodate her husband Nelson's wish for a son, enduring each dripping, popping, and sometimes furiously weeping pregnancy after the other, giving birth to each of her daughters willingly, happily, and fearlessly, pushing them out into the world until the marrow of her youth had been sucked out of her bones and she had begun to take on the air of a good barnyard animal (like one of the spotted cows they would see in the fields of the countryside), her life having long been reduced to the cooking of meals, the washing of clothes, and the rearing of her vibrant daughters.

A small but full-figured woman, she had borne each of her daughters with the stoicism of a man like her father, Don Emilio,

in Cuba. Like him—for he never missed a day of work—she had
met her wifely duties with diligence, tending to her husband and
daughters as if that were her only calling in life. She worked at
motherhood as if the fecund interior of her body, thick with
organs and tissue and blood, was a cavernous workhouse, all to
please her husband, whom she had met so many years ago in
Cuba.

Having given birth to so many children during so many
furious days, she knew intuitively the stages of a baby's growth,
at first feeling a bud parting within her, petals separating, roots
turning and implanting in her womb as if on the most fertile
ground; and then she would begin to discern the beating of a
small heart, a small echo of her own, and the slow growth of
those limbs which would be the legs and arms, and then a tiny
rump pressing against her interior, a warmth there, too, and the
beginning of a great weight and the stretching of boneless fingers
and toes within her, until a slight turn of the softest head coiled
like an emerging bloom. And then from these vegetable ridges,
humming like the soft earth, came the slow formation of bones,
so that the form rippled with ossification and with those fibrous
muscles forming at the joints, and at the same time she would
feel that a soul and mind were occupying her, because just then
the baby, floating in the purity of her womb, seemed to take on
a rudimentary personality, yawning or crying while eyelids, hair,
and nails began to grow and mouths sucked the placental fluids
of life. Then came the further hardening of the bones, and the
limbs grew fatter and the eyeballs fluttered in their sockets, while
the brain convulsed with the forming connection of the senses
and memory, and the hardening spine grew stronger, the head
—and she would hear an inward cry—shifting with an awareness
that the world, good or bad, was waiting outside. And by then
she would know if she was carrying a male or a female. They
had so often been females that when Emilio Montez O'Brien's
testicular body began to emerge it was as if Mariela were being
injected by an unknown perfume, or occupied by the flower of
another aroma, and his body was so strong even then that it
turned and contorted and stretched, as if it were a troubled soul,

making this birth, that of the last of her children, the most cumbersome and painful.

When their mother screamed, the plump Irene pressed to her forehead a dampened cloth, and the younger sisters put aside their toys and, with the religiosity of the very young, began to pray, imagining that through the house guardian angels floated, doctorly, protective, loving in their regard for the woman who once again was bringing life into the world. That night, as on the many other nights preceding it, when the great sighs filled the halls, a sound began to overwhelm them—not the breath of an exhausted woman, not the phrases she uttered in Spanish as if speaking to her mother and sisters in Cuba, not the low hum of the stars or of the moon floating curiously outside the window as if to peer in, not the rustle of the trees or the cicadas clustered at one end of the field, not motions from the rafters of the barn, where the mute gray bats hung upside down—but a kind of continual whisper, far in the distance, discussions perhaps among the angels, as if the firmament above that house, as in tales of the Nativity, in which all the world awaited the birth of the Saviour son, was dense with a many-tiered angelic hierarchy: trumpeting angels, angels of fire, angels floating in the clouds, angels emanating from the stars, angels with swords, great legions of them spiraling down, entangled like the angels hanging suspended from strings over the Crèche displays that the sisters had seen in Philadelphia department-store windows and in the fancier Catholic churches (not like the simpler displays in handsome Father Mancuso's church, for the Catholics of that town were few and for the most part poor).

For her part, Mariela Montez saw herself at the center of a swirling and sometimes beautiful life, as if she were the pistil of a flower and they the petals, formed around her in a circle and protecting her from the ill winds of the outside world with their love. Yet the pregnancies were often difficult, and as the days would go by, her face, ever pensive but flushed with health, would show the pain. And then there was the expansion of her belly and the distortion of her form—they'd see her sometimes in the bathroom naked as she prepared to take a bath; the distension of her breasts, the clawlike stretch marks exploded from her plump nipples, and the striated markings over the great moon of her belly, her thin legs livid with blue, wormy veins and looking frail and thin, as if they might snap under the weight of her body. Seeing her daughters, she'd try to cover up, one hand on her breasts and the other on the burst of hair below, until, making a decision, she would uncover herself and, extending a hand, ask them to help her into the tub. The weight of her engorging breasts and of the baby would bend her spine, and she would suffer in the simple act of crossing a room or getting up from a chair, and that would make her moody and she'd shout out orders, and sometimes, when she had just finished suckling a baby on her breasts and things around her were too noisy or one of the daughters had snapped at her and she was plagued by a general nausea or suffered from the weight of the child pressing on her lower abdomen, she would feel like crying and, despite her love for the family—for love sometimes turned to air—she would wish to God that she could have had the independent life of a woman like Miss Covington.

Carrying Emilio in pregnancy had been especially difficult. From the beginning, he was heavy inside her, as the others had been, but at her age, when she had first felt his tumblings in her belly, she imagined that he liked to jump up and down inside her, imagined that he could somehow reach up through the placental womb to yank on her ribs and bend her back low, so strong was his force. She was always tired and often slept through the mornings; her dietary habits changed and she developed a taste for snacking on jars of mustard and honey. At night, she'd rest in bed, her husband's hand on her belly, and when he would ask, "Are you sure it will be a boy?" she would tell him, "Yes, I'm sure." But then a nervousness would seize her—Of course, a boy, she would think—and she would twist around in bed with the agony of knowing that she was too old to endure yet another birth, and the anxiety of thinking that her baby would be another girl plagued her.

But she sometimes felt a deep pleasure. A sense of elation would flow through her. She was not an intellectual or a saint, but she would look around and feel such a sweetness, such a connection with what she saw as the continuity of the world: all this would be passed on to the boy, everything that occurred within his endlessly diverting body, all that occurred out in the world. And it was that feeling that sustained her in the days when she was carrying the baby who would be their son.

Earlier on the previous afternoon, Nelson O'Brien, thinking that the birth would take place a week or so later, had gone off to Philadelphia, as he often did, to buy photography supplies and to pick up the week's films from a distributor. He had wanted to get back to the Jewel Box for that evening's show, but he had experienced a mechanical difficulty with the engine of his automobile, an oft-used excuse, or he'd decided to park his car near the Thirtieth Street Station and hit one of the speakeasies there, a place called Irish Bill's, where the password was "King MacCool," and having perhaps one too many, trusted that the sisters would know what to do with the movie house that night, the big feature being Charlie Chaplin's *The Gold Rush*.

That night, as the pangs grew more intense, the very moment when Mr. Chaplin sat down in a shed in a snowstorm to dine with great daintiness and aplomb on the tethered laces of an old boot; just as her husband, Nelson O'Brien, lifted to his mouth a frothy-headed stein of bootleg beer, wiping his lips and speaking with authority on the vicissitudes of war—the details and dangers of his journey to Cuba would grow more spectacular with each sip of the brew and each passing year; and just as Margarita, now married, was planting on her husband's navel a tongue-tipped kiss, which stirred his valiant masculinity; and as sister Maria, feeling the need to use the Jewel Box Movie House ladies' room, got up from the piano, which she had been playing as accompaniment to the aforementioned film, switching places with Jacqueline—just as these little things happened, their mother had started to go into labor with Emilio. That was when she thought that her guts would split apart, when she soiled the sheets beneath her and wept with shame (it had been Isabel and Irene's work to lift her off the bed, clean her, and replace the sheets), when even the presence of those sisters in the house was not enough to calm her. As the night wore on, all the sisters, save for Margarita, at home with her husband, would be there, either asleep in their cribs or waiting out on the stairwell landing. They had put up a Chinese screen with lotus-blossom fabric so that the younger ones would not peek in and see their mother crying out, as if in a prayer, "Ay, ay, ay," that ululation becoming all distorted (so that some of the sisters such as Isabel, ever protective of her mother, heard "Why, why, why!" and imagined Mariela asking, "Why am I here in such great pain?" and "Why did I ever leave Cuba!"). Their mother had been especially worried, as had the others, for that was a time when many mothers died in childbirth or the babies died, strangled on their umbilical cords or born "blue." And the sisters had been happy when Miss Covington arrived with her night bag to sit in vigil down below not an hour after their mother's contractions had started and the doctor had been alerted. Miss Covington, with her New Englander's sense of propriety and order—a bit of a restraint when the girls wanted to make merry in their parents' absence—was a godsend, even if she was a Protestant, for her staidness, her levelheadedness were a salve on their fears; Miss Covington, an elegant lady of great feminine inner strength, could maintain order and calm even when the screams of childbirth filled the house, sending the black birds out of the trees.

By then Mariela started to shake and cry and feel a terrible chill, when the boy Emilio, wide-shouldered as a bull, began to move inside her. She asked her daughters for something to relieve the pain, to relax and free her from the symptoms that suddenly beset her, for that night she was suffering from languor, nausea, and a deep-set feminine fear, almost hysteria. She had begun to see sparks, like popping fireflies, floating through the room before her eyes; she felt a dizziness, a dread of some impending evil, and palpitations of the heart. To alleviate these symptoms, they had rubbed into her muscles a liniment called Angel Oil, composed of vegetable oils and electricity; and until the doctor arrived and gave her something stronger, she was administered the medicinal called Larson's Vegetable Cure for Female Weakness.

Then she received many kisses, the sisters prayed, Emilio

pushed, and in the swelling crest of life on which she wanted to
remain afloat, Mariela Montez, racked by the pain of childbirth,
drifted toward the light of maternal fulfillment.

*

Held aloft, young Emilio was passed from Margarita to Isabel to Maria, and then to Jacqueline and Olga, to Helen, and
then to Irene, and from Irene to Sarah and Patricia, and then to
Veronica, Marta, and Carmen, but not to Violeta and Gloria, who
were too little and too excited to hold him. They had kissed his
puckered face, unfurled his toes, and played with his fingers,
laughing wildly and with great shyness when he shot an arch of
piss into the world through his strange and diminutive instrument. And then they had watched as the good doctor, who had
examined them during so many different times of illness, with
his silvery beard, his bifocals, and his raven-black waistcoat, bent
low to their mother's ear to convey instructions in his gentle
German-accented English, saying, "You know, Mrs. O'Brien,
that now you can rest. And you must, understand, for you've lost
a lot of blood this time." Their mother, despite her claims that
she did not always understand English, knew exactly what he
meant and nodded, the expression on her face, buoyed by the
sound of the healthy baby's cry, that of a woman who'd returned
from a distant place. Earnestly relieved, she touched the doctor's
strong hand in thanks.

The fourteen sisters would think of this gathering as a reunion because, some months before, their oldest sister, Margarita
Montez O'Brien, had married Lester Thompson, and her visits to
the family had since become infrequent. Having slipped under a
trellis of lilting roses into the life of a newlywed, she had lost her
virginity and learned about love in a flowery room overlooking the
cascading mists of Niagara Falls, where they had honeymooned,
and now she lived in a good section of town, where she spent many
of her days wistfully in the parlor, wearing a robe, naked underneath save for her gartered legs—how he loved that—awaiting the
arrival of her husband and the fulfillment of his pleasure.

During those hours of the night that her mother, Mariela

Montez, was in labor, Margarita, absorbed in her own life, had been in bed, daydreaming about what her mother had said about love: "Your heart burns when you love somebody, your soul becomes restless, light enters your every thought, and when you close your eyes, all you can see is your man." But that night, as had often happened before, she had closed her eyes and, resting beside her naked husband, he with his lean, matty-haired, smooth body, his sonorous and ever-alert masculinity adrift and awaiting her nocturnal touch, she did not think about him but rather about her family.

*

That morning in 1925 she was in her parlor sipping tea. She had just taken a sponge bath—on the dressing table before her, a Spanish Bible, a wedding gift from her mother, inscribed in her mother's meticulous and elegant script: "*Para la joya de mis sueños*," "For the jewel of my dreams." And beside that a small jewelry box and a silver hand mirror of baroque design. Her plump breasts, whose purpose just a few months before had been more of a mystery to her, were sore to the touch, tender from biting, and faintly aureoled with a purplish hue. Her vagina hurt, and her rump hole smarted from when, carried away, he'd jam his fingers inside. Men were funny, and her husband, Lester Thompson, whom everyone knew as a gentleman, a high-society "catch," a grand and promising businessman, well connected and the inheritor of this earth's bounty, lived to pursue a secret life with her in the bedroom—obsessed with her bodily parts and secretions and scents.

Thank God they'd arrived. Bells for the first services had already rung, people were on the street on their way to church, when her sisters Isabel and Helen came into town to tell her the good news that a brother had finally been born to the family and to take her back to the house. When her sisters tapped on her door, her husband was calling to her from an upstairs bedroom: "Come on in, honey, your man is waiting for you." That night he really wanted to "bugger" her—where he'd gotten that notion, she did not know, but he seemed fascinated with her rump; he'd even told her, "You know, the women of Spain and Italy let their husbands do it that way all the time." But that had not convinced her. He would get angry, then they'd make up and settle for the more conventional forms of love.

*

Their first words that morning—"Margarita, Mama's given birth to a boy!"—sent her back up to the bedroom, where in the half light her naked husband rested atop the mangled sheets, his masculinity alert, and when he saw that she was putting on a dress, he asked her where she was going. Telling him, she saw that he was growing moody and discontent, twisting on the bed and reaching over to a side table where he kept a decanter of whiskey, from which he poured himself a little Sunday-morning drink. The strong brew burned his gullet, as it would on many a night—for he liked to drink to calm himself—and, coming into a newer, cheerier mood, he complimented her on how pretty she looked in her flowery dress and sunbonnet. Helen and Isabel waited below, and as a kind of reward she knelt beside him on the bed and took him into her mouth, and within a few minutes he'd gotten what he'd wanted. (She was aware that the door was slightly ajar and was worried that the world would somehow know, because it was a Sunday and the clarions were ringing and the shadowy nature of her life with this man had begun to depress her, even then, during the sunny days of this, her first marriage.) Satisfied, he rested back in bed and she stood again before the mirror to reapply some oxblood lipstick to her pretty mouth, and even though she felt he was admiring her and perhaps really loved her, she was anxious to slip out—planning to spend the day with her family and her newborn brother.

It was on the way to join her sisters below that she heard a most shocking thing. "Enjoy yourself, honey," he'd said. "Maybe I'll drive up later to see the kid myself." And then, in his offhand way of presenting ideas to her: "I kind of like little tykes. Maybe we should have one of our own, my darling."

*

So that day his many sisters kissed, pulled, tugged on Emilio, and in a celebratory mood played music boxes and musical instruments, their chattering voices cutting through the powerful wailing of the baby boy.

And they were present when their father, Nelson O'Brien, arrived, a little the worse for wear, his automobile chugging to a halt. Nelson, who had seen his share of suffering and who moved through life sometimes with a forlorn expression (advancing, as if against the storm of a winter's day, against the female brilliance around him), was led by two of his daughters up the stairs and, hat in hand, approached the bedroom where little Emilio rested with his mother, suckling her breast. They were present when Mariela's exhaustion seemed to leave her at the sight of her husband, and happiness entered her eyes as she knew that after so many female children this boy would please him. She told him, in Spanish, "*Mira, tu hijo.*" Dumbstruck, he loomed over mother and son, smiling, and said, "Well, I suppose I should kiss the lad," and with his large hands lifting the boy up, he planted a kiss on his cheek. As he did so, the light seemed to shift in the room, for the sun had momentarily moved behind the great maple tree and, emerging, sprinkled the room with the promise of hope, of future happiness.

Then he put the baby down and, though he felt a great elation, the pain of new love and fatherhood came to him. Slipping through his bones was the knowledge that with his paterfamilias, as per the methods prescribed in *A Gentleman's Guide to Love,* he had helped to bring another new and helpless being into a world thick with joys and sorrows—and he said a prayer to himself that, though he was not a bad father to his daughters, he would be an especially good father to this boy, God willing.

And Margarita, like the others, would remember the afternoon of the first day of their brother's life. After they'd dined on a summery meal of cold cuts and watermelon and nearly overripe peaches, little Gloria, sitting out on the porch blowing soap bubbles with Violeta, had propped open the screen door as a support to her back as she played. She watched bubbles with coronas of pink and forest-green light float by, and as she did, two swallows came flying into the parlor of the house where the other sisters were gathered, and circled around, chasing each other as if madly in love, flitting without hitting the walls, as birds caught inside houses sometimes do, circled tranquilly until, having made their presence known, they returned to the trees in whose high branches they belonged.

Margarita's Discovery

DURING THE YEARS of her young brother's childhood, Margarita had the displeasure of finding herself in an increasingly unhappy marriage, and she thanked God that she could return to the house in which she had lived with her sisters, to find solace in their company.

In those days, she learned that one of Lester's motivations for marrying her in the first place was to rankle his ever-proper family. That had been a source of satisfaction to him, had nourished his glee (his mother and father ashen-faced and embarrassed when they first met her), and he'd even told her so, one night in 1926, when, a little tipsy, he said: "You may be my little dark rose, but to my mother and father you're a thorn." He told her this while suckling her breasts and fondling her bottom. "You don't know my folks; they die a little bit inside each time they think about us, which is just fine with me." And he laughed, and even though they'd proceeded with an energetic coitus and he'd covered her body with kisses (she did not doubt that her nakedness made him feel a genuine lust), she'd felt herself demoted from wife to parent-rankling device.

Still, he relished her "delicious body," as he'd call it, and though that very night she'd started to regret their marriage, she would tell herself a thousand times a day, "I am his wife," a vocation she identified with compliance. She mainly felt that during the act of love. Coming home from the store or from his business trips, he'd let down his suspenders, pull off his trousers, and rest back on the bed so that she could rub his feet and wipe his naked body down with a dampened cloth; then their love-making would take place—and on a few occasions when she'd hoped to God to make him happy, she'd let him "bugger" her.

She did so in the belief that in her kindness to him she would somehow help change his demeanor, as she wanted the marriage to work, and wanted it so badly that she put up with just about anything he demanded. Yet, no matter what she did for him, each of their evenings became more and more of an ordeal. He'd make her wear tight bodices and red ribbons around her thighs, demanded that she be always prepared for him in bed. And there were real humiliations, such as when Lester, returning from a trip to New York in the spring of 1927, produced an electrically operated "giant power belt" with an ornate rim and leather backing, with electrical wiring and a loop that dangled down from its buckle, "a spiral suspensory" through which, once switched on and wrapped around the base of his member, an eighty-gauge current would flow.

That night, straddling her husband, she began to feel a pure astonishment at how quickly the promise of her marriage to Lester, comfortable in so many ways, was unraveling before her. It turned her stomach to think how she had confused the desire to escape and make her way in the world with love—how she had allowed herself to be lulled by the gentlemanly and accomplished surface that her husband had presented to her. Further, she could not understand what he had seen in her. Yes, there was her pensive and slightly mischievous air, to which he would allude from time to time, his attentions lavish until he'd gotten what he wanted, when he would groan and shake and then turn away to sleep, leaving her to contemplate, at three in the morning, the promising/unpromising progression of her days.

There was another reason for their troubles: Margarita, her fecund mother's daughter, could not have children. And because of that, a certain logic came to her, a logic that forgave Lester's growing contempt for her (she could not fault her virile husband).

Dr. Schultz, who had delivered every one of her sisters, and who was therefore familiar with her mother's fecundity, at first refused to believe that Margarita could not have a child.

He prodded and probed her interior, and as he had had a late-nineteenth-century medical education, he reluctantly pronounced in the end that her womb, while normal in every other respect, had a certain misalliance of the ovaries. Perhaps, he had told her, an operation might cure that, but it might almost kill her, too. So he advised her to drink a concoction of milk and eggs and sugar and prescribed certain bromides said to promote fertility, but she never was to become pregnant, and this had not made her husband happy. When a bad mood came over him, or he was dissatisfied with her in bed, this great gentleman would tell her, "Not only can't you have children, but you can't even satisfy me anymore," carrying on in this way until he reduced Margarita to such a state that she'd ensconce herself in the parlor with her beloved books from the library (how she would envy the solace of that place).

In time he would seem, in the manner of his parents, to behave around her with more and more detachment, but he always wanted to impress her family, with his natty clothes and the very fancy red Nash sedan that he'd take the children for rides in and with his air of prosperity and earthly success. He won the younger children over with bagfuls of candy, crinkly, frill-trimmed, heart-shaped boxes of chocolates, and occasional gifts of dolls and board games. Because he'd turn up at the house with a fancy purse from Philadelphia or New York for their mother and had on various occasions presented her with a wide assemblage of hats, shoes, once in fact whisking her away from the house to a big Philadelphia department store, where he'd bought her a nice new dress; because of all this, and the way he was so courteous, and because he sometimes attempted to speak some Spanish, phrases he had learned from Margarita, her mother found his "respect" and generosity overwhelming and had come to like him very much.

Margarita could never complain, appearing at the household every so often with him by her side, holding hands, even laughing as they carried on in some mutual charade—though some of the sisters such as Isabel and Helen (my, but he always liked to look at her) sensed her unhappiness, but they never said a word.

Maria, Olga, and Jacqueline, mermaids swimming through a sea of music, were oblivious to him. Fat Irene was too far away in some other universe to appreciate her oldest sister's situation. And the younger sisters and the boy, Emilio, seemed enthralled by this man who cut such a grand figure. So when he walked in the door with Margarita, the younger ones would overwhelm him with affection, so much so that his wax-tipped mustache would quiver with delight and the hardness of his eyes would seem to melt away.

(The man would display a critical narrowing of the eyes when, standing naked before a mirror, she would begin to sing or to take a little dance step to amuse him, or when, in the interest of rekindling their romance and to reinvoke past discussions about their plans for European journeys, she'd show him the travel brochures she had mailed away for. He would become maudlin and his gloom would heighten and he'd accuse her of having taken him for a ride because he was rich.)

Another Moment of Happiness, 1928

THE UNHAPPINESS of their marriage only strengthened her love for the family. She'd look forward to her visits with them, and began to live for those moments when she could return to the house, turning up with some books and sitting out in the yard with the younger sisters gathered about her, contentedly teaching them to read. Those visits were often the only events in her life that made sense to her. She made it her habit to drop into the photography shop in the late morning, and she was frequently seen at the movie house on weekends—for that was when they did their best business—to keep her sisters company. They'd show films a few nights a week and all day on the weekends, and she loved it when her sisters worked the shows and she would leave her house and fool around in the back with them, as if she had never lost her virginity, and when, as her next-oldest sister, Isabel, put it, she refused to act her age. She'd even join in the flirtatiousness that had made certain of the sisters—even the darker ones—famous in the town. They'd sit in the back of the theater watching the movies, or else by the caramel-popcorn counter, amid a display of give-away novelty items—tin soldiers, lace-haired dolls, and George Washington and Theodore Roosevelt plates—fooling around with a Ouija board and sometimes laughing so loud over the answers of the spirit world that some of the patrons would come out and shush them, or else they'd play rummy or hearts, passing the night until it was time to open the exit doors and preside over an orderly closing down of the theater.

And she would take French lessons from Miss Covington and for a time put together a literary society which would gather in her parlor on Tuesday and Friday afternoons. She had decorated the parlor of the Thompson house with lace curtains and a chintz sofa and love seats with cushions whose flowery needlepoint coverings said things like "Home Sweet Home" and "Mother," and with elegantly mounted prints of birds and scenes from nature, a bridal photograph of herself and Lester on the center wall. Gathered by the window, where the light was greatest, they would drink tea, eat biscuits, and read aloud to one another, the gentility of the situation often making Isabel, who was not bookish but who loved her sister and worried about her, yawn, while the others, her sister Maria and the twins and sometimes younger and most beautiful Helen, would sit about, enjoying the relative calm. Other friends had joined, a certain well-off girl, Sally Smithers, recently wed and ever interested in the trappings and rituals of society, and sometimes Miss Covington. In this way, Margarita had read Edna Ferber's *So Big*, Margaret Kennedy's *The Constant Nymph*, Willa Cather's *The Professor's House*, and, among many other books, *Coming of Age in Samoa*, by Margaret Mead, the name Samoa sounding in a whisper off her lips as she walked down the streets of Cobbleton, all this in 1928.

(But, more beautifully, she would remember an afternoon in late April 1926 when she, heartsick, had gone to the house. Out on the porch with Maria and her mother, she watched the

children play, Emilio in Patricia's arms, and, just like that, she'd
wanted to take Emilio for a walk in the field. He was a heavy
baby, and as she carried him along, his head falling back with
a great weight—she was afraid that his head would snap off—
the baby gurgling and spitting bubbles, she thought to sit on a
favorite spot on her father's land where there was a stone wall,
an old, crumbling property divider. From there you could see
other farms, cows grazing in the pastures beyond. Holding
Emilio, she whiffed the sweetness of his skin and hair, rocking
him in her arms until he began to coo and reach for her face,
pulling with his soft fingers on her mouth and nose, so sweetly
and innocently. He touched her breasts and had seemed to want
them very much, his baby mouth reaching. She pulled away and
he started crying and turning cantankerously about. "Sisters do
not breast-feed their brother," she told herself, but feeling sorry
for the little creature, who was so hungry and innocent, she
decided to undo the buttons of her blouse, exposing her breast.

Years later she would remember the Y-shaped vein that
seemed to lie below the surface of the skin of her breast, its
plumpness and the womanly fibers leading to his mouth. Her
breasts were bulbous then, but she had no milk. Emilio did not
know that. He suckled her until her nipples became prescient
with a fecundity that she would never have. She had sighed, and
although the sucking had left Emilio content, his tiny nose
squinting and a nearly undiscernible snore rising up through it,
a few moments later she deemed it inappropriate, but better, so
much better, than the suckling of her husband.)

Emilio Montez O'Brien and His Sisters

Gloria

THE SISTERS WOULD ALWAYS remember how for many years Emilio had seemed inseparable from Gloria, the youngest of them, and how he, growing to be tall and broad-shouldered, cocky and handsome, had come to tower over her. She was thin and, like her mother, pensive, frail, and diminutive, with a tea-spoon face and large, honey-colored eyes. In photographs, she would stand demurely in the background, her hair in braids, and had so delicate a presence and such a look of haunted distraction as to give the impression that, like her mother, she could read minds. Small-boned (Emilio, if he wanted to, could wrap his hands around her waist), she'd had the misfortune of entering her feminine maturity in poor health, having developed, from an early age, a great number of allergies. Dust, the pollen of the flowers she so loved, the ordinary mildew of life, afflicted her with a swollen face and teary eyes, and the sting of a yellow jacket, such as those which sometimes inhabited a barrel of kin-dling wood in the barn, would send her to bed for a week. Even so, she had always done her share of work in the household and, despite her discomforts, had pursued the activities of daily life, going to school and accompanying her mother to church on Sun-day, where the smell of the beeswax candles made it difficult for her to breathe. Taking pride in her determination and wanting to show the family that she could do as well as anyone, she'd work at the Jewel Box Movie House, the theater air thick with perfumes (rose, lavender, violet, lemon scents, which made her feel dizzy) and cigarette and cigar smoke floating like a blue-cresting haze before the projection booth. And she went to dances and sometimes stepped out to the back alley of the town hall and allowed the boys to kiss her, later paying for such fun with nights spent wearily in bed with a throbbing headache thanks to the inhalation of their cologne and hair tonic.

She used to sleep in a room on the upper floor, two doors down from her mother and father's bedroom, sharing that corner space with its low-hanging beams with her sister Violeta and her brother, who had a bed across from them. His portion of the wall was covered with pictures of baseball players and old framed etchings of scenes out of the Wild West which his father had put up when Emilio was three—cowboys busting broncos and herding buffalo, great clouds of dust rising up from their hoofs. They shared that room for many years, a box of tin soldiers underneath his bed, until Nelson thought it better for the boy to sleep alone. Then he inherited the room in which Isabel had once slept with Margarita and Maria. His father had always been squeamish about the boy's masculinity. It had startled him that Emilio, his flesh and blood, felt so at ease around the females of the house, that the boy seemed so to enjoy their company.

He did not need to have any such fears for Emilio, who would love women too much, and not always in the most fraternal way. The world seemed quite simply a female invention intended to bring him affection and pleasure. From the time he was little, his sisters' love for him riddled the curtains of the house, whipped and breathed through every piece of linen and cloth; it had radiated in the glassware, in vases, in the tulip-shaped electric lamps, in the scent of their dresses, slips, and underdrawers, which, hanging off laundry lines in the yard, were like the flags of a beautiful and luxurious nation. He would twist happily in their lumps of clothes, jump up and down on their beds, dangle off the hems of their skirts, lose himself in the scent of their feathered and ribboned hats and parasols in the cedarwood closets. Their love was in everything, from the morning buttermilk which he consumed by the quart (the kitchen aromatic from pancakes, sweet with blueberries and maple syrup, prepared by Irene) to the bread, thick with female tenderness and affection, whose dough they kneaded on flour-covered boards, to the chicken baked in their stove, to the very stockings that his older sisters would pull onto his feet, their hands forever tender and reassuring, whether combing his hair, making it slick with tonic, or gingerly teaching him the business of buttoning up his trousers. It wouldn't much matter that the faces of his sisters seemed interchangeable; what mattered was the female tenderness of those hands which would roam, soapy and diligent, over his body when they'd take him out for a bath in a tin tub in the yard or wash him inside the house, the boy squirming in the liquidity of that pleasure, then bundled in a towel and left to dry off in the sunlight or to rest, years earlier, in his exhausted mother's arms, suckling her.

He was unable to walk by a mirror without taking a glance at himself and had been so touched by the benevolence of his world it seemed that even the rooms around him and all they contained were approving of his arrogance, that the pink and yellow lace-hemmed curtains, the hand-woven rugs, the knobby, curvaceous divans and chairs hummed with happiness in his presence. His sisters had bathed him, they had combed his hair, they had taught him to wipe his bottom; they had taken him for walks in the fields, the older sisters lifting him into their arms, all loving him.

The sight of bluebirds alighting on a branch would remind him of the happy birdsong on those mornings of his youth when in the good weather the sisters would sit out on the lawn, lazing about on chairs or on blankets, reading their magazines under ribbon-brimmed sunbonnets and gossiping—the vista of fields and hills in the distance and the many wildflowers that grew everywhere an extension of the women gathered there. In his sisters' company, he'd experience a sensation of pure happiness and it would seem that everything around them emanated from those females, the world itself a fertile living thing, the earth beneath them humming with its unseen life: roots and stems and burrowing insects and worms aerating the soil, and flowers striving to reach the light, and the soft grass surrounding them reaching up toward the sun, in the way that his hands would reach toward his sisters' faces. Moss and lichen covering the very stones on which he would sometimes sit; dragonflies flitting through the air and in the trees around them—the birds swooping between the branches, and the animals of those trees, chipmunks and squirrels, scampering about, attending to the commerce of life; even the tepid water in the muddy-bottom pond in which he, in short pants, and his sisters Gloria, Violeta, and Carmen in their sunsuits used to bathe in the hot summers, its ripples cresting out from around them, bristled with femaleness.

Everything Arranged to Please Him

TWO OF THE SISTERS especially doted on him; they all did, even Isabel, big-boned and plain, who kept a watchful eye on him as he charged through the yard chasing the hound with a stick, and who would proudly hold his hand when the family headed out to church on Sunday, dressing him in short pants and a navy-blue jacket, bow tie and shirt, the boy with a bit of sunny rouge in his cheeks and brilliant blue eyes like his father's: the oldest, Margarita, and Gloria, who, closest in age and living to impress and win his heart, would feel melancholy whenever they were separated.

Their childhood was happy. Off to the county fair, to dances, to swim in Tucker's Pond, to go into town and sit in the ice-cream parlor, taking a booth and watching passersby on the street. Or having races, which he would lose on purpose, even while she would go wheezing along, the two playing cards or, under the guidance of their sister Patricia, seeking to contact the spirit world with a Ouija board. Little Gloria would linger by the door, waiting for him to come back from the Young Citizens' Club meeting, a kind of Boy Scout outfit that Emilio had joined at Nelson's insistence; or she'd wait outside the bathroom for him

to finish his business so that they might go out and play. She loved
being around him and regarded his robustness and his good-
natured and quiet demeanor with joy. She loved it when, as an
infant, he would slowly wake up, eyes still heavy with sleep, thick
head of dark hair falling over his brow, and she would lead this
docile and splendid being by the hand and make sure that he
brushed his teeth before taking him into the kitchen, where they
joined the others for breakfast. She liked it very much when they
would nap in the same bed, and she would listen to his strong
heartbeat. And on those days when she could hardly get up, lips
and nose chafed from kerchiefs and the scent of medicine, when
she found herself crying for no reason, and the outside world was
beautiful with sunlight, Emilio would come play with her.

But there came a time when he left their room, when his
physical maturity became evident and he had to shave at least
once a day, and in the mornings he'd gotten into the habit of
turning his back to the sisters, Violeta, ever so curious and of a
mischievous nature, asking him, "What are you hiding?" in a
singsong voice, while Gloria, ever respectful, would avert her
eyes—foolishly, for both sisters had already intuited that in the
mornings the curvaceousness in his pajama trousers was not a
hip, or a buttock, or any other feminine entity. If truth be told,
he was not even aware of it, having been so accustomed to the
tribulations of growth that many nights, sleeping face down on
his bed, he did not know what was going on. He would feel
confused by the assertiveness of pleasure, his body shifting
against the mattress and pressing into heaven-knew-what (Gloria, awake at three in the morning, observing this through the
twilight of the room), the healthy young lad, as his father might
have called him, discovering in the fabric of the bed a feathery,
heated response, so delightful that, without wanting to, he could
feel a liquid turning inside him, like cream poured onto a cast-
iron skillet, a kind of froth shooting up from the base of his spine
and into his head and back around again through his body, as
if a thread of sensation were looping through every stem, every
rib, every muscle. He'd shake, feeling as if he were being carried
away in some odd dream, his heart beating as if he were running

up a hill with a sled in a foot of snow, as if suddenly he was falling—and he'd cry out. And Gloria—what did she know about men except the occasional remark from her more worldly sisters ("They're all babies," she'd once heard Olga say)—would swear that her brother was suffering, as he would moan and his head would rise in some contortion of pain and his boyish expression would become gnarled and fierce, and she would want to wrap her arms around him and bring him peace.

By the time he had his own room, his maturity had been more or less widely noticed in the household by his sisters, with many laments. "He was such a darling boy," Carmen would say. "He was more precious as a baby," Irene would say. "He's lost his angelic features," Maria would say, but for all that, the sisters had to contend with the barbed masculinity which was their brother. He was tall and lanky, and though he would one day consider himself a graceful man in movement and character, he became an awkward though welcome presence, knocking things over and, miscalculating his gentleness, lifting his sisters up in his arms as if they were dolls. He was six foot two by the time he was sixteen, and most Irish-looking, with a symmetrical, high-cheekboned face, a cleft chin, and his father's blue eyes. At the same time there was something of his mother in him, in his eyes, that suggested her ancestry, and a cast about his face when he was deep in thought that, in his mother's words, seemed *"muy, muy español."*

Taller than his own father and broad-shouldered, he seemed like a giant when he entered the femininely adorned parlor. Gloria, who was no more than five feet two in height, had loved to stand by him when he was a boy, but in time she found his looming presence a little frightening.

When the lengthening of his bones and the onslaught of his sexuality had begun and great surges of natural strength came to him, Gloria had lamented the loss of physical parity with her brother. For his part, he had begun, perhaps from the age of ten or so, to feel as if his maleness amounted to some form of exile. When his body began to "shoot up," his physical size changing so much with each year, he would have odd dreams. In them he

became so large that, as in a fairy tale, he, with bent back and
thick limbs sprawled all about him, took up the interior of the
parlor and, expanding, crushed all the furniture, smashed the
windows with their lacy curtains and vases and lamps, and, with
his immense head pressing upward, burst through the roof of
the house.

He became more cautious around his sisters, for on certain
days when he caught sight of some piece of dainty laundry hanging on the line in the yard, he found the titillation a little startling,
and he began to understand his father's queasiness about ladies'
things left around in the house, and his demands that his youngest daughters, who had remained at home, follow the rules of
propriety, as the older sisters had: that they not get careless about
dressing, that even in the hot summer months, when they would
sometimes leave their beds in the middle of the night to cool off
on the porch, they wear a robe over their slips and be very careful
about closing the door when bathing—for what good would it
do for their father or brother to be given the sight of their unclad
fannies, what good would it do to know which daughters possessed brown rather than pink nipples or that Veronica with her
red hair and freckled back had a pubic mound covered with hair
the color of cardinal feathers, or which sisters had moles on their
bottoms, or who, naked, had the featureless beauty of a young
angel, or whose bodies would quiver with voluptuousity, whose
Venus mounds burst with the thickest Andalusian or dark Irish
or blond hair? He began to understand why his father had been
strict with the troublesome Violeta, whose idea of a fun afternoon
was to sunbathe in the front yard in a pair of white short shorts
and a blouse that she would roll up, exposing her belly to the
sun, her body protuberant and beguiling to drivers passing on
the road.

Walking with his sister Gloria, he would often wish he was
so little that she could carry him in her arms, as she used to. It
would have made her happier, he would think, and less edgy.
Sometimes, while puttering in the yard, putting a new chain on
a bicycle, or just raking the leaves away from the lawn, he would
see Gloria watching him, diminutive and nearly closed off from

the world, and wish that he could pick *her* up and put her into his pocket, walk away, and, protecting her, go about the business of being a man.

Little Gloria, Years Later, and Her Sisters

GLORIA WOULD NOT BE like her naughty sister Violeta, a young voluptuary two years older than herself, who, by the beginning of the Second World War, would fashion her image after the fast girls the movie posters in their father's theater described: "She was a fun-loving bobby-soxer and he was a handsome naval officer!" Violeta, who tortured her father with her free spirit, seemed to live, to his exasperation, in the town drugstore, dancing in front of the jukebox—she in her tight sweaters and Lindy Hop skirts, soft white stockings and low-heeled shoes—and (in his opinion) trying to arouse the attention of the GIs on their way in or out of the war who would pass through Cobbleton and spend the night in the hotel. Violeta came home one evening in 1942, after a dance, reeking of so much whiskey that, reluctantly, her mother, Mariela, had to drag her by the hair into the kitchen, where she washed her daughter's mouth out with soap before presenting her to Nelson O'Brien. He, most reluctantly, too, beat her into sobriety with a belt. (Even then, Gloria would remember, Violeta had not changed her habits; ushered from the parlor to the stairway, Violeta passed by, her fleshy burgundy tongue sticking out in jest.)

And she was nothing like her older sisters, who were already making their way out into the world. Her second-oldest sister, Isabel, had moved from the house, having found herself a husband—in Cuba. (How twisted was the family history, that love coming about under the saddest circumstances, when in 1932, after so many years' absence from Santiago, their mother received by cable the news that her poor Poppy, Emilio Montez, after whom she had named her son, was ill, suffering from a "bad heart." And all of a sudden, after having gone from year to year discussing such a trip with her husband, Nelson, and deciding against it for one reason or another—it would be too expensive, there were too many children to look after, or she was pregnant and in no condition to travel—she found herself making hurried preparations to go to Cuba with Margarita and Isabel and Emilio. Their visit lasted several months, and while there they stayed in the family house on Victoriana de Avila Street, keeping the old man company in his last days. Isabel, on the verge of matronhood, twenty-eight and still a virgin, made the acquaintance of a kindly-hearted Cuban fellow, Antonio Valdez, some ten years her senior, a pharmacist and family friend, who looked at her as no man had ever looked at her before, their romance flourishing during a most funereal time. And when the day came for her mother and sister and brother to head back to Cobbleton, she decided to stay behind, taking work as a seam-stress and falling more deeply in love—with Antonio and with Cuba. And one day she'd married him, with several of her sisters in attendance, and became the sister in Cuba.)

Nor did Gloria possess the tremendous urbanity of Maria and the twins, Olga and Jacqueline, whose life as self-styled singers and instrumentalists blossomed during the 1930s, when, despite the misery of the Depression, they became regular per-formers at local weddings and society (what was left of it) affairs. The sisters would switch instruments—Olga playing the harp, Jacqueline the violin, and Maria the piano, and were also known to appear in the exotic cities of Philadelphia, Baltimore, and New York, where they had taken an apartment together. Not only did they wear beautiful gowns and glittering jewelry and perform in places like the Waldorf-Astoria and sometimes at the Paramount Theater, but they had the distinction of being the first of the sisters to make regular crossings to Europe as singers aboard the *Queen Elizabeth*. And there, like young Anita Loos, they met their share of European counts and barons and rich gentlemen and great stars like Nelson Eddy and Noël Coward, tales of whom they would relate to the sisters when they'd come home for a holiday, laden with gifts and always with the mischievous air of beautiful and talented women who had laughed over flirtations in Parisian cafés, sisters who were so devoted to one another that, though they were wooed by many men—and sometimes dangerously so, as with Maria's great second love in Paris in 1937 —they would remain stubbornly, gloriously together.

And Gloria was not like Irene, corpulent and happy with her husband, their butcher shop and little babies, and she was not like Sarita, whose life had taken an unexpected turn when she became the subject of the affection of Rafael Garcia, that earnest young man who had first fallen in love with Margarita years before. A lawyer in Philadelphia now, quiet and businesslike, he had remained a friend to the family, and returning again and again with his father to visit the household, he had transformed his earlier love for Margarita into a love for Sarita, composing poems that she would read with wonder, for it was known in the family that he had done the same with Margarita, and she felt flattered (and a little wary) receiving them. But he courted her with sincerity, and though she suffered from an occasional ringing of the ears that went back to a day in 1922 when she had fallen through the ice of Tucker's Pond (and gotten very sick as a result), she heard his words of devotion clearly. She had many doubts and fears, but she married him nearly ten years to the day after she had been a twelve-year-old bridesmaid at her older sister's wedding.

Nor was Gloria, despite the mystery of her expression and the prettiness of her face, gifted in the ways that Helen and Patricia "the living" were. From the time that she was a little girl, Patricia had been aware of her predecessor, the other Patricia, who'd left this world before ever having the chance to enter it. She would say years later, in an interview with a spiritist quarterly, *The Angelic Voice* magazine, that while sleeping at night she could feel the spirit of the dead Patricia flowing through her body, and that the other Patricia, in the capricious ways of the spirit world, lived vicariously through her, so that whenever she experienced a simple moment of earthly happiness—the bite of a sweet autumn apple, a delicious late-afternoon slumber during a rainstorm, a first kiss, among so many other things—she knew that the little spirit was also enjoying it. And it was the other Patricia who helped her to "see" and "hear" things. Knowledge that she had this ability came to her slowly. She had never been visited by premonitions, had never been enchanted by a fortune-teller as a little girl, never had an eccentric old aunt who could foretell thoughts (their aunts in Cuba were only a few lines of information in the letters her mother received over the years), had attended no mentalist or Theocratic society meetings—nothing at all to put such ideas in her mind. But it started to happen when she was seven years old, and the first of these events led to many others.

One afternoon, while taking a short-cut through the cemetery with Irene, Patricia noticed for a brief moment a beautiful red-headed woman in a white lace dress moving sadly among the half-toppled tombstones, her sadness so powerful that Patricia began to hear weeping, and as quick as a wink, when she turned to point out the woman to her sister, the woman was gone. She would think about it for days, sleeping fitfully though she shared a room with Sarah and Veronica, and eventually she had forgotten (her childhood days were endless and dense with events), when, in the middle of another night, as she got up to use the toilet, she saw the same woman standing at the door of her mother and father's bedroom in an aureole of light, her hands extended and shaking, for she must have been very cold, and her kindly face racked with confusion. Then she went away, stepping back into the shadows. This event Patricia reported to her mother, Mariela, who had reacted by saying, *"Ay, no me diga, hija!"* Knowing the identity of the apparition—Mariela had seen her back in 1902, when she and Nelson had first settled in this house—she sighed and patted her daughter on the head, saying, "It's nothing, child. Just a dream. Now, why don't you go out and play?" Obedient to her mother, she ran out into the yard to play with a *diablo*, a donut-shaped piece of wood on a string which she would spin around her head and try to catch on a peg. And then it happened. Her mother always lamented silently to herself the fact that she felt a sadness while sleeping in her canopied bed with Nelson, as it was in that room, years before, in 1897, that her husband's sister, Kate O'Brien, died from pneumonia. That thought spontaneously settled in her daughter's mind. She had even "heard" a name, Kate, though she would not know the details of the woman's death until years later when she was of an age to discuss it with her father. Now she knew that the lady in the hallway was the very same woman about whom her father, Nelson, never spoke, whose portrait he kept in an oval-shaped, gold-leaf frame in the parlor, Aunt Kate, dead and long gone from this earth, but, for a few like herself, still present.

(And on this subject, of all the sisters it was Patricia who would have the suspicion that Aunt Kate was not in truth an "aunt," and that her father had been not a brother suffering the loss of a sister but a widower; but if it was so, the secret would follow him, as they say, to the oblivion of the grave.)

Though it would be many years before Patricia would attempt to parlay her otherworldly gifts into a livelihood (or what some would call a "scam") and though she had never made much of her ability, wishing to be like the others, she had become the sister known for her uncanny luck at carnival games, especially wheels of fortune—she was much disliked by the games men, who would tire of giving her dolls and teddy bears, as she'd "guess" the right numbers nearly one out of every three tries— and for the casualness with which she would predict at two o'clock the arrival of a Bible salesman at three-seventeen, or that the postman would be delivering a letter from Cuba at four. And while these were the kinds of minor intuitions that would give Patricia her legend within the family, she would also suffer from such foreknowledge, knowing, with some sadness, that the kindly Miss Covington would be run down by a trolley car while visiting her brother in Boston in 1933 ("My dear, why are you so sad?"), and that her mother would one day receive a cable from Cuba containing the news that Don Emilio was dying. All this became a burden and she got into the habit of keeping things to herself. But her powers developed regardless and even affected her appearance. A brunette with clear dark eyes, she had a high forehead and high cheekbones. She was pretty, and exerted like the others an inevitable female influence, but her skin began to take on a translucent quality, so that, when looking at her, one became vaguely aware of the flow of thoughts and blood, the gleam of her powerful soul, underneath her skin.

Mainly, she got used to knowing about things. She'd re-member riding the train into New York, as she and Helen and Margarita (with her lousy marriage) did in 1926 so they could join the crowds thronging the streets outside the Campbell Fu-neral Parlor, where Rudolph Valentino's body lay in state, and predict to herself that the young and handsome college student sitting across from them would pull from his satchel two books, Melville's *Moby-Dick* and Twain's *Huckleberry Finn*, that the latter's cover would have a stain shaped like the bottom of a coffee mug, and that tucked inside that book was a kiss-off letter from a sweetheart. She knew, too, that his name was Johnny. Or, years later, riding the same train, that the ticket taker pos-sessed not only a cheerful disposition but a sex as long and textured as a loaf of bread, that the secretary and executive who had entered the rail car were having an affair, complicated by the fact that he felt estranged from his wife but was very close to his children.

As she was working in the movie house, behind the popcorn stand, a profitable concession, a man would hand her a nickel and she would hear his heart wheezing; or another fellow, a truck driver headed for Youngstown, Ohio, would walk away and she would know that he was suffering from a bout of syphilis.

And years later, during her maturity, there were the young men of the town, worried about money and thinking an awful lot about sex—for in the back rows of the movie house the couples would sit in the darkness, necking. One look and she could tell whether they were "good" or "bad," and while she had never thought an unusual amount about love (on some days in the house the rooms were thick with love, the sisters daydreaming about future husbands, and about sex, too, and love for each other), there came an evening when a lanky, awkward blond-haired hayseed fellow, with serene eyes and an air of innocence about him, came to buy some popcorn and instantly she knew that he, a feedhouse worker, an honest and hardworking person, was going to be her husband, a flush rising in her face.

It came true. When she was eighteen—in 1932—he would come back to the movie house seven weeks in a row before working up the nerve to ask her out for a date (to go by buckboard to a picnic in a beautiful field near Farmers' Crossing). In time he unburdened himself, explaining to her that he worked so hard he'd hardly ever given much thought to girls; that he would feel honored by the pleasure of her company. And so it went: an old-fashioned romance ensued—it was three months before he kissed her—and in 1935 they were married.

Helen and Veronica

LIKE HER OTHER SISTERS, Gloria had felt wonderment at Helen's presence, not so much for her beauty, but because she had always been so self-confident and robust—it was as if life's ordinary troubles had passed her by. Tall and statuesque, and altogether satisfied with her physical appearance, she had passed her teenage years in a revelry of male adulation. Even their father, Nelson O'Brien, who seemed largely indifferent as to which of his daughters was most beautiful, took so many photographs of her in his studio that years later they would fill three cartons. Nor did he seem to mind it when she would enter and win beauty contests. She had been Miss Spring Rose in 1925, 1926, Miss Autumn Harvest in 1927, and, in 1928, the Pennsylvania entry for the Miss America Pageant, which had taken place on the Garden Pier in Atlantic City, New Jersey, many of the sisters in attendance. She did not win. But with her participation came offers to work as a model; a gentleman from New York, an agent, approached Nelson and proposed that if Helen could spend a month in New York, he would certainly be able to find her lucrative assignments as a magazine cover girl and in advertisements. ("Imagine her picture, plastered up in Times

Square," he'd told them.) She was eighteen then, and excited about living another life, but Nelson and Mariela were reluctant to give her permission: New York could be a little rough for a young, inexperienced girl. But Helen then settled into such a lethargic, life-was-over gloom that after several months Nelson and Mariela changed their minds and prevailed on Isabel to accompany her for the month, the two sisters taking rooms at the YWCA.

She was so good-looking—as Isabel related the story—that when they walked along the streets of New York nearly every man would tip his hat or smile, the more aggressive types following them for blocks, men always holding doors for them and offering to give them a hand up on the Ninth Avenue trolley. At the Metropolitan Museum, which they'd wanted to visit, as it was something their mother often talked about, Helen saw herself in a sixteenth-century portrait of a Florentine princess. A middle-aged man from London, a lawyer on holiday, a baldish fellow with a thick Ottoman mustache, was so taken by Helen that he had started to follow them around through the exhibition rooms. Unable to contain himself, he approached them in the cavernous lobby as they were about to leave, insisting that he be allowed the privilege of taking them out. He seemed suave and nice enough—and they didn't have very much money, wanting to save what they'd brought along for the variety shows on Broadway— so they accepted, joining him for dinner in a French restaurant in the Fifties where they tasted for the first time in their lives creamy escargots and beef bourguignon, the gentleman explaining that he was a widower on holiday and very happy to be in the company of such pretty young women.

"Especially you, my dear," he kept saying to Helen.

Helen had found French cuisine much to her liking, and that meal (impressed, they'd asked the waiter to wrap up the remnants so that they could have a second late-night feast in their room) would be the first of many—so many that years later Helen would find herself bored by the "usual French fare" of New York restaurants: yet, at the time, she regarded everything about New York with delight.

True to his word, the agent soon parlayed her physical winsomeness into money. But a decision had to be made as to what name she would go under. European names were greatly in vogue then, and because the name Helen O'Brien was so typical, they settled on the more exotic Helen Montez, a funny choice as far as the sisters were concerned, because Helen, ever confident and full of herself (though never unkind to her sisters), had always been the one to set herself apart. Walking in town with her mother, she made it her habit to maintain her distance, either moving ahead briskly or lagging behind, and when her mother would rush ahead or wait for her, taking her hand, she would feel embarrassment, often pulling away and saying in English, "Mother, please. I'm not a child anymore." (Her mother knew what went on—she had seen it, too, in her older daughters, even those who spoke Spanish with her—that they were sometimes ashamed to be identified with her; anxious, fumbling in English, she took it in good stride. And although she always loved the little ones, like Gloria and the boy, Emilio, she would often feel angry with Helen for ignoring her, and one day, exasperated, she had simply told her in English and Spanish, "*Pero, chica, nunca olvides que yo soy tu mamá.* Never forget I am your mother.") But for all her feelings about her mother, she capitulated to her agent's suggestion, her name becoming Helen Montez. She modeled sleeveless dresses with skirts cut at the knee, in Saks and Bloomingdale's, posed (scandalously, but for good money) in a Kestos brand brassiere advertisement, her head anonymous and turned away from the camera; and with penciled-in eyebrows, mascaraed eyes, and ruby-lipped mouth, she appeared mysterious and agelessly beautiful in cosmetics advertisements that would adorn the windows of many a beauty parlor in New York.

Isabel, bored and a little wary, did not like this world and was often shocked by the way women were treated. At a showroom on Fortieth Street and Seventh Avenue, she would sit off to the side while the models got dressed, Helen, ever private, going behind a screen to put on a dress, while the others, more seasoned and perhaps a little jaded, would pull off their dresses and slips and sometimes stand bare-chested in the middle of the room with gruff floor managers and front-office accountants all around them, pencils wedged over an ear. And department-store buyers would happen by, some having the nerve to stop and chat as if in fact the young lady to whom they were speaking was not naked under a slip. This Isabel found intolerable and she would ask her sister, "Are you sure this is what you want to do?" They got to know other models and heard stories about how, to get the best jobs, one had to sleep around, and heaven help you once you began to lose your looks. And yet Helen maintained a certain dignity about her. There was nothing cheap about her person— innocence, yes, but also a certain elegance and an almost aristocratic air that, were she to confess it, she owed to the example of her mother in her better, calmer moments.

Slowly—it would take her two years—she began to get better work. It wasn't easy for Nelson and Mariela to live with the idea that their daughter would be more or less alone in New York. Margarita and the musical sisters would make it a point to visit her from time to time—but Nelson decided that New York and her career were something that Helen would get out of her system, given that she must certainly feel lonely at times and that the stock-market crash put a lot of people out of business, making such work more difficult. But Helen had luck.

She would never grace the covers of magazines like *Vanity Fair* and *Vogue*, nor become a model for such artists as Erté— Romain de Tirtoff—but she became quite popular with the advertising boys. There was something about her wholesome and secure looks that was perfect for the climate of the times (the racier, sexier ads of the late 1920s were out), and she began to go under the name of Helen O'Brien again, posing as a young, concerned mother diapering a baby, a practical but lovely wife mopping the floor, a toothpaste girl with a "pearly smile," the lovely sweetheart perched atop a hill with her boyfriend, smoking a Camel, a "Weaver of Speech" telephone operator wearing a headset for the Bell System (her creed, "The Message Must Go Through"), and, more lucrative, "The Pause That Refreshes" girl for Coca-Cola.

She changed, becoming the sister whom Gloria and the others would remember as an occasional presence, an angel, triumphant in an ocelot coat with blue fox sleeves, dropping in to report on the sophistication of the outer world. She'd come back to Cobbleton at least once a month, arriving by train, and usually her father would pick her up at the station. But one day she drove up to the house in a shiny Packard. She was in the company of a man, about thirty, who seemed, in his gleaming black English shoes, very far removed from the troubles of the times. He was a straightforward and polite fellow (the way her mother liked them), with a seaside scent about him, a partner at the Field & Lowe Agency, for whom she had sometimes worked. They had met during a photography session and he, "smitten by Helen," as he told the family that day, had invited her to dinners which she had at first refused. She did accept an invitation to attend a Christmas party at the agency in 1931, a densely packed, joyous affair (though she would say that one "felt rotten as all hell," making one's way through the pencil sellers on the streets below) where they drank a "tangy Christmas punch" and danced all night, her face pressed close to his, the bulbs and holiday lamps of the twenty-foot tree in that hall aglow, couples necking everywhere, and with her friends, other models who had been invited along, telling her: "He's quite a catch."

Whether this fact impressed her, the family would never know, for she was very private about her affairs. But the day they had come to visit, they were "engaged" and Helen, possessing the ability to feel ever assured and certain of her happiness, continued to move forward through the world.

*

Her sister Veronica was, it would seem to Gloria, the most compassionate, the story of Veronica's veil, which their mother had recounted, making a great impression on her. She was a redhead (red like Christ's blood, red like Aunt Kate's hair), and though she was almost as quiet a presence in the household as Gloria, she was so aware of the meaning of her name that she had torn out the page of a religious magazine, putting above her bed (in the room that she shared with Patricia) a lovely rendering of St. Veronica placing the renowned veil over the face of Jesus. In 1940, she put an ad in the Cobbleton *Chronicle* offering her talents as a seamstress. She felt that the business of sewing and cutting materials to the precise design of a pattern, and proper repair, was an art. (It was Veronica who took it upon herself to mend the hems of skirts, to take in or out her father's trousers, who would run around at the last moment to sew up a thread in the seam of a wedding dress.) During the Depression, loving to mend things, she would sit in the basement of St. Anthony's Church in town, darning the stockings, blouses, shirts, trousers, skirts, and underwear that had arrived as donations for the poor, and could not help but work each stitch so carefully that the garments seemed like new. She was thin and almost ascetic in appearance, though when she turned twenty in 1936 she filled out, in a late bloom, her bosom larger and her hips and bottom more enticing. When bums and hoboes came to the house begging for bread and food, she would stand on the porch, shy and proud, distributing leftover food to them. In the winter, when families roamed the countryside, she would sometimes set out in her father's old Model T with provisions—food and clothing—looking for them. The hoboes got to know her as the nice young lady, an angel of mercy, whom they would find here and there in her auto or out by the fence of the Montez O'Brien house giving out goods ("This is for you, these trousers for you, this skirt for you"). She was so attentive to these unfortunates that her mother, Mariela, sometimes thought her too "good," and worried that some slick young hustler would lure her away and take advantage of her. And so, seeing Veronica, she would call out to her from the porch of the house, "*Venga! Venga!* Come inside."

The Handsome Young Man in Rags

ONCE IN 1939, when a handsome young man in rags had fallen exhausted on his knees before the front steps of the house, she had brought him inside, pulling him up over the porch steps,

past the screen door, and onto the lounge in the parlor where
the aviator had once rested, and attended to him, scrubbing his
forehead, hands, and feet clean.

He would come back looking for her six years later.

*

And there was Marta and Carmen, homebodies for the most
part, who seemed destined to live quietly forever in their town,
a common fate for young girls who were not outgoing and too
comfortable in each other's company. The two living tranquilly
at home, passing their time in the shadow of their more flamboyant and lucky sisters and only gradually coming to fear the
prospect of spinsterhood. As they got older, they would stoically
go about tending to their looks and acquiring for themselves a
proper young woman's toilet, with pomades and vanishing
creams, the two venturing out together into the world, nicely
made up and beautiful, but ever modest, nothing like the musical
sisters, or the much more forward Violeta, their excursions to
dances and church socials no longer marked by timidity, their
choices few. They were cautious, even when life in the house
seemed the same from day to day, a terrible feeling gripping
them sometimes at dinner, when their father, presiding, would
notice their mood and announce, "No matter what happens in
this world, don't you worry, for I will provide for you."

During the Depression they relished the security of their
house—they were not lacking, as their father's theater always
provided an income. But during the war, when it was easy to go
off to a USO dance in Philadelphia and fall in love with some
young man about to see action, they held off, wanting neither
the quick romances—though they were often approached—nor
the heartbreak of the war widows they would see in town. And
so they remained in the house.

Emilio in Cuba, 1932

THAT HE WAS HALF CUBAN (behind that thought, his mother's
words, "Being half Cuban is better than not being Cuban at all")
meant little to him. Even during the family journey to Cuba in
1932, when his mother presented him to the frail, white-haired
man who was his Cuban grandfather and namesake, those days
were merely a sequence of moments in which the boy played on
the back patio among the jade plants, digging into the earth with
a stone, chasing after iguanas and the chameleons skulking along
the wall, the history of that house—his mother's first home—
unknown to him, its voices and those that he would hear on the
streets sounding to his ears as if from another world. He'd remember going for walks with one of his aunts, who did not speak
English, and with Margarita and Isabel—sightseeing tours of the
city of Santiago, strolls down to the Marine Park, where bands
sometimes played, up a cobblestone road to look at the antique
stone house in which, Isabel explained, Hernán Cortés, con-
queror of the Indies, had once lived. And often in the late evenings they would make their way up to the Cathedral Plaza and
sit at a café (the Venus), watching the passersby, his mother
sighing in concern over the poor state of her father and preparing for the vigil which she and her sisters and mother would
undertake when, returning to the house, they would light holy
candles and sit in high-backed chairs saying the rosary for the
soon-to-be-departed soul. His sister Margarita sighed as well,
while catching the eyes of the gallant gentlemen in their straw
boaters and linen suits, lamenting her marriage to Lester, which
everybody in the house, even the littlest children, knew wasn't
working out. Sorrow plagued both Mariela and Margarita,
whereas Isabel, the family wallflower, found herself happy in the
company of a gentleman whom Emilio would remember for his
hands, which smelled of soap, and the absolute cleanliness and
order of his being, not a stitch out of place. While the Cathedral
bells rang on the hour, and birds flew around the Cathedral

towers and musicians played guitars and sang, moving from table to table, the boy would grow restless, feeling out of place and far from home. He'd remember taking a walk with his mother down the hill from where the family lived, going through a market and coming to a street where she pointed out a shop window and in her best English told him, "This is where your father once had a studio. This is where I met him, many years ago, before you were born."

Of course, they took along a Kodak camera and posed at many of the aforementioned places, Emilio and his Irish-looking sister, Isabel, the tall blonde who was falling in love with the Cuban (that was something his mother and Margarita seemed to joke about when Isabel's suitor, the pharmacist, came to the house in the evenings to keep Isabel company), blissfully smiling in a way that she had never smiled before, their blond hair and fair faces, as they stood together before the window of the shop that had once been their father's studio, nearly washed out by the brilliant light. As it was at home in Cobbleton, so it had been in Cuba, very little being denied to the boy, but just the same he felt restless, even if it was interesting to accompany his Aunt Vivian's husband and their sons to the jai-alai matches, or to walk by the harbor and watch the fishermen coming into port. They'd even gone to see an Edward G. Robinson movie in a local theater, and the boy was shocked when Robinson could speak in Spanish. He'd never seen anything like it, and for days wondered how all the American actors and actresses in a gangster film had come to learn Spanish, when he himself could not speak more than the few phrases that his mother had coached him in. ("*Abuela, abuelo, estoy muy contento de haber venido aquí*, Grandmother, Grandfather, I am very happy to have come." And: "*Yo te quiero mucho*, I love you very much"—phrases which he would often say in those days and which would remain with him for years, though he could not say much else and did not know what the people in Cuba were saying to him, only that they were very nice, as the world was nice to him in his youth, the pure affection that he felt in Cobbleton duplicated in Cuba.) It was Margarita who would explain the principles of dubbing to Emilio—that Spanish actors went into booths and spoke the words for their American counterparts, and that had fascinated him then and would years later when, having become an actor, he would be sitting in his California bungalow looking in the TV listings and find one of his movies, *Desperation*, listed as *Desesperación* on the Spanish-language channel, the man watching himself in that more-or-less mediocre potboiler speaking his lines in a Spanish whose origin he could not determine, the high-pitched fluency of that other Emilio Montez O'Brien impressing him and then leading to a depression, for in later life, long after his descent into obscurity, he would wonder how much he had missed in life because he, like his younger sisters, did not speak Spanish.

Yet, in those days, he was getting along well in life without that language, even if he was never certain that his mother truly understood him, or was never sure what she was saying to him, even in later years, when their conversations were of a practical and simple nature, the feeling that he did not know her making him sad also.

On one of those nights, he had spied on Isabel and the pharmacist, Antonio—who'd always give him candies—as they sat on the back patio in courtship, the man whispering to her in a low voice and from time to time pulling her close and giving her a long kiss, his murmuring speaking of a desire which was clear to Emilio even then. And despite the grief that came over the household when a cry was heard in the middle of the night, his grandfather finally shutting his eyes for good, he had loved the journey itself, the busy terminals, the rail trip to and from Havana and then the boat out of that port city back to Key West, Florida, where Margarita, ever kindly (and a little seductive) with Emilio, bought him a rubber alligator at the rail station and they made their way home, north to New York and west to Cobbleton.

Nelson O'Brien's Chagrin

DESPITE THE BIRTH of a son and the love of his daughters, his father, Nelson O'Brien, had failed to find within himself a feeling of real contentment. Maybe he had seen too much suffering during his early life. He'd seen his share of it back in the days of the Spanish-American War, and with the onset of the Depression had pitied his fellow men, the ranks of the unemployed, hoboes, who would get rousted from the freight cars and come drifting through town looking for work and, when they could not find that, for a handout. He would sometimes get a man to come in and clean his shop window, hand the fellow a buck for mopping up the floors, or, even when it wasn't necessary, hire a small crew and have them scrub down the walls of the movie house, mop the floors, maybe put a fresh coat of paint in the rest rooms. He'd have one of his daughters cook up a pot of stew, get a case of "near-beer," and feed these men, so that the unfortunates would have at least a few days of decent food and some work, but there always came the moment when he would have to let them go, slapping their backs and wishing them the best of luck. Sometimes he'd had trouble. He'd hired someone to work in the studio, and a few of the nicely framed photographs that he'd put up for display would be missing, or some boxes of candy would disappear from the movie house—but nothing more.

Thinking about the family and his standing in town, he would judge that, given the troublesome times, he had done well enough for himself. His daughters had turned out to be good women, though he'd worried about Violeta, whom he reluctantly classified as a "floozie," and there were many days when he worried about poor Gloria's health. And there was Margarita's marriage to Thompson—whom were they trying to kid? The family treated the man well enough when he came to the house—what else were they going to do?—but Mariela would sometimes spend half the night in bed going on in Spanish about her daughter's unhappiness, and "with such a good man," she would tell him in Spanish, a wishfulness in her voice. He would listen and tell her, "He's a drunk." And it was true—who the heck did he think he was fooling, coming to the house ever so subtly drunk, a slight roll to his eyes and malevolence in his voice.

It takes one to know one, he would think to himself.

But Irene had married that nice butcher and he had become a grandfather and his other daughters had done well enough—though he could not help but worry about them.

The thing about life, he would think, is that there's much that's lovely and much that brings one pain. He'd always found little ways of telling his boy, Emilio, this truth of life, and he'd wish to God that there was a way he could guarantee happiness—if not his own, then the happiness of others.

He never wanted his son to notice his little habits—bootleg whiskey and bottles of Relaxation Heightener. A swig or two every hour until the last moments before bed—someone usually finding him asleep in front of the fireplace. He'd gotten used to hearing the sisters saying, "Daddy's in an eccentric mood." And why? Just because he would sometimes talk to himself as he sat watching the fire? He'd tried to quit, but bootleggers and speak-easies in Philadelphia, where one could buy a bottle of whiskey for five dollars, had always kept him well supplied, despite Prohibition; and there was the curative potion, which he had been drinking for many years and kept stocked in their cellar and in kitchen cabinets as well. It was his friend in time of need.

But he had to admit there were times when he'd gotten carried away, when he would move through the rooms of the house and have to gird himself to offer the appearance of normality. Some days, when he crossed a room, he'd suck in his stomach and concentrate on maintaining his balance so that he could walk into the parlor, where his daughters would be gathered, without "letting on." Still, there were those nights when he would find himself roaming the field outside the house, all confused under the stars and thinking himself back in Ireland, near the Bridge of Echoes (and the River of Sorrows), Kate somewhere waiting for him. Or he was in Cuba, near Las Guásimas, roving in search of a trench to relieve himself, and suddenly he would hear a voice, or feel a hand shaking his arm, one of his daughters, or, in later years, his boy, his one and only son, Emilio, pulling him along, and as if he had been slapped in the face, he would soar out of these reveries and tell himself, "Come to your senses, man."

He'd supposed he was fooling himself in thinking those

bouts were his little secret. Even his wife, Mariela, unbeknownst to the children, promised to leave him if he didn't change his ways—though she never did. Besides, he would go for weeks without touching a drop of anything; after all, he needed all his senses intact to carry on the business of supporting the family, and in that he took great pride.

When his son was eight, his hair started to turn gray, and although he wanted to assure the boy that all was well in the world, regardless of his personal habits, there were times when his tragic side took over. It was a funny thing. Always affectionate with his daughters, and sometimes vocal about it—"Now, listen to me, you come here and give your father a kiss"—he had not been very open with them about his life. With Emilio he behaved differently, confiding in the boy. My God, on some evenings he would sit with his son and tell him grand stories about his youth that always drifted toward the darkness (dim recollections coming to him that the next day would make him feel terrible)—the boy sometimes squirming in his chair and wanting to go away, but he would hold him by the wrist.

What could he have said?

He'd taken pride in teaching Emilio all about the photography process. He'd even sent his son to take care of a job when he could not, and he'd brought the boy along on his journeys to Philadelphia to pick up canisters of film for the movie house.

And yet—

Emilio, his flesh and blood, a fine, strong young man, gregarious and happy with his sisters, always seemed a bit on the somber side with his own father, and Nelson had remained careful about pressing him for conversation, preferring to go through their days offering common bits of advice. But as the boy got older, entering young manhood, his father had started to question him about the future.

"You know, there's always the management of the movie house for you to think about," he had said to the boy in 1939, when Nelson was already past sixty. "I've always said one thing to myself, boy, and that's if there is anything I can do for the family it's to leave them a means of support."

Then: "You're interested, aren't you?"

"Yes, Father."

His son's response always heartened him, for as Nelson got older, he wanted to know that everything in the lives of his children would be in place.

"Just remember, too, that when I die, should any of your sisters be wanting in any fashion, or if your mother needs support, I want you to take care of them. You understand?"

A Slight Excitement: Gloria

HE HAD TO GIVE his father credit—the man did teach him about the photography trade and the movie house—and in the days when Emilio had come of age his father (to remove any doubts from his own mind about the boy's "maleness," for who could say how a young man so subjected to the female influence might turn out) took him to a countryside brothel, the lady taking care of him a little sad, and reminiscent in his mind, because she was so dark and deliciously proportioned, of his older sister, Margarita. At the sight of this woman, who couldn't have been more than thirty, in garters and with her thick bush prominent under the veil of her panties, he had thought about Margarita, not with incestuous desires, but with a strong memory of the days when his oldest sister would bring him over to her house and he would play, rolling a truck along the floor, and his oldest sister would come into the parlor, all dolled up, as they used to say in those days, carrying a book.

"You must learn to read, Emilio. Now come for your lesson."

And he would sit on her lap, everything about her full and soft, the silk of her dresses touching him, and, if the truth be told, a slight excitement—though he confused it then with love for his sister—coming over him. Sometimes Gloria, his beloved companion, would join them, or Carmen or Violeta. Sometimes all the younger sisters would be gathered in that room where Margarita's literary society met, the windows happy with light and the crystal objects in the room gleaming. But sometimes they were alone and the smell of her perfume and the sweet touch of her hand brushing his hair away from his eyes as he would lean forward to see the words better would make him feel like wrapping his arms around her and giving her a kiss—as he often did.

"Oh, but you're affectionate," she would say.

(Scent of violet perfume.)

He was not bookish, reading bored him, but for many afternoons he endured the ritual just so he could be near Margarita, always so tender with him, and sometimes staring so deep into his eyes that he would feel she was trying to enter inside. He would blink.

They would be alone, sitting together. His sister Margarita, with her grand wardrobe (and sadness, even then he could sense it), making him lunches of warmed chicken with mayonnaise and salt and pepper on rye bread and chocolate cookies and Coca-Cola, and the two of them afterward sitting, he on her lap, always on her lap, with a warmth rising up through her skirt, much peace and the monotony of the words, a happy time, until, unexpectedly, Lester, her husband, would come home, nervous and agitated from having spent the morning in the department store without having seen a single customer. He'd announce, "I'm here, honey," and, "Where's lunch?" and, in a shirt and bow tie, sit at the parlor table, munching on a chicken leg and pouring himself some liquid refreshment from a decanter. Afterward marching across the room with his suspenders down, he'd pat Emilio's head and say, "Now, we're off for a nap. You stay here and play. And if you're good, there's two-bits for you."

On one of those days (perhaps several), he had gone upstairs and, crawling along the rug, had come to their bedroom and peered in through the slightly ajar door. What he saw was a dresser and mirror of an ornate design, a tassel-fringed electric lamp, and a bed, a man (Lester) kneeling on a rug before that bed, his head bent down and apparently concentrating on kissing or licking the outspread, brunette center of an unidentifiable being, whose legs fell over his shoulders, and he heard cries, "Ay, ay, ay," and noticed, like a detective, that the subject of these attentions was wearing a pair of red leather high-heeled shoes with tassels, and through the brilliance of deduction, and because the woman raised her head to declare, "You're biting too hard," he saw it was his oldest sister, Margarita.

Of all the details, it had been the black thickness of her pubic hair that he remembered. In the brothel where his father had taken him, the prostitute, in garters and stockings that rose to her hips and with a brassiere that could barely contain her dimpled breasts, seemed most exciting to him. She had pulled her panties up high so that an uninitiated young man would see the fabric kissing the whorls of her labia. He stared and she tugged tighter. Strands of her black pubic hair radiated such promise that he wanted to mount her. She had reached out to suckle him, rolling her tongue about her lips, but he felt terrified. Laughing, she laid back on the bed and opened her legs wider: between her thighs and stretching across her feminine opening was written WOMAN, and he did not know whether he should stand back or leap. He stood back. She waited and then took hold of him, putting him into her mouth, and after a long time she declared, "I give up." But he suddenly felt empowered and, not really knowing what to do, began kissing her as she guided him into her plush center. He blinked, thinking of his sister, guilt paralyzing him. Fortunately, Mother Nature prevailed.

*

In time, a new kind of brazenness and energy overtook him. He would run charging across the fields in bursts, hopping over stones and going on for long distances until he'd exhausted himself. One afternoon he ran for nearly an hour and a half, making his way to one of the farthest hills, where it occurred to him that he wanted to keep running forever—imagining, in the distance whose silence would be cracked open by the occasional train whistle or a crop-duster crossing the sky, that there would be many other houses with brunette ladies awaiting him. On one of those days, with two dollars in his pocket, he ran back to the countryside brothel and spent his money there, his initial reservations and his boyish sense of propriety and deep respect for women giving way to a languorous appreciation of the female body, and unlike the other men who frequented the place, men who acted as though the whole business were "dirty" and the women employed there were "dirty" as well, this lad went about the act of love with great courtesy and diligence, as if he were studying some new craft. For several years, he'd go there every month or so, and during that time lost the last traces of his boyhood habits. He suddenly began to see the limits of childhood and to lose interest in being the "little brother."

The sisters noticed this—his daily routines had started to change. It seemed that he was rarely in the house and showed much less patience when he would walk out the door and Gloria, always following him, would ask where he was going. She still loved to spend her time with him, while he simply wanted to be alone. But thinking himself cruel, he lacked the heart to dismiss her on those afternoons when he would go to town with the hope of running into certain girls, mostly high-society debutantes, the daughters of bankers and factory owners, who kept summer houses in the beautiful hills outside Cobbleton. They would walk to town together, Gloria frankly daydreaming that they would always be together and that one day they would pursue the most glorious adventures—traveling to the big cities and even to Europe, as some of their sisters already had, God willing.

She thought him "experienced." Why, he had already journeyed as a boy to Cuba, a place as distant and mysterious as China (during the two loneliest months of her childhood), and though he remembered little about it, his journey gave him, in her mind, some credence as an adventurer; and because he was so strong, as she was not, she fancied that one day they would make their own journey together, her brother protecting her. In her daydreams, she and Emilio would pack their bags, and in the way that her father, Nelson, and his sister, Kate, had once traveled to America, they would set sail to many wonderful places where cities and people were so beautiful that she would forget her bodily woes and live a life of bliss. It was a daydream, for the world in those days was changing rapidly. Events in Europe, which they followed with rapt interest (listening to the news on

the radio and watching the newsreels in the movie house),
seemed, in the late 1930s, to be heading toward war, and yet the
world in which she imagined themselves traveling existed outside
all that, an endless array of perfectly painted vistas like the backdrops in movies or on the picture postcards that they'd receive
from the musical sisters when they were in Europe. They would
move through the future, like young couples making their journey through life in the wishful ads for places like the Alexander
Hamilton Institute, which offered a course in business management—a man and a woman walking along the road of life,
crooked and jagging, but heading toward a paradise of rolling
hills and sunlight.

She thought about this often, especially during the days
when Emilio seemed to be pulling away. "A stage he's going
through," she heard Veronica saying one day, and she wanted
to believe that. She had her own life—work in the movie house
and dating from time to time—but in the end she simply preferred the company of her brother, hating it when he would
disappear and she would find herself waiting and so distracted
that her own mother had said to her, "Let him do as he pleases,"
and in Spanish, *"No te mortifiques."* Still, on many a lonely
afternoon in the household with her sisters, Gloria would pine
away for him, her body tensing, her symptoms—when she had
them—worsening, as she thought that, were she to become
gravely ill, her brother would rush to her side, never to leave her.

She'd pass through great torments, resting in her bed and
sighing, her head filled with speculations about his changed demeanor. It would come to her as a relief to hear that he had
spent the afternoon in the photography shop or had gone out
with his father on some job. But all else—that he was roving
about without her, youthful, vibrant, and handsome—troubled
her, and the plans that she'd fantasized with in regard to her
brother would unravel. What if he met someone who caught his
fancy, so that, later on, this unknown person became the beneficiary of his company, "stealing" him away and going on all
those journeys which she had planned, leaving her alone in the
house with her mother or settled into a mundane kind of mat-

rimony with some nice, normal fellow, who, for whatever reason, had found her charming and perhaps pretty. She would shiver, wondering, Why is he running away from me? She'd even feel concerned if he went to Margarita's house to perform some chores for her, aware of Margarita's seductiveness with Emilio. (And it was so. Gloria had accompanied Emilio to her older sister's house, the house by that time sad and loveless, for many years had passed since the days of her happiness. And her sister, well into her thirties and childless, would appear in the parlor, as it happened, just closing the buttons of her blouse or hitching up her skirt, so that something of her very female body could be seen by anyone in the room. Her sister's marriage was so loveless that Margarita would spend many a night at their house, especially on evenings when Lester was in a bad mood or had gone away, lamenting his misfortunes. The department store was doing badly and they had moved from the grand house to a smaller, more humble dwelling. They did not get a divorce because it would be too expensive, but also because Lester was often away managing one of his family's textile factories in Philadelphia for weeks at a time. By then this bookish older sister, feeling that her life was over, that she was married to an unhappy, foppish man, and—this went back years—without children of her own, took a special interest in Emilio. He had passed many of his childhood days in her company, days when Margarita, so it seemed to Gloria, had been a little more than sisterly with the boy, as if she wished to take him away for herself—away from the household, away from her.)

And although she loved her oldest sister, just the thought that she was spending time with their brother was enough to make her unhappy. By then Margarita seemed very old to her, yet Gloria entertained tormented visions of Emilio leaning his head against her breast, as if he were an infant again, and who knew what was going through her oldest sister's mind?

It did not help matters that she had been aware of Emilio's maturity for a long time, that she'd watched him writhing in bed and once opened the door to his room to leave a chocolate bar on his pillow and found her brother with his trousers down around his ankles, holding a book—whose cover read: *A Gentle-man's Guide to Love*—in one hand, his other fist fiercely working the ardent, veiny, and shocking appendage that was his sex organ. She closed the door as quickly as she had opened it, but despite the brevity of the incident, she walked around with that image strong in her mind and could not look him in the eye for a month, his male development, which she had intuited and caught glimpses of in the days when they all shared a room, so startling her—for "it" and "he" seemed so overwhelmingly powerful—that her thoughts unraveled, brushed against temptation and fantasies, how and why she did not know. It was just that she would find herself desiring contact with that strength, which confused her, as she loved him like a sister (his favorite, she liked to think). But no matter how many times she dismissed her re-action as the normal shock of discovering something intimate about the opposite sex, even one's own brother, she could not get rid of certain thoughts that might not be considered "nor-mal," and berated herself for them.

(She did not know that Violeta had had a similar experience, encountering Emilio as he stepped out of the bathroom one after-noon, covered only with a towel that did not do much to hide his attributes, and she had blushed and laughed and gone into the kitchen, thinking, My goodness, while she washed the dishes.)

Gloria reasoned that if she could entertain such thoughts—she would slip into a daydream of joining her brother in bed so that they could "embrace" as they used to as children, and she would reach down and touch him: "Stop thinking this, Gloria!" she would tell herself—certainly her oldest sister, Margarita, who had always been seductive with Emilio, must have had similar ideas as well.

These speculations made her jittery in Emilio's absence and depressed her. If not Margarita—and certainly nothing was really going on—there would be someone else. Perhaps one of those sporty tennis-playing types in town—for when they walked along the main street of Cobbleton, she was always aware of the way the young women looked at her brother, and she had seen them making eyes at him when he in his usher's outfit would lead some of the ladies to their seats, and when they went into the ice-cream parlor there was always a little group of girls to start giggling, as if he were (and this would be funny enough) some movie star like Clark Gable or Joel McCrea, whom people always said Emilio resembled.

And it would bother her to learn that on certain weekend afternoons her father and Emilio would load the car with fishing rods and tackle and cans of worms, driving off to fish by the Susquehanna, or simply to get away, out of the house—away from her, she would think.

On days when he would tell her, "Come along," they would go happily to town together and he was nice to her—it wouldn't matter if Carmen or Marta accompanied them—it would be as if she'd never had such thoughts of abandonment, their rituals moving along in the same way, off to the ice-cream parlor and to browse through the magazines in the pharmacy, or, when she had it completely her way, to look at the wedding gowns and pretty dresses in the Silver Bells Bridal Shop, or, quite simply, to see their father and to sit, keeping him company in his studio.

Now and then, she would say to him, when no one was around, "We'll always be together, won't we, brother?" and he would tell her, "Yes," but a flush would come over his face and he would quickly change the subject, the two of them walking on quietly and at times with such formality that it would seem he was walking home a date he had not known for very long. But each night around nine-thirty, when they'd all finished listening to President Roosevelt on the radio or to one of the funny variety shows out of New York and it was time for them to go to bed, Gloria would leave the parlor just after her brother, each time planting on his cheek a kiss and saying in a singsong voice, "Nighty-night." She would linger in the hall until he'd close his door and in a revelry of self-satisfaction go to bed in the room that she shared with Violeta, sighing happily, because he had been so nice to her, as if she had fallen in love.

And Margarita Loved Emilio

MARGARITA ALSO LOVED Emilio very much, and although she may have been too casual around the boy, sometimes greeting him at the door of her house in a slip, she never entertained any sensual thoughts about him, even when he was turning out to be quite a good-looking man. She was careless in the way of a racy aunt, and perhaps a little absentminded—her life with Lester had made her forget she was quite a beautiful woman—but, if anything, she felt almost maternal toward him. She was the sister who had once allowed him to suckle her, but if he knew that, he never let on. All he knew was that, despite the torment of her marriage, Margarita could be counted on for advice.

On days when he would visit Margarita at her house—the poor woman passing the monotony of her days reading books— or when she would come to visit and they went picking flowers in the field, he would talk about his ideas for the future. The hard times did not give him much recourse, but it weighed heavily on his heart that he really did not have much interest in continuing on in his father's business. The photography trade and moviehouse work were good for the time being, but not at all what he really wanted to do.

This was before the Second World War, and although he would graduate from high school in 1942 (they'd have a grand party in the house, a reunion of just about all the sisters, marked only by the absence of Isabel, who was married and living in Cuba), by the time he was fifteen or so, in 1940, he'd fallen under the influence of the flamboyant trio, Olga, Jacqueline, and Maria, who would sometimes come back to town to perform. He had no musical talents, but he very much liked the business of the stage and the idea of making people happy by getting up in front of them. Developing certain skills over the years, he learned sleight-of-hand tricks, with which he entertained his sisters and the intermission crowds at the Jewel Box, and for a time he dabbled with more formal magic apparatus, having acquired for himself a kit from the Apex Novelty Company of Brooklyn, New York—fine hobbies, as his father would say. And spending so many hours in the movie house, where he, like his sisters, worked in many different capacities, he became enamored of certain actors, much admiring comedians like Charlie Chaplin or Laurel and Hardy, but aligning himself, because of his good looks, with the matinee idols of the day, fellows like Cary Grant and Errol Flynn. He was always happy when his father rented out the theater to a traveling troupe of players, the boy delighting in all the business that went on backstage, and he'd relish those visits to New York when he would stay with his sister Helen, who had married well, and they would go see shows on Broadway. Though he would attend these performances with the younger sisters, and they enjoyed them, too, such exposure made much more of an impression on him.

So he joined the high-school dramatic society and would spend his time studying the lines of plays. He was always carrying around a copy of *Romeo and Juliet*, and he used to visit a rich girl, a sweet little blonde, and they would lie on a blanket on the lawn of her house, reciting their lines, and when out of sight of the adults, they would sometimes kiss. He'd even appeared in a school production of *You Can't Take It with You* and, in the words of his teacher, had shown "flair."

What he had mainly liked about the experience was that it was a way of getting out of his own skin. He'd inherited some of his father's gloominess, the torpor that comes from spending too much time around a man who was sometimes "not all there," and he could feel, while moving through the house, his own mother's nervousness, which, unknown to the others, sometimes possessed him. Besides, he felt in tune with his mother's and father's creativity. Then there was his simple vanity: long accustomed to being the center of so much female attention, he had naturally assumed that his presence on a stage or in a movie (that's what he, like so many other young men and women in those days, dreamed about) would have the same effect more generally.

And yet he had his doubts—particularly when it came to the

notion of conveying such hopes to his father, and because, in
any case, he knew that in all likelihood nothing would come of
it. His main advantage—though he did not think of himself this
way—was his handsomeness. But that in itself guaranteed
nothing.

He also felt a little troubled about Gloria's reliance on him
for her happiness, and on many of those days he felt like saying,
"You must learn to get along without me."

Back then, he had no intention of leaving her, but it had
often made him feel a little queasy when she would look at him
in a certain way; what would she do in the future, whatever his
decisions about a profession, when he simply left the household?

Margarita would listen attentively to her young brother, and
although she was not really in a position to give advice and was
not especially religious in those days, she would counsel, "God
will provide for you," and hold him close. That's all she could
do, besides making him a sandwich and a glass of iced tea whenever he was hungry and in such a mood.

The End of Margarita's Marriage, 1941

FOR MARGARITA, things were resolved when her husband,
Lester Thompson, met "another woman" in Philadelphia—a
show girl, a model, a factory worker, she did not know, only that
during one of his visits home in 1941 he announced after sixteen
years of marriage that he wanted a divorce. The oddest thing was
that, once he'd gotten all of it out, he seemed to become once
again the gentleman who had so impressed her, kindly, introspective, courteous, and optimistic about the future—his future.
He pleaded that he once loved her, that the troubles of the world
had brought out his mean-spiritedness, that he'd never intended
to hurt or offend her, that, aside from wanting a child, which she
could not give him (his woman, she would later find out, was
pregnant at the time), there had been the financial pressures of
the Depression, but now things might shape up again, for his

family's factories were being refitted to prepare for the looming war, and of course, a financial arrangement could be made. She sat listening to him as he paced about the parlor of their house, perceiving the sudden sadness in his brow, and recalling the bawdier, more affectionate, and sometimes upsetting sessions of love that had marked the first years of their marriage, she felt pangs for the old sweetness—or what she had confused with a nostalgia for her own youthful hope for love. And for a moment she remembered when it was their habit to make love many times a day and how, with time, that had dwindled to nothing, so that for the last three years his occasional presence in the house seemed quite strained, and they would pass entire afternoons together without saying very much to one another, he content to sit in the parlor over some ledger books with a glass of wine, she nervously trying to read and improve herself. For many an hour, she would pass the time reading certain pages over and over again, because whenever Lester was in the household she found it impossible to concentrate, the sense that something disastrous was going to happen blurring the letters. Then she would find herself pacing the rooms, waiting for Saturday and Sunday to pass and the clock to ring at 6 a.m. on Monday, when he would get up and prepare to drive back to Philadelphia. She would watch him move down the street, the years of her life spent with him already feeling like time wasted. Life-loving and good-natured, with her own daydreams of becoming like those worldly women she would read about—the ladies embarking each year on liners for Europe—Margarita had become another kind of lady, the unfortunate, ignored "wife," the best years of her youthful beauty squandered on the hope that things would change.

But she found strength in certain memories—what was it that Miss Covington used to tell her: "A woman doesn't necessarily need a man to find happiness in this world." She had believed that and had tried to maintain her calm through all those days, spending time with her family, watching their lives change and basking in the affection she felt for her young brother, who would sometimes come to visit and find her so lonely that she felt like crying in his arms, an impulse which she always resisted.

It was hard for her to think about her sister Isabel, with whom, without knowing it, she had been very close. She felt much happiness about Isabel's discovery of love in Cuba and was consoled when one by one her sisters seemed to be slowly finding their way in the world. The love she felt for them seemed certainly more dependable than the love of courtship and romance, no matter what novels said about such things. On those days alone, she would miss Isabel (on whose lap she had sometimes cried when her spirits were low) and remember their months together in Santiago de Cuba, where for a time she had partaken of the love of her mother's family, even while her father was suffering. In those days she became aware of how different her life might have been had her mother, Mariela, never entered a certain photography shop on the corner of a market street in the year 1900, that she might have ended up like her Aunt Vivian, content with her children—but would she have had any of her own?—and the quiet security of that life. Maybe a different love would have been her destiny and perhaps she would have been passing her days on a small farm in the province of Oriente, lamenting her life there. She did not know. Or what if she had been born in Ireland? She'd read books about the place—histories going back to the days when the Danes plundered and settled the island and when Druids and fairy folk were everywhere—and she knew about the famine, and Parnell and the Insurrection of 1916, and would drift, wondering if the pain she felt on certain days, the pain of an idealizing love skewered on the thorn of reality, would have come to pass. On certain days she'd laugh, finding herself staring out the window, like her mother. She would watch the clouds moving from one end of the horizon to the other. An airplane would come sputtering along and she would think about the pilot whom she'd taken a girlish fancy to, some twenty years before, and wonder what would have happened if he had fallen in love with her. Would they have entered a life filled with light, or gone tumbling through endless space thick with charcoal-bottom clouds? She would wince at her own cynicism, her own unhappiness, and berate herself, for did not everyone in the world have troubles?

Her husband: the last time she committed the act of fellatio on his person had been on a balmy summer afternoon in 1938, and when he was ejaculating, she could feel through the stem of his sexual organ a shimmering rush of foaming, excited sperm—his seed rushing up into the world, and for what?

In appraising her marriage to the man, she would wonder if she'd really even wanted to have children—his children, in any case. The idea of having a child, she supposed, was to bring forth a little human being who would embody the virtues and mutual love of the mother and father, the baby to be nurtured and suckled and brought along in the world to perpetuate more love. Had she loved Lester in the first place? Or had she suffered from a kind of moral laziness, finding in him the means to get certain things? This would make her feel a kind of shame, but as she got older, she had less and less patience for the nonsense of self-deception. In marrying Lester, she had fancied that she would become an inheritor of the earth and that she would somehow loom as a success before her own sisters, that her mother would feel some vindication in seeing her sometimes mischievous daughter get somewhere in life—that the mysterious process of love that had started when an immigrant Irishman married a young Cuban woman, many years before, would continue through her and her offspring.

And for what? So that she could pace the floors, regretting the turn her life had taken? So that, before visiting her family, she could collect her nerves and feign happiness, as she did not want the family to think anything was wrong?

He told her, "There's someone else. I didn't want it to happen, but you know that things have been a little shaky between us, anyway. And it's for the best. We're both getting a little older and we gave it a good try; sixteen years is a long time.

"A very long time. I feel a little sick about it, but there's no other way. I just want you to know that I will miss you and your family. I'd thought of going there myself to inform them of my decision—tell your mother that I've regarded her with only the highest sentiment—but I decided it would be better to keep my distance."

Putting some papers, "documents," on the parlor table, he told her that at some future time, at her convenience, he would come back to collect his things. She could, of course, choose to remain in the house, as she pleased, or to sell their possessions, though one cedar closet, which had been in his family, he would like for himself. She watched him drive off and then sat at the table reading the documents, duly noting that "mutual incompatibility" was his reason for the divorce. She sat reading and rereading the documents and decided that she never wanted to see him again, wanted nothing of his money—though she would end up with ten thousand dollars as a settlement—and that on whatever day he returned to collect his closet she would be away.

She was not a drinker but poured herself a glass of Napoleon brandy from his decanter, and she drank it down and then had another. The day became suddenly calmer, the light through the window the way she imagined the light of the Mediterranean from postcards. She suddenly became aware that birds were chirping in the trees and that the trees were rustling in the breeze. Then she remembered the Mennonite farmer who had once declared everything around them the "work of the Lord," and her mother telling her that He had his ways.

Around four-thirty that afternoon, her brother, Emilio, came knocking at the door. She greeted him as if nothing had happened; he was there to tell her that she was invited to dinner at the house. That night, with her brother and youngest sisters present, she related the incident of the day. Her mother gasped and her father declared, "The bastard!" Afterward she went walking in the fields, Emilio by her side. The sun was just setting, the world at dusk quite beautiful, with bands of orange and red streaking across the sky. They went walking, and coming to the spot where they would sometimes sit, they both stared for some time at the sad face of the rising moon. He didn't know what to say to her, or why she had singled him out from the others, and he spoke, as he often did, about a movie he'd seen over at the Jewel Box, some love story (he figured he could've played the leading role). It was in the midst of this luminousness that she took his hand and said, "As Mama would say, '*Se acabó*'; that's

Spanish for 'It's over.' " And she squeezed his hand, holding it for a long time, before a chill in the air inspired their return to the house.

Nelson and Emilio, 1943

SOME DAYS STRUCK Nelson O'Brien for their splendid physical beauty—for a kind of buoyancy that would come over him when all seemed well with the world. He could sit back and reflect that, despite his personal flaws, things had gone well for him in life; a little arthritic pain, on occasion, and terrific headaches from his indulgences, but many days came blessedly. He had lived to the age of sixty-five, long enough to see his children grow, and could look forward to an honorable retirement, if he so liked. He'd closed down the photography shop in 1942, relegating his craft to the occasional foray into "artistic photography," and though he'd hoped his son, Emilio, might take up his work, he listened to Margarita, who one day confided in him that his son did not have an interest in the photography trade or in the movie house. That hurt him, but he would think of himself as a young man of Emilio's age when he'd had no desire to continue the operation of his father's roadside inn with its little pub and dry-goods store.

So, after much rumination, he'd decided to step aside and allow his son to do what he liked—a young man should choose his own life, he thought. Besides, he could continue to run the movie house without the boy and still make a fair living.

His son wanted to be an actor. "An actor?" Surely, he thought, such fancies would pass. Having exhibited thousands of films in the movie house in the past twenty-nine years, he knew something about the fortunes of the trade, that many an actor came one day and left the next. He'd liked Ramon Novarro in *Ben-Hur*, the biggest star of all time for a moment, and then gone. Then there had been Rudolph Valentino, taken from this world in 1926, his absence causing such grief, with pictures of long lines of mourners in all the newspapers. Who even mentioned the fellow now, except to recollect that day? Thinking about movie stars, he could name dozens who had appeared in one or two films and then vanished off the face of the earth. His personal taste had always leaned toward the "sweet ladies" of the screen—Lillian and Dorothy Gish, for example; they were reminiscent of the way he'd thought of his own daughters—wholesome and earnest. He'd seen them come and go, and though he had never been particularly interested in the appeal of movie stars, whose photographs he would sometimes distribute, he could see how a young man like his son might be attracted to such a profession, as even he had noticed how the young girls in town admired Emilio's good looks.

(And there was something else. Blunt in his fashion, open in his expressions, he would deal with the world as happily and open-mindedly and as hopefully as possible, afterward withdrawing into the privacy of his photography studio—a shed he had converted during the 1930s, which stood near the barn, where he kept his cartons of old photographs and a table where he could fiddle with the hand-coloring of photographs and with memory. On a day when he once again talked to his son about the possibility of his going into the business, he began to feel a little discouraged, and, as was his usual recourse, went into his shed, drank a few sips of whiskey, and imbibed a few mouthfuls of Dr. Arnold's Relaxation Heightener. Mainly it calmed him down, and he would forget about his misgivings—the many times he'd been unkind to his wife, Mariela; his lapses in mood, when he would move through the tremendous femininity of his household feeling disempowered, times when he would look at his son, Emilio, his flesh and blood, as he lounged in the yard and, with a great rage, would want to remind the boy that the legacy he was rejecting—the photography shop and theater—was the product of many hard years of work. And yet that day he walked out into the field with an eccentric, or drunk, look on his placid face, in one of those moods when, regarding the flowers, he would swear that they were growing because of him; and things which seemed to be in place, like the old buckboard in which he had photographed many of his daughters, came loose and moved. Then he looked toward the house and saw Kate O'Brien standing there, arms held out and imploring, as if it were 1897 again and the winter storm that would bring on her pneumonia was coming. And he thought, blinking, that death was lurking; why trouble the inhabitants of this world with one's own sorrows or needs? Another blink and he perceived a shadowy figure hiding behind a chestnut tree, and then a breeze rose and everything seemed normal again. He went back to the house and sat in the kitchen eating some stew—Carmen had set it out for him—and he thought about his son and asked himself, "Who am I to make trouble for him?")

Well, good luck and an honest demeanor were not enough to succeed, but to show his son, Emilio, that he would help him, Nelson had written a few letters to his friend Harrington's son in California. Harrington had gone out there to make pictures back in the 1920s—this tall cowboy of a man whom Nelson had met in Cuba in 1898. He had died, but his son had taken over his modest studio, Starr Pictures. To please Emilio, he sent off a few letters of inquiry, and he was delighted when Harrington's son responded with a most laudatory letter, saying, in part: "My father used to speak of you with the greatest respect. If there is anything that we can do at Starr in the future, by all means, let me know."

He tucked the letter into a jacket pocket and found his son in the ice-cream parlor with Gloria. Sitting down beside Emilio, he said that he wanted to "reveal a confidence," and they went outside. Standing across from the hotel, Nelson, his hand shaking, told Emilio about the letter.

"Now, isn't that good news?"

"It is, Father"—Emilio answering him in his "best" way, in imitation of his father's Irish intonations (he was lost when it came to speaking to his Cuban mother).

"But there's something I have to tell you."

"Yes, son?"

"I've signed up."

"Signed up?"

"For the army. I went over to Quarryville one day. I think
they'll take me."

"You couldn't wait for the draft?"

"No, Poppy"—his mother's term for her father. "I wanted
something different."

*

The sisters were not happy with his decision—death notices
of young men were everywhere in the newspaper, memorials
announced on the radio. But Emilio Montez O'Brien wanted to
have his way, so many days spent in daydreaming about the
challenges of life and the rituals of being a man. He was barrel-
chested and tall, sometimes taking work as a carpenter's assistant
for the money, or working on a construction crew in town,
hoisting beams and carrying sledgehammers and bricks in wheel-
barrows, and feeling hearty with the rest of the fellows, and sitting
around with them, hearing about how the war was ending the
Depression, bawdy jokes being told, and corny ones, too ("Say,
I got one for you, son. 'Whaddayou call a camel without a hump?
Humpfree"), and smoking cigarettes with them and giving the
up-and-down when a pretty woman came walking down the
street, some fellow always saying, "Boys, that's what we're fighting for," the fellows with whom he worked lost in speculation as
to whether they would make the grade with the draft board, for
they wanted to get the Japs and the Nazis; just about any branch
of the service was fine as long as they didn't turn up like one of
those poor sailors in Tiger Bay, eaten up by sharks or tortured
by the cruel Japanese ("Heard this story about this fellow, an
Aussie—that's what they call the Australians. They plugged his
bottom up with tar and sewed shut his peter; they sewed up his
nose and his mouth and left just a small opening so they could
pour rice and water down his throat. They did that until he burst
open, I wouldn't want that"). Or end up on a B-24, them Luft-
waffe boys shooting them down left and right like fish in a barrel.
And there was always one older fellow who'd remember the First
World War and say, "At least they're not using mustard gas
anymore. You know, that stuff gets into your lungs and makes

the veins inside expand and burst"—and many more descriptions
of terrible ways to die. Yet the prospect of glory seemed beautiful
and ennobling, even if you did die, carried home like the Spartan
on his shield in the history books.

He'd listen, feeling, despite his occasional doubts, that it
would be appropriate to do his bit for the war; and wanting very
much to be a man and get the hell away from the female influence, for as much as he loved his sisters, loved the tenderness of
their hands and how it was nice always to have someone pretty
to look at and someone to take care of the trivial chores of the
day, he had felt, over the years, softened and pampered by all
this. It would make him a little annoyed to see the picture his
father had taken of him a few months after his birth, when the
sisters had dressed him up in the most lacy and sweet-looking
clothes, his baby face so bright-featured that he resembled a little
girl instead of a male. He'd sometimes swear that his bones and
limbs and organs were somehow softer—and thanked God for
the healthy recourse of the bordello, where he could prove himself, the ladies always impressed. But there were many days when
he'd have the strangest dreams: that he possessed insides made
up of soft flower petals and like a young prince found himself
roaming through the rooms of a house filled only with female
things, dresses and ribbon-brimmed hats, slips and step-ins,
brassieres and stockings rising up and wrapping themselves
around him, the female influence in which he had flourished as
a child a source now of terrible self-doubts.

Not that he thought that he would go fairy like a certain Mr.
Belvedere, who, unmarried and delicate, ran the music shop in
town, the very shop where in earlier years his musical sisters had
bought their instruments, returning them for repair or adjustment
from time to time, the boy sometimes accompanying Olga or
Jacqueline, when she would buy a new set of violin strings. Mr.
Belvedere, with his snuff box and high forehead and wax-tipped
mustache, and his tendency somehow to have the air of a butterfly, was ever so enchanted by the presence of his sisters when
they looked particularly pretty on a given day, but was always a
bit more overwhelmed when Emilio would enter the shop with

them, the man clapping and clasping his hands at the sight of him, declaring, "My, what a beautiful child you're turning out to be." This gentleman was well liked by the sisters, and, in fact, aside from failing to exhibit a thorough masculinity in his every movement, there was very little about him that was different from other men, for he lived a quiet life alone in an apartment above the shop. Yet this did nothing to stop rumors that whenever he left town it was to have a lover's rendezvous with a young college boy of similar inclination. Emilio would wonder if Mr. Belvedere, too, had been raised with a powerful female influence—not the kind that makes a man grow dizzy at the prospect of love or makes a man feel crude and hopelessly ungenteel by comparison, but the kind of influence that would produce an inclination for untoward behavior.

He did not think about this often, except on days when he'd had those dreams and he found his sisters too doting or when his mother would tell him to wear a muffler even though it was not particularly cold. Wanting to prove himself then, he would charge across a field and on certain days, to test his physical strength, he would attempt to lift the front end of the Model T (he could never do it), regularly impressing his father with the ease with which he could carry his black trunk of photography equipment and his willingness to work for local farmers, mending fences and helping with the harvest.

Yet, while doing such things, he never felt particularly close to the brotherhood of man, the vague feeling coming over him that he was almost ambassadorial in their midst—a feeling that, quite frankly, he did not have when he was around women. In fact, he preferred their company, though he felt he would do best to keep his distance. Sadly, for on many a day when he had his doubts about life and something of his father's melancholy came over him, he would feel like resting his head on a tender female lap. Of course, he avoided doing so, being a man. Better to get out of himself, to become someone else—that's what, years later, he would say attracted him to the idea of becoming an actor (*Movie Life* magazine, August 1954).

For all his lack of experience, his few dalliances on the stage in long-forgotten high-school productions had put that idea firmly in his mind, and yet, for the time being, he, with his own self-doubts, had wanted to be toughened up by experience. He did not much look forward to the drudgery of barracks life and training, not to mention the very real possibility of getting killed, but he thought joining the army was necessary—even if he would have been called up in any case.

A Love Affair, 1943

SOMETHING ELSE, a love affair with a young woman, had helped him along. A traveling theater troupe had come to Cobbleton in 1943, mounting a production of William Saroyan's *Time of Your Life* for a two-weekend run in the Jewel Box Movie House, and Emilio, working backstage, had made the acquaintance of a young brunette actress named Spring Mayweather, a dark Irish beauty not much older than himself, a stand-in, who worked alongside him as a stagehand, in a shirt with rolled-up sleeves and ordinary blue jeans.

She was five eight or so and, like many actresses, a bit of a chatterbox. She loved to talk while they worked and had such a sweet way about her that her voice fell on his ear like a kind of music. She talked about the business, having danced in USO shows—he knew about that kind of work, for his sisters Olga, Jacqueline, and Maria were always performing for the boys in New York—and how she had gotten into show business. "Stagestruck, I guess," she said, her history amounting to a little summer stock and a few bit parts in a WPA theater in Albany. She was about twenty and had come from a small town in Upstate New York. Stricken with actorly ambitions, she hoped one day to make something of herself. Emilio, loving women, listened to her with great attentiveness and compassion. Her hopefulness was beautiful and he found himself nodding "Yes, you will do it," yet sensing that she would never get what she wanted in this life, fading instead into the oblivious periphery of the theater world.

One night he invited her to dinner in the Main Street Hotel, spent $7.32 on that meal, and amused her with a few card tricks (he always carried a deck of Bees in his shirt pocket), saying little about himself ("Yes, I have a large family. I've got fourteen sisters, three cats, and three dogs, though right now there're only a few of them at home"). Feeling most complimentary and happy after a few bottles of beer, she told him that he "looked like a movie star," and he answered, with some humility, "Well, maybe so, thank you. The girls look at me all the time and I don't mind it, but when it comes to doing something like what you're doing, I don't know if I'd have what it takes." And although he knew about the general demeanor of women from his sisters, and something about intimacy from the countryside brothel with its coal heater and smoldering wallpaper smells, he felt ill at ease, being one of those men who feel nervous until they find their release in the act of love.

After dinner, they'd gone for a walk, Emilio taking her by the hand to a tranquil spot in the countryside, explaining a little bit about his family—that he had an Irish father and a Cuban mother ("Cuba, I think I once heard of that place," she said) and that, although he could pretty much stay in that town for the rest of his days if he so liked, carrying on the family businesses, he didn't much like having things so easily set out for himself. He became a little sad, thinking about his father, who'd never as much as laid a finger on him all his life, and who would sometimes look at him as if he, and not his sisters, were the future of the family. That night, he stood in one spot, near a chestnut tree by a hill where in the winters he and his sisters sometimes went sledding, and she kissed him out of pity and loneliness, surprising him with the heat and strength of her tongue, that first kiss returned many times over, and Emilio, ever polite and respectful, sighing as her hand groped in his trousers and she said, "Oh, darling, this is perfect, isn't it?"

And because it was late May in 1943 and few lights were to be seen at that time of night because of blackout shades (most people were in bed for the night anyway), the sky was very clear and all across the horizon came streaks of light, falling stars.

They sat down on soft, dewy grass that left their clothing wet, holding hands and peaceful as if they were resting on the cots of a slightly rocking ship—the sensation of the world's movement beneath them—and soon enough they'd started to kiss again and Emilio began to feel glorious, and she, liking him very much, opened her plaid skirt and the blouse she'd bought at Macy's in New York, worn especially for the occasion ("I wanted to look pretty for you"), and lifted off her brassiere and suckled him on her breast (how he liked that, the soft flesh against his cheek, her nipple growing rigid and dense in his mouth), and told him in a voice that seemed to betray her many fears about the uncertainties of the future, "Take care of me now."

Her youthfulness, his strength, her softness, his ardor, her naughtiness, her compliance, his reckless thousand kisses, his large "bone," the scent of her hair, her quivering and sweet femininity, saliva, kisses, the churning of hips and cries.

They were inseparable for the next three days, his father vaguely aware of the young lady's presence, Emilio reluctant to hang around to help, walking about in a delirium of love, his every thought on Spring: not his sisters, his actorly ambitions, or Errol Flynn, or Cuba or Ireland or anything else. She was good to him; whenever they could get away, they'd meet and go off to their tranquil spot and she was tender and affectionate. But at the theater she begged Emilio to show discretion, not to stare at her with such obvious intent and to pretend that they weren't up to anything. Her fellow actors seemed to know what was going on—he had seen the players' sideways, winking glances and slowly began to deduce that the ardor of Spring was a pattern. He didn't care, but on their last afternoon, with Emilio swearing that he had fallen in love with her and on the verge of declaring his intentions, she said: "Well, I guess this is our last time together."

"Last?"

"Well, we're off to a few more towns this month, and then we go to Ohio, and from there we just keep on going."

"Will you come back?"

"I don't know. I'll write you. Maybe we can figure something out."

His handsome features drooping in consternation, his expression sad: "But I thought we had something going."

"My goodness, don't you know I can't get tied down. In any case, you're too young to get all tangled."

And when he was silent, she added, "For crying out loud, men do this kind of thing all the time to women, especially these days. Now, can't we just enjoy ourselves?"

They made love for a last time on a hot Sunday evening, and in the days that followed, his spirits were so low that he loathed himself—and this would get him in trouble over the years—for a tendency to feel easy attractions and to fall in love too quickly.

Another Reunion

AND THERE HAD BEEN the day in June 1943, before Emilio was to report for service—boarding a troop transport in Philadelphia and heading out to Fort Myer—when another reunion took place in the house, with those sisters who had been away converging on Cobbleton. Olga, Jacqueline, and Maria had been living in New York, working now and then for War Bonds and USO shows, entertaining the soldiers with a musical review that revolved around the compositions of Gershwin, Berlin, and Harold Arlen, though sometimes they would also perform a song like "La Vie en Rose" and on occasion, when they knew that in the audience there were some Cuban and Puerto Rican boys from New York, they would perform songs like "Perfidia." Sarah in Philadelphia and Helen in New York had gone to work as nurse's aides, and Margarita, who had moved from the house in which she had lived with Lester to become a boarder in a house in the factory town of Warrenville, near Philadelphia, with her sister Veronica. They had gone to work together in a parachute

factory, her evenings taken up with night-school courses in Philadelphia, as in those days, divorced and past forty, she had begun
to think about becoming a schoolteacher. They all came, and
Irene, too, turned up with her butcher husband and her three
children, arriving with a carton of steaks, which did not sit well
with Nelson, who always carefully observed the war rationing.
(He also maintained, in the spirit of the cause, a modest Victory
garden—growing potatoes, corn, lettuce, onions, and tomatoes
—and made it a practice to allow servicemen and their dates into
the Jewel Box for free.)

All the sisters except Isabel were present that afternoon,
Marta and Carmen having baked a chocolate cake; their mother
and father opening the house to old friends. García the butler,
regal and old, and ever kind to Mariela, visited with his wife and
sons (his oldest boy married to Sarah), consoling Mariela (they
went walking, as they used to, in the field, Mariela as always
confiding her concern for her son). The family ate a good meal
and then gathered in the yard for a photograph, Nelson behind
a portrait camera, with pneumatic bulb in hand, preparing to
take a picture.

That day Emilio stood uncomfortably between his mother
and his oldest sister, who, holding on to Emilio's arm, kept leaning over to whisper, "I'm so proud of you," while his mother, on
the other side, clutched his arm tight, saying in Spanish, "I'm
going to be praying for you every night." Gloria stood next to
Margarita in something of a state of shock, for when she had
first heard about her brother's enlistment, she withered, a slew
of new and mysterious symptoms overwhelming her. The poor
young woman feared more than anyone for her brother's safety,
withdrawing into a shell and feeling as if she were now locked
up, as if her brother's emergence into the world had confined
her to a small and narrow closet. Posing for the shot, she was
nervous, and kept hoping he would turn around and say, "Come
here, sister," but he didn't.

Italy

HE HAD BEEN ATTACHED to the 36th Infantry Division of the
Fifth Army and was among that contingent of unseasoned re-
cruits who, under heavy fire, landed on September 9, 1943, on
the beaches of southern Italy, the coastal stretch between Amalfi
and Paestum. The Salerno beachhead invasion, its goal to secure
the mountain road north from Salerno to Naples, left many
Americans dead and wounded, the casualties mounting to five
thousand in the following weeks. He knew this because he had
been assigned as an orderly to a Major Strong, an intelligence
officer whose job it was, in part, to collect such data. (With the
ground shaking under him, bursts of red and yellow light in the
night sky—not falling stars, but the shells from Panzer tanks—
and the cries of mutilated, wounded men in the distance, he
would roll on the ground, his hands cupped over his ears.) His
job was to receive casualty reports by radio, listing the men by
name, rank, serial number, and battalion, and sometimes when
he'd be sitting about despondently and a detail was going about,
collecting the dead, someone would call out to him: "Can you
give us a hand?"

And he would, day after day.

By the time the Fifth Army entered Naples, in early October,
the young soldier had so many memories of corpses—American,
British, German—that every night for several months he experienced a disquieting dream in which, as if watching a film, he
saw himself running through a muddy field toward the house in
which he had lived with his sisters, an artillery shell exploding
in his head.

With Major Strong in Naples

FOR MANY OF THE SOLDIERS of the Fifth Army, the Italian campaign was a slow and hellish succession of battles north toward Rome and beyond, for the clever General Kesselring, who commanded the Reich's forces in Italy, found the Allied strategy predictable, its generals conservative, and though often outmanned and outgunned, he had maintained a fierce defense, Allied casualties outnumbering the Germans' three to one.

Emilio would remain with Strong and his company in Naples for seven months, his work to chauffeur his commanding officer to and from the overcrowded *pensione* in which they were staying (officers and soldiers dozing in the hallways), to intelligence headquarters (an ambience of strategy boards, cubicles, radios, orderlies running about, clipboards in hand). The city was in chaos, disorganization rife; the streets thick with the hungry, sanitation ruinous and typhoid prevalent, a black market thriving, and prostitutes from all over southern Italy offering themselves everywhere. Off-duty, Emilio Montez O'Brien would wander pensively in the streets, losing himself in alleys and pathways, exploring the antique chapels with their statues of the Virgin, the stones cracking and the blossoms wilted, always good-naturedly distributing candy to the hordes of children who would follow him around begging for money or whatever he might have (much in the same way that his father, Nelson O'Brien, finding himself in the American-occupied city of Santiago in Cuba in 1898, had been followed by packs of hungry children), feeling quite bad when he had to use force to discourage the boys from rifling through his pockets (and ever careful not to get too drunk on Neapolitan wine in those saloon brothels like many a soldier who, wandering drunk out into the street at three in the morning, would fall asleep in the gutter and wake the next day to find himself stripped of every cent, every document, every stitch of clothing).

Years later the names of streets would settle vaguely on his memory—he was not one to keep a diary or any other such written record—and the words Via Toledo or Piazza Olivella would descend on him out of the blue. Putting from his mind the daily arrival of bodies stacked in linen bags on lorries, he would remember instead the impression that he was in a purgatorial city of many languages and accents—walking along and hearing, for example, all kinds of English, as spoken in the Southern drawl of soldiers out of Mississippi, or in the dialect of Britishers from Manchester, who, to his ear, spoke English as if their mouths were filled with bread. Then, in the cafés, he would hear French spoken by contingents of troops from the French colonies, from Madagascar to Algiers, their language falling as strangely on his ears as his mother's Spanish, and he would wonder what his sister Maria (or Jacqueline or Olga), who had spent time in Paris before the war and who had developed something of a European worldliness about her and an impressive ability for languages, might have thought. (Once, while visiting his sisters in their West End Avenue apartment in New York, he overheard Maria on the telephone to Paris, speaking an idiomatic French, sprinkled, he had thought, with endearments, and so fluently that he felt like an awkward small-town boy; all he knew of French was *"Mon cher,"* *"Bonjour,"* and *"Magnifique!"* which he'd heard her saying as a matter of course.)

But there was also Italian—all kinds of dialects spoken in that city, Calabrese, Sicilian, Neapolitan, Roman, Tuscan, Milanese, accents all awhirl to his ears and sounding vaguely like Spanish.

He was in a bar, too, when he overheard some GIs speaking Spanish. It had intrigued him enough so that he walked over, bought them drinks, and introduced himself, getting drunk enough with them to confide that his mother was Cuban and that he had fourteen sisters. One of the GIs looked him over and declared, "Yeah, well, holy shit, you don't look it!"

And feeling accused of being a liar, he produced from his wallet a picture of his mother sitting on the porch of the house in Cobbleton (a shot that he himself had taken), dark-haired, dark-eyed Mariela with her Andalusian face and deep pride.

("Very nice," one of the soldiers had said.) He'd surprised himself by going into an explanation of how the family bloodlines had converged or split among his many sisters, citing that, for example, his second-oldest sister was blond and quite Irish in her looks but that she had settled into a marriage in Cuba and spoke a beautiful Spanish, while his sisters Marta and Carmen, who much resembled their mother, looking, in the parlance of the day, like pretty little *señoritas*—like him, they did not speak Spanish.

One of the soldiers, Raúl was his name, asked him, "How come you didn't?"

"Well, I came out of a small town in Pennsylvania and there just weren't many Cubans or Puerto Ricans around."

"But what's the matter, you never spoke to your own mother?" And: "What, were you too good?" And that had flustered him.

"I just hadn't given it much thought."

Still, they got along well enough, drinking, Emilio listening to their plans about what they were going to do when the bloody war ended. That's when one of the soldiers had said he was going to work with his father running a bodega, and the other fellow said he was going to finish high school and try to get a decent job in the construction business, the two of them slipping off into Spanish whenever they wanted to say something private. (That happened when Emilio confided that he would like to be an actor of some kind, and one of them had turned to Emilio: "Oh, yeah, what are you gonna play, Zorro?") Then the military police came into the bar, rousting the soldiers so they wouldn't get too drunk, and they made their way off down the road.

That exchange saddened him. His lack of Spanish wasn't something he'd think about very much, but in the days when he thought he might see action and the possibility that he might be killed had come to him (first at boot camp and then on the crowded deck of a transport ship), he started to feel regret that, for all the years he shared the same roof with his mother, he had never really gotten to know her, not in the same way as he'd known his sisters, or in the way he knew his father. His mother had somehow been relegated, in the dense activities of that household, to a minor role in his life. The afternoon he'd said goodbye, she took him by the hand and led him into the field, her phrases half in English and half in Spanish, confounding him: *Si tú supieras las cosas que estoy pensando ahora mismo, y que el corazón de tu mamá está lleno de lágrimas* . . . I want to tell you something, son. It's just that the words don't always come out correct. *Es que yo le pido a Dios que te proteja. Te quiero mucho, hijo.* I love you. *Y voy a rezar cada noche por tu protección, voy a pedir al Señor que te sostenga durante esta guerra.*"

And he nodded, as he always nodded, without knowing what his mother was saying to him, and remembering their last moments (indeed, all his farewells, that difficult business of saying goodbye when he did not know if he would return), when his mother had said: "*Que Dios te bendiga*," he'd felt gagged and bound by his own limitations, pulling her close and saying, "I will be thinking about you, Mama."

*

Certainly he looked more like a man, cutting a dashing figure in uniform (some soldiers would give him a hard time, calling him "pretty boy"), but he was green and would remain so. He had survived the landing at Paestum, but the war news that came over Radio Tripoli and on the BBC, reports on the fighting as the Americans and the British converged on Kesselring's Gothic Line, left him impatient with the general monotony of his days, when he would drive the major about and wait, drive to the mess and wait, drive him to the hospital and wait, all that time wondering about the luck of his circumstances. He'd gotten used to the sight of Vesuvius floating in a mist in the Bay of Naples and was most curious about Capri. He remembered a story that his oldest sister once read to him, some tale from a romance magazine about a nobleman who, while posing as a sheepherder, falls in love with an American tourist on Capri, at Tiberius' villa. Some days he sat in a piazza, church bells ringing and (on occasion) the ground rumbling from the weight of tanks as they moved along on the Via Toledo, the sun feeling nice on his face. He'd take off his sunglasses, tilting his head back, and with his eyes closed enjoy a few moments of happiness. Thinking how the house in which he had once lived seemed so far away, he would feel pangs of homesickness, and the word Pennsylvania would sound like Cuba or Ireland or Mars.

Sometimes he'd get careless and lean too far back in a chair, catching himself just before he fell, and with his eyes open again and the world coming into focus—the outline of a church, the medieval roofs around him, the archways with their shadowy recesses, suddenly so new—he'd wonder, feeling a great pride in his circumstances, what his father, Nelson O'Brien, would have made of such a place. He'd imagine the kindly, slightly addled man roaming about the square with his camera and tripod in arm, looking for an appropriately artistic shot. (Behind that, a boyhood memory, Emilio in his father's shop, looking over some very old photographs spread out before him—some of the hundreds that his father had taken during his four years in Cuba, his father telling him, "But, my God, I was so young then, and interested in everything, my boy.")

And yes, his mother walking among some women on their way to market—not in Cuba but in Naples, or Napoli, as he'd heard it called. His mother chattering away, far from Cobbleton, in Spanish, and somehow fitting in perfectly.

He'd imagine his sisters dancing in the square.

*

Among the gifts he received from home was a Spanish grammar that Margarita had sent him. In a letter, he had mentioned the encounter with the Puerto Rican soldiers and she wrote back that it might make him feel better to learn something of the language. And so, in his spare moments, he began to study the book, his goal to compose a letter in Spanish to his mother. Each day he worked on it, trying to put together certain phrases (as best as he could judge), but not being bookish or at ease, and constantly distracted, he composed a hopelessly mangled letter and could not bring himself to send it. He would write a letter to the household every month, a letter to his sister Margarita (the news within to be conveyed to Veronica), letters to Olga, Jacqueline, and Maria, and to Helen, and from time to time a letter to Gloria, that one composed very carefully, as he knew that she cried herself to sleep every night with worry about him.

*

Eventually, he left Naples and was posted near Cassino— the area pacified. His sisters were happy to hear that news.

That was in August of 1944. Earlier, on May 11, the Allies, pursuing a spring offensive, had launched their fourth attack on Cassino to the north. Even though heavy bombardments had long ago leveled the town, there were new bombardments, and the Polish Corps and the Eighth and Fifth Armies, after nearly two weeks of fighting, had taken the town and its surroundings. Even earlier, in January, the Allies, thinking that the Benedictine monastery on Monte Cassino housed the German high command, reduced it to rubble, and the Germans had killed four thousand Poles defending it.

One afternoon he found himself on the parapet of a medieval tower on a hill, gathering intelligence. It was his duty to scan, with a pair of binoculars, the hills and valleys before him in search of potential enemies, Germans who might have gone into hiding, for most had long been rousted from the great fortress of the mountain or withdrawn. Yet, if he caught anything in his sights, it was a farmer leading his cow across a field, or the local priest, head bent in meditation, or a woman and her children, buckets in hand, on their way to a well.

He was to report any activity that might be of military importance, but the days passed without incident, so much so that the summer heat and the strong scent of wisteria in the air induced in him a kind of torpor. Red poppies appeared in June. He'd remember that, and sometimes, out of boredom, he would spread pieces of bread along the tower ledges, ever happy with the descent of birds, who pecked along, getting their fill, blinked in the sunlight, and flew away. Yellow-winged butterflies rose out of the balmy fields, fluttering up beyond the umbrella pines and cypress trees to visit him in the tower, and he would wonder, What can one feed them?

Now and then he would hear gunfire—troops bored in town having set up a firing range—and from time to time the rumble of trucks making their way into the mountains. He sat there, with the apologies of his commanding officer, from six in the morning until five in the afternoon, and was happy whenever Strong, feeling compassion, used him as a driver.

Sometimes Emilio would drive Strong back down to Naples along the Via Napoli, but one day they rode up to the monastery, to view the ruins, climbing the crumbled walls from which one could see halfway across Italy. The commander, reveling in history, had been unforgiving that the Allies had bombed it—a tactical necessity at the time, it seemed. Standing on a particularly scenic spot, he handed Emilio a camera and asked, "Do me the favor?"

Antonella, His Italian Love

AND WHAT HAPPENED to Emilio in that pacified region?

As he was walking down the street of the small town where he was stationed, love hit him like a sniper's bullet. It was toward dusk, the cobblestones rolling with the elongating shadows of the houses, the town peaceful and brilliant with an orange light, in the distance dogs barking and from the barracks window some bebop swing. Heading back to the mess, a rifle slung over his shoulders, his helmet in one hand, he was sunburned and powerful-looking—though there was a kindness and generosity about him that made him famous with the children of that town. He passed the church and, hearing the clatter of utensils, looked up: there, framed in the narrow window of a medieval house, stood a beautiful and serene woman who couldn't have been more than eighteen or nineteen years old, in a simple housedress, hair falling down over her shoulders, a baby in her arms, the child reaching up and touching her face. And then she moved away from the window, returning, he supposed, to the business of their evening meal. There were voices, mainly female, and although he did not understand Italian ("*Buon giorno*" and "*Grazie*" the extent of his vocabulary), he listened for her voice, sweet and mellow, and heard her saying, "*Vengo subito*," and he found himself standing there for a long time, trying to pick out the gentle intonations of her voice among the others. Her voice was like a length of silk, slipping out the window and wrapping around his heart. He stood there for nearly an hour, listening and hoping that she would return to gaze out the window again. And as the heavy bronze bells of the church in the central piazza of the town had started to clang, he heard another voice, perhaps that of her mother or grandmother, saying, "*Antonella! Non c'e' piu risotto?*" And again: "*Antonella, hai fatto bene.*" And: "*Antonella, vieni qua col bambina.*"

In the barracks, after their evening meal, Emilio and his fellow soldiers usually passed the time playing cards and listening to radio broadcasts over the short wave. Through the static, the slow and inevitable progress of the war was reported, and some nice entertainment shows, too. Feeling pangs of loneliness—he'd not been with a woman since Naples—he surprised himself with the vagueness of his own recollections of Spring Mayweather, whose stupendous influence during the brief time he had bedded her down had now waned. Instead, he was thinking about the woman in the window, Antonella.

The fellows were laughing and talking mirthfully (and with some embarrassment) about a club in Naples, Il Capro, famous in its time for its floor shows of beautiful young women and for the way these women serviced the men. They'd all gone there. You paid a few dollars to get in, had all the wine you could drink, and, sitting at your table, which was on a raised platform, you would wait for one of the young ladies to come along: standing on a narrow walkway that passed under all the tables, the woman would slip under the tablecloth and in a kind of gleeful game "blow" one of the men. A fellow would be sitting there laughing with his chums and in the next moment feel a hand opening his trousers, a *pompino* ensuing, as his penis was taken into the woman's mouth and sucked, the idea being to keep a poker face and watch the show while this was going on, until a head flung back, face grimacing, the others laughing, betrayed the act. It amounted to an interesting kind of roulette, because, on entering the club, one never knew if one would be chosen, or, for that matter, if, one by one, each of the men sitting in a row would be serviced.

But a kind of philosophical problem arose when it became common knowledge that the army closed the club down because the beautiful and curvaceous young women with their worldly mouths and soft feminine lips were, in fact, beautiful and curvaceous young men.

"You're kidding me," said one of the boys. "I don't believe it," said another, the pleasure taken, the lascivious "maleness" of the situation, diminished.

Although Emilio listened, his thoughts were on Antonella. How could he meet her? She had a child, but did she have a husband? Many Italian men had been killed in the war. But even if he were to meet her, what did he want from her?

A funny thing: He remembered that when he was driving Major Strong through the countryside outside Naples, the major, who'd trained in engineering and architecture, liked to stop from time to time to examine the interior of churches. Emilio must have seen fifty—so many that he would find himself a little bored as Strong walked about, examining the ceiling vaultings, trying to date the brickwork. ("That wall, with the crenellated, criss-crossing pattern, was made of Roman brick, while that chapel wall is medieval.") During those trips, Emilio had become fond of a certain kind of fresco that adorned many a church—depicting the Holy Mother and the Infant Jesus. Some did not compel him at all, the workmanship ordinary, and some were too polished. But in a little church (whose name he could never recall) near Sorrento, while the major had conversed with the priest, for he spoke a serviceable Italian, Emilio found himself languorously disposed toward a fading, paint-flecked fresco in whose surface he had seen an expression of pure affection. The Virgin, in a blue gown, with a halo, and with cherubs fluttering about her head, was gazing with absolute love and compassion at the Infant, plump, healthy, and with angelic locks of hair, his pudgy hand reaching toward her lips. The woman poured all her love into the child, and her eyes revealed that she, in that moment, certainly knew that the Child in her arms would become the man on the cross.

He felt an odd empathy for the scene, thinking that women (his sisters and his mother) were delegated to the comforting of men before the storm that would be their lives. He sat there, adrift in his despair and wishing that, for all his other longings, he could pass into the corridors of perpetual love.

Antonella's House

HE GOT INTO THE HABIT of stopping before Antonella's house—always looking up at that window. And when he trekked up the hill, making his way toward the tower, he'd hope to see her, but it seemed as if she never stepped outside her door. One late afternoon he was in the square, where he would often sit, pull off his boots, and wash his feet in the fountain where water poured out of a bronze lion's mouth. He was rubbing his immense toes when he saw her walking down the street. She did not look at him, did not smile, but when he called out, "Hey!" she turned, waiting. She was plumper than he imagined. Standing before her, he fumbled awkwardly for candy and cigarettes, saying, "For you."

She took a deep breath, appraising the American soldier; she looked him over with her almond eyes and smiled. *"Grazie."*

He watched her walk off and watched her coming back. And when she walked by him again, he clutched at his heart. "My name is Emilio," he called after her. "Emilio."

GIs were always falling in love in those days. One of his fellow soldiers, a Private Haines, had something going with a young widow in town; but mainly the soldiers, looking for companionship, would make forays into a nearby town where there was a bordello. Emilio, however, could not get this woman out of his mind. He kept his vigils, waiting outside her house, sometimes encountering her on the road, though few words were exchanged between them. He gave her candy and cigarettes and Superman comic books and imagined that she thought him "simple." And then, just like that, she had stopped by the fountain, saying, *"Venga,"* and although he did not know Italian, he followed her. They came to the doorway of her house, three hundred years old, and he was soon entering another world. The rooms were cool, with a crucifix on the wall in every room, reminding him of his grandmother's house in Cuba. He did not know what she was saying when she introduced him to her family—grandmother, grandfather, her mother, her father, and many little children running about—but he surmised that she had described him as a "kindly soldier."

They'd dined on pasta and cheese and the grandfather had produced a bottle of wine. And he had passed the night shifting positions in the chair of honor, and oblivious to what they were saying, nodding, nodding as he always did with his mother when she spoke Spanish. By the evening's end he, with his courteous humility, felt certain that a door had been opened, that he could court this woman.

Later, when she took him downstairs, he blushed, lowering his head, and said: "Antonella, I want to get to know you." And she smiled. "And I hope that we can do this again. I can bring you things, canned meat, chocolate, whatever you want, and"— she had straightened his cap—"I want so many things with us, so many—"

She cut him off, saying, *"Lei è molto simpatic. Grazie."*

But when he tried to kiss her, when he took her by the hand, she told him, *"Non posso."*

And then abruptly, at ten-fifteen on that evening in 1944, the door closed.

(Sometimes he would remember that event differently, Antonella detaining him by the doorway, her baby in her arms, and speaking ever so sweetly. On her face the expression of a woman who wished that she could get to know the young man. That's

when she started to cry, for her husband, though absent from
the household, was still somewhere in the world. And though
she knew that she could easily fall in love with him, it was an
impossibility. So what she did, in the way that he preferred to
remember her, was to pull him close, giving him a long and
tender kiss, and in a state of torment and agony, had told him,
"I will never forget you." And then she left him standing outside
her house.)

He walked back to the barracks and happened on the fellows
as they were leaving by jeep for a late-night excursion to a brothel
in another town, and seeing that the affable Emilio was in an
unhappy, daydreamy state, they invited him along, their jeep
making its way along the dark, unsteady dirt roads, the soldiers
drinking merrily. In the brothel, he went to bed with a woman
of ingratiating proportions and stoic manner, in whose skin and
scent he lost himself, thinking often that night about Antonella
and wondering how he could have fallen in love with her, when
really all she was was a pretty woman framed in the window of
a medieval house, holding a child. He had gotten along with her
in a small way but he could never understand her, and he convinced himself, with his penchant for self-deception, that the
woman of forty or so with the pendulous breasts and the wild
head of black hair was almost like Antonella. Years later, when
remembering that night, his mind fogged by drink, he would not
only have shared a tender kiss with Antonella but believe that
she, too, had fallen in love with him. In that invention of memory,
when he left the house she went walking with him toward the
church, and there, in its back garden, among the pear and fig
trees, she rested on the ground and he covered her with kisses.

It must have been five in the morning when they'd returned,
and because Emilio was to leave for his post on the tower at six,
he saw no point in trying to sleep. Not one to drink in those days,
he had fortified himself that night with too much cheap Chianti
and was a little unsteady as he made his way toward the tower.
A cool breeze had resuscitated him, the first birdsong greeting
him, and Venus, the morning star (which his mother had always
pointed out), up in the sky. He had looked forward to his ritual

of spreading bread crumbs along the ledges for the birds and to watching the butterflies rising over the field (it would make him feel a little like St. Francis, on some days). But, climbing the narrow stone stairway leading to the tower, he faltered on the top step and slipped back, tumbling down. He landed badly, and broke his right arm at the elbow, the bone and sinew tearing through the skin.

He came to within the hour and reported to the medics, who gave him some morphine, and he seemed to have slipped into a dream as they went about setting the bone, or trying to, for over the next several months it healed oddly, his elbow slightly distended and a deep scar where the skin had been penetrated. Soldiers who noticed this would ask him if he had "caught one" in battle, and he would most often tell the truth, that he had fallen down a stairway, but he so wanted to get out of himself that he would sometimes say he had been hit by a sniper down in Paestum during a clean-up operation.

Newsreels, 1944

NEWSREELS OF THE WAR, a Betty Grable film, a short with Leon Errol, a Bugs Bunny cartoon, and next to Margarita the smartly dressed officer whom she had met at a dance which she'd attended with some of the other girls from the factory. The night before, the night her brother dined with Antonella's family, she got into a nice dress and went to a beer hall and, in the spirit of patriotism, danced with a lot of the servicemen, who didn't seem to care if she was past forty. She felt so taken by this break from her routine that she flirted, laughed, and drank with them—and then she had met the officer, a Marine from Pittsburgh, a fellow who had seen action in the Pacific, "stuff that would make your skin crawl, but let's not talk about that, let's talk about your pretty face," he'd told her, and though she had been to bed with only one man in her life—Lester Thompson, who had made her think "To hell with them all"—she accompanied the officer to his hotel room and spent the night. He had a hard and muscular body, his skin smooth save for a star-burst scar over his right shoulder, and he was virile, suckling her breasts like a hungry baby; the rocking, the penetration, and the fact that she had not lost her ability for pleasure exhilarating her in those moments.

Gloria's Little Romance

THAT NIGHT his sister Gloria experienced the tedium of yet another evening of worry about Emilio. Even though he was safe in a beautiful part of Italy near the monastery of Monte Cassino, she lived in the fear that he would be reassigned and sent to the front or that some freak accident would take his life or hurt him badly. By then she had drifted into such a state of gloom that even her mother, Mariela, became concerned. Encouraging Gloria to have faith in God, she urged her to get on with the practical business of life. And Gloria tried, heaven help her, as she would always try. Though she was sometimes a wreck of nervous symptoms, real and imagined, she would get dressed up and go out on dates, with one boy in particular, a schoolteacher a few years older than herself, a fellow who had been too myopic for the service. She had been sitting with Carmen in the ice-cream parlor, feeling Emilio's absence deeply, and as she was sucking up a vanilla ice-cream soda through a straw, this schoolteacher came to sit beside her, apologizing for his rudeness but saying that he could not help himself. He was a genteel-looking man, thin-faced, with soft eyes and wire-rim glasses, and had sand-colored curly hair reminiscent of the movie actor Leslie Howard (who, having become an RAF pilot during the war, had been reported lost over the North Atlantic). He was about twenty-five and new to the town. Seemingly much taken by the delicate presence that was Gloria, he confessed an interest in taking her out, to an afternoon concert in Philadelphia, and though she felt that her life had become one long wait for the return of her brother, she liked his manner and (truthfully) wanted some companionship.

They dated for six months and the man adored her. Of limited means, he was always buying her gifts—"ladies' things": mirrors, compacts, mother-of-pearl-inlaid boxes ("So that you can keep the letters I send you"). Love letters, of a more cerebral, nearly Victorian bent, confessing to the ardor of his heart and the sublime and pure affection he felt toward her, that each and every day he woke up thinking about her and thanked heaven that he'd been so bold with her. She liked the attention but did not once invite him to the house, as if that would violate the sanctity of her past life there with Emilio—as if the house had somehow become Emilio's realm alone. During country rides, they would stop on a hill and look out at the valleys—beautiful days when most anyone would have felt elated, and yet, when he kissed her, her body would go limp, her mouth passive. Still, they would kiss for so long that she would begin to show some signs of interest, kissing him back. Once he had even worked his teacherly hand under the buttons of her dress and felt the softness of her breast. And although she had much enjoyed that sensation, a wall came down between her and her teacher friend—his name was Harold Downs—so that, while she wanted him to touch her some more, she felt it too inappropriate and told him, that sweet and gentle soul now perspiring and with a flush in his cheeks, "Please, I just can't."

"But one day you will, won't you?"

She smiled and buttoned her dress and suggested that they drive back, her schoolteacher suitor collecting himself and making the best of things, whistling the melody of a Mozart adagio as he steered his automobile over the hills. That's when he told her, "I just don't understand you—don't you think this life is beautiful?"

"Of course I do."

For all her reticence, he fell in love with her and proposed marriage some fifteen times: she told him no. And hurt that she would not invite him into the house even though the family knew something was going on, he showed up several nights, knocking on the door and sitting with her out on the porch, frustrated and unable to understand why she would not let him into her heart.

Finally, he'd given up. They would pass each other on the street or find themselves in the same shop and he would merely tip his hat, say "Hello," and walk away.

Sometimes she would sigh, thinking about him: perhaps she had been a little cruel, too protective of the circumstances that Emilio had left.

One night, as Gloria sat quietly reading a *Life* magazine, with articles mainly about the war and the domestic lives of family and wives at home, her mother, in her best English, said to her: "You're going to be crazy if all you can do is sit around and think about your brother. Just remember, that's who he is, your brother. Don't forget that."

His Return

THEY ALL HAD PRAYED for his safe return, and at the war's end their prayers were answered. His sisters were at the station —much palpitation of the heart and cries of happiness when Emilio, sunburned and handsome, military pins and ribbons on his breast and corporal's stripes stitched to his sleeve, stepped off the train with his duffel bag. He flew into their arms—Margarita, Gloria, Helen, Olga, Maria, Jacqueline, and the others who had come to greet him, covering his face with kisses. His mother, neither elderly nor young, wrapped her arms around him, squeezing him so tight that she'd surprised him with her strength. And his father, Nelson O'Brien, had been so elated by his arrival that he was unable to resist a few celebratory sips of drink, his face slightly flushed, but grinning with pure happiness. And Emilio? He was welcomed as a hero, his picture in the Cobbleton *Chronicle*, and he slept very late—having sat up with the family until five in the morning becoming reacquainted with them.

During the months that followed Emilio's return, his youngest sister, Gloria, tried her best to reassert her place in her brother's heart. And indeed at first, because he was so kindly and had

missed her and the family and had not forgotten the surprising
solitude he had felt in their absence (though he did have his
moments when the prospect of adventure and the allurements
of the future had excited him, little moments when aboard ship
he'd make his way along the crowded decks to stare thoughtfully
into the water, or when standing on a mountaintop in Italy he'd
looked out over the endlessness of the world, and he'd felt a
connection with all the other men who'd come to stand on the
same spot, and he found that heartening), Emilio Montez
O'Brien had made it easy for Gloria. The two had once again
become inseparable, Gloria happily accompanying her brother
through the routine of his days, on his trips to town, where he
basked in the feelings of appreciation that the townspeople
showed their returning soldiers—his money was "no good" in
the ice-cream parlor or in the hotel bar, and he was the guest of
honor, along with other veterans, at celebrations mounted by the
Catholic, Lutheran, and Mennonite churches and was invited to
parties thrown by the Farmers' Association and the Ladies' Society. She was his companion, sometimes to his annoyance, when
the Good Citizens' Club held matchmaking parties for the returning soldiers, Emilio turning up in uniform with Gloria by
his side and dancing with her until one of the young debutantes
of town would tap him on the shoulder and ask him to sign a
dance card. Sometimes Gloria would be left alone in the corner
while Emilio danced a waltz or jitterbugged with one of the local
young ladies. But he'd always come back to her, sensing her low
spirits, pinching her chin and, taking her by the hand as the
music started again, saying, "Come on, now." (She remembered
that sometimes, while being twirled around by her younger but
much larger brother, she would feel herself in the swirl of romance, an odd feeling of both desire and hopelessness coming
over her. And he would remember dancing to a slow song with
one of the more beautiful local girls, an elegant brunette who
under other circumstances would never have given him the time
of day, and he'd swear, as he pressed close to her, that through
the thick cloth of his uniform, through his shirt and his sleeveless
T-shirt and in spite of his dog tags—he still wore them around

his neck—he could feel the tips of her breasts against his chest. And at the dance's end, when he released her to her next partner, a fellow named Mackenzie whom that beautiful dame would end up marrying, he'd had the chance of romancing her, if only Gloria had not been so punctual about appearing at his side, for his partner looked her over and said, "Well, I don't want to keep you.")

The Mayor of Cobbleton had even invited Emilio to a banquet at his house, which he attended with Gloria, other veterans being toasted and fêted, and Gloria, ever nervous and wondering if he really wanted her around, sipping too much champagne and getting so sick Emilio had to help the poor girl out. There was something about feeling his arms around her, as he escorted her to the car, that made her feign an even greater illness, moaning with such terrible pain that for a few moments Emilio thought of taking her to the doctor, though an Alka-Seltzer from the local pharmacy and a brisk ride through the countryside soon fixed her up.

Even though he sometimes found Gloria's presence restricting, he decided, being a good brother, not to let on. He'd never forgotten their childhood together, and though he had both delighted in and been disappointed by two tormenting loves—with Spring and Antonella—he felt tempered by those experiences, brief as they were. He was, in that period, dedicated to the exercise of caution toward members of the opposite sex. In a way, he'd started to regard Gloria's infatuation with him—he was very much aware of it—as a kind of buffer between himself and the female world.

(For this reason, he liked to be around Margarita, who would come down on the weekends and in the late hours, after everyone else had gone to bed, sit talking with him. In her eyes there was a feminine wisdom—she was smoking too much in his absence—and as she had a practical, bedded-down air about her because of her years of marriage to Lester, and had suffered much and survived, Emilio came to think of her as strong. He felt that he could open up to her, speaking softly on the porch of his self-doubts and of his desires to do well for the family. He liked the fact that she, in her forties, divorced and childless, would speak about her own plans and seemed able to dismiss the sadness in her past life with the detachment of someone flicking a too long ash off the tip of a cigarette, which she often did. He wanted to become an actor, he'd told her on those nights, and also that he was sometimes afraid.

"Well then, you must do it. Never get yourself into a situation of entrapment, such as I had for many years. Do as you like, for time passes in any case, and you will succeed, one way or the other. You don't want to end up like me." Then he would reach over to hug her, and she would feel her hands tighten around his back, pulling him close, tobacco and perfume rising off her, and say, "Don't be worried, you'll always have me.")

*

So when Gloria tagged along and seemed too doting, he remained tolerant, and set about, at the lordly age of twenty, to decide what he would do with himself. The army would afford him a chance for an education through the GI Bill, and though during those first months back he entertained the idea of attending college (he had been seventy-seventh in his high-school class of one hundred, much to the consternation of the family, as Margarita had been number one, Isabel number twelve, Maria number eight, Olga number twenty-two, Jacqueline number seventeen, Irene number thirty, Helen number twenty-seven, Sarah number twenty, Patricia number seventeen, Veronica number eight, Marta number forty-two, Carmen number twenty, Violeta number twelve, and Gloria number thirty-three), he started to daydream again about becoming an actor and wrote to various schools in New York asking for an application. There were drama workshops of every level there, theatrical schools sponsored by the WPA, schools connected to New York theaters, schools that were part of the YMCA curriculum. He had written to them all and one day received an acceptance from the Greenwich Village Dramatic Society.

His Plans for New York

WHEN HE MADE PLANS to stay with Maria, Olga, and Jacqueline in their big apartment on West End Avenue and Eighty-eighth Street, he tried to dissuade his sister Gloria from joining him. The day he announced his intentions, she feigned a gripping illness, suffering chills, growing puff-faced (as if through an act of will), and took to her bed, and then (as this did not work, for he would sit on her bed, joking and cheering her up until her symptoms ebbed from her body) she announced her intentions to make her own way, independent of her brother, to that city.

"What will you do?" her father asked her at the dinner table one evening, and scrambling about for a plan, she reminded them that she had done very well in bookkeeping in high school and told them that, unbeknownst to the family, she had received a certificate of bookkeeping from a mail-correspondence course. She would use this skill to find a job, as she was tired of Cobbleton. Her father said, "But, child, you can come and work for me," but she remained adamant, impressing them with her resolve.

"Well then, where will you stay?" he asked her, and as if she did not know that Emilio would be going, she said, "With Maria and the twins." At the table that night, Emilio, face turning red, excused himself and went for a walk to the farthest reaches of the property and then passed half the night pacing in the yard. Later, when he came back to the house, Gloria was waiting for him on the porch. Speaking in a low voice, he said, "Gloria, don't you think that it would be better for me to go to New York alone? It's not that I don't want you around me, but this is something I've been thinking about for a long time. I mean, I have no idea what it's going to be like, sister, and, in any case, I don't even know if I'll have the time to go around with you. Besides, don't you think it might be better for you—and me—to find our own ways? It's not as if you won't see me again—heck, I'd come back to visit pretty regularly, I don't see what would be so bad about that."

He could not look her in the eyes, and when she said, "You don't want me around, do you?" her sadness and the helplessness which seemed to come over her in his company began to tear him up. My God, but how he wished he could walk away without having a moment of worry about her well-being, to go and do as he'd like, without the sense that he, her brother, would be committing a terrible wrong. Maybe it was Catholic guilt, he did not know, but he found himself softening toward her, and he began to revise his feelings. He couldn't bear the idea of leaving his poor sister behind. At the same time, he had a feeling of doom, for, though he felt love for his family, the notion of hurting Gloria raised the possibility that there would be less love in the world for him. And yet he knew that not every brother in the world assumed the care of his sisters.

What would happen, he asked himself, when he inevitably moved on?

"Well, I suppose we could get along well enough. But understand, I can't guarantee to spend a lot of time with you." And sighing, he said, "I suppose it will be okay."

"Are you sure?"

"Yes."

And with that she wrapped her arms around him in the same way she used to when they were children.

A Distant Sadness

THEIR MOTHER, Mariela Montez, had watched them that night. She had sighed, a little worried about her youngest daughter. At one time or another, she had worried about all of them, but she liked to think that God would help them find their way. That's what she'd started to feel as she got older. She was then sixty-one—and had begun to think herself much like her paternal grandmother, whom she remembered vaguely from childhood, as a woman of traditional values who had learned, during trou-

bled times, to move stoically through the world. Or perhaps Mariela was now like her own mother, Doña María, who had died
during the Second World War. (In the grief of those days, she
dreamed of her mother's ghost—an odd relief from her concerns
for her son's safety—for on the night when her mother died, a
gaunt, thin, white-haired woman had appeared in the bedroom,
not five feet from where she slept beside her snoring, tipsy, but
beloved husband, the woman unrecognizable in a simple cotton
dress, holding her arms out to her and speaking in an inaudible
whisper, eyes wide and sad, as if to ask, "Don't you recognize
me?" She had sat up, experiencing palpitations of the heart, and
had gone downstairs to sit in the parlor by a lamp, reading, with
the help of a dictionary, with her bifocals low on her nose—the
way her father used to read in Cuba—whatever magazines were
in the house, *Life* and *Time* and *Screen Life*, among others, until
her eyes grew heavy and she felt that she could sleep again. But
no sooner had she fallen asleep once more than she became
aware that the woman was entering the parlor and this time,
when she looked up, she was only a few feet away, and still she
did not recognize her, and in a kind of terror she made her way
back up the stairs, passing the rest of the night sitting up with a
light on and watching the door. The pattern repeated itself for
two more evenings—the white-haired, gaunt skeleton of a
woman making herself known by leaning so close to Mariela's
ear that she could hear the whisper: *"Soy tu madre."*

That it had been her mother was verified when, through the
tangled wartime communications, Mariela received a cable from
Isabel in Cuba conveying the news that her mother, María Montez, had passed away three days before, of cancer.

And that certain knowledge, she supposed, made it unnecessary for her mother's ghost to appear again before going off
into the peaceful kingdoms of heaven and memory. What had
shocked Mariela was her mother's condition, never alluded to in
letters from her sisters or her daughter Isabel, for her mother
had always wanted to spare her the grief. Then a week later, a
letter from Isabel had followed the cable, explaining that toward
the end her mother was unrecognizable. Her hair had turned
white, she had become skin and bones, and the color seemed to

have drained from her eyes. But she had been taken into God's arms, and God would restore her whole.

Mariela had become stoic. Even when Patricia came to the house one morning to tell them that she had been feeling a communication from Cuba, though she could not say what—as marital happiness and the presence of two children, Henry, born in 1938, and Clara, in 1940, with a third to come in 1947, and the chores of her daily life would cloud her visions for a long time—Mariela had already guessed the identity of the woman in her dream, and when that intuition was borne out, Mariela felt some kind of relief—another proof of spirits and the world awaiting them all.

She had been unable to undertake a second journey to Cuba. To console herself and her family, and to satisfy her daughterly guilt, she'd said many novenas and rosaries and offered many Masses for her mother's soul. She had felt heartbroken after her journey in 1932, and not just because her beloved father had died. During that visit, she had started to grow reaccustomed to Cuba, feeling a comfort and familiarity that, even after so many years in Cobbleton, had never come to her there. She had wanted to stay behind, wishing that she could transplant the life of her family; and on their return to Cobbleton, old pangs of longing plagued her for many months. (The family thought she was pensive over the loss of Grandfather Emilio.) Now a certain resignation seized her; at least her life in Cobbleton was bearable. She was no longer the colorful lady on the streets, timid and sometimes unreasonably angry in the shops, but a citizen like the others, with her own family, a husband of responsibility and stature, and daughters—and a war-hero son—who were known to all.

Their Mother's Concerns

KNOWING THAT some things were beyond one's control, she had watched Violeta lose her air of mischievous and curious virginity and, once she was of age, become arrogant about going out and doing exactly as she pleased, her dresses too tight, and her sweaters (in Mariela's opinion) giving her an alluring but cheap appearance. There was nothing to do, for she was over twenty-one and a woman. What could she do, beat her (as she had a few times before), or send her off to a prison for foolish young women? Or, with much pain, send her out of the house? The house which with each passing year was becoming emptier and emptier.

Mariela did find some consolation in the fact that Margarita often tried to intercede ("Whatever you do, Violeta, do not get yourself pregnant," her oldest sister said. "And don't be so trusting of men. Believe me, I know"), and one day Patricia, sensing her mother's concern, told Mariela, "Don't be worried about Violeta, as I know she'll end up just fine." But, all the same, she braced herself for the worst: the news that her daughter, who would stay out all night in the dance halls of neighboring towns, had gotten a swollen belly from some dashing officer or cheating husband, or, even worse, that she would end up like one of those unfortunates slashed up by some crazy man and left in a roadside ditch, as the newspapers reported from time to time, she carefully deciphering their contents.

(She'd first gotten into the habit of sitting down with a dictionary and a newspaper back around 1910, when Halley's comet would appear at night, brilliant in the sky, and the Cobbleton *Chronicle* featured weekly installments of scientifically speculative articles about the celestial event and its effect on human and animal behavior. Hounds barked everywhere, horses stirred in their stables, insects seemed to teem under the ground in greater numbers than before, and the nature of time was reported to have changed, some clocks inexplicably ticking more slowly. The incidence of suicide went up, too, for the electrodynamism was exerting its influence on the brain. She would look up and think about the monk Theocratus on the planet Mars and the splendid beings who were supposed to live there, look up blinking, and think about Cuba—those thickly written texts too difficult for her to decipher, so that after hours of effort she would simply give up and ask her husband, who doted on her in those days, to read the articles and explain their contents in his best Irish-brogued Spanish.)

She prayed for Violeta, finding it nearly unbearable when she would enter the parlor with a certain look of carnality in her eyes. (One day that carnality was most pronounced, for on the previous night she'd met a fellow at a dance and afterward they'd gone to a bar, and because she'd had a few too many highballs, she sat with him in his parked automobile and they kissed and "fooled around," though, contrary to her mother's worst fears, she would not go "all the way," as they used to say in that epoch. But they were so drunk that, between the kisses and his attempts to undo her dress, she began to lock her legs together, and things were on the verge of getting bad, with the man attempting to force himself on her, when she resorted to a compromise, undoing the fellow's trousers. She did not much mind the act and found it much more convenient and in a way more satisfying, as she delighted in the fact that while Rudy Vallee or Bing Crosby was crooning away out of the dashboard radio, she could make a man's penis fill up and thicken and rise bit by bit, with her mouth, until she would feel siren-like and powerful, especially if the man was larger than most of the other fellows, if he had a particularly striking and virile inguinal vein or a beautifully shaped glans—some were even pretty. Just the sight of it, engorged and livid red, would make her feel as if she were the most alluring woman in the world, and not just one of the sisters. Then she would bring the gentleman around—that part of the business a bit of a chore—until the man was satisfied and, feeling more kindly-disposed, as happened that night, drove her back through town and to the edge of the Montez O'Brien property on Abelmyer Road.)

Mariela was troubled not only by her daughter's changed air and by the worries she felt for her future (she did not know, and this would make them laugh one day, that she would marry a Protestant minister) but by the fact that her daughter's youthful and sinful zest reminded her, from time to time, that she was becoming old. She'd feel this more and more as each of her daughters reached the age when they would naturally begin to leave the house.

Even Marta and Carmen, who never seemed to mind living at home, even they began to look around for a place of greater and more exciting opportunities. Now and then they would visit their sisters in New York and seemed happy with the prospects of getting around, if not to New York, then to Philadelphia to visit with Sarah. But they'd gotten a taste of another world when in the summer of 1945 they went to visit their snooty sister Helen in Newport, Rhode Island, where she and her advertising executive husband kept a house. They'd come back after a few weeks of the good life—swimming, going out on a sailboat, followed by dinner on the veranda of the beach club—filled with gossip, tanned, and bursting with health and a hunger for adventure.

The evenings would find them looking at train schedules and fares to points west, and it became their regular habit to discuss places they would love to see. (These included Niagara Falls, Lake Michigan, Hoover Dam, and the cities of San Francisco and Los Angeles, among others.) They'd even begun to entertain the idea of taking a vacation "down Cuba way," to visit with Isabel and see something of their mother's country; and that, for a time, prompted something of a studious demeanor in them. Much to their mother's surprise, these two sisters bought a Spanish textbook, which they would read to each other in the evenings, their mother sitting with them, trying to help with their pronunciation. (Sometimes Margarita, visiting the house, would sit with them.) But neither seemed to make much progress, for their accents were deplorable, so bad that in mid-lesson their own mother would let out a sigh, and turning so many years of lifted eyebrows and "What did you say? Can't you speak English?" around, she would get impatient and dismissive, saying, "Maybe you will be better off with English, because I don't think anyone in Cuba will understand the way you speak Spanish."

That would leave them stunned, but Margarita, more encouraging, would prompt the continuation of the lessons, these two daughters with their most Cuban appearance and Cuban names studying on, and Margarita, confiding, would say (as if her mother, listening from the other room, could not hear), "You must forgive Mama. She's getting old and I don't really think she wants you to go anywhere."

Then: "And, like Poppy, she's getting moody."

("Moody": what was that? Her mother, carrying on her lips the sound of that word, "moody," which she had heard many times in her life but never bothered to learn in terms of its exact meaning, opened up a Spanish–English dictionary in the kitchen and found the phrase *de mal genio*, or "of a difficult turn of mind.")

What could they expect, she found herself thinking, after so many years of looking after them, of selfless concern for them, of sitting, tongue-tied and nervous, with their teachers in school without knowing half the time what had been said in confidence or the true drift of an expression or a tone of voice, especially during those early years, when she did not always have her husband by her side and her oldest daughters were reeling from her linguistic influence and were having their own troubles (though she was proud of them), after so many years of worrying about what would happen to them once they'd left the household, of having lost sleep over their illnesses, of having, in her own way, to counsel them about the turns of life, and of attempting to offer them some inspiration through her creativity. (Had they forgotten the painted-glass years?) Or that she, in her quiet way, had always pursued the art of poetry, filling notebooks which they would never see until after she was gone? And what about the example of her dignity? Even on those days, when she thought she was sometimes considered a fool, she would walk through town with them and elegantly smile, head and posture straight, despite her impression that someone somewhere was speaking poorly about her. Or that nearly every morning, on waking, there would be a moment when she would feel that she was young again and back in Cuba and the world seemed so new and everything seemed possible, the spell falling away and a tinge of sadness coming to her. Yet, despite those feelings, she always met her motherly responsibilities with affection and care. What of all that?

Now the house was emptying; and she'd begun to realize that, after so many years in that town, few friends remained.

Even the Puerto Rican butler García had finally retired. He had moved away from Cobbleton in the middle of the war, pension in hand and savings in the bank, and journeyed back to live in Puerto Rico, near the town of San Germán, writing her thoughtful letters about the happiness of his days, and always lamenting the distance between them. (Their mother's little secret: The day García showed up at the house to say goodbye, his wife by his side, they took a last walk in the field, as they did over the years, and she found herself shaking at the thought of his absence. The day, so sunny, suddenly clouded with her own fears of loneliness, the prospect of all future days less promising, as she asked herself, "Who will listen to my little verses?" Not even her own husband, as hard as he would try, seemed to have much of a taste or patience for her poems. She never knew if they were any good, but García always listened intently, his brows furrowing in concentration, the man nodding as if they were very good indeed. "Excellent, excellent," he would say. "A work of outstanding virtue and talent." And that had always been enough to give her a measure of self-satisfaction. Then, after so many years of friendship, this gentleman, with whom she had spent so many hours of earthly happiness, was telling her goodbye, and she had come to the verge of tears. "Don't be worried, child," he consoled her. "I'll be back every so often to visit my boy"—he was referring to his son the lawyer, who'd married Sarah, the eighth of the fourteen sisters. "And to visit you, of course." Instead, he had chosen to remain cozy among the palms in a nice house on a hill, living like a rich man, and perhaps he planned to visit, but she would never see him return, the gentle being who had been García now absent from her life.)

And Miss Covington had been gone since the day she left to visit her sister in Boston and was run down by a trolley car, her presence in the household now no more than a few plumed hats that she once left as gifts.

And Father Mancuso, the young and handsome priest to whom she could confess her sins, was now a refined and regal monsignor in a Catholic parish in a Frenchified township in Maine.

She consoled herself by thinking that, even if Carmen and

Marta and Violeta were to leave, she would at least have the companionship of her daughters Irene and Veronica. But Veronica had also fallen in love. Some six months after the war ended, the very same young and forlorn-looking young man whom Veronica had once been kind to on one of the hungriest and most lost afternoons of his life in 1939, came around looking for her. The man was more prosperous and cleaned up now, with a fresh haircut and a brown suit, driving an automobile and appearing at the door inquiring if the young woman who had once shown him so much compassion, Veronica O'Brien, still lived in that house and would she mind if he left a letter for her? The man had spent the war years working in a factory and then gotten himself into the construction business in Illinois, and he was damned if he could not at least treat the woman to a good meal. That was how their love started, though it could be argued that it had begun that afternoon six years before when she had been startled by the hard times and pain in his eyes. She had thought about him through most of the war—a stupid little memory—and though he eventually prospered and could fend well enough for himself, rarely a day passed that he, too, had not thought about the redhead who once led him into the living room of the Montez O'Brien house for a meal before sending him on his way (tucking five one-dollar bills into his hands; she could not bear the suffering of others).

When he returned another day, this man, Rudolph Williams, found Veronica in the house and they sat talking over old times. He recounted his freight-car hobo life during the Depression and they laughed, as all that suffering seemed so far in the past. That night—it was a Saturday—he took her to the best restaurant in town, at the hotel. The next day he would be driving back to Illinois, he told her; and that he was looking for a good woman and she was the kindest woman he had met in his life. Ever a gentleman, he brought her home that evening by ten o'clock, and for months afterward he would come back every three weeks or so to visit with her in Philadelphia for the weekend, just so he could thank her some more for her kindness and take her out. And things between them got to the point where he said it would be much easier if she could be nearer to him, that it would really be something if she would consider becoming his bride. Up to that time, she never thought much about marriage with anyone; she thought more about making dresses and about the countless hours she had worked beside her older sister, Margarita, in the parachute factory. But she had told her family about him.

The prospect of her marriage to a virtual stranger troubled her mother and father, so, though she wanted their approval, she simply decided to elope with him.

*

More or less accepting the lives of her children, Mariela, feeling exhausted, decided that she would not meddle—and, besides, she would tell herself that the young do not always value the wisdom of their elders. She became stoic in the sense of allowing herself to take things in with some detachment: she did not want to be hurt. She became like a piece of *pan con ojos*, an expression her mother from Cuba sometimes used—meaning "bread with eyes"—promising herself that she would observe and appreciate the blessings of her daughters, keeping her misgivings to herself. She would not, for example, mention the travail of Margarita's divorce from Lester Thompson and that she sometimes faulted her daughter for not being strong enough—if he was so bad, she should have gotten rid of him long before, so that at least she could have pursued a life with another man. (She forgot how, for many of those years, she'd refer to Mr. Thompson as a saint.)

Even as the house emptied, she believed that she could always count on her daughters' visits. Perhaps she could persuade her husband, who had become very set in his ways, that they could make some journeys of their own. She would take note of the aging, white-haired man sitting in front of the fireplace and recall that he had once been something of an adventurer.

New York, 1946

THROUGH THE TRAIN WINDOWS, the brilliance of the countryside flashing, the faces of their fellow passengers blanching
white and then darkened again by shadows. A Hamilton watch
advertisement, among others in a row above the luggage rack
across from where Gloria and her brother, headed for New York,
are sitting. Out of boredom she reads the ad, *"To Peggy—for
marrying me in the first place . . . Darling, here's your Hamilton
with all my love, Jim."* The woman, a pretty blonde, is kissing a
love letter and in her hand is the precious Hamilton that her
wonderful husband has given her in gratitude for the happiness
she has brought into his life. Gloria reads all the copy and sees
that the man is grateful for their children, for all the socks she
has darned for him, and all the meals she has cooked—happiness
exuded, a simple moment, speaking of things that Gloria believes
she will never have.

And, later, out the window, a simple scene, quick in the
meadows and quick by the crashing streams: a woman running
alongside the rushing train, a healthy, robust woman charging
through houses and fences and stone walls. The woman who can
do anything: Gloria, dreaming about herself.

*

In a Pennsylvania Central railroad-car seat, her brother,
Emilio, dozes, lanky and uncomfortable, a brown felt hat pulled
low so that it covers much of his face, the striations of light kept
out of his eyes. He has fallen asleep, the car rumble and sudden
braking, the tooting of the locomotive sometimes stirring him.
For a long time, everything is dark inside his head, then a clearing
and he sees himself as a boy, fascinated by the careful presence
of his father, Nelson O'Brien, looking out through his archaic
bellows-type camera, ready to photograph the sisters posed before
the house, the boy crawling about and feeling himself lifted up
and set down on the porch steps, a draft of heat and an inex-

plicably pleasant aroma wafting through his nostrils—a draft of pure femininity, the ladies of all ages hot in the early-summer heat, and that draft, that combination of sweat and juice and impatience welling up and transported his way by the slightest breeze.

He looks over toward the far end of the porch and sees his sister Helen, tall and elegant, in a white sleeveless dress, the ever beautiful Miss Spring Rose of 1925, shifting her posture, and as she moves to favor one hip, there slips down along her right leg, from under the umbrella of her skirt, a single drop of sweat, descending like a tongue over the curvaceousness of her legs, settling on the instep of her foot. Margarita is wearing a sun hat and sunglasses, which strikes him as exotic. She, too, shifts her weight and fans herself, feeling uncomfortable in her dress, so much heat being generated by the humidity of the day and by the sunlight and the brassiere and slip she has to wear, her fingers pulling every so often on the inner "bracing" that itches and makes her perspire—her fingers stretching the elastic band and snapping it back again. And there is Irene in a girdle, to make her thinner, scratching at her arms and waiting, waiting for her father, mumbling under a black cloth, to take the picture.

The heat of the day and the extra heat produced by his sisters. There are in this dream, or recollection, some lines from a magazine story about the Indians of the Wild West that Margarita once read to Emilio: "A fine and noble people, the Indians had lived in tepees, and in the harsh winters they would gather in their tepees and warm themselves by a central fire . . ." That's what it feels like to him, sitting on porch steps among so many women. He looks around and swears to himself that under the restlessness of their skirts a kind of fire is burning, its heat, flowing out from under the layers of their undergarments, exciting him.

In the train Emilio feels himself falling down through a cloud of skirts and lacy undergarments, his hands grabbing at the items around him as if they were petals that will hold him aloft as he drifts through the clouds of femininity, floating in his head, waiting, as he always does, for his feelings of anxiety (and excitement) to abate, squirming in an uneasy sleep, his heart palpitating, as it always does in times of uncertainty—yes, as in the moments before he first went to bed in the countryside whorehouse, and before bedding down Spring Mayweather, and during his other encounters with women during the war—until he feels his sister Gloria shaking him awake to tell him that they will soon be coming into New York.

With Their Sisters

THEY SETTLED INTO their sisters' apartment, whose walls were covered with the souvenirs of their lives: posters, flyers, and photographs. The twins, Olga and Jacqueline, shared a bedroom, while Maria had her own. They put Emilio in the maid's room and brought a bed into Maria's for Gloria.

Looking out into the sunniness of West End Avenue was their parlor, ornate with potted plants, a grand piano, a harp and music stands, and, on every table, the flowers which Maria would buy; there was a pleasantness about the room and Emilio liked to sit there in the mornings, having his coffee and taking in the perfumed air. Because they were performers and worked mainly at night, Maria, Jacqueline, and Olga tended to have their days free, though they would sometimes give music lessons to children, who would come by. They weren't famous but were professional and well liked. By the time of Emilio and Gloria's arrival, they had taken on the air of operatic divas. There was a delicacy and tenderness about the three sisters that seemed to endear them to their employers. Their faces were refined, their cheeks perhaps a little too rouged, their bodies exuberant and a bit overly plump. Olga carried a Spanish fan, her arms glistening and heavy with bracelets ("The gifts of admirers," she would say). And when Olga liked something, she would say, "Ooo la la," their trips to Paris having made an impression on her. Jacqueline, the most buxom yet demure of the twins, would sway about, her wide hips an asset. (Though she and her twin, Olga, had nearly the same

bodies except in the hips, Jacqueline, during the war, was the
one to show a "little leg" to the troops.)

Otherwise, they seemed, as far as Emilio could determine,
to spend their days going to lunch appointments, to movies, and
window-shopping. Every now and then, they were off to work
on the *Queen Elizabeth*, but mainly they seemed to be earning
a good living performing here and there in New York.

Sometimes men, Emilio observed, would come to their
apartment. Their manager, a slender, bald-headed fellow who
liked blue-serge suits, showed up on Monday nights for dinner
to discuss possible singing dates, radio slots, and special events,
such as weddings or a performance at a society cocktail party.
("Jack Benny—a doll.") Would-be suitors, men of middle age
with money, so it seemed, would turn up in tuxedos and suits,
with bouquets of flowers, to escort one of the sisters out. On their
free nights, one or the other would be off to the opera or dinner
in a fine restaurant, a car and driver down below—and Emilio
(and perhaps Gloria) would look out the window, watching them
below. For all these suitors, though, there never seemed any
movement among them to get married. They were middle-
aged—Jacqueline and Olga were thirty-eight in 1946 and Maria
forty—but they seemed to regard these men as diversions from
routine.

Mid-afternoon would find them in the parlor playing sere-
nades on their instruments; they would perform what Maria
called "the more elegant music"—pieces by Mozart and Bach
and Schumann, among others, a serenity filling the apartment.
Maria's favorite composer was a Frenchman, Gabriel Fauré,
whose piano études she found "heavenly," and she liked the fact
that he was quite a religious man. She was always playing his
vocal works on their record player, sitting quietly on the couch,
listening intently and raising her right hand in swirls as if conducting the choristers herself. Emilio would watch her—if only
for a moment, as he passed along the hall—wondering what
brought such peace of mind to her expression. Having none of
her "class" or, for that matter, her knowledge of music—she very
much liked popular composers like Cole Porter but also took

sustenance from the operas of Verdi and Mozart—he had no idea
what would make her drift off into another world, far from her
origins, far from their time. Once, when he asked her why she
liked the choral compositions of Fauré so much, she had given
him an answer that went far over his head: "Because he composes
with the religious fervor of a Fra Angelico."

He nodded, he smiled, then went into the kitchen and looked
in the refrigerator for something to drink.

Sometimes the three sisters played around with opera, *Così
Fan Tutte* being one of their favorites. Or, when having a dinner
party, they would slip into the living room and, someone asking,
"Sing for us," let loose with the lovely melody of "La Donna è
mobile." He was fascinated by their singing and sometimes felt
overwhelmed by their talent. He would sit with Maria, his favorite
of the three—for she was talkative, while the twins tended to be
more cautious, ever friendly and affectionate but never really
telling him anything about themselves. He was interested in Maria's romantic life, as it was a well-known bit of family gossip
that she had once rejected a quite famous and glamorous man,
who had courted her in Paris before the war. Whether she loved
him or not, she always dismissed his name—"And what about
Antoine Rameau?"—with a bit of laughter, saying, "He was like
all men in some ways." Yet she kept a framed photograph of
herself posed beside him in a Paris photography studio, the two
with their faces pressed together, she with a curly-helmet hairdo
and translucent, happy eyes; he, incredibly dashing, as they used
to say in those days. This photograph was kept in a gold frame
atop the piano, and always near flowers, as if they were there to
honor the portrait. Emilio, in thinking about the few years he
lived in that household, would always remember that each time
he looked at this photograph he knew that his third-oldest sister
had once been deeply in love.

Maria's Second Love:

Antoine Rameau

ONE NIGHT IN 1947, Emilio had come home from a late evening out to find that there had been a dinner party. The long oak table in the dining room was covered with the remnants of a meal, many brandy and wine glasses, crumpled napkins and dessert plates everywhere; and though his sister, Maria, was moderate in her consumption of food and drink, he found her in a rather intoxicated state, sipping brandy in a long gown, her feet up in the air over the back of the couch, wriggling her toes.

It was two in the morning, and yet Gloria was sitting up, as she did many a night, waiting for the arrival of her brother, or perhaps she was simply there to keep Maria company. But when Emilio saw Maria in such a state and asked Gloria what had happened, she told him, "This fellow, Antoine Rameau, her old beau, came here tonight and, in front of everybody, proposed marriage to Maria."

*

Maria fell asleep—suffering greatly the next day—but that night she had perhaps thought about her first meeting with the great Antoine Rameau in a cabaret in Paris in 1937. She had been thirty-one then, but didn't look her age, and the history of her life in Cobbleton had been largely obliterated by the diversity of her travels. She could speak Spanish, Italian, and French and was accustomed, as were the twins, Olga and Jacqueline, to the overtures of rich and presumptuous men. Never taking the idea of romance lightly, she was prone to sad bouts of memory about her first love, the tenor Henry Maine, and believed that she could do very well without further heartbreak. Although she never intended to make herself attractive, as a performer it was her business to convey a certain elegance and an otherworldly, angelic presence to men.

The night she met her suitor, the second great love of her life, she was wearing a chiffon gown of Parisian design, its soft material glittery with fake nonpareils, a veil of fishnet material falling over her cleavage, and a Majorcan pearl necklace. The cabaret they attended was renowned for its impromptu performances. Singers from all over Europe, and some from America, frequented the place, and it was not unusual for the emcee to invite one of the stars to sing.

Edith Piaf had been the headline performer that night, and in her formidable aftermath, the sisters, then going under the name of the Three Nightingales, were called to the stage. There, before the crowd, they sang through a program of George Gershwin tunes, to much applause, for the French loved that music. This happened on a night when Maria's earnestness and strength and sweetness as a woman coalesced with her beauty and the allurements of her form and manner, to which she never gave much thought outside of a professional context. There had been a buzz in the crowd when the singer and actor Antoine Rameau, gallant lead in many a French musical film, the Bing Crosby of France, archenemy of Maurice Chevalier and veteran of a dozen M-G-M films in America, walked in.

Dressed in a tuxedo, and in the company of a female acquaintance, he sat near the stage and watched the sisters performing, his posture never changing, his chin on his hand, his deep blue eyes blinking occasionally. She had noticed him, and as he had seemed unmoved, never applauding when the audience did, Maria thought him cold. When the sisters left the stage, the emcee called out to Nelson Eddy, who was vacationing in Paris, to sing—but Maria did not feel like watching the rest of the show, and so she and the twins retired shortly to their hotel.

On another night, however, while the sisters were performing in the cabaret room of the Ritz, much frequented by American tourists, Rameau appeared again, and although he sat through their performance with the same indifference, he afterward sent Maria a bouquet of roses with a note saying, "I must have the pleasure of meeting you." Romance did not interest her; nevertheless, she joined the great star at his table. In a French-accented

English, he assailed her with praise: "You are more of a divinity than a thousand Aphrodites. Venus would be your house servant. You are beauty pure."

Perplexed, she listened, nodding, and when she spoke French with him, he seemed charmed. But she wanted nothing from him. Instead, she had wanted to return to the comfort of her hotel room and the company of her sisters. He had told her, sensing her indifference, "Most people know me as a popular singer and movie actor, but in fact I studied opera in Milan." And right there he began to sing an aria, and the face that she found so handsome yet predatory seemed transformed, a saintly nobility coming over his features.

He asked her, "Will you dine with me?" and she said yes, and the two walked along boulevards and over bridges, the river lamplit and misty.

He seemed a perfect gentleman, but she knew his reputation. He had been married to an American movie star, to an heiress, and in his youth to a Milanese contessa. Lifting her hand and dropping it on his left shoulder, he asked, "May I kiss you?" and although she had her doubts, she allowed him to.

But that was not all. When he started to press against her —they were under a bridge by the Seine, the walls about them leaking rainwater, and couples here and there necking furiously—she said no, thinking in those moments about her first love, who drowned in Lake Constance many years before, his lips pursing and his arms gesticulating as if he were singing an aria, bubbles of air rising around him, life and all his music leaving him forever.

Soon she felt Rameau's erection against her leg. He was adamant, even then asserting, "I know what people say about me, but it's not so."

"Well, then, *s'il vous plaît*, take me back to the hotel."

They made a date: he would pick her up two nights afterward at six-thirty. He arrived at her hotel in a carriage, its hood covered with blossoms.

Off they went down the Champs-Elysées—automobiles honking, men in carriages tipping their hats, passersby on the sidewalk watching them as they went by. He owned a grand house on the Right Bank and there they dined. That night, feeling nervous, she had, for the first time in her life, gotten drunk. He was handsome. As the movie advertisements would say, his was the "face that felled Helen of Troy."

No lines, no signs of anxiety, pleasant angles, manly surfaces, a great and pleasing symmetry to his mouth.

Though he was in his forties then and without his movie makeup, he still seemed a quite fit man of thirty. She would look at him and feel as if, yes, she wanted to lean over and kiss him, and, yes, give in to his allure.

He tried to kiss her again, and she tried to turn her cheek. (But he succeeded in slipping his tongue in between her lips and, touching her breasts, he led her, in this embrace, to the couch.) Courting her, praising her, he tried one last gambit: he leaned over, saying, "I will die without you," and they awkwardly kissed again, her face blushing, hands shaking.

"Take me out of this place, please," she told him.

It went on. The sisters were in Paris for another week. She agreed, because he was so famous, to see him twice more. By their last meeting, he was bitter. She would not go to bed with him. By that time, she had fallen in love (or as close to love as she could imagine, for to reach her heart he would have to penetrate the thickest walls of comfort and habit, her passion for music, her pain, and the simple affection and loyalty she felt for Jacqueline and Olga). On their last date, sitting on a bench, he rested his head against her breast and she felt a tenderness toward him. His surliness, she decided, came from a lack of family warmth, his arrogance from insecurity. In those moments she started to think fondly about him, and because of her good heart, she thought about taking him to bed.

They went walking along the river, and as if it were a natural habit in that city of love, they found a shadowy place under a bridge and began to kiss, and then, for reasons she did not understand—the smell of his cologne, the taste of his tongue— she allowed him to lift up her dress. She gasped, for he had pulled down her undergarment and thrust himself into her, so that in a moment they were like so many of the *amoureux* they had seen wrapped and clinging to one another here and there in the night. They made love standing—an uncomfortable and nerve-racking experience—and while she felt much pleasure, having thought about what it would be like for years, she afterward felt gloomy and wished that she could walk into a church and kneel down on the floor to pray. They walked back to her hotel in silence, and by its entrance he asked her if she would stay in Paris with him.

She told him: "I'm sorry, my darling, but I can't," and turned away.

The odd thing was that he kept trying to find her, whatever his reasons, in Geneva, in Amsterdam, in London. Long-stem roses would arrive in ribbon-tied boxes bearing messages gushing with endearments, bracelets or pearl earrings tucked inside. Her heart ached for him—or for the idea of romance or from desire, she did not know—and she spent many a restless night remembering their lovemaking by the river, and sometimes she would daydream about a life as Mrs. Rameau. She would think about a photograph she had once seen of him in a magazine, playing polo, a white helmet on his head, his silk scarf aloft in the wind. He owned a villa near Nice, on the Riviera. He knew movie stars, counting Charlie Chaplin and David Niven, who had taught him how to water ski, among his friends. He knew the royalty of Europe and was a rich man, and yet she could not abandon her sisters, nor did she want to break up their happy life, as she could always be certain of their devotion. But it had not been easy and her decision would weigh on her.

She was on the deck of the *Queen Elizabeth* on the way back to the States in 1938 when she happened on an English gentleman, Noël Coward. She had been standing by the rail, watching the endless waters—depressed not so much from the experience of her love as from the fact that her little interlude with Rameau constantly tempted her to abandon Jacqueline and Olga.

Coward, in a blue blazer and linen trousers, had been on deck for a smoke—in fact, running over the lines of dialogue for a play. They already knew each other from different cruises and had spoken casually and sometimes sat down together for a dinner with the captain, a great honor for her, but he had never really talked with Maria Montez O'Brien. When he saw her by the railing, though, he walked over and, tapping a cigarette free from a gold case, looked around the horizon and said, "Splendid, yes?"

Maria nodded and Mr. Coward stood beside her and for a long time just stared out over the sea. The moon's reflection on the waves left an interesting pattern of light—almost hieroglyphic in form—messages in broken squiggles that asked her, *Do you love him, and does he love you? And what if you're making a terrible mistake?*

Wishing to break her gloom, Mr. Coward said, "My dear, there are days when life may seem dreary, but only for a bit, and romance is a fleeting thing in the end, just another sweet memory. I've been to the States on many crossings and each time I have a moment when I look over the railing and think that our lives are rather like the cresting waves, with highs and lows, that the moon illumines the night as emotion brings a glorious flame into our hearts. But what one must do, when the thrills are gone, is not to let our joys be destroyed by sentimentality. Curious, isn't it?"

His presence made a difference, his amused, capricious face looming above her, a cigarette poised in his hand. He gently touched the back of her neck and that made her lift her head up. There, against the backdrop of the rolling sea (there was nothing else, metal walls behind them), she told him about her first sweetheart, who had drowned. She said that she had been happy with her life, but that she might be forming an attachment to a "fellow, much renowned," who, against her better judgment, had won her heart. He listened intently, his deliberation, in the end, that sometimes a brief encounter with a passing flame was only an illusion, for it takes many years to find a true love.

"Scoundrels, rakes, common romancers drop down into life like fruit from a tree. Forget him and come along, ducky, and have a drink in the bar with me."

*

Before that night in 1947, she had not seen him in eight years. He had come looking for her in New York in 1939 and telephoned the apartment, begging that she see him. By that time, she had decided that he was quite simply a man who could not accept rejection, and by then much of her feeling of love or desire was a faded thing. He asked to meet her, anywhere, and finally she agreed. She did not want to see him and yet she felt curious. It was around Christmas and the sisters were going to Mass, so she decided to meet him outside St. Patrick's Cathedral at noon. For a year the letters and gifts had kept arriving, and these she would send back to his Paris address.

Snow fell that day, a steady, gentle, drifting snow—and soon enough, after hearing High Mass offered by Cardinal Spellman, which she'd attended with her sisters, she found herself standing alone on the steps of the cathedral in a fur-collared coat and a felt, fur-trimmed hat, its veil falling mysteriously over her face. As the cathedral bells announced the hour of noon and all the world that day seemed covered with white, Antoine Rameau appeared before her, dapper and elegant, his face contorted with pain.

Once again, as he had repeated a hundred times in letters, he told her he was in love, and again she said she had made up her mind. She was not cruel, and when he started to shake, she wiped a tear from his cheek, and, with that, he knelt down in the snow, asking her to love him. It was a curious thing. In those moments, she thought of a passage she once read in a guide book about the Emperor Charlemagne being forced to kneel in the snow, to beg the Pope's forgiveness—and as that scene flashed through her mind, she took him by the hand in her own doeskin-gloved hand and said, making a clicking sound with her tongue, "*Mon cher*, you mustn't do this to yourself." And when he had composed himself, she added, "I'm sorry, but I must go."

*

By the time, years later, when he visited the apartment, he was a different man. The war and his sympathies for the Vichy government in France had led to the ruin of his career; he was

in New York en route to California, where he was to audition
for a minor role in a film. This Antoine Rameau wanted to humbly pay his respects to Maria—perhaps out of loneliness and
despair. He had married and divorced again in the intervening
years. His hair had turned white and his nose took on the raspberry coloration of a drinker.

*

What happened? Shocked by his presence but never unkind,
Maria felt pity for the man, asking him to join the sisters and
their friends for dinner. He sat in a high-backed chair, putting
on a good front, much of his urbane conversation devoted to
reminiscences of his life in Europe before the war; and in the
course of the meal, quite civil, he drank several bottles of good
French wine which he had brought along, and he singlehandedly
finished off a decanter of Courvoisier. His mood changed. He
could hear or see no one else at the table and the edges of the
room were blurry. Perhaps he was merely drunk and had lost
his common sense, but he got up and, swaying as drunkards do,
raised a toast and declared that he was there to open his heart
to the true love of his life. Maria had tried to calm him, but he
went on about the cruelties of life and, declaring that "happiness
must be seized," made his way over to Maria and, kneeling on
the floor, once again proposed marriage.

Saying, "The poor man's drunk," she excused herself and
left for the refuge of her bedroom, Gloria following after her.

Their manager helped Rameau to his feet and suggested
that they leave. Down below, he gave Antoine a ten-dollar bill
and hailed him a cab, which drove down a few blocks and turned
east at Eighty-sixth Street. And so he left her life forever.

The next day, Maria was quiet and terribly hung-over. And
while this would be one of the few truly unpleasant episodes of
her life, something better forgotten, there were moments, her
sisters and brother noticed, when the happier elements of that
brief love affair came back to her. Standing by the window, she
would remember how low she had felt by the railing of a liner
crossing the Atlantic one night, and the kindly words of a gallant

Englishman who by his presence helped to make the anguish of her heart more tolerable.

"Cheers!" He toasted her that night. "Here's to all the bloody messes of love!"

Greenwich Village

IN HIS DAYS AS AN ACTOR in New York, Emilio Montez O'Brien much enjoyed the bohemian atmosphere of Greenwich Village. On one of his first mornings in the city, he went browsing along Fourth Avenue, where there were many old book and print stores, and saw the actor Vincent Price foraging through a bin of old etchings—looking for Dürers. Three days a week he would take a West Side subway down to his acting workshop, which was in a second-floor studio on Tenth Street, off Sixth Avenue, and there his overworked instructor tutored him and his fellow students in the correct and lordly enunciation of Shakespearean dialogue. These workshops lasted the whole afternoon, and on days when they weren't held, he took elocution lessons on West Seventy-ninth, concentrating on the movement of the tongue against the palate and the enunciation of vowels. ("Ooooo" for "O," "Ahhhhhh" for "A." "When you read a phrase in a script and it ends with a period, that means that you should stop . . . And remember, as it is written, there is a pause between one word and the other. If a word ends with a consonant, there should be a sharpness, a finality. You must remember that the mumbling speech that we take for granted confuses the listener in a theatrical setting. Now repeat after me, 'A, E, I, O, U.' Now again . . . No, no, open your mouth for 'O.' Have you bread in your mouth?") Riding the subway or strolling about the downtown neighborhoods with a few pages of script or a much rumpled and water-stained copy of a drama manual, he'd go to a little café, where, with beret on his head, and feeling like a Continental, he would sip a coffee or drink beer, watching life passing on the streets. There were many Ukrainians and Italians and Jews in those neighborhoods; college students, too, and a surplus of what he would call the "artistic" community—painters and actors and musicians, as well as a great number of introspective types— intellectuals who, he imagined, were college professors or philosophers or poets, their brows heavy with thought, as if trying to solve a crucial issue of life.

And there were women also. Young ladies making their way along the sidewalks sometimes gave him a sideways glance, appreciative of his blue eyes, which could be picked out, distinctive, from across the street. He would watch them walking by in their plaid skirts and ruffled blouses, and in the simply designed dresses, shaped like bells, that were a holdover from the war, and he would see in each something beautiful.

On some afternoons, he would fall again under the spell of the feminine influence and swear that the world and everything in it emanated from a female source. The paper flowers, rounded and curvaceous, that the café owner put out on his tables, the undulating and fancy script of a menu, saying "Cappuccino, 20 cents," the circular motion of a rather devastated, street-worn pigeon, following another over the curb. He would step into the rest room and notice the ovularity of the toilet's shape, of the mirror, the sanitary tissue, the octagonal tiles, notice every hint of rounded motion, even in an unsavory facility, all suggesting the female presence in the world.

What was ugly in life, he thought male. Even the most winsome-looking men—like himself—he considered crude in appearance (though he was always happy when a woman stared at him). He'd once watched a man with his girlfriend come into a café and take a corner table, in the darkness the man fondling her under her sweater. He heard their laughter, and looking over from time to time, noticed later, as they walked out, that the woman, with her Lana Turner breasts, was beautiful, and he thought that the man, with his fledgling erection evident inside his trousers, seemed grotesque by comparison.

Well, God bless them, he thought.

He'd get lost in the labyrinthine streets, on his way to a dramatic reading put on by some actor friends, and waiting for a traffic light to change, he'd find himself appraising the architecture of a street lamp, its petal-like ridges, its blossoming rims, female. And he would look up and swear that the finial of the lamp, bursting with electric light, resembled a woman of the Victorian era wearing a slightly pointed hat. The moon over the rooftops; a cat in heat perched on some garbage cans, raising her rump in the air—all female.

(Of course, he was aware of the hard-edged contributions of men: a particularly ugly postwar high-rise seemed male. The Empire State Building, to whose observation deck he had once ascended on a sightseeing tour with his sisters—he had looked out to the south, naïvely imagining, for a moment, that he might be able to see as far as Cobbleton—had struck him, with its phallic eminence, its similarity to a hypodermic needle, as powerful but vaguely depressing. Then a view of all the square-topped apartment houses, going on into the distance, and a look at the Chrysler Building, with its jagged ornamentation, an edifice touched equally by the male and female influence, mostly pleasing him with its female characteristics. It would remind him of the Statue of Liberty, sitting out in the water with its crown, its flaw, in his opinion, the manly arms and hands of the Lady.)

Some days found him in the company of friends to take in "culture." He went to art galleries and saw modern paintings, some odd configurations of geometric forms, others squiggly and stormy. He would look them over and sigh. And yet the most vaguely curvaceous paintings interested him. (He would remember something that his commanding officer had once said to him: "There is nothing more beautiful than a circle.") He was not by nature a thinker, and on his walks along the streets or on his way home to the apartment, these notions would bring back the same feelings that he'd always had as a child, an ambassadorial sensation that he, Emilio Montez O'Brien, could never articulate to himself, but which made him feel like a well-loved but minor functionary in a sometimes good world whose creation and whose better aspects had nothing to do with himself or others like him: men.

He'd study lines of dialogue, practice enunciation. And

often, lost in thought, he would look up to find a pretty young woman sitting at a nearby table. His reaction, as it had been for many years when his sisters got his attention, would be to smile, for he did love women.

One late afternoon, as he sat in a café, a plump, red-cheeked brunette, wholesome as the German farm girls he used to see in Cobbleton, asked, "Pardon me, but haven't I seen you up around Dobbs Ferry?" He'd said no, but moved over to sit beside her, asking, "Do you mind?"

They talked, and she mentioned that she had noticed him reading a script, and that he must be an actor. He listened, his eyes on her eyes and her lips—a plump and cheery-looking mouth, suggesting, he imagined, that, despite the Depression and the war, she had never gone wanting. He further surmised, during their conversation, that she was in New York to become an actress but that her decision did not weigh well with her family, and that she was lonely living in a boardinghouse. She was very young, maybe nineteen or twenty, but there was a nervousness about her, her lovely hands shaking slightly when she sipped her glass of iced tea. Focusing intently on her and looking away only when an airliner was heard above, he told the young woman that, like her, he came from a small town, and impressed her with the details of his life in Italy during the war.

When he asked for her name, she told him "Katherine," and the demure tone of her voice moved him. Reaching over, he tapped her shoulder and said, "Well, Katherine, don't be worried. I think your life will turn out fine."

She was tender. She was interested in him. She talked a lot about her family, who had been disapproving of her chosen profession. ("They've given me two years to make a name for myself. My dad's a judge and he sends me a hundred and fifty dollars a month as support—money that I'll pay back. But they keep waiting for me to come home.")

He took her out to see a couple of Broadway shows; he seemed wealthy. Receiving two hundred dollars a month from the government, he thought nothing of buying her little gifts, or treating her to dinner. He was always polite and a little reserved;

bringing her back to the boardinghouse, he would shyly say "Good night" and she would double the effort to win him over, giving him a sweet kiss.

One night, at two in the morning, after attending an Italian street fair—spending twelve dollars at a stand, he won her a teddy bear—they slipped into a restaurant, Sorrento. They were drinking wine, and his memories of Italy flowed into him. They ended up sitting in a corner, necking, and that led them to an Eighth Avenue hotel room. As he rested back on the bed, she told him, "I don't know what to do." All the same, she had stripped off her clothes, and while he lay there, fully dressed, she let the weight of her brunette plumpness settle on him. As she undid his shirt and trousers and all the rest, it struck him that she had fallen for him. Her fingers stroked the curls on his head, and though he considered her a delicate and refined person, he suckled her breasts. He noticed that her bottom ridges were quite sweaty as the fingers of his right hand slipped from the low knob of her spinal column down her body. She said, "You are the kindest and most handsome man I have ever met in my life, more handsome than Errol Flynn." With that affirmation, he grasped her by the hips and shifted her position, and with the strength of one knee, the left, he opened her wide, telling himself, "No matter what, my boy, you can't fall in love."

He was going out with three other actresses at the time, insecure, flamboyant, and hopeful young women with whom he worked and who, in various incarnations, reminded him of his first great love, Spring Mayweather, women whom sooner or later he took to bed. (Making love on a lounge couch, in a room filled with bits of scenery, and doing it quickly, because they could hear the stage manager's footsteps sounding louder on the rotting wooden floors; making love after twelve rehearsals, backstage when the others had left, almost standing up, with his right knee getting bruised against the rim of a prop crate, or in the large walk-in closet of a producer's town house on Eleventh Street, against a bundle of clothes, or, in the spring, strolling in Central Park, on some downy meadow, ever nervous that a cop, twirling his nightstick, would come across them in the act while walking his beat; and making love, hurriedly, in a dressing room, some of those women so wanting distraction that now and then an actress would invite the youngest Montez O'Brien into the room to help zip up her costume, the touch of his warm hands producing more warmth on her back, so that she'd turn around and, saying, "Oh, fuck it," pull up her dress and rest back on a chair, a matty rug, or a couch, her anxiety and fears for the future alleviated in the muscular quivering of her legs, her hands pressing against the small of his back, and asking for more—Emilio on some nights left confused by his power but always willing to go along, for it seemed the manly thing to do.)

His evenings were so broken up with dates that he would come home to his sisters' apartment at five in the morning, opening the door quietly and finding, more often than not, his sweet sister Gloria on the couch waiting for him.

His Debut, 1947

ELEVATED TO an advanced level after a year of conscientious studies, and assigned by his drama coach to a role in a reverential production of Bernard Shaw's *Caesar and Cleopatra*, which was to open in a run-down Bleecker Street theater, Emilio, the son of a Cuban mother and an Irish father, was to play Britannicus, Caesar's secretary. As written, Britannicus was a tall, solemn fellow of about forty, hair grayed, and sporting a white beard. He would appear dressed in a blue toga. Miscast and somewhat deficient in conveying the wisdom of the man, Emilio had one saving grace. He did not forget his lines and made quite an impression on that contingent of the audience composed of his family—his mother and father and all the sisters who'd shown up to give support and applaud loudly, their clapping rising above the polite response of an otherwise indifferent audience, during the curtain call.

The occasion marked not only his first appearance on the New York stage—he threw up before and after the performance—but one of the few times that his mother and father would venture outside of Cobbleton to New York, the family finding accommodations in Helen's Park Avenue apartment and with Maria, Olga, and Jacqueline. That his mother had shown up seemed miraculous, for, despite many previous invitations from her daughters to visit them in New York, she'd always been afraid of leaving her husband alone.

At sixty-nine and still working as an "exhibitor of movies," Nelson O'Brien showed the symptoms of senility—forgetfulness and indecision becoming more common in his behavior, so that Mariela, his wife, began to fear that if she left him alone for even a single evening he might, while lighting his old Dutch pipe, set the house on fire. (He had started to talk with more frequency about going on to his heavenly reward, and made it a subject of their bedtime conversation, so that, while he would eventually fall asleep, she would spend the nights awake, wondering how she would feel in his absence. On the other hand, these symptoms seemed to come and go—weeks would pass during which they would sit on the porch together and talk as they used to, when they were both young, about what they might do in their retirement. Their children's desire to see something of the world influencing them, they would sometimes make vague plans for excursions around the country. "Maybe out to the great West," where he wanted to go as a younger man, Nelson would say. And she would listen and nod, taking hold of his ruddy and bigknuckled hands and squeezing them tight.)

Emilio's first performance did not receive good notices, but the cast party after the opening, held in their teacher's Barrow Street town house and thick with fledgling actors and their friends and fellow students, was joyful. There were punch bowls of a potent mix (his father grew happy-eyed from its effects), and young pianists and singers took turns at the kind of casual performance that Emilio would always identify with his happy days. Stubby Kaye showed up, singing by the piano, and later, in came Zero Mostel, passing half the night in the corner telling naughty jokes. The sisters themselves swooped down into the midst of this affair with shopping bags filled with baked pies, compliments of Irene, and some Cuban-style dishes which Maria, having access to the ingredients in New York, had prepared in great quantity. (In Helen's magisterial Park Avenue kitchen, as big as a living room, Maria, with her mother by her side, cooked up a large kettle's worth of paella and another of black beans. And in the kitchen during the party their mother, taken by the activity around her, spent an hour frying plantain fritters, which went out in great platters and disappeared soon enough into the mouths of the grateful, celebratory, and hungry aspirants to the stage. She had been struck by the little trip she and Margarita and Maria made up to 116th Street and Lenox Avenue—the neighborhood where García's New York family once lived—and she marveled at all the food shops, some Italian, such as she had seen during a rare earlier trip to New York, and at others whose awnings announced themselves as bodegas, where she had felt a little stunned to hear the shopkeepers speaking in Spanish, and to see that their racks were filled with fruits and vegetables that she had not seen since she'd visited Cuba in 1932. Above all, she had felt a little surprised at how many Spanish-speaking people there were in New York, for in 1902, when she and Nelson had first passed through the city en route to Cobbleton, she thought it mainly an Irish, Italian, German, and Jewish place— in fact, there were no more than two thousand Puerto Ricans and a handful of Cubans living in the city at that time—and she marveled at how, during the years she spent in Cobbleton, the outside world had changed. At one shop she found herself inquiring if the owner happened to know a certain Herman García, the butler, and she was pleased to find that he did, and right then, as Margarita paid for their groceries, she had felt pangs of longing for "her people." This mood followed her throughout the day and into the theater where Emilio, looking quite strange, first stepped on the stage and recited his opening line in a deep and solemn voice: "*My master would say that there is a lawful debt due to Rome by Egypt.*" And as she watched her son attempting to make his way in the world, she saw him as an absolute American, like certain of her daughters. As he crossed the stage following Caesar about, declaiming his lines, she regretted that neither of them seemed to know the other. What had she been to her son, and to some of his sisters, but their mother, from another world?

She had always tried to remind them that they were half Cuban, regardless of the way their bloodlines made them look, but she supposed that to her Irish-looking son those words did not make much difference. As she watched his faulty and unconvincing portrayal of the Briton, the cadences of her husband's pronunciation of English coming through, she found herself losing track of the play. Taking in his performance with a remote appreciation and hope for what her son was trying to do, she sighed and asked God to bless him and to carry him off on the wings of success so that he at least—she would wish this for all her children—could thrive in the country which to her seemed so complicated.)

The party lasted until three-thirty in the morning, Emilio passing the night chatting amicably with his theater friends and enjoying the camaraderie of his fellow aspirants, dreamy unknowns drinking and singing and doing bits from the shows and plays they knew. (He loved musical-comedy actors and actresses, and wished he was not so clumsy when it came to dancing, and that his voice was decent, which it was not.)

He adopted an actor's air, having bought for himself a fedora and a cape, in the style of a European count, an affectation he acquired from his teacher. But on his walks through the streets of Greenwich Village he had also seen the actor John Carradine, tall and lanky and crag-faced, making his way along, reciting Shakespeare to his friends in his fine bass voice, physically impressive in a cape and a crimped hat and cane. Emilio forgot the cane but adopted for his wardrobe not only the aforementioned items but an ascot, a silk shirt, and a tweed jacket.

That night, Katherine turned up, too; and Emilio, who had broken her heart, was surprised to see her. (He ended things with her for reasons she would never understand, just at a time when she had become really accustomed to him, going about by his side to auditions for plays and musical shows, and getting quite used to going to bed with him, and the violet coloration in her nipples when he would kiss them. She could not understand what he meant, one afternoon in the park, when they had been dating for three months—April to July 1947—by saying their love affair was "too distracting." And even though she started to cry and he held her close, saying, "Now, be calm about this," he did not, just the same, change his mind, though she was a sweet girl, walking away from her with a heel's expression on his face and, she hoped, some regrets.) She happened to have walked over, on the arm of a young actor, at a moment when Emilio was standing with a group which included two other women whom he had also taken to bed dozens of times, and as if a kind of radio communication had risen among them, Laura Hathaway, "willowy and as tall as a drink of water," to quote *The New York Times*, and Ellen Conners, "a gypsy who deserves the central spotlight," seemed, in a spontaneous revelation, to know that Katherine Dempsy, "a worthy supporting player," also made love to him.

There were a dozen individuals standing watching Emilio Montez O'Brien perform some sleight-of-hand and card tricks —he could "guess" the card picked from a deck, effortlessly— and these three women, shifting their positions, drifted together. And he saw them standing off in a corner, Laura recounting to the others how she liked to be kissed in a certain way, and Ellen, with her gaunt white body, recounting how, when she mentioned that she did not much like her bottom, the lick of his tongue had moved along her buttocks and he had told her, "You're delicious." And he saw that Katherine was not happy at all, that she must have told them the whole story, for they began to stare at him with murderous intent, their disdain for him so powerful that he felt a buckling of his knees and a waning of his spirit.

As some young and frantic musician banged out a Hoagy Carmichael tune on the piano, they decided that the earnest actor, whose seeming lack of guile so moved their hearts, was just like so many of the other men they'd met: perhaps they'd wished him some future lonely hell.

*

That night of Emilio's debut in New York, most of his four-teen sisters showed up (Margarita, Maria, Olga, Jacqueline, Helen, Irene, Sarah, Patricia, Veronica, Marta, Carmen, Violeta, and Gloria—only Isabel, in Cuba, missing). And how they had fawned on him. Only Gloria, who seemed enchanted by his performance, kept her distance, bent on allowing him the free-dom he so wanted. Sitting off to the side, engaged in a conver-sation about the aspirations of actors in general with a sweet, vaguely effeminate young man, Gloria would look around for her brother. She admired him and felt grateful that he allowed her into this world. She wished him well, she hoped that he would thrive, that he would fall in love and be happy, but at the same time, with so many women about, she wanted nothing to change.

Margarita, beautiful in a red dress and happy to jitterbug with some professional dancers, would sometimes plop down on the couch, fanning herself, exhausted and happy. Then she would say to Gloria, "Maybe you should dance, too," but the youngest sister would shake her head, as if she found great comfort in playing the demure wallflower. That night found her making frequent trips out to the back garden of the town-house apart-ment—it was on the ground floor—to take the air, for the fumes of cigarettes and cigars and the women's perfumes were making her a little ill. For all that, she did not want to leave, and revived by the night air, she would come back inside, always looking for her brother.

His father, Nelson O'Brien, stood near the punch bowl in a gentlemanly way, nodding and offering to ladle more of the brew into cups and trying to think what he would say to his boy. In the dead center of the evening, when Emilio came by with a young woman on his arm, he said: "Well, you did good, son." And Emilio gave his father a hug, the older man feeling most tactful and happy that he had been coy enough to lie, for he slept during the performance. He was the ever-cheerful Irish gentle-man, raising his cup of punch in a toast to those who happened by, saying, "God bless you," and "Ahh, back for some more. Well, good, then."

Everyone in the family had a good time, but eventually there came a moment when the happy partygoers all began to leave and Emilio found himself walking with his mother on his arm, his father by his side, and the sisters following along, with the moon over the rooftops and a few stars in the sky. Emilio looked at his mother and asked, "What did you think?"

And she said, "Good! Good! My son," speaking to him in her clipped English, thinking that he would not understand anything more complicated. He'd consumed too much punch and was almost as tipsy as his father. Bewildered by his debut, Emilio secretly wondered if he succeeded only in humiliating himself, but at this moment he had looked off, swearing that it was a great pleasure to be so young and to have aspirations and to be in love with the future. That night, as he climbed into a Checker cab with Gloria and the Chanteuses, he tried to define the quality of the blue sky that seemed so enchanting to him, the distance that seemed like his future. A blueness zooming in through the taxi window; the blue of those storybook illustrations that Margarita, ever the lover of books, would show him as a child. Not the black-and-white skies of cowboy fantasies, not the blue of vacation brochures, but the blueness that he recalled from an illustration in the *Arabian Nights*: a tower, phallic and powerful, at the summit of a hilly Arab town, cutting into the horizon, and the sky a deep and mysterious blue, dotted with feminine, adoring stars.

The Happiness of Their Days

THE SISTERS WOULD REMEMBER those years for the happiness of their days. (The oldest, Margarita, attending night school in Philadelphia, was working toward a degree. Isabel, in Cuba, had her third child, a girl. Helen, affluent and ever elegant in her Christian Dior New Look dresses with their nipped-in waists and short Chinese button jackets and planet-Saturn hats, enjoyed playing the New York society lady. Patricia had her own baby, as did Sarah. Veronica seemed content enough in Illinois with Rudolph Williams.)

And Gloria, close to her brother, was also happy, waiting on him, doting and ever loving. Proud (and anxious) to prove that she could take care of herself, she had gone to work as a book-keeper for a doll manufacturer, a tedious job, as her boss was a terribly disorganized businessman who for years kept his receipts, invoices, and orders in barrels, and every morning she would come into the factory to try to put these chaotic records into some kind of order. She did not mind the endless nature of the work; it was a way of marking time. And on good days she would leave the factory (on Thirty-eighth Street, off Sixth Avenue) in the afternoon and walk up to sit on the steps of the Public Library on Forty-second Street, eating her wax-paper-wrapped sand-wiches and a soda and watching the passersby, seeing in a half hour more human beings thronging the sidewalk to and from their offices and shops than lived in Cobbleton, whose population had risen to just over eighteen thousand. All kinds of people, too, venders and cops, and Bible salesmen, office executives and buxom, brainy-looking secretaries, students and GIs heading up the library steps toward knowledge, messengers and bank clerks, advertising-agency workers and many bookkeepers like herself, stunned and happy to be out in the light. And she would some-times meet with one of her New York sisters, one of them turning up to take "the poor thing" out for lunch. They liked to go have a bite at the Horn & Hardart, where one could eat nicely with only a handful of nickels for the soup, sandwich, and dessert vending machines. Or, if Helen came along, Gloria would ask her boss for some extra time, for they would dine in some fancy joint over on Madison or Lexington Avenue, where the food was good, the service languorous, the waiters polite and self-effacing. Helen, the sixth-oldest of the fourteen sisters, who had never really known how to relate to Gloria, would urge her to take better care of herself, to dress with more style. And to that end she would sometimes promise to meet with Gloria in the late afternoon so they could visit dress shops, a process that Gloria, with her love of simple clothes, found a little self-indulgent, though Helen was generous, always paying for the purchases. She'd begun to feel the pressures of "growing up," a natural step, and of becoming desirable to men. But she had no interest in men, even on days when she was feeling well and put on lipstick and eye makeup and seemed quite pretty. (Some lonely book-keeper like herself would slip a section of newspaper down on the library steps close to her and sit down, attempting to strike up a conversation: "Have you the time? A nice day, isn't it?" But she tended to respond with mere politeness, for even if the young man was the nicest fellow in the world, well-intentioned and simply wanting some pleasant company, she would turn away.) And though many a handsome man passed in the crowds—and quite possibly "the right man," as magazine stories used to say —she did not, like so many other girls, get dressed to the hilt on the chance that on a particular lunch hour "Mr. Right" would walk into her life. Gloria did not pay that kind of hope much mind, even when she did catch a man's eye and he tipped his hat and smiled.

Her happiest lunchtimes were spent with Emilio. He'd take odd jobs, selling ties out of the Times Square shops, or working as an usher at one of the big movie houses, day work that he'd get through a temporary agency, a job that would leave him free to attend auditions or to study whatever he liked. And sometimes when he was in the neighborhood he would come by to see Gloria. Even though she might have seen her brother the evening before at dinner, those lunches, when he would sit beside her on the steps, seemed very special, as if then, among so many strangers, they shared a kind of anonymity and she could have him to herself. He, like the family, knew that it was not good for Gloria to shut out the world. And he knew that there was something vaguely unsisterly in the way her eyes became so happy at the sight of him, or when he said to her, "You look very pretty today, Gloria," a blush coming over her face, or, when walking by his side, she would hold his hand and swing it along with hers, as if they were teenage boyfriend and girlfriend. He'd tried to interest her in the company of one of his cronies at the workshop, a good-looking actor Gloria's size, a nice fellow who came along to join them for lunch—a mistake. Gloria thought the fellow pleasant enough, but for days she felt betrayed and angry that Emilio had allowed someone else to intrude on their special time together.

It was a strain for him, as she wanted to know everything about his life: which plays he was auditioning for, whether he would have classes on a given night, or if he had met someone. Dutifully, he would report on the first two items, keeping the third a secret, as he thought it would make her jealous and unhappy and because, on those occasions when he opened his heart to her, mentioning the few infatuations or loves of his life, he had the sensation that such admissions cut through her like broken glass. (He knew, for example, that on nights when he came home quite late from a dinner or a party, she would have spent the night unable to sleep, listening for sounds in the hall. And his love affairs with the young sweet women of his profession—his way of marking time—would intrude on the delicate balance of her heart and mind. He'd talked about it—with Maria and Margarita—and each had cautioned him to be careful. A few times he had moved out of the apartment, to share a place with some fellow actors in the Village, and each time Gloria would slip into such a state of silence and discouragement that Maria or one of the twins would call him up, asking Emilio to come talk with Gloria; and each time, having a good heart, he would decide to return to their apartment. They knew that something wasn't right about all this—even Gloria knew it—but what could they do? Maria had spoken to Margarita about the sisters pitching in to send Gloria to a doctor of the nerves, and one day Maria had mentioned this to Gloria, who was unable to accept the reason for doing so: "Why, just because I care and worry about my brother?"

Sitting on the Fifth Avenue library steps, Emilio would remind Gloria that, if things went well for him, he would be heading out to California to try his hand as a movie actor. There was their father's connection in California, and he had a feisty agent who in those days sent out his growing resumé and 8 × 10 black-and-white glossies to the different studios. Emilio gave himself three years of apprenticeship—for he liked New York and was not in a rush to go West. But that was his eventual plan. In Gloria's company, he tried to prepare her, but at the mention of California, she would become so happy. "Oh, I've always wanted to go," she would say, and Emilio would feel even more confounded.)

Back in the factory, she would spend her afternoons taking care of paperwork in a little office with a window that overlooked the factory floor. Down below were some twenty tables where women, mostly Italians and Puerto Ricans, assembled the dolls and sewed their dresses, tagged and packed the finished dolls into boxes, their overflow on any given day arranged in a row along racks. Cry-baby dolls and Little Sis dolls, with their pretty blue blink-open-and-shut eyes, were the first sight that would greet her when she came to work in the morning, and the last, watching her mutely as she, waiting for her boss and the floor manager by the door, would click the lights off, one by one.

Gallant Heart

IN 1949 IT HAPPENED that M-G-M was casting for a new film, a romance (*Gallant Heart*) about the love affairs of American GIs and British women in London toward the end of the war. The actor cast to play the small role of an Indiana farm boy, with some eighteen lines of dialogue and one "kiss-off" monologue (in which he convinces the sweet farm girl he loves that he is secretly a heel, so she will forget him before he goes off into his uncertain future), had been pitching a baseball game with some actor friends in Santa Monica when a hard-hit line drive caught him on his right knee, and he was laid up, with smashed bones and torn ligaments, for three months. His bad luck worked to Emilio's advantage—it was as if a prayer was being answered. In California, the producers, exhausted and in the crush and panic of pre-production, told their casting people to find a last-minute replacement. With most of their contract players tied up in other movies, they decided to look through a portfolio of faces, many of them from New York, choosing a few whom they might bring out for a screen test.

One of their scouts, a woman, knew Emilio as the romantic lead in an Actors Equity Showcase the year before and had been impressed by his naturalness. By that time, he'd been in twelve plays, none running more than a few weeks, but he had received some good notices, the most positive citing him as "an earnest and athletic-looking actor . . . possessed of an inward quality that might one day invoke pathos." And though he had, to that point, no outstanding success onstage, he learned to comport himself like a professional, and had slowly developed the kind of presence and charisma that women liked. Strong in heart, he seemed vulnerable and self-effacing; and, above all, there was something so earnest about him that the female scout from M-G-M would think him Cooperesque.

One morning, as Emilio was dressing for a day-long stint as a temporary file clerk in a midtown office, his agent called him to say that M-G-M wanted him to test for a role. Doubtful, he did not say a word to the sisters, but made his way downtown to the agent's office, where he was presented with a copy of the script. He sat out in the hall with the screenplay unopened on his lap, hoping to find on the first page the name of a Hollywood director he much admired. (His three favorite directors were Preston Sturges, John Ford, and John Huston, one of his favorite films being Mr. Sturges's *Sullivan's Travels*, which had played for two weeks in his father's movie house, the Jewel Box, in 1942. Whenever he could, Emilio would watch that film intently, studying the casual, natural acting style of Joel McCrea. He enjoyed the director's urbane and lighthearted version of the Depression, and daydreamed about doing the role of Sullivan, dreamed about taking to the freight trains to experience firsthand—even though he knew that he was watching a movie—the calamity-ridden landscape of America.) But there was no great name on the screenplay, and it even struck him that the script for *Gallant Heart* was a little weak.

Its lengthiest lines were the monologue, which his agent had

underlined in pencil: "*Becky, I've come here tonight to say goodbye. And not just because I'm shipping out tomorrow, but because
I want you to know the real truth. Ever since the time we were
children, it seemed as if you and I would always be together. In
all those years there's not been a single day when I haven't treasured
our precious love, but I figure that since I might not come back, I
may as well level with you. I've been what those big-city magazines
call a playboy, in my own way. I've been disloyal—don't want to
say with who or when, but that's a fact. And even though I know
this breaks your heart, I tell you now so you don't get your hopes
up while I'm away. Now that I'm going off, it's time for us to grow
up, you and me. Well, goodbye—I won't be looking back.*"

He sat with the script for two hours. It was summer and a
great heat was rising off the Manhattan streets, and he had begun
to feel so fatigued that when his agent came out into the outer
office, saying, "Come on, Emilio; what have you got to lose?"
the young man, then twenty-four, agreed to fly that very evening
to Los Angeles.

Back in the apartment—none of his sisters was home—and
in the heat of the day, he packed some clothing. He made one
telephone call to his family in Cobbleton, reaching his mother,
but he hung up unconvinced that Mariela had understood everything he said. His flight was scheduled for 6 p.m., with a change-
over in St. Louis. At four-thirty, when Olga and Jacqueline
walked in the door, he tried to explain, but there was a tightness
in his throat, from nerves, and he was afraid of missing the flight,
as if that might unravel his stroke of good luck. Dallying in the
hallway, like a soldier off to war, he related the possibility that
he might have a part in a movie, and the twins had smothered
him with kisses. Later Gloria came home, and asked, "Where's
Emilio? Hasn't he come in yet?" And they had told her, "He's
gone off to California to try out for a movie."

"Yes?" In the bathroom, running the water in the basin, as
its sound seemed to keep her company, she remained there,
sitting fully dressed on the toilet for a long time, wanting to be
alone, and then the thought of her brother's turn of good luck,
his chance in life, his big break, took her breath away and she

began to shake, sighing over the intimation that his absence that day was the beginning of a much longer separation.

Hollywood

A STARR PICTURES POSTER circa 1955, which his oldest sister Margarita would take out of its frame in her father's movie house and keep, rolled up, for many years. In it, an artfully rendered color painting of her brother, Emilio Montez O'Brien, working under the name Montgomery ("Monty") O'Brien, as a private detective, in rumpled trench coat and bent-brimmed felt hat, a busty Jane Russell brunette in a torn dress facing him with a gun, the electrified caption reading: "She was passion gone wild!" And: "A Private Eye under the spell of love!" The poster commemorated one of the four pictures in which he played Lance Stewart, private detective, in his decline.

She would remember that he had also made, for the same studio, two Tarzan films, *Tarzan in the Land of No Return* and *Tarzan in the Opal Kingdom*—the kind of pictures that her poor, talented brother had taken for the money in 1955–56.

*

During the first five years of his time in Hollywood, he would appear in forty-two films. For the family, they were years of absence (and not because they missed his physical presence, as he would fly back East as often as possible for the holidays, but because, far off in that different world, the Emilio they had known had begun to change). He'd worked steadily, marching through the tedium of *Gallant Heart* for M-G-M and graduating some three months later into the romantic second lead in a film called *A Springtime Love*, also for M-G-M. Both pictures did badly. His notices had been good, however, and he made some money, so he drifted from M-G-M into work for other studios, playing two- or three-day bit parts under heavy makeup: a Napoleonic lieutenant, a knight of Richard the Lionhearted in the time of the

Crusades (and, in the same film, a Saracen horseman), an American Revolutionary under the command of General Washington, among many others. He played gangsters, cowboys, and once, hired to work in a movie about Billy the Kid, he played a deputy sheriff.

Now and then a better part would come along.

Years later he would belabor himself most for having taken the Tarzan roles. (As a much older man, he read a television review: "Tarzan again, on a vine, yoiks!") In 1952 he made his best movie for Starr Pictures, a low-budget affair called *On Saint Anne's Street*, about a handsome Catholic priest, Father Byrne, who falls in love with one of his parishioners. An unconsummated love on the screen that had been, however, continuously consummated offscreen in his trailer: he had fallen in love with the actress, Hedda Holmes, who played the role of Mary. (That affair started because of their desolate loneliness between takes, he staring at her, she smiling. And then one day he invited her to lunch in his dressing room. Eating salad, Emilio, in priestly garb, started to kiss her, and she, in the midst of swallowing a piece of lettuce, kissed him back.)

Ten weeks to shoot, that movie made money. Because his character ultimately resisted temptation (the Conference of Catholic Bishops had put it on their recommended list), in the fadeout the priest, having told Mary that their love is impossible, watches her meeting up with a nice guy on the street; the camera then follows him into the interior of a church, where he kneels in prayer, contemplating a crucifix above the altar, a heavenly choir swelling, and the camera fading out on the crucifix as the chamber fills with a light as blinding as love. The New York *Herald Tribune* called his performance "elegant and biting." After playing unnoticeable secondary roles, Emilio had suddenly found himself lauded; a year later (1953), he made a second Father Byrne movie, *The Boys of Amsterdam Avenue*, but that film, about the priest's good work with a band of street urchins, was bereft of passion and a love interest, and it did not fare as well as its predecessor.

But it, too, made money and was popular enough with the

public that for the first time he began to receive fan mail, mostly from young girls. Some letters were mundane and some outrageous—letters of proposal and letters in which he was propositioned—but he answered each with a signed photograph, hiring a secretary to mail them out all over the country. (During his biggest month, in June 1954, he received 1,220 such requests; during his worst, in February 1957, eight.)

Stardom

STILL, HE'D STARTED TO FEEL like a star. He posed for cigarette and automobile ads, and now and then he would be asked to escort some rising young starlet to a Hollywood premiere, or some ladies' club in San Francisco or Seattle would invite him to speak at a luncheon. He bought a little bungalow, not far off Sunset Boulevard, in West Hollywood, where he would meet reporters. Two photographs—one of himself as a teenage boy posed with his family ("Monty's folks") in front of the house in Cobbleton, another as a GI during the war—found their way often into his life stories. Few profiles of Emilio ever went very far into his family past, though some reporters worked in the fact that his mother, Mariela Montez, was a "lady from south of the border," one writer using that item to explain why he, an Irishman, had Latin-lover appeal. Because he was one of Hollywood's most eligible bachelors, there were always snippets of gossip about him. He'd been linked romantically with a number of starlets: Randy Jenkins, Betty Reed, and Vida Ramsey, among others—actresses with whom he'd fall madly in love for a few months, before a kind of femininely-influenced fatigue would settle on his heart and he'd move on.

While he was not always confident about his acting abilities, he had come to know something about seducing women. His movies, bad or good, made little difference when it came to his personal appeal. Whether attending a party at the Brown Derby or in some producer's house high in the hills overlooking the

city, he'd always meet someone. Even when he was shooting a
film, getting up at five in the morning, he would often end the
day taking someone to bed, his eyes heavy and his mood cantankerous for the next day's shoot. He bedded down so many
women in that time—actresses, extras, stand-ins—that on many
a night he not only forgot his original aspirations but began to
forget his family: his mother and father and his fourteen sisters.
Though he had been conscientious about writing and calling his
sisters, the very fact that he missed them so made him, on bad
days, feel resentful. Slowly, his contact with them faded—partly
because of his work schedule and partly because he had become
quite an active man about Hollywood—dwindling to the occasional late-night telephone call and then, for months at a time,
nothing at all.

(Even when he flew back East, during the happy time of
Christmas, there was a new remoteness about him that confused
his sisters. Polite, respectful, and ever generous—for he would
make epic shopping trips in Manhattan and come back to the
apartment on West End Avenue or to the house in Cobbleton
loaded down with expensive gifts—he seemed all the same to
have lost his ability to appreciate the simple enjoyments of affection that had so marked his youth.

He did not like discussing his career, preferring to talk about
the movie stars he had met: Cary Grant was a gentleman, Mickey
Rooney was funny, Stan Laurel and Oliver Hardy were "gems."
He was friendly with Errol Flynn, who would sometimes spot
him in a crowd and cheerfully call out, "Hey, chum, over here."
They'd shake hands and clink champagne glasses, Flynn still
"gorgeous" and always with a young woman on his arm. They
met at a party in 1951, and Mr. Flynn, talking about many things,
drifted into the subject of Cuba, where he had spent much time.
He reminisced about his "splendid" days in Havana, where he
was a friend of Hemingway, and Emilio told him his mother was
Cuban. Errol Flynn felt no deep nostalgia for his past, but that
night he told Emilio, after many drinks, "I'll never forget my
amorous adventures in the arms of the beguiling Cuban ladies,"
and this somehow made Emilio all the more like Flynn. From

that time on, Flynn, who liked to keep an entourage, would call up his new "chum" and invite him along on his outings about town. He would see other movie stars—Fred MacMurray, Claudette Colbert, James Mason, and Laurence Olivier—chatting in a corner, and he even met Joel McCrea, who looked him over and said, chewing on a cracker slathered with caviar, "You know what, you look like a cousin of mine," then walked away. All this excited Emilio, but after a time he became so accustomed to these famous people that their company began to mean nothing to him and his eyes would scan the room for unattached women.)

His sisters loved his stories, but they were worried about his life out there: Was he eating well? Was he working too hard? Gloria took the solemnness of his moods to mean that he needed someone like her to take care of him, and on each of his visits she would offer to come out and keep house for him, but he'd always explain that things were quite all right. Knowing of his romantic proclivities and the brittleness of his heart, Margarita thought quite simply that what he needed was to settle down, a sentiment shared by the others. Patricia kept to herself the thought that her brother's moods were due to some unconscious awareness of a dreadful future personal loss (in dreams, she would see fire), while Violeta, ever flirtatious and vain, thought mainly of herself, reveling in his company, especially when he would accompany her to town. His musical sisters, Maria, Olga, and Jacqueline, were always happy to see him, and, knowing enough famous people themselves, and having seen what sometimes happens, simply hoped the trappings of his profession would not go to his head. The others, like the plump Irene, simply loved him. And yet they noticed he seemed troubled.

Even his mother, off in her own world, sensed this. She would watch him sitting pensively out on the porch and wonder just what her son was thinking, whether he was unhappy because he was too famous or whether he was so sad because he was not famous enough. What was it with the boy?

Although he was not yet thirty, he felt a vague disappointment with the way his life was turning out. He'd remember the days of aspiration, when he had first daydreamed about acting and perhaps making a movie, as having been very sweet—the hope much more glorious and fulfilling than the actual deed. As for matters of the heart, which also weighed on him, he felt nostalgic (and would to his last days) about the first loves of his life, and his more recent romantic escapades seemed to him like mad dashes to re-create those simple joyous moments; or perhaps he had never gotten used to living in the world itself, far removed from the potent love of his sisters, who smothered him, for so many years, with affection. Whatever the cause, a kind of torpor and a feeling of inadequacy as a man, movie star or not, would overwhelm him at times, and he would grow impatient with his days of idleness and look forward to getting back to work.

Visits, 1953–54

HELEN AND HER HUSBAND and two children came out to see him in Los Angeles in 1953, and he had taken them around the city and up into the hills in his shiny Cadillac and onto the set of one of the pictures he was working on, a pirate adventure starring Burt Lancaster. He would remember their visit as being most pleasant. The kids in particular were enchanted by the activity on the sound-stage sets and by the notion that perhaps they were around real pirates, and Mr. Lancaster himself sat the boys down and amused them by juggling four rubber balls. The studio photographer, as a favor to Emilio, or "Montgomery O'Brien," had photographed him with his beautiful sister Helen and her family, on the mock deck of a ship, a picture that turned out quite nicely. He had to admit that he liked to come home and find them waiting for him, but was a little put off by the incredible stiffness of the kids, who referred to Helen as Mother, as in "Mother, may I have a glass of juice," and he found her a little too reserved with her own children. He was surprised by his own fondness for them; they called him Uncle and that had made him happy and determined to amuse them even when he felt exhausted after a long day's shoot. He'd sit on the rug of his living room in front of his radio and television set, performing sleight-of-hand tricks (something which was very successful with women, for on occasion he would pull from their sweaty navels a pair of earrings or from the beautiful wreath of their pubic hair a pearl necklace). While wondering if what he really needed in life was a home and children of his own, he had enjoyed their company, driving them out to the beach on his days off and dozing on the sand, content to hear their voices around him.

Helen wanted to make the rounds of the most exclusive nightclubs and eateries of the city, and Emilio, ever the sport, could not refrain from paying every one of their bills, even though he knew his brother-in-law, with his yachty face and perpetual sunny cheeks, was a millionaire. And though he had been surprised by his sister's formality and realized that he did not really know her—she was fifteen years older than he—Emilio was touched by her concern for him. By the end of their ten-day visit, Emilio, "*sans* women," as his friend Flynn would say, began to feel a little impatient, though their presence had released him from his feelings of solitude, that sensation which he simply equated with being a man. And he nearly cried—why, he did not know—when at the airport his sister Helen gave him a long and sustained hug. He had watched her, in her Dior outfit, making her way to the airliner, amused by how a sister, remote and distant in one moment, could become in another so important to one's life. And when her children, in their blue suits and caps, waved ecstatically at him, off to spend the rest of the summer in Newport, he blew them a fond and avuncular kiss.

The following autumn, his oldest sister, Margarita, came to see him. By then she had graduated from college (at the ripe age of fifty). Grand parties had been held in New York and out in Cobbleton, which he did not attend. She arrived buoyantly happy with a certificate to teach Spanish. And she had just returned from a triumphant first journey to Europe, having traveled through Spain, where she found herself involved in an autumnal romance. At that time, she exhibited the physical propensities of their mother, having aged little. She liked to wear a big sun hat, and in her tight polka-dot dress (and girdle), and with her good figure and unlined face, she did not seem much older than a woman of thirty-five. She brought her movie-actor brother a bottle of Spanish brandy as a gift, and because she arrived in California not more than a week after her return home from Europe, she was bursting with the energy of one who has passed successfully through the fire of a new and dazzling experience.

Ever since childhood, Margarita would refer to her brother as "*hermanito*," as Emilio, as "sweetheart," but her time in Spain had inspired her to call him "*mi vida*," "my life." He had picked her up at the airport, puzzled by the glow about her. As he sat beside her in his automobile, it seemed as if some unknown scent was rising off her skin, as if she'd just come from a spice-ridden country, and he realized soon enough, recalling his own past, that she was scented with the fragrances of Europe and perhaps of love. That Sunday morning he drove her to a restaurant, and he was so happy to see her that, though he had to get up early the next day, he'd inaugurated a series of visits to different restaurants and bars around town. By the time they made their way to his bungalow, the world, for both of them, seemed aglow with the sweet promise of the future. On his back patio he opened a bottle of Spanish brandy and there they enjoyed the nearly Persian pleasures of the afternoon, a happy time, during which Margarita related that she was newly in love.

During her travels in Spain, and after a happy week along the south coast, she boarded a train to Valencia to see the orange groves outside that city, and there, while dining in a little restaurant, she met Luis, the owner of an automobile mechanic shop in Havana, who had been visiting relatives in Andalusia and was heading north to Barcelona. Watching her dine in a restaurant, he was amused by her befuddlement over the outrageous anatomy of a pomegranate that she ordered as dessert, smiling and saying to her in Spanish, "You mustn't eat the seeds, just the soft flesh." With a pomegranate of his own, he'd demonstrated the correct manner in which to eat that fruit, and soon enough he joined her at her table.

The night Margarita recounted to her brother the story of

her romance, she asked Emilio about his life, commenting as-
tutely that whenever she had seen him back East he always
seemed preoccupied.

"Work, that's what I mainly do," he said to her. "People
think making pictures is easy, but, really, you have to put up with
so much . . . Seven or eight takes. If that goes well, then four
different angles of each shot . . . and, under the hot lamps, you
have to look as if it's the most natural thing in the world."

"But," she asked, "isn't it a pleasure?"

"No, it's a living."

(He said this, longing for his joyous apprenticeship days
performing onstage.)

A long silence.

"Well, cheers," she had said. "Or, as they say in Spain,
Salud!"

And they toasted each other.

Curious about her brother, and with her own head filled
with so many happy sentiments, she could not help returning to
the subject of love. She started to chain-smoke Chesterfields and
asked him: "Do you have someone now? Someone to take care
of you?"

"No."

"Well, is there anyone who interests you?"

"No."

She blew a plume of smoke toward a cluster of roses, some
wilting, some alert and blossoming.

"But don't you think, *mi vida*, that it would be a good thing?"

Just then he threw a fit, repeating, "No, no, no!" and he
went to take a shower, leaving Margarita alone. She sat there,
sipping at her brandy, thinking about her years of marriage to
Lester Thompson, that loneliness—vivid, enchanting, and
excruciating—coming back to her in a moment, and she had
laughed to herself.

*

She'd also remember her brother's little surprise. Early one
day he asked her if she would mind if a friend joined them later

for dinner. She was to fly back home the next day and he had decided that they would celebrate her last night with dinner at Ciro's. She was sitting on his couch in a flowery dress, reading a newspaper, when her brother's friend, Mr. Flynn, followed him into the living room. Her brother, beside himself with wicked glee, said, "Errol, may I present you to my sister Margarita."

"My God, but you're a beautiful lady." Flynn, dapper in a white suit and cream-colored shoes, bowed and kissed her hand.

In Ciro's they dined and drank champagne, and when the orchestra played a sweet version of Cole Porter's "Night and Day," she and Mr. Flynn stepped onto the floor and the touching of their faces—for Mr. Flynn liked to dance close—induced in her a kind of splendid revelry, a thrill akin to the feelings she'd had when years before she had first laid eyes on the handsome aviator. She sighed, for there she was in the arms of a once-great movie star who in youth had been so devastatingly handsome that women fainted when he entered a room. But this Flynn was aged, his face heavier, more mature and engagingly rugged. What struck her most about him, however, was his sadness, an intense feeling of disappointment that he communicated through his alcohol-bleary eyes. And although she would never forget her delight in the man, she felt pity for him. There was a kind of absolute solitude about Flynn; he had the air of a man cut off from the world, and she'd wondered, watching Flynn and her brother, Emilio, if the lives of such men were, for all their fame, destined to be unhappy.

*

It was also in 1954 that Gloria, the youngest of the fourteen sisters, arrived on vacation with Marta and Carmen, the sisters loving not only the climate of California but the Hollywood life of their brother. They visited the set of his second Lance Stewart film, *Desperation*, and joined him at cocktail parties, where the sight of movie stars made them giddy. They enjoyed the seaside communities of Venice Beach and Santa Monica, and were so elated at seeing something new of the world that in a short time Carmen and Marta had begun to entertain the idea of moving out there.

During the time when their brother was at the studio, they were perfectly happy to drive off sightseeing in their brother's convertible—he owned two automobiles—happy in the mornings as they'd pack a bag with their bathing suits and suntan lotion and sunglasses and sandwiches and wine, for a day at the beach. Accompanying them on these outings, Gloria, who thought the point of the visit was to see her brother, felt cheated by his absence. And while Marta and Carmen romped in the surf, dashing into the powerful California waves, fascinated by the colorful cabanas and the atmosphere of health and happiness of the Californians, Gloria would sit under a beach umbrella—for she thought herself allergic to sunlight—morosely passing the time with movie and women's-interest magazines, waiting for the day to end, so they could return to their brother's house.

He'd come back about seven in the evening, exhausted from the day's shoot and ever preoccupied with the direction of his career, but he was still their movie-star brother and happily took them around. And on nights when they stayed in, he was content to enjoy a simple meal with them. He had been pleased to see that his sister Gloria, about whom he sometimes worried, seemed changed, more confident and mature. She was still attentive toward him and there were times, when crossing the room, that he was aware that she was watching him with more than sisterly fondness. At other times, when she'd be sitting on the couch and a sadness would come over her, and he would ask, "Gloria, is everything all right with you?" she'd answer simply, "Yes."

Used to her life in Manhattan without him, she left her job in the doll factory to work in the bookkeeping department of Macy's, which in those days offered its customers and employees many amenities. A guard would open a door for her when she'd arrive at eight-thirty each morning, and at Christmastime, she told her brother, the store would give her a bonus of a week's salary and a turkey and a basket of candies and jams, all wrapped up in crinkly paper. But when she told him that she was happy there, her voice quavered. She had been delighted by the idea of seeing him again, of spending ten days in his company, but promised herself to maintain a proper and sisterly distance; still, there was much that she wanted to tell him.

She was then thirty-one and quite womanly. It had surprised him to notice that his frail and delicate sister had in the last few years filled out, become more buxom. As he sat up one night alone in the living room memorizing some pages of script, she startled him. She was on her way to the kitchen for a glass of ice water, wearing only a slip, her dark hair, which she'd often wear in a matronly bun, unraveled, so that it hung down over her shoulders. She appeared to be naked under her slip, for he could make out the shadow of her pubic mound and the pronounced roundness of her breasts, the darkness of her nipples, and her bottom quivering under the sheeny fabric. She yawned casually and returning through the room had said, "I'm sorry if I've disturbed you, brother."

"Not at all."

She then made her way back to the guest room, as if it were the most natural thing in the world for a man's sister to display herself. In fact, she had been sitting up, unable to sleep, fully aware that her brother was in the living room, and though it was true she was thirsty, before leaving the room she removed her brassiere and panties. She'd wanted him to see her, as if to say, "Look how your sister has become healthier without you." She did not think about him in the other way that used to plague her many a night over the years, when she would remember how they had bathed together and slept snuggled in the same bed, so much so that she would feel a physical queasiness. Still, she would often take the cache of letters that he had written to her during the war and in his first years in California, filled with affection, and reread the pages until she felt she was full of the spirit of her brother. And whenever one of his movies opened in New York, or when she went home to Cobbleton and they went to the Jewel Box, she would sit watching his movies three and four times, and retiring to her bed, she would feel his absence intensely.

On such nights, she would lament her lack of what she would call physical charm and would feel tired of her own demureness and the way dear Mother Nature had made her too sickly for too long, and it was as if, on one of those nights, she had willed her

body into a womanly fullness. Her sister Margarita during a visit
to Cobbleton had noticed this and said, "My goodness, Gloria,
but I do believe you've bloomed." And though she considered it
one of nature's caprices, she sometimes told herself that it had
happened so she could be more attractive to her own brother.

That's what she had wanted to show him that night.

The change was evident enough. One late afternoon around
Christmas the year before, the floor manager of the doll factory,
a brusque and pushy man, invited her into his private office,
where the bosses would gather on Friday evenings for a few
drinks, which he'd pour out of a Four Roses bottle, to unwind
from the week's work. It was a claustrophobic place removed
from the clutter of the factory, with its machines and worktables
and barrels of eyes and doll parts, with four highly placed windows that looked out onto the gray walls of another building.
That evening, when he asked her to join them, even though she
had no taste for whiskey, she, flattered to be included for the
first time in such a gathering, said yes.

After drinks, the bosses decided to leave the building together, locking up as they usually did, and when they reached
the street, the floor manager, Mr. Bruno, a married man, insisted
on walking her to the subway. He had never especially noticed
her before, but that night he asked her, "How about going out
with me sometime?" She had said no and thought that was the
end of it, but for the next few days Mr. Bruno would call her at
home, an edge of secrecy in his voice, asking her again to go out
with him. And when she got back to work the following Monday,
tending to her usual business, he started to ask her into his office.
"Really, Miss O'Brien, I don't understand why you're suddenly
so afraid of me. After all, we've been working together for a long
time, nearly seven years, and you must know me as a gentleman.
I don't want to make anything out of the fact that I'd like to
socialize a little more with you, and I don't like the idea of using
the fact that I'm your boss, but the way you've been so unfriendly
makes me think you don't like me very much, and I don't think
that's very good for employer-employee relations. The fact is, I've
never given you a hard time about all the sick days you've taken

in the past, and I think I've been pretty reasonable about letting you off for your doctor's appointments and such, but to tell the truth, your lack of gratitude has gotten me to think that unless certain things change between you and me, well, your days here are numbered."

And he sat back in his swivel chair, smiling and raising his eyebrows, as if to say, "I mean it." She passed that afternoon knowing just what he wanted, and being a creature of habit and accustomed to that work, she began to fear a change. She was making a hundred dollars a week and taking care of herself, and she had never been penalized for sick days, when she would wake up feeling too ill to make her way to the office. She liked that job. The owners had been generally fair to her, and it was nice to have access to so many dolls—she would take some home on the holidays and give them to the children in her building. But what he wanted her to do was unthinkable, and at three-fifteen in the afternoon she gathered her belongings, emptying out her desk, and tendered her resignation in a note that cited Mr. Bruno for his ungentlemanly behavior. She asked that her week's pay, and the vacation days owed her, the amount of which she had calculated, be sent to her home address, and with that she bid her fellow employees goodbye, bid farewell to the dolls, and made her way out into the new maturity of her life.

Her Love

SHE'D WANTED SO BADLY to tell Emilio about her love affair with a nice man she'd met when she'd gone to work for Macy's, a job she'd taken a month after leaving the factory. She did not like idleness, and while she could have gone back home to Cobbleton, she enjoyed living with Maria, Olga, and Jacqueline. In her new "incarnation," she started to take better care of herself, even picking out sexier dresses and trying out different cosmetics. Part of it was that she had begun to enjoy the way certain gentlemen would tip their hats when she'd walk by, but she also decided

that her infatuation with Emilio was a delusion, that she'd allowed herself to drift too deeply into territories that weren't quite
correct. She still loved him but decided she would be better off
moving on. It was around this time, with her brother far away,
that the idea of a romance began to interest her, and she'd promised herself to become less closed off to men.

One of the men in the store, a fairly prosperous two-and-a-
half-percent-commission salesman in the furniture department,
would make a point of often talking with her in the employees'
lounge. He was from Canarsie, in his mid-thirties, and always
wore a white carnation in his lapel and bright red bow ties. With
a natural and open way about him, and never using pressure, he
was successful with customers, who considered him trustworthy.
He lived with his widowed mother, a powerful woman who still
regarded him as a child and would become inconsolable whenever he'd talk about moving out to find a life of his own. When
he lost his father fifteen years before, his life had become a stormy
affair, his evenings spent at home with his mother in silence, his
heart filled with anger and regret. Little by little he'd confided
all this to Gloria, and slowly, distracted and moved by his plight
and by the way he had admitted so much to her and made her
feel like a special confidante, she allowed herself to think more
and more about him. And there was something else: just seeing
him through the glass partitions of the payroll office, standing in
the lines of employees on payday, would make her happy. And
when they sat together at lunchtime, or went strolling along the
congested streets, his physical proximity made her feel as if she
wanted to go off into a private place and kiss him.

This young man, whose name was Arnold, helped her to
stop thinking about her brother. Slowly, and at a cost to his life
at home, he would sometimes date her after work. They would
take in a movie or go to a nice restaurant, he always apologetic,
as he was intent on getting back to Canarsie at a respectable
hour. ("Otherwise, Gloria, my mother'll have one of her fits.")
Meeting always in public places, they rarely ever kissed, and
when they did, it was a fumbling, awkward process. He was timid
and shy, and quite possibly even more frightened of a kiss than

she. They had been going out for six months when it occurred
to Gloria that the apartment on West End Avenue would be
empty on the weekend—her sisters Maria, Olga, and Jacqueline
off on a six-day cruise to Bermuda, on a job—and she invited
him to visit her on the Saturday. She was to prepare him lunch
and perhaps afterward they'd head out to a movie. She greeted
him, and as he sat on the couch, hat by his side, she went into
the kitchen to fix him a drink, where she made a sudden decision:
a few minutes later, she entered the living room carrying their
drinks, naked.

"Come on, my darling," she said, and she led him into her
bedroom, with its little shelves of dolls and plastic flowers and
photographs of the family, and he followed her, overwhelmed
and sweating, and there on the bed he, to that day a virgin, helped
her to lose her virginity; and she nearly exhausted him with her
passion, pent up for so long, her body exuberant; Gloria, shy and
demure and a little remote, feeling as if she now possessed one
of the healthiest and most desirable female bodies in the world.

*

Nothing more happened. That night in California when she
had wanted to show off her woman's body to her brother, she
went back to bed slightly surprised at her own boldness and lay
there listening for his footsteps in the living room and hall, as if
on the way to his bedroom he might pause by her doorway and
quietly knock, her fantasy placing him by the bed, where he
would kneel before her and say, "I wanted to say good night,"
and in this fantasy he would spy her breasts through her silk
gown and, parting the top buttons, take one of her nipples into
his mouth. Why she had been thinking these things, she did not
know.

(The milk of her health, her new life, flowing into him.)

In memory she would see her brother, troubled, distracted,
and ever courteous, pacing about with a script in his hand, needing love. When she thought about that, she would remember
how divided she felt, telling herself that in her desire for him
she had been a little crazy. She'd decided that her moodiness

during her visit with Marta and Carmen involved her feelings about missing Arnold from Macy's; but she sometimes appreciated the fact that Arnold, in terms of "manliness," could not begin to touch her in the way that her memories and longing for her brother did. She lay in bed, lifting the hem of her gown up past her navel. She sighed.

For his part, Emilio was busy enough that each day seemed a prelude to the moment when the three beloved sisters would be preparing to leave, when their closets would be emptied of their sundresses, suitcases packed, when he would look about while eating a meal with them and notice Marta's and Carmen's deep tans, and comment one last time how happy he'd been that they had decided to visit him.

Having liked California very much, Marta and Carmen would come back for good in a few years, finding work down near Anaheim.

And Gloria would settle into an on-and-off-again romance with Mr. Arnold of Macy's.

In B Land, 1955

HE'D TAKEN ON THE ROLE of Lance Stewart for the money, nothing else. The character, with his trench coat and colorful speech—"Look at the gams on that dame"—bored him, but he needed work. Despite the success of his first priest movie and the occasional good notice, he was never given a chance to act for a first-rate director, and the B-picture scripts he received— for he was now considered a good B actor—he read with a mixture of pity and contempt both for himself and for the poor writers who'd been forced to sit and produce such material. Not that he always felt dissatisfied, but as he moved from one film to the next, he had the feeling that he was on some kind of forced march, that it was his unpleasant destiny to linger in B land. He tried to test for some really classy movies—he'd played a small part that year in a Gary Cooper Western—and yet, as his days became clouded with work, romantic escapades, and weekend drunks, he sometimes felt that things were hopeless.

Drinking seemed to help for a day or two, and then his darker feelings would come back to haunt him. Sometimes he felt so disempowered that he would move through the tedium of his scenes with total detachment—it would seem that he was inhabiting someone else's body. A feeling that he was leading a strange life came to him so often that he began to long for—and at the same time resent—the days of his youth, when he had luxuriated in the attentions of his sisters, when the world seemed an orderly, harmonious, sometimes raucous place. But hadn't he begun to feel a mounting disappointment with the actor's life?

A kind of shame began to come over him; despite his successes, for he was making a good salary and truly enjoyed some aspects of his profession, he felt the old desire to run off. His romantic dalliances, his earthly joy in bedding down some new and lovely woman, would satisfy him for a time, but he would greet each new, passing love with more and more cynicism and started to feel that his frolicsome partners were part of a disheartening trap. He was so troubled that he consulted with a then-prominent Beverly Hills psychiatrist, Dr. Zeno, who'd listened to his story and, over a series of sessions, discerned that what Emilio was lacking in his life was a "true and fulfilling mature love."

Listening intently, Emilio nodded, gushed appreciation, paid the doctor his heavy fee, and then, leaving Dr. Zeno's majestic office, drove back to his bungalow to sit with his fan mail and drink down a bottle of gin. He'd remembered waking at three in the morning, thirsty and groaning, for his head ached and he would have to get up in a few hours for another day's work. He'd been awakened by the voices he'd heard in a dream—his sisters' voices calling to him as a child, "Emilio! Come here! Emilio, I have something for you!" voices filled with affection, voices beguiling and sirenic, their influence on him confusing but powerful, coming back from the incalculable distance of his past.

*

On Lake Tahoe, away from the heavy lamps and cameras of a movie set, a few months after his sisters Gloria and Marta and Carmen had gone home, Emilio was rowing out into the waters. With four days off from his latest film, he'd flown north with a young actress, taking a room in a lakeside hotel, where they spent most of their time in bed, drinking champagne and dedicated to their mutual pleasure. He made love to her three times one morning. (Her breasts were so full that after they had made love in every other way, she pressed them together so that they nearly had the amplitude of female buttocks. Having covered them with some sort of oil, she played a game: pressing her nipples down as he passed himself through, she would "kiss" him with each.) Then Emilio, needing to be alone, left her in the hotel room, taking a rowboat out into the lake.

Around him and spreading over the waters, many trees and their shadows were reflected. Down below, and as far as he could see, wavery depths, and at the bottom, plants. He'd laughed to himself, for he felt like diving in. Instead, he allowed the rowboat to drift. He leaned back on the bow, musing that in two days he would have to go back and play Lance Stewart, private detective. And for a few brief moments he thought of himself floating across the lake on the kind of fairy-tale vessel that he had once seen in a storybook, a boat shaped like a swan and piloted by a goddess. Pure comfort awaited him on the shore and he felt that the sunlight beating down on his eyes was human, female. The warmth of the water, and the pull of the current on his hand, which he was dangling over the side, possessed a kind of female nature. He fell asleep. The rowboat drifted out toward the edge of the lake, and when he woke up, a wind had started to rock the water. He looked around, trying to discern his future, and could not, for the life of him, determine where he should go.

His First Marriage

HE WOULD MARRY TWICE. His first marriage came about because of a piece of fan mail that he received one day in 1956, a letter from an eighteen-year-old girl who, gushing great love for the actor, had invited him to her forthcoming wedding in a small Montana town. *(". . . I've never written to a movie star before, but I couldn't keep myself from writing to you. I've always loved every single one of your films, some of which I've seen three and four times. But the reason why I'm writing to you is that I am going to marry my old sweetheart, Jack, in September. My mother told me to invite anyone I care to, as long as that person is important to me, and because I've been one of your biggest fans I was wondering if you would be at all interested in attending my wedding. I know that you probably get asked this kind of thing all the time, but nothing would make me, or my family, happier than if you would consent to be a guest. We could put you up at the hotel if you like, or you can stay with my family, although I would understand if you wouldn't want to . . . In any case, I've enclosed a formal invitation for September 12, 1956, and, as I've said, nothing would make me happier than if you could accept. It would be the thrill and honor of my life, and I just want to say that, even if you can't, I will remain your most devoted fan. With sincerest regards, and high hopes, Sally Monroe")*

The letter had arrived in late July, on a day when Emilio was feeling restless. Now and then he'd receive similar requests and ignore them, but fan adulation had of late been tapering off. From the twenty or so letters he received that week, he set that one aside. She had enclosed a high-school graduation photo of herself, from the previous year, and what he saw appealed to him: an innocent and pretty, freckle-faced blonde in blue gown and mortarboard, exuding the kind of small-town purity from which he was now separated. He was making a Tarzan picture at the time and carried that letter about with him for several weeks. Then, on a whim, as he sat around, bored between takes, playing cards with the grips, he decided to accept. Lounging about in his loincloth and his robe, and feeling that his greater acting aspirations were behind him, he'd written a brief note saying that he'd been moved by the invitation, that, though he did not usually do this kind of thing, he, being "touched by her sincerity," would make an exception.

A few weeks later he drove to Sally Monroe's town of Crystal Falls, Montana. He had not minded the long drive and had, in fact, enjoyed the break from his usual routine. Envisioning a grand reception for himself, he imagined all the townspeople lining the sidewalks waiting for him, for Miss Monroe knew that he would arrive sometime on the afternoon of the eleventh. Instead, he found a town so sleepy and deserted that a great gloom came over him, the kind of feeling that would settle on him when, on an impulse, he would succumb to the female influence and, for the hell of it, pick up a woman at a party, even if he did not particularly like her. His delicate and manly ego suffering its first defeat, it occurred to him that perhaps he had made a mistake. As he turned off the main road, looking for the street where Sally Monroe's family lived, he realized that once again he had allowed himself to be taken in by his own desire.

Dressed in a tan suit and wearing a shirt with an open collar and an ascot, he arrived at the Monroe residence, a two-story white clapboard house. Tall, tanned, and radiant before their screen door, he heard much commotion from inside even as his footsteps sounded on the porch. Sally's father opened the door, a pleasant man in his fifties, a lawyer, greeting Emilio, "Well, my goodness, Mr. O'Brien, please do come in."

In the parlor, a radio was playing and a table was set with cold cuts and a bottle of champagne in a bucket, and an arrangement of flowers glowing under a lamp. In a corner, there was a framed photograph of a soldier—he would learn it was Sally's oldest brother, killed in Korea—and a little cabinet with a few medals, a Purple Heart and a Silver Star, and a miniature American flag on a stand. Pictures, too, of more elderly relatives, in oval frames on the wall, the kind of house, he figured in those moments, of one of his typical fans—and it occurred to him that in part he had driven all that way to see how his "most ardent fan" lived.

Then he met Mrs. Monroe, a matronly woman with deep blue eyes—Irish, he imagined—who must have been quite pretty in her youth, and she said, "We're all just so amazed that you would take time out to see us."

Mrs. Monroe called up the stairs, "He's here. Mr. O'Brien is here," and all of a sudden Sally Monroe, beside herself with happiness, came down into the parlor, all dressed up, with ear-rings and makeup, her blond hair in a coif. She gave Emilio Montez O'Brien a peck on his right cheek and, blushing, said, "I can't believe you're really here. Oh, thank you, thank you for coming."

And because she did not know what to do, he took her hand, saying, "It's my pleasure," and kissed her forehead in greeting.

At dinner, in a place called the Mountainside Inn, Emilio passed the evening answering questions about Hollywood stars for Sally's Aunt Ethel and her husband, Herbert, and for her quivering teenage friends. He went through stories about his friendships, which movie stars were nice and who was snooty, rarely speaking about himself. He got through the evening—Sally sitting beside him, and her father across the table—by drinking. Back at the house, they'd opened their bottle of cham-pagne. Everyone else seemed thrilled with one glass, but he drank three, and when that was gone, he went out to his automobile to retrieve a bottle of good, high-priced French brandy for them—or him—to drink. At the restaurant earlier, he'd also con-sumed a heavy sweet wine that was nearly undrinkable, and by the evening's end he was a little drunk. (He'd remember that the groom-to-be, Jack, had shown up with some of his friends to say hello and that he had stood up at the table, ever handsome and earnest, to shake the fellow's hand, saying, "Well, you're very lucky, my friend.")

In the waning hours of the evening, Emilio became quite silent—he did not want to say anything because he was afraid he would betray his condition by slurring his words—entertain-ing many inward thoughts: the house in Cobbleton and the sen-sation of walking into the security of the parlor when all his sisters were there, with their feminine, nurturing presence; or driving up the rocky dirt road to Monte Cassino with Major Strong, and looking out into the distances of Italy, where, with the buzz of cicadas in his head, everything seemed possible; and those days when he had fallen in love with Antonella and his heart beat so rapidly when he passed her house; or cutting back to some party on Barrow Street in New York with actor friends, circa 1947, and remembering that first moment when on a certain

night he had met, by the punch bowl, a pretty actress who was
having her troubles, and that they would sit on the couch talking
quietly about their desire for a life in the theater and in film, and
that later he would blink and find himself suckling her tart red
nipple; or thinking in an instant what his mother, Mariela Montez, and his father, Nelson O'Brien, were doing while he sipped
at his wine, the two very old now and perhaps at the end of their
days, feeling that he should have been a better son—why had
he gone to Crystal Falls and not just flown to Cobbleton?—or
thinking about his sisters and wishing each well and in an instant
reviewing their lives in his mind, all the while looking around
the table, his eyes met with endless smiles.

Mr. Monroe suggested that they put the actor up in the hotel,
but Mrs. Monroe, friendly and motherly, asked that he spend
the night with them. Sally, eyes wide and happy, concurred. "Yes,
stay with us!"

It would be easier, for his automobile with his luggage was
still sitting in front of their porch, and in any case Mr. O'Brien
was tired and would probably dislike the inconvenience of check-
ing into the hotel. And so it was agreed that he should stay with
the family, that night before Sally's wedding. Later they led him
to his room—kept intact from the days when Sally's older brother,
Robert, was alive, with model airplanes hanging from the ceiling
and collections of baseball cards and technical manuals, all still
on the shelves, a narrow, claustrophobic room on whose bed
Emilio Montez O'Brien could finally lay down his tired body.
Mrs. Monroe showed him in and he undressed, looking out
through the window at the darkness of the night in that middle-
of-nowhere Montana town. He was dozing off when, about three
in the morning, there came a rapping at the door.

And there she was, on the eve of her marriage, Miss Sally
Monroe in a nightgown.

"I didn't want to bother you, but I couldn't sleep, thinking
how nice you were to come all the way here from Hollywood for
my wedding. I just wanted to let you know that it means a lot to
me, and if you'll allow me, I just want to give you a thank-you
kiss."

"You shouldn't do that, honey," Emilio found himself saying, but she knelt before his bed, moving her fingers through his wavy hair. "I've dreamed of doing this for a long time," she said and gave him a long tongue-kiss, and he started to caress her breasts through her gown and, loving it, she whispered, "I cannot believe this is happening, with you." They kissed again and Emilio reached around, his hand slipping under her gown and into the terrific heat lingering there beneath lamb-soft small-town girl panties. But she said, "For the life of me, I can't. It feels so good, but I can't." And she went on like that until he grew bored and, aware of the strangeness of the situation, allowed his head to fall back on the pillow, and he said, "Maybe it would be better if you went to sleep."

Then, blushing and ashamed, she left the room.

*

By morning—her father awakening him at the door—Emilio regretted that he had come to this wedding. But he was a gentleman. Forgoing breakfast, he remained in Robert's room, biding his time, and at eleven, as the family prepared to head for the church, he appeared, resplendent in a white silk suit. When he entered the church, his presence in town was widely known, and people whispered and murmured and went over to him to say hello—he, ever cordial, shaking their hands. After the ceremony, they all retired to the reception hall, and that's where Emilio Montez O'Brien got himself into trouble.

Sally Monroe's father made a speech, thanking his guests for coming, and at the end he mentioned the presence of "a certain actor, whom we all know and love . . . an actor whose films have moved us all, Montgomery O'Brien." As the celebrants applauded, Emilio noticed the longing expression of the bride, who would beam at him from time to time—awakening the memory of their brief moment of near-intimacy on her dead brother's bed. He had also become aware of the attentive gaze of one of Sally's friends, a tall and buxom brunette who had been trying to make eye contact with him for much of the afternoon. She was wearing a tight sequinned dress and spent much of the reception with her family and friends at a nearby table, sipping cocktails through a straw, her escort beside her looking a little bored (they were on the verge of breaking up). As the afternoon wore on, and her escort went off to the men's room, she had walked over to Emilio and said, "You are the most gorgeous man I have ever seen in my life and I would do anything to get to know you."

"Really?"

Later, she and her escort argued and the poor fellow left the reception, and as the Crystal Falls Hot Cats began to play a Tommy Dorsey number, she went over to Emilio and asked him to dance. He should have known better, but entertaining the fire chief and his wife with yet another story about Hollywood did not interest him, and so he made use of the opportunity to escape. Still, there was a bluntness about this woman that shocked him. Shortly after he'd learned that her name was Betsy MacFarland, she joined him at his table, saying, "It was my idea that Sally invite you here, and when she told me you would be coming, I nearly died. When you went out to dinner last night, I was supposed to come, but my boyfriend likes to keep me on a leash and wouldn't let me go, and we had such a fight about it that it left me in tears. He wants to get married, and though he's a nice guy, like so many of the men in Crystal Falls he's a bore, and I just know what my life would be like with him. If you want to know the truth, I would brush off a hundred guys like him just to have a moment with someone like you. I've been in love with you ever since I saw you playing that priest, Father Byrne. I sleep with your picture under my pillow and I have collected every single itsy piece about you from the movie magazines and I feel so in love with you that I would do anything for you, do you understand, anything, and even though I know you're beyond me, your life is so impressive I want to be with you, if only for a night."

"Are you propositioning me?"

"I most certainly am."

The revelation that she had been behind the wedding invitation, that Sally Monroe was doing her friend a favor, slightly disheartened him, for he felt touched by Sally's essential purity, even if she had come into the bedroom to kiss him good night. (He supposed that she couldn't resist the idea of having a little treasured memory for her future.) He was used to the ambitions of young actresses, who would attach themselves to him, but (thinking of womanly strength) he had been impressed by Betsy MacFarland's straightforwardness and said, with a slight weariness in his voice, "What do you propose?"

She lifted a Hawaiian paper umbrella from her frothy drink and said, "My family's got a little house about twenty miles from here, a real private place. Why don't you come see me there tomorrow, say at eleven." She told him how to get there and thereafter, so as not to appear conspicuous, left him and rejoined her friends.

Photographers snapped his picture sitting at the table, and he posed with the bride and groom and was interviewed by a reporter from the local newspaper. ("It's not every day that the folks of Crystal Falls see a movie star like you. What brought you out here?") Later, as the party wound down and the bride and groom went off in a '56 Chevrolet with a "Just Married" sign hanging off the trunk, the actor left with his hosts, Mr. and Mrs. Monroe, who drove him back to their house. Sitting with Emilio out on the porch, Mr. Monroe told him: "The house is going to be pretty empty from now on. You know, Mr. O'Brien, we lost our boy, Robert, at Inchon, in Korea." And he looked off into the distance, sadly. "But Sally, she found a good man in Jack—he works for a gasoline distribution company—and I suppose that soon they'll be having kids and those kids will be coming over here on Sunday afternoons, running around the halls and raising hell. Which would be fine with me. Do you have any kids?"

"No, sir, I don't."

"Well, it's a heck of a pain in the neck, I'll tell you, but in the long run it's worth it, bringing life into the world and all that. And it makes for pretty cheery Christmases, most of the time."

"I know the feeling," Emilio said. "I come from a big family. I was the youngest of fifteen children."

"Fifteen?"

"And fourteen of them females."

"Fourteen sisters?" That made Mr. Monroe guffaw. "My Lord, must have been all hell breakin' loose *all* the time, in your house."

"Yeah, I would say it was kind of pleasant and cheerful."

And Emilio went on to describe how life was turning out for his family, with his sisters here and there, and his own feelings of separateness from the world making him unhappy.

"The crazy thing is that when you're an actor, making pictures— Have you ever seen Gloria Swanson in *Sunset Boulevard?*"

Mr. Monroe shook his head.

"A great movie—I'd give my eyeteeth to work with a director like Billy Wilder—you wake up feeling like yourself, whatever that might be, and then an hour later you're becoming someone else. When your daughter invited me to her wedding—"

"It was wonderful that you could come."

"—I was working on a Tarzan movie. You know what it's like to wake up in the morning—I get up at five-thirty on days when I'm working—and come out of a dream that makes you think you're a kid again and it's 1932 and you're moving through the rooms of your childhood and everything seems so real, your family sitting around in the living room, one of your sisters playing the piano, another reading a book, and in the dream you swear that now is back then, but you can't tell if it's a dream from childhood in which you're imagining your future. Do you follow me?"

"Yes."

"And something happens. I have this sister who's a great cook, God bless her, Irene. And whenever berries came into season, Irene would go out into the field behind our house in Pennsylvania and poke around for blueberries and blackberries. She'd spend the afternoon collecting what she could find into a basket, and when she did not have enough, she'd go to the Farmers' Market in town and buy some more, and the next thing you know, she would be in the kitchen baking pies or making jam. In any case, I remember a pot of these berries, which she'd cook up, and she'd call my sister Gloria or me or one of my other sisters over and she'd let us have the pot, and we'd eat up the filling. It was so good that I find myself, years later, tasting it still, the sensations so pure, and then the goddamned alarm goes off and an hour later I'm on a soundstage in a mock-up of African trees, and because it's a low-budget picture, we have to do everything in fast takes. You can't forget for a second that you're not in Africa, and you feel a little stupid, because everything inside you is set aside. We had one scene where I'm playing Tarzan and I leap into a river, and what you see onscreen is Tarzan diving into the Congo, but all I'm really doing is jumping down into a safety net. I remember jumping and thinking about the taste of jam, and for one moment I had the sensation that at the end of this take I would open my eyes and find myself back in the house where I grew up, in 1932."

Mr. Monroe nodded. He did not wish to impose on his famous guest. So he said (stifling a yawn): "Well, it's been great talking with you, Mr. O'Brien. I better get inside here, but before I do, I want to thank you again for coming out to Crystal Falls. I hope it's not been too painful for you."

"No, sir, not at all."

"Just one thing. I noticed that you made the acquaintance of Betsy MacFarland. I don't know what you or she said to each other, but, as I consider myself a friend of yours, I caution you that she's quite a handful."

"How's that?"

"She's beautiful, you know that. And even though she's one of my daughter's best friends, I have to tell you that she's had a dozen boyfriends in the last three years. I don't know much about her private affairs, but I can guarantee you she's a bit of trouble, in my opinion."

"Well, thank you, sir. Good night."

"Call me Bill, please. No formalities here."

"Good night, then, Bill. And thanks again for your advice."

Love

ARRANGING HIS SCHEDULE so as to leave before eleven, Emilio found himself driving out of town along the road that Betsy had mentioned in the instructions she'd written out with a gushing fountain pen on a napkin at the reception. At the juncture of Route 22, he could choose to turn left for the Interstate or right toward Route 17. And just as he thought he would be better off going back to California, he decided to visit her. It took him a while to find the house. He passed through flatlands, eighteen miles of fields thick with hay and wheat and goldenrod, then came to a sign reading "The Falls, 2 miles." He followed that route, the road rising gradually into a locally popular recreation area, where streams and brooks cut through woods, and there was a small lake. As his automobile rose up into the hills, he saw Crystal Falls without knowing it, a rush of water cascading down over a ridge of jutting prehistoric rocks. He drove past that, to level land, where the farms seemed immense and the houses few. He drifted into a memory of a film he had liked very much, *Sons of the Desert*, which starred Stan Laurel and Oliver Hardy, two of his favorite comedians. (He was sitting between his beautiful oldest sister Margarita, perfumy and elegant, and the youngest sister, Gloria, in a print dress, and he was laughing and happy in the knowledge that his other sisters were also there, Gloria, ever so slight, shifting her weight against him whenever the audience laughed.)

He could not help but think that he was heading for a fine mess, but he drove on. The house was situated high on a hill up a driveway that veered into a wood. He had stopped to examine nearly every mailbox along the way, and when he came to the name MacFarland, he paused, wondering if he should turn back. But a great longing prompted him on. When his automobile, a 1954 white Cadillac convertible, turned into the driveway, Betsy was sitting on the porch reading a magazine. As soon as Emilio stepped out of his car, though, a crazy elation came over both of them and he found himself charging up the steps of that house into her arms, and soon enough they were kissing and dropping their clothes on the floor.

What ensued was so scandalous that Emilio, a B-movie star, imagining the carnalities of their meeting in a film, would have censored much of the proceedings. His large penis had never been [censored] and she, open and delighted, had never so cherished [censored], and she lifting her rump [censored] and he trying to make sense of a quivering muscle on the inner side of her thigh, [censored] and she, raising and lowering her head over him in the act of [censored], had never squealed with such delight, his [censored] maleness impressing her, and she had smeared baby oil over his body and declared, [Censored], rolling up the sheets afterward . . .

They had been making love for nearly two days when Betsy, blunt as ever, asked Emilio, "Why don't we go to California and get married?" And he, drunk for two days and elated with her body, said, "Never thought I would, but for you—yes."

*

During the court proceedings four months later, Betsy MacFarland's lawyer asked Emilio Montez O'Brien if he considered certain sexual acts normal. And he named them.

"I do, sir."

"And will you admit that you participated in these acts on a fairly regular basis?"

"No, sir, I did not."

"And did you, Mr. Montez O'Brien, ever consider the discomfort of your wife on those occasions while performing certain hideous acts?" (A voice saying "Objection," the judge instructing the jury to strike the word "hideous" from their memory.)

"And were you aware that your bride was only nineteen years old at the time of your elopement?"

"No, I thought she was twenty-two, maybe twenty-three years of age. That's what she said on the license."

"Why did you marry her in the first place?"

"Because I was drunk."

"I see. But once you married this young lady, the former
Betsy MacFarland, you saw that marriage as giving you the right
to do whatever you felt like doing."

"No, sir, I did not."

"Will you deny that you would often force her to bed, as she
has so sworn in her affidavit?"

"No, sir, I thought that she loved me. That's what she always
said."

"And you loved her?"

"Yes, sir, I believed so."

"May I then ask: If you loved your wife so much, putting
aside the cruelties you subjected her to in the bedroom, why were
you seen leaving the Pacific Beach Motel on three different occasions in the company of a young woman whose name, correct
me if I'm wrong, is Mildred Miles. Do you deny that you were
having a love affair while your good wife remained at home
waiting for you?"

"No, sir, I do not. We were working on a picture, and when
you spend so much time together, a kind of bond forms
and—"

"These girls are easy picking, yes?"

"I didn't say that."

The trial went on and on, the details of Mr. Montgomery
O'Brien's personal habits making all the Hollywood newspapers,
the worst calling him a Gigolo Movie Star, unfaithful husband,
and "bedroom deviant," the publicity harmful and intrusive and
nearly as painful as losing the case, which wiped out his savings
and left his wife, Betsy MacFarland, with quite a favorable ali-
mony settlement. Perhaps she had, all along, entertained such
an eventuality.

At the time of their marriage, he hadn't thought about the
potential for disaster. Enchanted by her carnality and her small-
town straightforwardness, he wanted to start life over with her.
His friends and family had been astounded by the suddenness
of his decision. ("And not even married in church!" his shocked
mother lamented.) It didn't matter; the sisters never got the
chance to meet her, settling instead for a few photographs of

Betsy that he'd taken of her in a two-piece bathing suit by the
beach, the consensus among them being that, whatever his reasons, he must have been in love. And though he kept telling
himself it was love, after a few months he and his bride were at
odds, bickering about the littlest things. After the initial flush of
their love, the tedium of being an actor's wife began to weigh
heavily on her; and when her husband came home after work,
she was always ready to go out. And he would take her out,
though after a while he started to feel weary of this. They would
pass many a night sitting next to each other in some fancy club
without saying a word. Soon their only communication took place
in the privacy of the bedroom—though they would sometimes
spend the night in a Santa Monica hotel, these last efforts at
romance often tense. Then, like a fellow in a tabloid story, he
started a little love affair with an actress, and like a tabloid wife,
she hired a private investigator to tail him at night, and armed
with evidence, she found herself a lawyer and a few eager Hollywood reporters to relate, though without any basis, her life as
a "battered sex-slave wife," a sweet small-town girl who left a
happy life in Montana to run off with a movie star who promised
her the world but gave her nothing but pain.

The worst of it was that in the end, after losing everything,
he felt like a marked man. It troubled him that news of the trial
and its seamy details would reach the family (as it did), and
though he wanted to head home to seek consolation and a little
privacy in the company of his sisters, the experience left him
numb with shame.

An Odd Dream, 1957

WITH AN UNFAVORABLE public image, he went into a kind of
seclusion. Scripts still came his way, mainly for horror films, low-
budget nuclear-age stories that name actors would not touch and
which he, having his pride, also turned down. For months after
his much-publicized divorce, reporters would skulk around in

his front yard and hound him like cheap gumshoes in the evenings when he drove to one of the big hotels to have a quiet
dinner by himself. He did not feel like dating and on many a
day could not keep down his food, so unraveled were his nerves.
Early one Sunday morning, with birds twittering in the rose-
bushes of his yard, he awakened from a dream in which he was
walking along a road when suddenly the sky, thick with clouds,
sent a torrent of fish falling down all around him. He did not
know what this meant, but it so unsettled him that he got out of
bed and poured himself a glass of orange juice and vodka in the
kitchen, and then another, a man walking about his living room
in a pair of striped pajamas, wondering what to do with himself.
He'd decided, feeling nostalgic for his youth, when he would
head to town with his sisters to Mass, that he would go to church.

A reporter had followed him, and as he left the service, a
photographer took his picture walking down the steps—that shot
appearing in the late edition of one of the local papers, with a
caption reading: "The Contrite Montgomery O'Brien leaving the
11 a.m. Mass at St. Agnes."

During the peace of the service he remembered how going
to church had once been a happy act, when everyone in the world
had seemed good, and in Cobbleton he and his sisters would go
to the ice-cream parlor after church, clean and sparkling and
sinless, to have their malteds and cones and to watch passersby
through the window. He'd experience something of that feeling
while making the Father Byrne pictures, in which he looked
devout and pious in priestly garb. Of all the parts he had played
in the past eight years, he was lauded most for his portrayal of
the priest. But now he seemed to have slipped into the opposite
role, the villainous husband who would be punished simply for
being a man.

He decided to avoid people, at least for a time. Even when
a friend like Mr. Flynn, with his own share of troubles, called
to offer condolences and to invite him out with the gang, Emilio
turned him down.

Then his sisters called him, the telephone ringing many
times a day. At first he was polite, recounting to Margarita, for

example, the travails of his heart. "You know me, sister. I can put up with just about anything, but this business makes me crawl out of my skin. I guess I'm just not lucky in some things, and I may as well get used to being alone."

"That's not so," she said. "Don't even think that, and always remember we all love you."

She'd urge him to visit the family in Cobbleton, but he always made an excuse—auditions, the possibility of a role, and exhaustion (but he was really just ashamed). Each of those calls ended the same way, with Emilio feeling worse than before, his manner and tone more severe, his patience, even with his beloved sisters, wearing thin.

As for work, he got only one offer that interested him—from, of all places, Italy, where his notoriety put him in the company of a long line of Italian ministers involved in scandalous affairs. It was an offer to play an American businessman on holiday in Rome, and though he had corresponded with the producer and said he'd do it, the project folded when the film company could not raise the funds.

Eventually he decided that just hanging around his bungalow—at least he'd gotten to keep that—would be disastrous, for in his solitude he tended to rely more than ever on drink.

North to Alaska

ONE DAY, he got into his automobile and drove to Seattle, then Vancouver, winding his way north to Alaska, where, enjoying his anonymity—Emilio grew a beard and was going by the name of E. M. O'Brien—he stayed for five months, earning a good worker's wage as a member of the crew of an oil rig and much relishing his contact with the ordinary people of the world, with whom he had lost touch. There he made the acquaintance of another young woman, named Jessica Brooks, who was neither an actress nor a small-town girl but an adventurous dame who had traveled out

to Alaska from Minnesota to open up a restaurant for the local
workers. And there, during his meals with his fellow derrick
workers, he would find himself drawn to her. She was a pretty
blonde, kept her hair in pigtails, liked to wear flowery dresses,
and had a beaming and sunny nature. But what struck him was
that she reminded him of his oldest sister, Margarita, not so much
in her looks—it took him a while to figure it out—but because
she was bookish and tried to stay informed about the world. And
now and then, when things were slow on his days off, on a Saturday afternoon, and most of the men were in the saloon starting
to drink their way through the weekend, he would wander over
to her place to use the pay phone to call East (for he always
feared that some calamity might happen, requiring his presence).
And more often than not, she would be off at some corner table,
with a gathering of children around her, reading aloud from a
book. He had been touched by this and by the shelf of books that
she kept behind her register and on shelves in her office foyer.
One day, he asked her how she had gotten into the habit of
reading to the children, and she told him, "I was a schoolteacher
for a few years before coming out here, and I guess old habits
stick."

With women scarce in those parts and with so many single
men looking for ways to spend their time and money, she was
always being asked out, some of the fellows working up the nerve
after an afternoon in the saloon, others leaning by the register
as she counted out their change from a dinner bill. Emilio, content to sit quietly in the corner sipping coffee and reading a
newspaper, maintained his distance, as in a film of that period.
This, and the fact that he was the only man to ask her why she
read to the children, had piqued her interest, and one Saturday
afternoon after he called Cobbleton and started on his way back
to the boardinghouse, she called out to him: "Mr. O'Brien, I'm
taking the night off and was wondering if you would be interested
in going over to the church hall with me this evening. They're
showing a couple of movies, and, well, I haven't seen one in a
long time. Would you like to join me?"

He sat with a raucous crew in the restaurant until about

seven-thirty. She left the running of the place to her waitresses, languorously bathed and got dressed up, meeting Emilio at quarter to eight in front of the church. A crowd of townspeople had gathered there, for there was not much else to do—there was a general store, a gas station, a saloon, and two restaurants along a broad strip of boardinghouses and residences—the night crisp, the sky lit with stars, mountains looming in the distance. The Protestant minister greeted everyone as they came into the church hall, piously nodding and genuinely delighted with himself for having arranged, through connections in Juneau, for the equipment and the films. Jessica Brooks and Emilio found seats on folding chairs toward the back.

First for the children, as Emilio's father did in the Jewel Box Movie House, the minister, working the projector, showed two cartoons, a Mickey Mouse and a Donald Duck, whose bright, happy colors brought a cry of glee from the children. Then, as he switched reels for the main features, Emilio and Jessica fell into conversation.

Frankly curious about him, she asked: "And where are you from?"

And he tried to tell his story without alluding to his more recent past.

"Well, I ask you," she said, "because you strike me as a little different from the rest of the fellows around here. I mean to say, you have a refinement about you that I haven't seen in a long, long time."

What could he say to that but "And you do, as well."

By then the lights were brought down, and as a roll of drums sounded, Emilio, resting back in his seat, pressed his hand to his brow and could not believe that, of all the films in the world, the minister had gotten hold of *Tarzan in the Land of No Return*, a film which he not only considered one of his worst but whose showing that night seemed likely to undo his disguise. As bad as he thought the film, however, the stock African footage in blazing color and the central plot of Tarzan rescuing a princess from a hidden city seemed to satisfy the audience. And even he admitted that, while he had not done much in the way of acting for the film, he looked quite spectacular (he'd put himself through a rigorous month of exercise in preparation). He wondered if Jessica noticed a resemblance between Tarzan and himself, but she said nothing about it at the film's end.

They stayed to watch a quite funny 1950 James Stewart movie, *The Jackpot*, but halfway through, Jessica leaned over and whispered, "I'm feeling a little tired. Do you mind if we go?"

He walked her back to the restaurant, where she kept a small second-floor apartment, and it was then, with a brisk wind blowing, that she asked, "That was you, wasn't it?"

"What are you talking about?"

"You're the actor fellow who played Tarzan."

"You're imagining things."

"I don't think so." She looked in his eyes. "They're the same. You're him, I know it, even with that beard and your heavy clothes. Which is fine with me—but what on earth are you doing here?"

When he did not answer, she said, "I want to hear this, sir. Come inside for a beer."

She opened the restaurant door and put on the radio and they sat talking and drinking beer until three in the morning.

*

In the last two months that he remained in Alaska, they were to spend many such evenings talking. She found out about his debacle, the source of his recent woes, but it did not make any difference to her. She saw him with the eyes of a practical, good-hearted woman who had once taught Sunday school and, like his mother and all his sisters, truly believed that there was a God in heaven. No matter how often he said to her, as they stood on the brink of a serious romance, "I feel like poison these days," she counseled him that he was only human. "Everyone in the world has bad breaks. And who knows, maybe these things happened so we could meet."

They were serene, resisting somehow the temptations of comforting each other in bed on the chillier nights. He discovered, working on the platforms on the open sea, that as the season

grew colder the elbow joint of his arm, damaged in Italy during
the war, would begin to ache—something about the way the joint
healed, a doctor once told him. But he was determined not to
fall easily in love again, and though they would sometimes spend
hours kissing on her parlor couch and a sort of delirium would
come over him, he would not take it any further. But he looked
forward to seeing her, even if just to sit nearby while she read
to the children, and there were days when they would embrace
endlessly, losing themselves in each other during those simple
moments of wordless contact. Her influence was good for him,
and instead of waking up in the mornings and feeling he was
poison, he came to believe he possessed a good heart, after all.

Like a St. Augustine, he realized that vanity had driven him
in his affairs with women, his history with them suddenly
unimportant.

His time in Alaska was nearly over. The oil company would
be closing down the works for the winter and he had been let
go. By then, he had started to think again about getting away,
not because he did not care about Jessica, but because he wanted
to know if his emotions were true.

She liked to go to church with him, and even though he
grew fond of the kindly words the preacher said, he went only
because they would sit together, that was all. (Like his mother,
he found Protestant services vaguely disappointing.)

On the last Sunday of his life in Alaska, he had gotten up
and shaved the woolly beard that he had grown in his time there,
a few scant traces of gray in its weave, and when he met her that
morning, she had cried out, "My God, you look ten years
younger!"

They went off to the service and later spent the afternoon
cross-country skiing, for the ground was covered with snow, the
exercise warming their loins. That night, he presented her with
a watch that he'd ordered from Anchorage, and she gave him a
Bible inscribed "For my love."

*

In Seattle, two days later, he happened by a saloon, and it
occurred to him that he had not been drunk in five months. At

a nearby table was a contingent of rather pious-looking fellows, sweet-natured young men, laughing loudly and oh so joyfully drunk—but they lacked the gruffness of bar drunkards. Emilio finished a bowl of soup and asked, "What are you fellows celebrating?"

One of the young men said, "We're monks sending our friend Brother Joseph here off to his new life."

Another voice: "Yes, he's leaving us Benedictines, traitor that he is, to become a Trappist!" And they roared. .

"Come and join us," said another, and Emilio, with nothing better to do, pulled his chair over and listened to the stories of the monks and their cloistered lives. ("If our superior knew we were here reveling, oh, my God!")

"The thing, my friend," said one of the Benedictines, "is that in God's Kingdom there are levels of devotion and discipline, and within His Kingdom we Benedictines can't match the discipline of the Trappists, but Brother Joseph here"—he was a red-cheeked fellow of about thirty, with a righteous but extremely drunk air about him—"has decided to pursue such a level of discipline that he will certainly one day ascend to the highest realm of heaven."

"Not so, not so," said Joseph. And he leaned close to Emilio to convey the reason for his decision. "I was on a religious retreat, up on a mountain. No one was around and I heard, after three days of solitude, a voice whispering to me, 'Come closer into my fold.' And I realized I had heard the voice of God."

And he blinked and nodded and lurched back into his seat, and another monk mischievously conveyed the essence of what his life would be: "So our good brother must keep a vow of silence, except for two days of the year—Christmas and Easter —and even then, such earthly pleasures as the drinking of a bottle of beer will come once on each of those days, and that's why"—and they all laughed—"we're here filling the good brother with enough beer to last him for one hundred years!"

Indeed, it was so. There were some twenty empty bottles on his table, and Emilio said, getting up, "Well, I wish you the best of luck, my friend."

And he bought them a round of drinks and later that night,

as he rested in bed in a hotel near the harbor, he felt intrigued by the combination of memories (two among many)—his friend from Alaska, Jessica, telling him, "I feel you are a good man, no matter what anyone else has said," and the simple image of a monk high on a mountaintop hearing the whispering voice of God.

With Errol Flynn

HIS RETURN TO Los Angeles was met with a bit of luck. Delighted to hear from him again, his agent had gotten him a few weeks on a film in which he played a courtier in the epoch of Elizabeth I. By that time the press no longer hounded him. And the studio people, if not the public, seemed to have forgiven him his unsavory divorce. He was happy to be working on a new film, but afterward there were few worthwhile offers and for the first time in years he began to think of a return East or back up north to Alaska. Writing letters to Jessica, he'd receive her loving answers with joy, and after a time he thought to bring her down to California to join him and the uncertainty of his life.

Work was slack, however, so when in the June of 1958 his chum Errol Flynn offered him a part in a film, Emilio was most interested.

"I've got this picture planned, I think we'll call it *Cuban Rebel Girls*, or something like that. I've had my eye on what's going on down there, have you?"

"Well, a bit. I've got a sister who lives there, but I haven't always kept track of things."

"Your loss, my friend. See, in Cuba," Flynn said, "there's been an uprising taking place over many years. It goes back a long time, and the latest hero, if I can call him that, is a fellow named Fidel Castro. Now, I've read up on all this stuff. One of their biggest heroes was this black fellow named Maceo, Antonio Maceo, who was once called the Bronze Titan. That was in the old days, when the Cubans—that is, the descendants of the original Spanish settlers, with some Negroes—were trying to throw off the yoke of Spain, back around the turn of the century." Flynn laughed. "And they'd been having these piddling wars for years, since about 1868, the whole thing coming to a froth in 1898, when you Americans with your Teddy Roosevelt sailed down there, taking the spoils."

"My father was there."

"Was he? Even so, my friend, things have boiled with discontent since then, and now there's this fellow, an insurrectionist, who's giving the current government a hell of a run for their money."

"I've heard as much from my sister."

"So I've written a script about the whole dilly, and I've got a little money and I thought of making this picture about some Americans who get involved in the bloody thing. Can't go into more details, chum, but I promise you the script is all the way there. I wrote it myself and I've got a good part for you. Are you interested?"

Back in Cuba, 1958

THE SHOOT, filmed largely in the Florida Keys, with some location work planned later in Cuba, was a fiasco. Emilio's role, that of a demolitions expert from the.Deep South, ended up on the cutting-room floor. Mr. Flynn's companion at that time, Beverly Aadland, a seventeen-year-old beauty, played an American beautician determined to help the Cuban insurrection. Unfortunately, in Emilio's opinion, she did not know very much about acting, and the script was so bad that, even though Flynn, whom he admired, had asked him to stay on, Emilio Montez O'Brien jumped ship.

And there he was, in the Florida Keys, so, after a few days' rest, he decided to visit his second-oldest sister in Santiago de Cuba. He called her from a Havana hotel and took a train east from the city—no gunshots which signaled revolution, though the train would stop for two hours at a time, on its chugging route, for no apparent reason, perhaps military personnel searching the cars for suspicious-looking passengers. When he finally arrived at Santiago's central station, he whiffed an atmosphere of seaside and bakeries that seemed vaguely familiar from the time of his youth when he had visited that city in 1932.

He had not seen Isabel since he was a boy of seven, and remembered her as an immense and sweet, matronly Irish-looking blonde, but the woman who greeted him on the platform, covering his face with kisses and saying, "Ay, my brother, my brother," was a whorl of flesh, and with her graying hair in a bun and her tropical-patterned dress, she seemed to have turned into an almost grandmotherly Cuban. Walking with him up the steep hills to the old family house on Victoriana de Avila, she seemed to know everyone—all the shopkeepers, the fruit sellers, the lottery venders, and the ladies leaning out their windows, chatting happily with them, saying, "This is my brother from America."

She had three children: two boys, one in Havana working as an attorney and another in Georgia studying engineering, and a daughter of fifteen, a lean and pretty brunette with her mother's blue eyes, whom she introduced saying, "Luisa, kiss your uncle hello."

And there was his brother-in-law, the pharmacist, Antonio Valdez, now retired but famous in the family for having rescued Isabel from an old maid's life. He came shuffling into the parlor, fresh from an early-afternoon nap, tall, heavy, and bald, his intellectual eyes growing wide. And he embraced Emilio. "Welcome, my boy."

He felt relieved to hear the pharmacist speak quite good English, for Emilio, as they knew, did not speak Spanish, and it had impressed him that even their daughter, though not as conversant in English as her mother and father, knew enough to carry on a rudimentary conversation and to ask her movie-star uncle if he had ever met the actor James Dean, whose picture she kept on her wall. And not minding the question from his niece, he had lied: "Oh yes, he's a very nice fellow."

They'd eaten, that day, a large and heavy meal consisting

of dishes that actors would do best to avoid, his arrival marked by a roast crispy-skinned piglet and rice and beans, and they had talked afterward out on the rear patio.

"This, Mr. Movie Star brother whom I love, is the house where our mother once lived. This is Victoriana de Avila Street. Most everyone who lived here has died. Do you remember your aunts from the time you visited?"

He shook his head.

"Or their husbands?"

"No."

"Surely you must remember them from the time you were little and they would take you out for walks."

He thought hard. "I remember this garden, where I would play."

"Oh Lord, don't you remember anything else?"

"Yes, the walks with you and Margarita."

But he also remembered that the little room just off the patio, with a rattan couch and flowery pillows and a vague scent of eucalyptus, was where he would sometimes nap; and that one of the bedrooms off the parlor was where his grandfather had died. And his mother telling him, while they were out on that patio, that she had spent many hours of her courtship with his father, around the turn of the century, sitting on these very same sinuous wrought-iron, plump-cushioned chairs. All this amounted to a vague connection with the place, this house in a provincial capital in Cuba, a country he hardly knew about except from some reminiscences of his father's about his days there during the Spanish-American War, or from his mother's encomia about the good household in which she had been raised, and articles about the Cuban Revolution which more often than not he would skip. And for a moment he wondered what his life would have been like if, instead of returning with his bride to the States, his father, Nelson, had decided to remain, making Cuba instead of America his new country. No doubt he would have looked very much the same, but his head would have been filled with Spanish perhaps and his demeanor and his heart might have been different, for he noticed an open emotionality to the people.

Isabel herself had changed, becoming more Cuban than her

sisters in the States, and proud of it, for she told her brother, "I love this place and the people here. They have brought me much happiness."

He would take walks with his brother-in-law after meals, and that kindly man, ever on the lookout for subjects of common interest, was delighted when Emilio brought up boxing. "Have you seen Sugar Ray Robinson in the ring?" Emilio nodded. "Yes, once in New York." This afforded his brother-in-law, Antonio, the opportunity to go into his knowledge of Cuban boxing, mentioning Martin Perez and Paquito Miró, Ramón Cabrera, and other fighters whom Emilio had never heard of before, fighters who were a part of his brother-in-law's happy memories of being a young man, when he would travel all the way to Havana to see the fights in the Arena Colón and at the Cuban Lawn Tennis Club.

Antonio considered himself something of an amateur sociologist and could easily slip into interminable lists of great Cuban singers, radio personalities—which actors performed in soap operas on the radio and which of those shows were the most popular—and ballet dancers, classical musicians, composers, dance bands, actors and television performers, and poets and novelists and playwrights and baseball players. And then he would launch into Cuban history, detailing the great men who helped make it, such as the Cuban general Calixto García, a hero in the war against the Spaniards, a man who survived a gunshot wound to the head and wore a cotton plug in the scar, so that it would not coo like a bird in the wind. With few exceptions, Emilio had never heard of any of them, but as they walked along, it was as if his brother-in-law was intent on impressing on Emilio the fact that Cuba was thick with culture and art, and that it should be a source of pride for him that his mother was Cuban.

As to the current political situation, with Castro fighting Batista's men in the hills, he would shrug. "Whatever happens," he told Emilio, "we will find a way to carry on."

Emilio would go wandering through the streets of Santiago, the same way he used to roam about the city of Naples, and on the way he would wander through the workings of his own heart, hearing the voices around him and imagining how, perhaps years before, his father, an Irishman, once also heard foreign voices around him and at a certain moment, with tripod and camera in his arms during a hike up the steep hills of the city, he'd been enticed to stay and had pursued his destiny of meeting a Cuban woman named Mariela Montez. And years later his movie-actor son would have the privilege of standing by a stone wall looking out, pensive and filled with wonder, over the splendid harbor of the city.

New York–Cobbleton, 1958

ON HIS WAY BACK TO California, when Emilio stopped off in New York, his sisters, in their usual way, welcomed him. He was relaxed and dapper, spending a happy week stepping out with them to make the rounds, to see Broadway shows and plays, and to return, with his sister Gloria by his side, to his old haunts, Greenwich Village and theater-district pubs and restaurants, where he encountered friends from his New York years: stage actors in their ever-struggling incarnations as waiters and bartenders, some successful and prosperous in the new medium of television, or now the stars of successful shows; others, defeated and anxious, weighing on his heart. And he came across ex-lovers, who, after so much time—more than ten years—remembered their liaisons with sweetness, for now they were passing beyond their youth, and life for many of them had crossed the threshold of early promise. At thirty-three he felt the most admiration for the character actors, like his friend Thurston Gould, who after years of struggle had finally become well enough known among producers and casting directors to be earning a modest but steady living. And those who encountered Emilio Montez O'Brien were newly touched by how a kind of serenity had come over him, for in those days, when he thought about the future, he was feeling optimistic again. With luck, he would make a few good films, maybe even get a part in a television

program like *Playhouse 90*, and he even began to consider a
return to the stage, as he always enjoyed the heartbreaking conviviality of an acting company, with its myriad intrigues, romances, and camaraderie.

At the same time, while he considered these possibilities, he
felt his heart being pulled northwest again to Alaska—for not an
hour passed that he did not think about Jessica. But before heading home to California, he had decided to visit his family in
Cobbleton first.

*

His father, Nelson O'Brien, having entered a senatorial old
age, was enjoying a contemplative and more or less solitary retirement in Cobbleton. Though Nelson O'Brien, tottering about
in the field, would still attempt to take pictures, he'd long ago
closed his photography practice, and a few years back, when his
family lost interest in the movie house, freed himself of the Jewel
Box, which had seen better days, selling the building to a young
businessman who owned a drive-in near Quarryville. In the first
days of that new life, he spent many hours in his shed, organizing
the numerous photographs he had taken during his lifetime into
groupings for posterity (Cuba, 1898–1902; The Family, 1902–
1935; Farm life, Pennsylvania, 1902–1940). Slowly he'd become,
or so it seemed, indifferent to the life around him. Busy in his
musings, he left family affairs to Mariela, for whom the telephone
had become one of the great amenities of existence.

There were nearly weightless movements within the house
at that time, his mother and father shuffling about in pajamas
and day dress, going about their daily business with the bewildered acceptance of people who have managed to live so long—
by 1958, his father would be eighty, his mother seventy-four.
With the exception of Margarita, who would sometimes stay with
them (she had a little apartment of her own in town), they were
often by themselves during the week, alone until the happy time
of Sunday when the sisters would swoop down to visit them.
Irene would bring her family, and Patricia, with two of her children and her hayseed husband, would come for dinner, and

during an afternoon the house would be full again and bursting
with life, as it had once been.

Carmen and Marta's Life in California

SOME OF THE DAUGHTERS lived too far away to make regular
visits. A year before, Carmen and Marta had finally made the
decision to leave Cobbleton and had flown out to Los Angeles
and taken a bus to Anaheim, where their cheerful personalities
helped to get them jobs as ticket venders at Disneyland. And
they settled there, delighted by the California climate and the
merriment of the theme park (one grand thrill, an employee
banquet in Cinderella's castle, where they shook Mr. Disney's
hand). Living in a garden apartment on the periphery of town,
each of the sisters would in time find a husband. One was a
Cuban souvenir-shop manager named Carlos, in Mr. Disney's
employ. Marta met him when this man, a widower, noticed her;
a woman quite Cuban in appearance if not demeanor, whom he
imagined to be somewhere in her thirties, though she was past
forty, walking along Main Street toward the Magic Castle. Stout,
good-natured, and courtly—he had left Cuba for Hollywood
many years before, hoping to make it as a film actor—he would
see her going by and move out to his doorway, past children
wanting to buy Mickey Mouse toys and bags of caramelized
popcorn, calling out, "Oh, miss! Oh, miss!" He managed to speak
to her often and they got to know each other and after a time
began to plan quiet dates out to the drive-ins, where, as always
with potential lovers, he related his circumstances and she her
own. Carmen's future husband was a regional convenience-store
manager named Chuck, who lived in Anaheim and drove about
the area in a Studebaker "Woody" station wagon. Involving himself in good causes around the city, he'd turn up every so often
at Disneyland with groups of orphaned children in his care for
the day, and with Boy Scout troops. Thick-necked and with a
crew cut, he dressed in a tie and jacket regardless of the heat

and the eye-tearing fumes that would roll off the freeway and hang in the still air near the entrance to Disneyland. She must have talked with him a dozen times before he showed up one day, noble and disarming, with a bouquet of fresh-cut roses, saying, "What time do you get off, if you don't mind my asking?" She told him six-thirty and he returned and they drove over to a good restaurant, the Welcome House, and there, over a lobster dinner, squirty and smothered with ketchup, he told her the story of his life. The son of a mail carrier, he had grown up in Sacramento during the Depression and seen action as a Marine during the war, afterward going to work as a clerk, then assistant manager, then manager, then regional manager of the U-Drive-In department-store chain. "And now," he told her one night as they were parked, watching the stars, "I'm ready for something more." These sisters, like Veronica in Illinois with her contractor husband and kids, would come to visit once a year.

Others, like the sisters in New York and Sarah in Philadelphia, visited every month or so.

Violeta

AND THERE WAS Violeta, who, for all the bawdiness and insolence of her bobby-sox nature, had settled down with a good man of the cloth, a Presbyterian minister. She had met him in 1951 at the ripe age of thirty, the glory days of her scurrilous GI and civilian romances behind her—none ever turning into the love that she wanted. One day she noticed the new minister in town, a temporary replacement for the more elderly Reverend Muller, then recovering from a heart attack. She was working in the movie house and despite her Catholicism, out of curiosity and some intuition, she started, to her mother's shock, to attend his services. (Better than none at all, her mother would think, as Violeta was a little lax about going to Mass on Sundays.) Sitting in the front pew, she'd raise her pretty head with such devoutness that the minister, up on the pulpit before his congregation, would glance toward her. Outside the church, where the Reverend would greet his flock, she would approach him, complimenting his sermons mightily, her skin perfumed and her eyes bright with interest. She would also turn up at the church's Saturday-afternoon teas at his parsonage, affairs attended by the more elderly members of his flock, these gatherings ending when the Reverend would lead the group in prayer. It was after one of these teas—though this can only be guessed, all of it a mystery to the family—that Violeta dallied late one afternoon, the two talking quietly into the evening. The next thing, the sisters heard from their mother (and from Patricia, and Margarita, and Irene) that Violeta had taken up with the Reverend Farrell, a man, as it turned out, who had spent most of his childhood in a Presbyterian home for orphaned children. Dedicated and grateful to the church for saving him from the streets of Boston, where he was born and abandoned, for all his thirty-odd years he had never listened to the calling of his own heart, until Violeta had come along.

(He was not troubled that she was a Catholic. He did not know if his parents were Catholics, whether he was an Irishman or a German or a Pole, just that his name, Thomas Farrell, had been pulled by the orphanage director out of a telephone book.)

As for the allurements of the body, however careful Reverend Farrell may have been about his saintly sense of propriety, he, at the end of his tenure in Cobbleton, asked Violeta to accompany him to his next parish, which was in Baltimore, where, with some of the sisters in attendance, they were hurriedly married, for, by the time she left the household in Cobbleton, Violeta was pregnant. And though their mother, Mariela Montez, admitted he was a good man, he had perhaps sinned and, having sinned, was to arrange a discreet ceremony, held without fanfare or the trappings of a large wedding, early in the winter of 1952.

Violeta sometimes came to visit, happy and fulfilled, with her three children—the sisters could only imagine the pious carnality of their couplings—and Mariela and Nelson eventually blessed this marriage between their Catholic daughter and their Presbyterian son-in-law, knowing that they themselves, coming from such distant origins, had in a different way done the same.

(In all those years, their second-oldest daughter, Isabel, though intending to, never once visited Cobbleton. Each time she planned to, some catastrophe would come along: Antonio broke his leg while climbing a ladder to replace a bulb in a ceiling lamp; or one of her best friend's sons drowned; or a week of storms caved in the pharmacy walls; or she was laid up with kidney stones; and on and on. Each of those years brought the many enchanting letters that Isabel wrote her mother in Spanish. Somehow the time had passed quickly—and beyond this, the happiness of her days had left her quite satisfied, this satisfaction bringing with it, to some measure, the inability to move.)

A Planned Journey

FOR MARIELA, after so many years of familial service, their freedom meant an opportunity to do the things she'd always wanted to do. Satisfied for a time with the fulfillment of her own creative proclivities, she would spend many hours of her day writing poetry, which, as she got older, seemed to circle back more and more to the beatific time of her youth and to personal musings. She also dedicated herself to religious devotions that would benefit the lives of her children and the souls of the dearly departed. (Having survived her two sisters and brother, her mother and father, she prayed for them daily. She had survived the butler García, who passed away happily in Puerto Rico in 1952, and prayed for the happiness of his soul in Paradise, too. And for that of Miss Covington.)

Each night, when they retired to bed, she would remind Nelson how they once used to talk about traveling together. That, with her urge to see all the children, brought about a plan to drive around the country, fulfilling the promise of their early years. At first he, solitary in old age and having done his bit to raise a family, was reluctant. "God, woman," he'd tell her, "can't you see I'm too old for that kind of thing?"

But in the end she prevailed, and Nelson, coming to like the idea, bought a sturdy Ford convertible for the trip. Now, finally, she'd get to see the expanse of the country in which she had lived for so many years, and he would get to visit those American cowboy places he'd always dreamed of as a young man. They planned a route that would first take them to Philadelphia and New York, and then to Baltimore to see Violeta and her family. From there they would visit the capital, Washington, D.C., to see the Lincoln Memorial, photographs of which always moved Nelson (Lincoln pained by the troubles of life, stern and yet compassionately understanding of his place in history), imagining that their hearts would burn with pride, for they were both citizens now. Then, after driving north to Newport to spend some time with Helen and her family, they would double back and head west to Illinois, where Veronica was living with her husband and her two children. Their idea was to keep going, through the Western states (where he was almost certain they would encounter buffalo and Indians), ending up in California, where they would be reunited with their son. (But that was not all she wanted. Why couldn't they fly, as so many people were doing, down to Cuba? Or why not make a journey to Europe, first to Spain and then to Ireland?)

They were to have begun their journey late in the spring of the previous year. But one afternoon, during the winter, while shuffling across the living room in a pair of flannel pajamas to answer the telephone, Nelson felt a faint, nearly imperceptible twitching in his brow and a burst of prickliness within, as if a small nodule in his brain had gone to sleep, and in a second this already doddery man began to feel the world grow more faint about him.

Picking up the receiver, he greeted his daughter Maria and was alert enough to hand Mariela the telephone. ("*Hola, mi hija*," Mariela cried out.) And while she sat speaking first with Maria and then with Olga and Jacqueline, Nelson had the sudden compulsion to build a fire, to compensate for the sudden chill in his fingertips. Laying down some birch and pine logs, he took to his favorite chair and watched the fire rising, the embers glowing and dimming and the smaller twigs crackling, the minutest sparks bursting in the hollow of the darkness, and he laughed, saying, "Oh, my Lord," and, in one of his last moments of lucidity, realized he'd suffered some kind of stroke.

Not wishing to spoil their journey, he said nothing about this, and though he seemed a little more distracted than usual, they went ahead with their plans, Margarita and Irene taking their mother into town to buy some comfortable travel clothes, joyful sunhats, and tennis shoes, so that her feet would not get tired during their walks in the most scenic places. For his part, he tried to maintain a certain orderliness in his affairs, packing a suitcase very carefully and then, forgetting that he had not just returned from some journey and feeling pleased that he had kept his clothing so neat, dutifully unpacked, putting his shirts and trousers and other items back in the closet and dresser where he had, not an hour before, found them. Another day, he decided that they would need money for the journey, and he set out to the bank in town, but, approaching his new 1957 Ford, was startled to find that it was not his brand-new 1908 Model T, the dashboard with its radio and automatic gearshift and space-age wheel baffling him. And he sat for a long time, vaguely recalling that he seemed to know something about that automobile, but what he could not exactly say. Then he suddenly remembered how to drive, took his automobile into town without incident, withdrawing a thousand dollars from his passbook account, and, elated, took the familiar turn in front of the town hall and headed toward Farmers' Crossing, the countryside as sweetly familiar as always and reassuring, except that it seemed to go on forever. By the time he recalled that his house should have been no more than five minutes up the road, he had been driving for nearly forty-five minutes in the wrong direction. With that, he pulled over and, backing into a farm road, retraced his route, thanking God when he finally reached the house, which for a moment no longer seemed to exist.

The next morning, a Sunday, while taking Mariela to church, he imagined that the sky had filled with beautiful, clanging bronze bells, and, looking up (a flock of geese overhead), instead of straight onto the road, he nearly steered the auto into a ditch. Later Mariela noticed something else: Nelson standing outside the church, speaking with the Fitzgerald family (Sally and Pat being friends of their younger daughters, and their father, Jimmy Fitzgerald, a fellow member of the Cobbleton Emerald Society), her husband breaking his sentences into his slightly brogued English and into Spanish. The next day she took her husband to the doctor, even though he did not want to go. (For most of his life, he had been in reasonably good health and in all his years in America rarely went to a doctor for himself. He'd bring a doctor into the house when his daughters were sick with flu or mumps or the croup, and when his wife went into labor or did not feel well during some of her pregnancies, but that had been many years in the past. Whatever the ills he suffered—shortness of breath, occasional discomfort in the chest, the ebbing feelings of an unidentifiable guilt—he would simply make his way to the pharmacy and buy one of his favorite tonics.) Now suddenly he found himself being examined, a light probing the pupils of his eyes, a hammer tapping his knees, the doctor's index finger moving in a line before his nose—and in the end the doctor said, "He's probably had a minor stroke."

They put him into the Cobbleton infirmary for a few days' surveillance, and on being released, he was prescribed several medications to reduce his blood pressure.

Mariela, beside herself with fear, asked, "What is he suffering from?" and the doctor told her, "Nothing more than old age, really."

*

So they'd never made their cross-country trip, and by the time their son, Emilio Montez O'Brien, came to visit, Nelson's condition had worsened.

Somewhat more shrunken than he remembered her, Mariela Montez was overjoyed to see her son, caressing his handsome face over and over. And although she dyed her hair and seemed much younger than her seventy-four years, so many days alone in the house with her husband had given her the air of a slightly weary caretaker. And when Emilio first approached his Irish father, it took Nelson a while to understand that this strapping man was the flesh of his flesh. Then he became quite happy, slapping his son on the back and welcoming him into the house. The evening of his arrival, Margarita came to see her beloved brother and it was she who pointed out, after dinner, that in the past year or so Nelson O'Brien's mental faculties had started to slip away.

"Maria told me about Dad, but I had no idea that it had slowed him down so much."

"Yes, and it's sometimes a little hard for Mama. Some days he walks about the house looking for someone; other days he sits before the television set watching and not moving except to use the bathroom—at least he hasn't lost that. And sometimes he cries for no reason, or decides to go walking in the fields. One night, in the middle of a bad rainstorm, he got out of bed and went to the shed to get his old-fashioned camera and stood out in the rain for hours, photographing heaven knows what. It was so dark that he couldn't see the house and somehow wandered into the woods and only found his way back when Mama woke up and went out to look for him with a flashlight. They both caught very bad colds."

(That night, awakening suddenly and finding the bed beside her empty, her heart palpitating, Mariela searched through the rooms of the house and in a panic put on a raincoat and, getting the kitchen flashlight, searched for him in the field, bravely venturing into the thicket of trees behind the white fence and descending downward, the ground muddy under her, roots tripping her, elms and oak trees everywhere, their dripping branches entangling her. But she had kept going because he was her husband, and though she could not see very far even with the flashlight, slashes of rain cutting through the light, and though the whorl-knobbed trees seemed fierce, she called out to him, "Nelson! Nelson! Where are you," until she heard his voice, "I'm here!" Following that voice as best she could, she found the poor man drenched and shivering, his camera and tripod clutched in his arms, and she took him by the hand, saying, "Come with me, my poor foolish love," and led him out of the darkness and back to the house.)

"On some days," Margarita continued, "he will speak only

in Spanish to Mama or to me if I'm around, and when you've finally gotten used to it, he'll suddenly forget it all. Sometimes he's perfectly fine, the poor man, and with embarrassment he'll say, 'If I become too much of a burden, please send me away.' But Mama will have none of it—'I don't care if he spoils his trousers,' she'll say. 'If he dies, he will die in this house.' And, brother, it's good that you are here, because nothing, and no one, lasts in this world, and it is certain that our Poppy is going to die one of these days."

Emilio remained with the family for a week, accompanying the old man on his walks in the fields, his father dressed in a suit with a shirt and bow tie and wearing a derby, hiking along with a wolf-head cane, for a hip had started to pinch him painfully. His presence seemed to do his father good, and he never forgot his name, Emilio. They'd walk along and his father would find a particularly beautiful cluster of violets in the field and, picking some, whiff their scent and, with his brow creased, tell his son, "I'll miss all this." Or if a bird alighted on a branch, its feathers bright, with a worm in its beak for its young, he would stop Emilio in his tracks to watch carefully, and say, "Quietly now, these birds are highly nervous creatures," his mouth breaking into a childish smile. He seemed delighted with the littlest things—a brook in one of the fields or the friendliness of a farmer's hound, snout prowling the ground for scents, tail wagging. He'd say again and again, "I'll miss this, boy. And you, and all the others."

While they were sitting on the porch reminiscing about the days when they'd worked together many years before, Emilio his stalwart photography assistant, Nelson O'Brien muttered, "If you only knew what I'm feeling these days."

"What's that, Dad?"

"It's a strange feeling—I had some of it when I was a young man, but I was too foolish to see it. My head was too filled with the troubles of my little life. I just couldn't appreciate anything."

"What do you mean, if you don't mind my asking?"

"There used to be this very kindly farmer who'd pass on the road, a Mennonite fellow I always remember for his happiness.

He'd always stop to speak to one of the girls, and, looking about on a nice spring day, say something like, 'This is the work of the Lord.' And lately I've been telling myself, 'It must be so, for what does it have to do with me? Did I invent a twig, or one of those sweet birds?' " Then suddenly excited, he said, "Can you imagine if we had to make all this for ourselves? I wouldn't have the slightest notion where to begin, would you?"

Emilio shook his head.

"Well, there it is."

Getting up, he said: "Now, boy, when I'm gone, take care of your mother and the others—you know, you'll be the man of the family."

*

He would see his father the other way. For he would seem fine in the morning, but by the late afternoon would sit for hours in his pajamas, staring at the television, as if it were on.

*

During that visit, Emilio began to feel renewed tenderness toward his mother. Knowing of his travails, she had always told him, "I've prayed for you, son." And she was happy, for the gossip of the family had been conveyed to her: "I have one _aviso_ for you: if you're in love, believe in it."

Many hugs, a nearly back-crushing embrace for his father, sweet kisses for his mother, more kisses for his sisters, and back, back to California and the purest love and pain of his life.

The Time Margarita Had Gone
to Spain, Years Before

MARGARITA HAD GRADUATED from the Proper Trust College in Philadelphia in 1952. During the war and afterward, she had studied education, slowly, with the idea of teaching one day, and then drifted, after meeting a Professor DeLeon, head of the Romance Languages Department, into studying Spanish literature, her head filling with the words of the great Spanish writers of the past. (Many years later, as if in a film, their spirits came to visit her at night—Quevedo pacing the floors and picking at his goatee, mulling over an idea; Cervantes employing her as an amanuensis as he dictated long pasages of *Don Quixote*.) Her studies were difficult ("You can speak and read Spanish, my dear," Professor DeLeon had told her, "but you must go beyond what your mother taught you"), but working each night with a Spanish dictionary, she gradually started to understand the complexities of the language.

When she graduated, there was a little celebration in Cobbleton, and then a much grander one with her sisters in New York, at which her most prosperous sisters—Helen, Maria, Olga, Jacqueline—drank much champagne and made her a gift of a thousand dollars.

It would take her two years to make her way to Spain. First she moved back to Cobbleton, finding a job in the local high school, where she taught civics and Spanish. Then she found an apartment in town, enjoying her life of solitude, for she would often tell herself, after the debacle of her marriage to Lester Thompson, that she did not need a man to find happiness. Margarita visited with her mother and father two or three times a week and made frequent trips to see her sisters in New York and her sister Sarah in Philadelphia, where she and her lawyer husband lived an uncomplicated and prosperous life with two children, dark-skinned but very pretty girls, who were being kept from the cruder forms of prejudice by being sent to private schools and by the amenities of a Chestnut Hill neighborhood where very few children ever insulted them (though they may have thought to), and where urbane society respected the accomplishments of her husband, a partner in a law firm.

She concerned herself primarily with the well-being of the family, wishing them much happiness (and daydreaming about the life of her movie-actor brother out in Hollywood), and was quite content to come home to her apartment at the end of her

day, her head buzzing from her efforts to teach her largely indifferent pupils, the sons and daughters of farmers, something
about the Spanish language, both the conjugations of the verb
estar and something of the history of Spain and of the countries
that Spain had settled. ("Does anyone here know about Puerto
Rico?") She'd take a hot bath, read a book. She was not lonely,
having decided that the company of books made for a much easier
and perhaps happier experience than the company of men. Here
and there, a man would ask her out, especially in New York
during her visits, when her middle-aged beauty and her femininity would draw the attention of men on her outings with her
musical sisters and Gloria to nightclubs and restaurants. Even
in Cobbleton, a most conservative place, where an unmarried
woman of fifty was considered, for the most part, an old maid—
a woman to be pitied—there were men like the owner of the
town haberdashery, a widower, who would come out and stand
at his door to greet her if she happened to be walking down the
street. And one of her fellow teachers, a Mr. Richards, who taught
arithmetic, a lonely man, was always asking her out, Margarita
always politely declining.

    She did not care. Her marriage to Lester Thompson, and
the supreme effort she once made to be a good wife during their
years together, left her with a yearning for independence. Self-
doubting—after all, she had been incapable of bearing him
children—she sometimes drifted into generous appraisals of the
man, wishing to God that things could have turned out differently. On the other hand, she would think about Lester with his
young wife, making love on the chaise longue of their town house
in Philadelphia. (She had visited him once, in 1949, and he and
his surroundings seemed quite prosperous. Even so, he fell to
his knees, wrapped his arms around her legs, saying, "Oh, Margarita, I've missed you so much." And even though he was married, he opened her blouse and kissed her breasts, and with the
authority of a man who was quite acquainted with her anatomy
and how Margarita would quietly moan before she came, he stuck
his hand down into her undergarment, his fingers working the
bulb of her pleasure furiously. She liked the sensation, and his

passion, but she pushed him away, leaving his house and never seeing him again.)

She was fifty-two years old when she arrived in Spain, and the first thing that touched and saddened her was the poverty that seemed to be everywhere, for Spain had hardly begun to recover from the Civil War of the 1930s and everywhere on the streets of Madrid she saw cripples, men and women alike, who'd lost a limb during the fighting years before, and this made her think how destiny had protected her. If her great-grandfather had never journeyed as a soldier to Cuba in the mid-nineteenth century, she—instead of sipping cocktails in some speakeasy in Philadelphia with her husband in 1937, listening to jazz, or idly sitting about reading fashion magazines, a little bored, in Cobbleton—could have been one of these unfortunates.

As she traveled about, taking in the tourist sights of Madrid and heading south by rail into Andalusia, with guidebook and camera in hand, she would begin to daydream in the heat—the sight of some distant tower looming over an olive grove inspiring the thought that at the time of that tower's construction, seven hundred years before, her ancestors lived somewhere in Andalusia, perhaps as farmers, and this would fill her with a kind of pride, a feeling that part of her spirit belonged to this place. Although she also took pride in the fact that her mother was Cuban, she sometimes found herself feeling more emotional about Spain.

Of course, there were things that bothered her: the Guardia Civil, with their machine guns and intimidating air; the fetidness of the toilets; the sometimes grueling heat, the deadness in the middle of the day, when everything closed down and there was no choice but to go back to one's hotel for a siesta. In the beautiful Moorish city of Córdoba, where she spent a morning lost among the forest of columns in the Grand Mosque, she stayed in a *pension*, baking in the heat of the midsummer sun, the room so hot that she could neither nap in the daytime nor sleep at night. Despite the scrubbed tile floors, the air was heavy with dust, and she found herself parched and craving ice cream and snow. She had not liked that. And there had been the incident at the rail station in Aguilar. She had finished using the toilet facilities in the station and was planning to sit in a café, to await the next train, when a short, wiry man with a crow's flitting eyes had come up behind her and grabbed her bottom, and when she turned around, the man was holding in his right hand what certainly appeared to be his penis, a short and stubby device which neither impressed nor frightened her, so that when he asked, "¿*Te gusta?*" she said, "No! But I'm going to find a policeman."

(An odd experience, almost as odd as the time in New York, while visiting her sisters, when she and Helen went for a walk in Central Park and were caught in a sudden downpour, and as they were making their way out of the park, they came across a man ecstatically masturbating onto a bush.)

Despite the occasional inconveniences of the journey, she not only took in many of the tourist sights but luxuriated in the pleasure of conversing day in and day out in Spanish: about the political situation in Franco's Spain, a subject which came up with everyone she spoke to; about life in America; and, inevitably, about why she was traveling alone.

She would remember that journey for the evening in Valencia where she met her dear Cuban man, but she would also recall with fondness how, while traveling along the southern coast, between Málaga and Nerja, she experienced an unexpected moment of elation.

One evening, as she was dining in a restaurant, its balcony overlooking the Mediterranean, an Englishman in a tan suit, with the clearest blue eyes, a Mr. Norris, struck up a conversation with her. (She was a little surprised to realize she had not spoken English in three weeks.) Drinking a dusty red wine and lulled by the reflection of stars on the sea, she and Mr. Norris nearly pursued a romance—but the poor fellow drank far too much wine. Not that she minded his company. Small talk about London, England, a civilized city which she had never seen, ended in his suggestion that she join him, as he would be motoring north to Barcelona. But she'd turned the man down, and the Englishman, ever a gentleman, excused himself and made his way back to his *pension*, falling on his bed from drunkenness and disappointment, for he hoped to bring the pensive and marvelous-looking American woman back with him.

Some Spaniards in the corner of the room had been watching her, the younger men whispering among themselves, and on her way out, they invited her to join them in a glass of brandy. While sitting with them, she asked the young men if they happened to know if there was a stretch of beach where a person might bathe alone, as she put it. And one of them, a fellow named Diego, told her about a little beach where people sometimes went to do just that.

The next morning she packed a lunch and a bottle of wine. She wore a ruffle-skirted sundress and a wide-brimmed sun hat which fluttered in the breeze, low-heeled shoes, and dark sunglasses, and looking very much like Ava Gardner, she tottered with some difficulty along a labyrinthine path by the water, climbing rocks and finding sandy tracks at certain points. And at last—it took nearly an hour—she found a deserted cove with a stretch of pebble-covered beach. There she spread out a towel and had a glass of wine and a sandwich made with cheese and Serrano ham on a good, hard-crusted bread, and when she finished lunch, she stripped off her sundress, her cumbersome Maidenform extra-support bra, and her panties, and charged mischievously and triumphantly into the water, naked. She floated on her back, her full, taut-nippled breasts, puckered from the sudden chill, quickly warming in the sun, the fleshliness of her body floating, thick black pubic hair coiling, rising, swirling in the gentle whorls of the sea. Eyes closed, she sent sweet kisses up into the Spanish sun.

Emilio

MARGARITA WOULD ALSO LOOK BACK ON those years and think about her brother, Emilio, and the way things turned out for him. Upon his return to California, he decided to give his heart fully to love and headed north to Alaska, where he found

Jessica in a distracted state of mind. She had thought about him constantly, too, and the letters they had written each other during their separation were so tenderly affectionate and truthful that, the very afternoon Emilio turned up, she closed her restaurant and the two retired to her little apartment upstairs and, barely able to restrain themselves, spent the next two days happily in her bed—this idyll broken up by short periods of sleep and dalliances in her tin bathtub, where they would scrub each other's backs and play like children in the soapy water. He so lost himself in Jessica, had so crossed the line of promise and love, that as he pressed his toes against the engorged nipple of her right breast he told himself right then and there that he would dedicate himself to her well-being. Other women would not exist, and no matter how much temptation might come his way, he would resist, because each dalliance chipped away at love. He was so carried away with the goodness of her heart that, ever impulsive, he proposed to her, and she accepted.

It would take her several months to get her affairs in order, for she would have to put the restaurant up for sale and in the meantime leave it to friends to look after, making her way in the spring of 1959 to California to join the actor. In the meantime, Emilio had tried to revive his sluggish career. He'd even proposed bringing back the character of Father Byrne, and spent many a day tinkering with a scenario—in which no one was interested. He managed to find enough work, bit parts and cameos on different television series, to keep himself going, but he reluctantly admitted that he had long since passed his peak in earnings, 1954 having been his best year, when he'd cleared just under a hundred thousand dollars. He accepted that his days as a leading man, even in B pictures, were over, and found himself taking on character parts, three days' work here, two weeks' work there. And slowly he began to gain a reputation not only as being easy to work with but as an actor willing to take any role. His humility, which endeared him to many a director and casting agent, proved to be somewhat of a boon, for his agent called nearly every week with offers of work, enough to keep him busy for a long time.

It didn't matter, for he would slip out of himself in a pleasant

way into the total devotion of love. By the time Jessica arrived
to join him, they'd already started to make plans—perhaps she
would open a little business in Los Angeles, a restaurant for the
stars, or go back to teaching. It did not matter. They were off on
a perpetual honeymoon, these two. Emilio Montez O'Brien and
his darling could spend hours together without saying a single
word. Yet even when they went walking along the beach at Santa
Monica holding hands, it was as if they were really locked in an
embrace.

He was so ecstatic that his voice chimed with happiness. His
sisters, especially Margarita, noticed their brother's serenity and
they all felt happy for him. And in Cobbleton his mother, Mariela
Montez, curious about this woman, his font of love, would ask
him, "When are you going to bring her to visit?" His answer,
hopefulness in his voice: "When we come out to get married."

They discussed it, the natural thing being that they go to her
family in Minnesota, or have, as his agent suggested for the
benefit of publicity, a splashy ceremony in Hollywood, but because of the advanced age of his mother and father, she agreed
to a civil ceremony in the town of Cobbleton in the fall of 1959.

                                    *

They traveled east together for another Montez O'Brien reunion, all the sisters and their families converging on Cobbleton,
and happy celebrations taking place in the household. Even sister
Isabel, after so many years' absence, finally flew north out of
Cuba with her family—things were changing in Cuba and the
deteriorated state of her father's health concerned her, too. (It
was a beautiful reunion. Isabel fell into the arms of her mother,
the two holding each other for a long time, memory of her life
there flowing into Mariela, and many kisses passing between
them. Then there were kisses for her father, who hardly seemed
to recall who she could be, and the joy of seeing her sisters—
that they had all aged somewhat astounding her, but all in all,
a happy time.) Jessica's relatives came in from Minnesota, and
a few friends from her days in Alaska made the journey, too,
these folks staying in the Main Street Hotel. There was endless

activity in the household, children running around everywhere, and Emilio's mother, playing the grande dame, bursting with pride that this time her only son would be properly married.

Between the two families, there were so many people that the group shots, taken by a photographer, would resemble a high-school graduating class in numbers. Emilio Montez O'Brien in a tuxedo; his lovely bride, which was how the local paper described her, sitting in the front row, with the parents of the bride, Mr. and Mrs. Brooks, beaming proudly behind them. Mariela Montez, elegant in a gown, gazed intently into the camera; her husband, Nelson O'Brien, distracted and trying to hold his own, also in evening clothes. (And the others? Margarita holding flowers; Isabel and her husband and three children; the musical twins, Jacqueline and Olga, in organdy gowns, their agent beside them; then Maria with an older gentleman, a certain Fabrizio Balzaretti, an operatic tenor with a nineteenth-century air. On the other side, Helen, her husband, and their two sons; then Irene, her husband, and three plump children—no longer teenagers, but anxious as ever to get to the buffet. Sarah and her lawyer husband and one of her two children; then Patricia, her husband and children; then Veronica with her son—her husband, working hard as ever, could not attend; then Marta and Carmen, in from California with their husbands; Violeta with her minister husband and three young children; and Gloria, wearing a furtive, slightly embarrassed expression, with her Macy's love. Then you had to account for Jessica's family, which consisted of three brothers, their wives and children—thirteen in all—and an uncle and aunt and two of their boys, as well as a few cousins and old friends who'd decided to attend the wedding.)

A flash, the shot taken, years later an item for an old woman's or an old man's trove of memories.

*

That was the good that Margarita remembered—the happy celebration. The bride and groom stayed in Cobbleton the next day, for they were in no rush to go off on a honeymoon, having lived one for several months. Then they spent a few days in New

York before heading back to California. The sisters themselves were elated with the reunion, though Margarita was a little lonely, for the man she'd fallen for in Spain was back in Cuba, and love somehow seemed too far away.

Their Brother's Happiness

HER BROTHER'S GREATEST MOMENT of happiness would have nothing to do with the movies but came when, a year later, in 1960, his wife Jessica gave birth to a little girl. They named her Mary Isabel O'Brien, the baby inheriting, he thought, her mother's beautiful and soft eyes, her face cherubic and pleasing, skin smelling ever so sweet. Surprised by his love for the child, Emilio doted on her, his bachelor's house completely changed. He'd covered the walls of the guest room with a pink swan-patterned wallpaper, hung mobiles from the ceiling, filled the shelves surrounding the crib with stuffed animals. He did not mind her spittle, her lack of coordination. Even the unmanly business of changing her diapers amused him, his enormous hands ever careful not to hurt her. When she cried, he would feel an even greater alarm than his wife, and lurching from his bed, half asleep, he would make every effort to calm his daughter and then sit, despite his drowsiness, watching his wife suckling the child. He'd even feel titillated—for he'd always loved her breasts—and at three in the morning the child's feeding often ended with the actor and his proud masculinity reengaging with his wife, the couple, enchanted, feeding on each other's tongues and lost in some world where only love and nothing else thrived. He was so enthralled that afterward, when all they could hear was the occasional ticking of a clock and, in the distance, the motor of some automobile on the boulevard, he would swear, loving her and his daughter, that they should have another baby.

(And another and another, each thrust saying to him.)

A more devoted father or husband could not be found, Marta

and Carmen, aunts to the child in from Anaheim for occasional visits, would report to the family. What else could they say after watching their handsome brother playing with the tot as she crawled along the floor or teaching her to speak or pointing out the simple wonders of the world; why, the man, reformed and good, tranquil and happy, would rush home from his day's shoot to spend time with his wife and daughter.

What he reveled in was life, simple life—the goodness of bringing such a new joy into the world.

In time his movie star's edge faded away to a more practical aura, and the new clarity in his eyes and his professional demeanor continued to be popular with casting people and directors. He was prospering, no part too small or unbecoming for him to play as long as he could continue to earn a living.

He was always taking photographs of his wife and daughter. When his sisters came to visit, he posed them out in the yard under an orange tree, his daughter dressed in lace on the lap of one or the other. (Yes, he would have photographs of Margarita, Maria, Olga and Jacqueline, Marta, Carmen, and Gloria posed in such a way, their expressions happy.)

There was more. Tired of making pictures, he and Jessica, naked in bed, would talk about opening their own business in Hollywood, a restaurant for the stars—as he knew many of them and counted some as his friends. She, her hair in braids, would nod and tell him, "My darling, anything is possible with us."

*

It was a happy time for their brother, and yet, in retrospect, sad.

Mary Isabel was about a year and a half when Emilio decided to take his family on a vacation to Sonoma County. They would stay in an inn, and when they were not driving around taking in the sights, they'd ride horses at a ranch. And they would drive around to different vineyards, tasting many wines, their skins by the late afternoon so oozing the fragrance of the vine that bees tended to follow them. (They'd wrap the baby in a blanket, say "Cootchy-coo" and tickle her delighted chin.) They had been there for three days when Emilio's agent called to say he was needed to work for a few days in Los Angeles, a well-paying job, a small but good role in a Yul Brynner picture—would he be able to do it? They had planned to vacation for another week, but Emilio, thinking about the money and the security of his family, decided to take the job and perhaps extend his vacation afterward. So he drove to San Francisco and flew to Los Angeles, his wife and daughter staying behind.

It was a Wednesday night. Jessica and Mary Isabel were asleep in a room that overlooked a great expanse of the countryside, a beautiful room in which the morning light seemed nearly celestial. At around two in the morning, a gentleman, also on vacation, lingered in the downstairs salon and, fatigued from a great wine-tasting tour that day, dozed off. Dreaming that he had dropped his cigar to the carpet, he was relieved to find himself waking just in time to put out the smoldering glow in the rug. He collected himself and poured the remnants of a Scotch-and-water over the mess; he would write a note offering to pay for it, he told himself, or forget it entirely. And so he retired to his room. But about an hour later, the antique floorboards of the structure, built, as a plaque described, in 1868, began to get warm. Then the line of heat prospered, and a fire began to teem through the walls. Within a few minutes, the hotel, thick with smoke, was ablaze.

There would be articles about the fire, demanding better fire codes, and an investigation would take place, and listed among the thirteen victims of the fire would be a Jessica and a Mary Isabel O'Brien.

*

Emilio, his agent by his side, in the hospital morgue to identify his wife and child, a doctor of forensic medicine lifting off a sheet and exposing their faces. Their bodies were intact, death coming by asphyxiation, their eyes closed, expressions surprisingly serene. There was a smile on his daughter's lips; perhaps, snuggled in her mother's arms, she had been having a lovely dream about sweets, or about playing kiss-daddy's-nose, when the walls had started to ooze smoke. And his wife—he stood looking at her for a long time, before the doctor and a deputy led him away—perhaps that night, before falling asleep, she had been thinking about him and all the years they would have to-gether and all the hours they would be able to frolic in bed, the pleasure of his tongue on her breasts.

All he could ask the doctor was: "And they didn't feel any-thing, did they? I mean, they weren't awake."

And the doctor said, "No, sir, they were in their beds. They didn't know."

Emilio was wearing a raincoat and dark glasses, his head lowered, when, as he left the hospital entrance, a photographer took his picture. He'd raised his arm to conceal his shattered expression and reeled around, shouting, "Come on, can't you leave a man alone?"

The photographer, a novice with a local paper who'd gotten a tip that a movie star's wife and child had perished in the fire, stepped back, stunned and ashamed. But the photograph was published, first in the local papers and then widely across the United States. An article using that photograph had appeared in one of the Los Angeles newspapers, headlined "A Hollywood Tragedy."

*

When they received his call, Margarita flew out to join him, as did Gloria. Marta and Carmen came in from Anaheim. The funeral was held in Minnesota, he numb with grief and incon-solable. When it was over, coffins lowered into the ground and the business of life resuming, Margarita returned East with her sister Gloria, saying to him, "Remember, God will preserve you." And: "Don't forget, we will always have each other"—unaware at the time that she would see little of her brother in the coming years.

Lost Happiness, 1962

ALTHOUGH HE TRIED to maintain a discipline in his life, one afternoon at around four, after several months of somber self-control, Emilio left his bungalow and, weary of his ebbing pain, his head filled with tormenting memories, he got into his automobile and made his way to the gaudy, neon-lit Sunset Boulevard Bar & Grill and in quick succession drank down three vodka martinis. By five, he'd started another round, and a woman sitting on a stool whom he'd hardly noticed before, a woman with bleached-blond hair, began to take on the allure of a goddess. She, too, had been trying to forget some desolate event in her life and, plastered, watched the actor and smiled with a haven't-I-seen-you-before glare in her eyes. She looked about thirty-five and was a little washed up when it came to love, but all the same, Emilio, pulling out a wad of bills and dropping them on the bar, told the bartender to get the lady a drink. And she, delighted to have yet another highball, pulled up her stool beside his. He looked her over. She was wearing a tight red cocktail dress. Her breasts were large—she opened the first two buttons of her dress before joining him—and she had nice legs and an almost pretty face.

"So what's your little secret?" she asked him.

And he'd shrugged and sipped from his drink, saying, "Nothing. What's yours?"

And she went into this long "Do you really want to hear it?" tale about once having high hopes about a career and love, and being dragged down by one man after the other, as in a movie script. And just before getting maudlin, for, like every other person in town, she had wanted to be a movie star and had never made it, she leaned close and placed her hand on his thigh, asking him what he did with his life. And he responded by sliding her hand up toward his crotch, and she could not help appraising, with a squeeze, that hearty bundle of fiber and nerve. That's when he said, "Listen, why don't we sit over in the corner," and there, in a booth, they ordered more drinks and a couple of hamburger platters, and she started to figure out who he was— "I know you. You're the guy who played that Father Byrne fellow!" They started to nibble on each other's lips, then they drank a lot more, and at around nine-thirty she returned from the ladies' room and sat down beside him, against the wall, and with a little smile on her face said, "I've got a little secret. Can you guess what it is?"

"I don't know," he said.

"Now just look."

And she took the hem of her skirt and rolled it up like a scroll, little by little, until high on her thighs he saw the beginnings of her pubic hair, and she laughed. Then she rolled her skirt down and handed him her purse, saying, "Now look inside."

Snapping the purse open, he found a pair of lacy white panties. She told him: "They're yours." And then: "Let's get out of here, honey." And that's what they did, making their way, one auto following the other, to his bungalow, the night spent in a crazy romantic tryst, the two drinking and kissing and all the rest, their drunken and rubbery bodies against each other, and Emilio, for a few brief moments, forgot his pain.

He became physically acquainted with other women and got drunk nearly every night for months, so that in time he started to change, the same way his friend Errol Flynn, once the handsomest man in Hollywood, had changed, the beauty of his youth giving way to a heavier, more worldly, ruined appearance. (Poor Flynn had died in 1959, and his last film, *Cuban Rebel Girls*, had been a terrible failure.) But this didn't seem to make any difference to the women who saw him through the eyes of innocence or of drunkenness. He was a frequent star guest at many a dive in Hollywood, the owners, flattered by his presence, giving him free drinks. And when he wasn't working and would feel the impulse to lose himself, he would go off on one of his trips, driving up along the coast—toward Alaska?—or south to weather-worn and dilapidated beach hotels along the ocean, and sometimes down to Tijuana, where he hung around saloons and got into all-night card games, staying until he'd decide to sober up long enough to check in with his agent, calling from some honky-tonk bar about work, and head north, resolved to straighten himself out.

At the beach, he'd lie out on the sand watching the kids hit the surf, and endear himself to them, buying them cases of beer. And he'd set himself up for a sixteen- or seventeen-year-old girl, torturously beautiful and womanly in her bikini, to press corruption charges against him. (A sixteen-year-old's nipples in his mouth, their sweet and youthful taste enchanting him, his hands around her young hips, he, blurry with drink, would lose himself in the splendor of her body.) He hadn't gotten into trouble with young girls yet, but if he did, what did he care?

He was well liked enough that some of his Hollywood pals tried to get him into AA and he attended a few meetings, that item getting into the newspapers, but mainly he did not understand the twisted logic of their meetings, nor why he should give alcohol up. His drinking had not made the tinderbox walls of that inn go up in flames, and giving it up would not bring his wife and daughter back. At least when he got very drunk he lost himself in a cavernous space inside his head, there both forgetting and remembering the death of his wife and daughter.

He would have his women and his drinks and the hell with it all, for he considered himself a bit too much on the feminine—emotional—side when it came to feelings. (He'd have a drink at two in the morning to get rid of his terrible headaches, have drinks at six to make the sunshine a little more radiant and to make the drive to his agent's office or to a studio, if he happened to be working, a little more pleasant. And if he had work—though as time went by, jobs would come to him with much less frequency—he'd have a few drinks in the dressing room to help him through the day, his bleary eyes, picked up by the camera, exasperating the directors. And then more drinks throughout the day.)

Even so, he would wake up on many a night, like the insomniac character he had almost played for an episode of the fantasy television program, *The Twilight Zone*. (Yes, that wonderful episode about a desperate man who believed that if he closed his eyes to sleep he would never wake again.) He would get so blind drunk that he'd forget his lines, and he looked like death, and with the actorly aplomb of a trained grizzly bear, he was hired for jobs only when old friends, who were aware of his troubles, put in a good word for him, as long as he did not cross them up, which he often did.

*

He was only vaguely aware of what was going on in the outside world. His sisters wrote and telephoned, but their letters and conversations turned to air. That his sister Irene was suffering from diabetes was a blur of a few lines; that her son Kevin had been hurt in a car accident on his way back from a dance meant nothing. Patricia counseled him to have faith in his own future, for she intuited that he would find happiness once again (as she had foreseen his tragedy: years before his wife and daughter died, without knowning exactly what would happen, her mind had sensed an acrid scent like that of burned cork, wood, or rubber when thinking about them), but her words seemed to him no more than the ramblings of yet another sister feeling sorry for him. He cared little that Veronica, out in Illinois, was having trouble with her husband, whom she loved very much but who'd gotten absorbed with a young woman working in the construction-company office, and Veronica, with two teenagers still at home, didn't know what to do about it. Nor did he focus on the fact that his mother, in her beautiful and simple letters, written out carefully in English in her minuscule script, spoke of her husband's failing health and told him that she was praying for the peace of his soul. Nor was he even aware of the travails of his sister Isabel in Cuba, disenchanted with the new government but loving her adopted country, her heart sick at the idea of having perhaps to leave one day, as her husband was concerned about the future of their children under the new system. And he did not know that his sister Helen's oldest boy had joined the Marine Corps and gone as a military adviser to Vietnam, where, during the act of advising, the pinky, index, and middle fingers of his right hand were blown off when someone passing his barracks in Saigon lobbed in an explosive device which wounded him and killed two others. Or that his sister Helen, the beautiful high-society dame, was so shattered that she started to go to a psychiatrist and take tranquillizers and her beautiful and aristocratic face, the face of the girl who'd never known very many troubles in her life, suddenly begun to show the strain. Nor did he particularly appreciate the efforts of Marta and Carmen, who came up from their jobs at Disneyland to cheer him—or, in any case, to try to keep him sober. (Because he loved them, he would pretend not to drink, resenting their visits but seemingly perfectly calm and reasonable, until his moods would sour, and he would send them out of the house, and they would leave in tears. He would remember the next day that something bad happened between him and Marta and Carmen, but what he couldn't tell.) Margarita had told him that on a certain Sunday evening the Chanteuses would be appearing on the Ed Sullivan Show to sing a few songs, and he looked forward to seeing them, as he was proud and loved them very much. But by the time they appeared, after the comedian George Carlin and before the acrobats of the Moscow Circus, they had been reduced to some blurred image of what he remembered the sisters to be. He did not know that it was them, and in the middle of their big number he got up to refill his glass (vodka and ice) and decided in the kitchen to call that nice humpable starlet he had met the other day, screwing up the number so that when he finally got back into the living room his sisters were gone and *Gunsmoke*, on which he'd once appeared, came on. And there were his conversations with tender Gloria, who would call him at three in the morning from New York, even though she would have to get up by seven-thirty to head for her job in the payroll office at Macy's, her voice loving and concerned—but he did not particularly remember them.

The Last Days of Nelson O'Brien, 1962

EMILIO'S TROUBLES persisted through his father's last days, when, eighty-four, Nelson O'Brien got into the habit of rereading *A Gentleman's Guide to Love* and his photography manual, books that had been in his possession most of his life. Every morning would find him sitting out on the porch, fully dressed, those books open on his lap, and he would switch from one to the other and lean back and close his eyes, happy with memories. And though he would join his wife, and at times his daughter Irene or Margarita or Patricia, who'd be visiting the house for lunch, or take a walk with them in the field, he would mainly find himself transported far away, like a child daydreaming.

He would often think that it was 1896 again and that, instead of sitting on the porch of a house on the outskirts of an American town in Pennsylvania, he was once more making his way with his sister Kate O'Brien, carpetbags packed, onto a ship in Dublin Harbor. Or thinking that she might still be around, he would wander in the hall looking for his sister Kate, and then remember that she had died in 1897 and grow sad; or, remembering his journey to America with his young bride, Mariela, and their newborn daughter, Margarita, he'd recall the clutter and discomforts of the Fourteenth Street customhouse in New York in 1902. The long lines, voices echoing, the random examination of baggage, the hurried processing of certain passengers, mainly American citizens, rankling him because, although he and his wife were exhausted and wanted to rest, they had to stand in a line for over two hours—not a single gentleman offering his wife a seat on one of the benches lining the walls. And at the customs desk he'd had an argument with a burly official, an Irishman who, while expressing sympathy for the young couple, kept on saying, "You must go to immigration." He remembered that their papers were in order—they both had their passports and proper visas—and since Nelson was a man of property and apparent means, he could give the official a twenty-dollar gold piece—and they were spared further discomfort.

Or how they had boarded a train at Pennsylvania Station for Philadelphia, where they took another train, and by two in the afternoon they stepped off on the platform in the town of Cobbleton and were pleased to discover that the sun, on that dreary day, was trying to peek out of the clouds.

And there were gaslights burning in the lobby of the Main

Street Hotel, where they would spend their first night. The hotel, on whose balcony a military officer had once given a rousing speech, overlooked the saloon and a row of simple houses and a general-notions store, and the street itself was deserted save for the occasional passing horse and carriage. The town was desolate, the sky gray, but it was America!

They'd occupied a pleasant enough room, with sweetly patterned wallpaper, and the management were quite accommodating about a basinet for the child, whom Mariela bathed.

That first evening in Cobbleton, they'd gone to the hotel dining room to have a meal of roasted chicken, scalloped potatoes, and apple pie. On the dining-room walls, among the quaint ink etchings and watercolors of the Pennsylvania countryside, there was a portrait of Abraham Lincoln, whose face his wife had never seen before. The waiter and hotel clerk addressed them as "you and your missus," the hotel clerk looking directly at Nelson and averting his eyes whenever Mariela looked back at him.

How hard and confusing it must have been on you, my darling.

While he'd smiled obligingly at the waiters and the clerk, she, always carrying herself with an aristocratic posture, could not. Of a mischievous bent of mind, she had told him that night so long ago, "To hell with these unrefined people."

But that night when he'd brought up a bottle of sherry so that they might celebrate their arrival and offered her a little glass to calm her nerves, she was shaking with distress and wanted to forget everything, perhaps go back to Cuba. And she told him so, in a rapid, biting Spanish which echoed through the hotel halls.

"Now calm yourself," he'd said. "You're being a bit of a child about things. This is a grand country, and a wonderful community of people live here." He had told her this in Spanish. "You just have to get accustomed. It took me some time, my darling, but you will see."

He'd speak to her tenderly and in her language, no matter his errors, when he wanted to calm her down.

In the flush of the sherry's warmth, like sunlight, she said to him, in a joking manner: "Yes, my husband, but why here and not some interesting place like Paris?"

"Uh? What nonsense is it that you're talkin'? We're here now and maybe for good." And, as an afterthought: "And you have to start speaking English with me. Otherwise, I won't say a word."

That night, he could not sleep, the baby's colic keeping both of them awake. So he'd watched Mariela breast-feeding their daughter, watched her changing diapers and, in the darkness, rocking the baby in her arms, as she would with all their children.

*

And Nelson recalled how the next morning he hired a horse and carriage at the local stable to take them to their new home. With the equipment and possessions they had brought from Cuba, they made their way through the countryside, past Fitzgerald's farm, and Dietrich's, and Tucker's Pond, and came to his house, off the road, on a slight incline and surrounded by oak and maple trees, the sky hectic with coloration.

Shutters dangling, the roof in disarray—a crow nested above the cocoons and spiderwebs of the porch.

"Well, this is it," Nelson said to Mariela.

A skeleton key that he had hidden some years before opened the door.

They stood in the parlor, and baby in her arms, Mariela looked out through the dust-covered windows, the house filled with drafts and the drapery jostling and billowing in the wind, America looming in the distance.

Then those first days of their new life: Mariela attending to the baby, and Nelson setting out to make repairs, sanding the pinewood floors and coating them with resin. He caulked leaks and replaced shattered panes of glass, climbed up on the roof and with a helper from town hammered in new shingles. In the storm cellar, he found the skeleton of a fox. When a trunk with Mariela's clothes and personal effects, smelling of camphor and the tropics, arrived from Cuba, she filled a closet with her muslin and cambric dresses and, among other items, her bonnets decorated with birds and seashells set in the brim, as was the fashion at the time. They lived simply. They bought a cradle and washbasin and spittoons, a pedal-driven, curlicue-framed Singer sewing machine, kerosene lamps, brass candelabra, and mirrors. New lace-trimmed curtains, a lacquered pendulum clock, a few dolls, a rattle for the baby.

Those Memories, among Many Others

AND IN HIS LAST DAYS he would spend much time roaming about in the hall, the light brilliant through the windows, Nelson a little confused.

He'd remember so many mornings and afternoons when, as he opened the door to that house in Cobbleton, one or another of his daughters would come charging into his arms; and now, lingering in the hall, he would feel something was about to happen.

He'd start to shout, to tremble, waiting for the moment when his wife, Mariela, would hold him, repeating, "*Cálmate, cálmate.*"

He would nod and sit quietly for a long time.

One of those days, she was touching his face and acting most kindly toward him when he felt the impulse to use his old photography equipment. And although it was much work and he had no plates and the camera was no longer operable, he took the equipment out into the yard and planned a grand portrait of his wife. She was used to these flights of fancy. She wore a white-and-blue dress that he had always liked, and her hair in a bun. A passerby on the road would see an old man posing an old and patient woman in the yard, but that passerby would have no idea what Nelson was seeing through the camera lens: the sunny yard of a photography studio in Santiago de Cuba, circa 1900, and, seated before a tiled wall on a stool, a pretty woman with long black hair falling over her shoulders, an oval face serene with intelligence, the lady wearing a simple white dress with a pleated skirt and puff-shouldered, butterfly sleeves, a yellow bow at her waist.

"Now smile, my dear," Nelson said, all those years later.

And because she never smiled while sitting for a photograph, he said, happily, "My lord, Mariela, you haven't changed one bit."

Then, behind the black cloth, he squeezed the pneumatic bulb for the last time in his life.

*

A few hours later, there came a rap on the door, but Mariela Montez did not hear it, and because she was concentrating so hard on her writing, he did not want to disturb her. So he got up, and when she asked him, "Where are you going, my love?" he'd told her, "Someone's at the door."

"Oh, I didn't hear."

There, before him, stood two official-looking gentlemen in black suits and derbies. One he recognized as the man he had worked with for many years in Ireland when he was a boy, a kindly photographer named MacPhearson, and the other—he could place his face—the town undertaker, a man named Quinn.

"Good day, sir," they said to Nelson. "A beautiful day, isn't it, with the sun shining and birds singing?"

"It is." Then: "And what can I do for you, gentlemen?"

And with a heavy Irish brogue, the smaller of the officials, MacPhearson, said: "We've traveled a long way to fetch you."

"And do you mind telling me why?"

"Well, sir, if you must know, to take you to the Land of Promise."

"I thought as much. Do I have time to speak to my wife?"

"Certainly. Come, Quinn, and let's smoke a pipe."

While the two men adjourned to the porch for a smoke, Nelson approached his wife and with great effort knelt down before her and, gently taking her hand, told her, "I know I haven't always been the most demonstrative sort of fellow with you, and

I haven't always been attentive, and now I just want to tell you
that I've always loved you, for all my moods. *Siempre te he queri-
do, mi vida.*" And he rested his head on her lap and felt her
stroking his head. And then she said, "Would you like to hear
what I've been writing?"

"Oh, yes, please."

"It's a little nothing, but it goes like this," and in a steady,
soft voice, she read her poem in Spanish:

> *Birds are singing today,*
> *a conference on Love.*
> *Sensitive flowers,*
> *dreaming in the Sun.*
> *Where do they come from,*
> *with their darling melodies*
> *and their powers to beautify*
> *our days?*

And happily she added, "It's my third verse this morning."

"Well, it's very fine, indeed." And getting up, he leaned over
her and gave her a kiss and said, "Very fine, indeed."

Then, as he walked to the door to join the waiting gentlemen,
there came over him a terrible dizziness, and when he turned to
his wife, the sunlight around her was so brilliant that it seemed
as if it would swallow up the world—and it did.

Heaven

AT THE TIME OF his father's death, Emilio had just finished a
bit part in a cowboy movie, *The Man from Tucson,* in which he
played a desperado; and just as the family was trying to contact
him, he felt the impulse to go away again. He was in a saloon
somewhere in Arizona, killing time while a mechanic worked on
his car—the starter was giving him trouble—and he sat around
from eleven in the morning until five in the afternoon, downing

shots of whiskey and listening to country music out of the jukebox. About halfway through the afternoon he'd started to remember his wife and how happy they'd been and recalled that
other saloon near the Seattle waterfront where he'd listened to
the tale of a monk on a mountain hearing the voice of God, and
he wished to God, if there was a God, that He whisper into his
ears and explain very carefully His reasons for the way some lives
turned out. And then, fortified by drink, he experienced a pleasant few moments reimagining the heaven he had been taught
about as a child, with pastoral fields and angels winging their
way through the clear blue sky, and he laughed.

It happened that two priests were passing through that same
town and were in the saloon, having a meal and a few beers, and
as the afternoon wore on, Emilio eavesdropped on their conversation. When they got up to pay their bill, he said to them, "Hello,
Fathers. I don't mean to barge in on your discussion, but I happened to overhear you mentioning something about a religious
retreat up in Colorado, and I was just wondering if you would
mind telling me where this retreat is, beause lately I've had an
interest in such things."

And one of the priests, thinking that the man seemed vaguely
familiar—he once took a class of schoolchildren to see a double
feature of the Father Byrne films during a snowy afternoon in
Chicago—cordially conveyed the retreat's location, near Boulder,
Colorado, adding that it was a place where priests and monks
and also laymen could go for spiritual solace. They'd been there
several years before and met the monk Thomas Merton, the priest
reporting that it had been an illuminating experience.

"Is it, Father," Emilio had asked, "the kind of place where
a man might find peace?"

"It is, God willing."

And with that they bid the actor farewell and made their
way into the dry heat of the day.

So he sat there drinking and told himself, with a drunkard's
logic, that these priests had appeared out of nowhere, like angels
of God, and with the name of the retreat house, St. Joseph's, and
their directions scribbled on a napkin, Emilio, weary and seeking

escape, resolved to drive to Colorado so that he, too, could hear the voice of God.

*

He drove northeast, and, many hours later, presenting himself to the father superior, he was admitted to the community, provided he make a donation and observe all the rules, particularly pertaining to the ingestion of alcoholic beverages. The retreat, at the foothills of the Rockies, consisted of a church, a central banquet hall, where a rule of silence prevailed, and a number of log cabins spread here and there, as well as a formal garden, with its patches of herbs and dying flowers and statues of Christ and the Holy Mother. Mass was said every morning and there was communal prayer. For one hour each day, between four and five, the rule of silence was lifted and the thirty brothers and priests and monks gathered to converse—he assumed, about the goodness of the Lord.

My God, but he tried. Each day arrived with the promise that as he walked in the garden or took a solitary hike up into the mountains, some great insight about the fortunes of his life would come to him. Counseled by a monk, who'd sensed the man's troubled heart, that spiritual contemplation would be much helped by a fast, Emilio did not have as much as a morsel to eat for five days, sustaining himself with water, and though he felt light-headed and "cleansed"—for he had been poisoning his system for many months—and would sit in a quiet place, the longed-for inward illumination did not come to him.

On the fifth day of his fast, he was feeling most discouraged after nearly two weeks in the place. He participated in the prayers, invoking the names of the Father and the Holy Spirit again and again, trying to tap into his mother's faith and straining to hear, amid the birdsong and the rustling of trees in the breeze, the whisper of faith, but pain still filled his heart. He decided to take a long hike, following a path that after some two hours would lead to a small chapel with a view of the surrounding mountains and hills—the glory of nature all around.

Many clear streams cut down through the hills—the water

so pure that one could drink it—and as he made his way along the path, after an hour or so, he heard laughter and voices in the woods around him, male and female voices crying "Wheee!" and "Come on, don't be a 'fraidy-cat!" and the sound of bodies splashing into the water. Curious, he followed the sounds till he came to the edge of a clearing, and standing quietly behind some bushes, he saw a sort of grotto, over the top of which flowed a waterfall, emptying into a pool below. He also saw three teenage boys and three teenage girls, some atop the rocks and ready to jump in, others already in the water, swimming about—they, innocent as the sunlight, with healthy and unspoiled faces, were all naked.

He watched the prettiest girl in the group, a tall, athletic brunette, her breasts gleaming with the damp of water and sunlight, pubis dripping wet, leaping off and doing a somersault in the air, legs tucked up and the femininity of her bottom protruding, during her tumble into the water, out into the world. And it nearly killed him, not because she was so beautiful, but because in so many ways she reminded him of his beloved wife, as many an infant reminded him of his own, breaking his heart. He watched them jumping, squealing, playing tag in the water —how beautiful women were, all thoughts of the Lord out of his head now—and he, with a prayer book in his bluejeans pocket, saw one of the boys standing up to show his girl, a blonde, his "boner." "Looky here, Lynn!" he'd cried out with the joy of youth, and she had answered, splashing him with water and squealing, "Get that thing out of here!" And it occurred to Emilio then and there that, for all his efforts, a life dedicated to the spiritual ascent into the enclave of heaven was not for him.

Hungry and craving a drink, Emilio made his way back through the woods toward the retreat, and he packed his suitcase and, reporting to the father superior, thankfully made his donation—and drove that late afternoon the twenty-five miles or so to Boulder, where he settled in a hotel for the night. In a restaurant whose walls were covered with cowboy memorabilia, he devoured a meal of steak and potatoes, smothered in gravy, and drank down a bottle of red wine, a disastrous way to break a fast, as the next day he would dearly pay for it with the worst headache and cramped stomach of his life.

But that evening he'd found the world pleasant, and though at first he missed the resolve with which he had decided, on an impulse, to go to St. Joseph's, by ten-thirty, as he was having an equally ruinous double Scotch on the rocks, his brief time at the retreat house and his attempt to resolve the aches of his heart through the resuscitation of the spirit, like so many other things in his life, had already started to slip away.

California and New York, July 1962

PITCHER OF MARTINIS in hand, he was awaiting the arrival of friends. Now, a few hours after he'd gotten back from his most recent trip, the telephone rang and Emilio learned of his father's death.

"Well, brother, I've been trying to call for a week now, with bad news. Poppy's gone."

He did not know what to say.

"We tried to reach you, over and over again by telephone, and we sent telegrams"—they were down by the mail slot, with letters and bills, in a pile that he had not cared to glance at. "And Marta and Carmen went to your house, looking for you. We called your agent, but she said that you had been shooting a movie in Arizona. We just couldn't find you. I'm so sorry."

"And Mama?"

"She's holding up very well, surprising us all, but of course she's very strong. She's been asking for you."

A flush of embarrassment, much shame. It sobered him.

"And what can I do now for the family?"

"Oh, lord, come out. Now you're the man of the family."

*

Full of sorrow, Emilio turned up at the house in Cobbleton after his long absence and laid his head on his mother's lap, weeping.

But she was so gladdened, despite the circumstances, that her son had come—"I'm sorry, I'm sorry, Mama"—that she simply rocked him in her arms, repeating, in her best English, "We're just happy that you're here with us now." And for a few days Emilio, pensive and sober, seemed a part of the family again. On the third day he drove to the cemetery with Margarita to his father's grave and stood for a long time before it, stricken by life's total uselessness. The cemetery brought other memories back to him—flames shooting through a tinderbox hotel, his little girl and wife perishing—and so he told Margarita, dropping her at her apartment, that he was going to spend the afternoon looking for a present for his mother.

But he, the new man of the family, after browsing in local shops, even going into the five-and-dime, headed over to the hotel and dallied at the bar for several hours, signing a few autographs and throwing back a number of whiskeys. When he got back to the house, he was nearly staggering, and though his mother's bones ached, she got out of her chair and grabbed her movie-star son by the ears and slapped his face, saying, "Why are you doing this to yourself? Why?"—in Spanish—"¿Por qué?"

And she pulled at his hair and tried to haul his heavy bulk into the bathroom, wanting to wash out his mouth with soap—and felt truly defeated by the fact that she did not have the strength of a man. Out of frustration, she filled a pot with water and poured it over him.

"Wake up and take care of yourself, boy. God will take care of the rest."

Focusing his eyes on her, he announced, "I'm tired, Mama. Maybe I need a rest." And as if nothing had happened, he gave her a sweet kiss and headed upstairs to one of the bedrooms to nap. Waking shortly before midnight, he was in the kitchen, looking for something to drink. The only thing he found was an old, unopened bottle of Dr. Arnold's Relaxation Heightener, whose contents he dispatched, and soon, as his father used to, he was roaming in the yard, his mouth open as he looked up at the sky, reeling and turning in circles and feeling some odd communication with the old man. The events of his past were swallowed up by the luminous benevolence now all around him. Why, he could close his eyes and swear that, opening them, he would find his father and mother in the yard having a barbecue, his sisters in attendance, the family posing for photographs with the blessedness that had once been his little girl. The wind blowing against his face, he'd swear that it was his daughter's hand touching his nose and chin, and when he looked up at the splendid blue haze surrounding the moon, he thought of the innocence of Mary Isabel. Then the feelings of elation ebbed and he went back into the house, again looking everywhere for something to drink—Margarita had taken out of the house what few bottles of wine and liquor they'd kept in cabinets. And he passed half the night trying to put everything back in its proper place, awakening in the early morning on the parlor floor, his mother sitting in a chair across from him. "Ay, son, don't do that to yourself."

For months after Emilio left for California, Mariela's prayers asked God to restore him. Beside her bed, Mariela kept a tarnished crucifix, a statue of the Holy Mother, and a receptacle with an image of the Holy Spirit, a dove, for blessed candles. In bed she prayed for her son; she asked God to protect him, to send into his life an angelic presence, a woman to help him through his difficult days. He was a good son, calling her on the telephone every so often, but his voice was slurry and hard to understand, his English often incomprehensible. She would lie awake nights, speaking to Nelson, who, in her mind, was not dead, and he would appear to her as a sad whorl of knots on the timber wall. She would speak to her father and her beloved mother. She'd remember Miss Covington and ask her, "What can I do?" Miss Covington, a benevolent woman, would speak mainly about Mariela's rights to pursue her own life, even without a husband. ("Above all, my dear, you must put out of your mind the unpleasantness of your life.")

She prayed and prayed, and one night the angels, as many

as the stars, came flying into the room, and God in His wisdom
directed one of them to intercede in the life of her son.

*

Mornings, given the strength of his mother's prayers, would
find Emilio newly determined to change his ways. Having
watched his career slowly dissipate over the past few years, he
would go for days without so much as one drink, trying hard to
forget the feelings that plagued him. But he was hiding out; that
was how he saw his life. And in the evenings, when he would
retire to bed alone, there would come over him an inability to
sleep—for abstinence left his nerves wrecked—and just like that,
the actor would get dressed, put on his sunglasses, and set out
in his automobile for some bar, where he would sit drinking until
four in the morning, until the bartender would roust him out.
Like the character played by Ray Milland in *The Lost Weekend*,
he endured more than his share of humiliations. A bunch of farm
boys in town for a good time, their faces glowering, picked a
fight with the former movie star; or he was kicked out of a fancy
restaurant because he dropped his third glass of wine on the floor
and, in a fit, turned over the table ("Monsieur, you must leave");
or, waking one morning in a strange apartment with a woman
whose name he could not remember, he thought to himself, My
God, and tiptoed his way out.

For all that, he was lucky. He had never been pulled over
by the cops for being intoxicated, or gotten into an accident—
though some nights he would drive without his headlights or
zoom at seventy miles an hour along the winding roads of the
Hollywood Hills—and he would thank God the next morning to
have made it back to his bungalow (or awaken parked along
some road) without having hurt anyone, his greatest nightmare.
On some of these binge days he would drink so much he'd forget
he was Emilio Montez O'Brien and that he had fourteen sisters.
Sometimes he would make like Lance Stewart, private detective,
and call himself Lance. Or he was Johnny Rogers from one of
his war pictures, or Craig Higgins from that film *Desperation*, in
which he played a jilted husband. And sometimes, walking along

the beach in his bathing trunks, trying to find a good place to watch the pretty surf girls and the tides, he would swear he was the most muscular and beautiful man in the world—after all, he had played Tarzan in two movies—and would feel like standing on the shore giving Tarzan's jungle yell.

He might forget for hours at a time the dense pain he felt in his heart for the loss of his wife and child, but blinking his eyes as he rested in bed, he would remember Jessica putting the baby in the crib and then crawling in beside him, whispering, "We're having a happy life, aren't we?" And that he'd wanted to take her and the child, when she was of traveling age, to Europe on a grand tour, his head filled with memories of beautiful Italy and his heart craving the sights of France and England and all those other places he'd never been. He had wanted these things not only for himself but for them. Then he'd swear that he could hear Jessica humming in the garden and race out, thinking that he would find her in Bermuda shorts, watering the flowers, little Mary Isabel playing in the grass. They would not be there.

And he suffered from all kinds of aches—stomach, liver, kidney aches—and when they got really bad, he would lay off for a few days and then, feeling all cleansed, empty his liquor cabinet.

On one of his worst days he looked up and saw his father, Nelson O'Brien, fiddling with his camera in the back yard, and he stumbled out, opening the sliding doors to find that his father was Mr. Perez, a gardener hired to plant some new bushes.

Things would get all swirly around him, as in those B pictures where a man is cracking up and, spread at the center of a spinning hypno-disc, he falls through an abyss of darkness, voices and distorted faces everywhere around him.

*

And then it happened. He woke one morning, his arms and legs and head covered with bandages and wired up in traction, in a hospital. Flowers in vases set here and there in his room.

He asked a nurse, "What happened?"

"Well, Mr. O'Brien, as best as we can figure, you were up

in the hills one night—and very drunk, that's what the lab tests say—changing a tire along the road; or maybe you were trying to flag someone down to get you back into town. You must have been standing in the middle of the road and some kids, joyriding in the hills, did not see you. You got pretty banged up, mostly broken bones—both your legs and your right arm, which, incidentally, the doctor reset. You had a protruding ulna, I suppose from an earlier injury. But that'll be all fixed up now. And you had a concussion, but a minor one—lucky for you that those kids just swiped you."

"And how long have I been here?"

"You've been here a week," referring to his hospital sheet.

"And did you notify anyone?"

"Well, you had the name of a place called St. Joseph's written on an old napkin in your wallet. And the name and telephone number of a lady called Jessica—"

"—Brooks."

"We tried that, but it was disconnected. Finally we got the name of one of your sisters in New York from an agency here in L.A. Five of your relatives are in town."

"Five?"

"Yes, sir. I don't remember who they are, but they usually come during visiting hours, at four in the afternoon, to inquire about you."

This had been at 11:30 in the morning. He waited and waited until the hour of four, when in they came: his sisters Margarita, Maria, Marta, Carmen, and Gloria.

"Thank God, brother," they shouted, kissing his unbandaged hand.

"*Dios mío,*" Maria had said. "We were worried to death about you when we heard. All of us prayed."

*

It took Emilio months to heal. He hired a nurse to help him in the house, for he was dependent on a wheelchair, and from time to time he received visitors, actor friends and his sisters Marta and Carmen, who would come up from Anaheim to visit him. His hours were spent, for there was not much else he could do, reading the books—novels, travel books, and a Spanish grammar—that Margarita brought him. Otherwise, he passed much time on the telephone, especially with his mother, who, gushing love, and happy with his forced sobriety, spoke admiringly of his strength. Though she never wanted to see him suffer physically like this, she was convinced that God's hand was in all of it. As He sent troubles into the world, so did He intercede to put men on the straight path in life: "You don't have to believe me, son, but it's the truth. You were being protected that night of your accident. Because Dios decided to put an end to your suffering, and He may have been harsh with you, but how else could He bring you out of your torment? He did so because of our prayers and because He is good. Now, never forget that, son."

*

All that was true. It was as if he had awakened from some other life.

He managed, when he was finally getting around again, on crutches and then with a cane, to get his hands on some booze. One of his movie chums brought a couple of bottles of vodka over, but when he took his first sip, it turned his stomach and he threw up. He tried it again, and it burned his gullet. Then he took another sip and found the taste so vile that he poured the bottle out down a sink, and though he tried again on other days, his old temptations coming back to him, his disgust became even stronger. He found himself regarding drink the same way he regarded the old distension of his arm.

*

He gave up on the profession of acting—but did not like the idleness of his days. With some money, about fifty grand, that he'd managed to save over the years, he started at the ripe old age of forty to look into a new means of livelihood. For a time he kept himself amused by practicing his old sleight-of-hand tricks and thought about putting together an act—but while performing here and there in schools, for children, to try it out, he felt a little ridiculous dressed up like Mandrake the Magician, with collapsing top hat and flowing black cape. Some old friends almost talked him into investing in a restaurant, à la Preston Sturges, who had done so in the 1940s, but as Mr. Sturges had been ruined, Emilio, despite offers of help from Irene, who loved to cook, decided against it.

One day he picked up a camera. He had been thinking about his youth in Cobbleton and the many hours he used to spend beside his father in his shop and going about the countryside, and remembering Nelson O'Brien's serenity when he set about his work. And in the same way that a glass of whiskey once brought him closer to his father, he found that looking through a lens did so, too. At first he took it up as a means of passing the time. He would drive south and into the desert with some fancy equipment, taking photographs and feeling at peace with the world. He accumulated the materials for a development lab, which he set up in a closet, and while dipping some negatives into the chemical solution, he found himself experiencing a sense of communion with his own family history, the old sensations of belonging again accruing in his heart like lights and shadows rising to the surface.

So, as if he had the blessing of his father, Emilio Montez O'Brien, former movie star, found himself a storefront on Wilshire Boulevard and, placing some advertisements here and there, embarked on a new mid-life career. His name, Montgomery O'Brien, was remembered well enough among the Los Angeles community. Old connections in the movie business began to hire him for promotional photography, and magazines, finding his former stardom alluring, would assign him to shoot photographs of the stars in their homes. He photographed Zsazsa Gabor, Kirk Douglas, Burt Lancaster (an old friend), Lauren Bacall, Cary Grant, Bette Davis, and Gilbert Roland, among many others. And the high-society folks out in Bel Air and Beverly Hills, enchanted by the splendidness of this former movie star, thought it prestigious to have Emilio, sober as wood, at their gatherings.

A Few

Moments of

Earthly

Happiness

Lastly, she pictured to herself how this same little sister of hers would, in the after-time, be herself a grown woman; and how she would keep, through all her riper years, the simple and loving heart of her childhood: and how she would gather about her other little children, and make their eyes bright and eager with many a strange tale, perhaps even with the dream of Wonderland of long ago . . .

—from Lewis Carroll's
Alice's Adventures in Wonderland

Cobbleton, 1967

LIVING IN COBBLETON and teaching high school at sixty-five, Margarita still wanted to leave that town. She often thought of going to New York to live out her retirement years with her sisters in their West End Avenue apartment, or of moving up to Connecticut, where her Cuban lover, whom she had met in Spain, and who was now an exile, lived. But after Nelson died, Margarita, ever loyal and dedicated to her mother's well-being, resigned herself to remaining by her side, and she gave up her apartment and moved back into the house, taking two rooms on the upper floor, one for her favorite furnishings and keepsakes, the other the room she had once shared with Isabel.

In that room, the dresser drawers, with their 1920s scent, were still filled with old camisoles and slips and cloche caps and stockings and underwear, and on the shelves were some of their childhood dolls and certain of the books that she collected as a young girl, with their pressed flowers and antique valentine cards tucked inside, just as she left them. Then there was the mirror before which she had stood naked as a young girl, proudly examining her body. That mirror, neglected for so long, must have been happy when now, as a woman of advancing years, Margarita, preparing for a bath, would stand before it again, her body so much more weathered by life, her legs covered with varicose veins (these coming to her like a mockery during the days when she first had to endure the discomforts of menopause, with heart palpitations and a heat so severe that she would break out in a terrible sweat), and her breasts less firm but with nipples that still hardened, even at her age, when, dampening a finger, she would pinch them until they swelled. Later, in the privacy of the bathroom, she would fill the tub and rest her body in the warm and consoling water. And as the water drained out of the tub, she would pull the curtains closed and turn on the shower, enjoying the intense spray on her belly and down below, where it was all tangly with gray and black pubic hair, her femininity, in old age, feeling as good under the force of that spray as it had in her youth.

Sleeping on her old brass bed, she would have uncanny dreams at night and swear that she would awaken and find herself a young girl again, the rooms of the house filled with a chaotic and ever-busy configuration of sister beings. On some mornings, when she would join her mother for breakfast before heading off to school, she would remember the days, during the painted-glass years, when the feminine influence of the house was so strong that automobiles would sometimes run off the road and skid into the thick oak tree in their yard, and once an aviator, his plane's engine losing power, brought his plane down in a field. (Though she liked to think that he'd been brought down by the allure of the women who once lived there together.)

She moved in with her mother to insure that Mariela Montez would not spend her last years alone. For her part, Mariela did not want to leave the house, even when her daughters Irene and Patricia offered to take her in. It was as if her mother drew some kind of strength and inspiration from her surroundings. Long accustomed to her life in the house, with her little *cositas*—her things—she seemed to take solace in her late husband's belongings; his clothes still hung in the closets and she liked to keep his pipe around, sometimes sniffing its scent. Set in her ways and content in the peaceful contemplation of her past, the writing of her verse, and the occasional company of her children and grandchildren, Mariela did not like to go out, except for an infrequent trip into Cobbleton or to New York to see her daughters there.

When she went to town to shop with Margarita, she'd walk regally along the streets with a slow but assured gait—for, while many things in the town had changed, she would always proudly remain the same. People did not stare at her now, as they used to years ago when she would come walking along with a pack of her children following behind her. And though she still did not enjoy speaking English, she now used it in the serenity of autocratic old age, to order shop clerks around.

Margarita would laugh, thinking about these things. A few years before, when their mother was eighty-one, they made a trip into New York City to hear Maria, Olga, and Jacqueline in recital at Carnegie Hall, the concert taking place on St. Patrick's Day, and on the morning of the parade, Margarita, Maria, and their mother, overdressed in fur hats and fur-muffed coats and boots, stood along Fifth Avenue to watch the procession of marchers with their Irish banners and shamrock-decaled drums and floats representing the Sons of Erin and the Emerald Society, and flank after flank of police officers, and brave fire companies wearing green-tasseled caps and cummerbunds, and musicians in kilts and grenadier hats, playing bagpipes and snare drums— beauty queens, too, and high-school boys and girls marching, green-dyed carnations pinned to their lapels—a grand Irish pride everywhere, and a slight chill in the air.

The daughters, half Irish, felt a surge of excitement, while their mother, perhaps thinking about her husband, watched the line in silence and then sighed.

Afterward they'd gone over to Bloomingdale's, to a sale of European blouses. Mariela tottered along the racks, inhaling the perfume mists in the air, and evaluating the silk, rayon, and cotton designs. ("Now, I know how to sew. The person who made this didn't," she would mutter in Spanish.) And Margarita would remember how one of the salesladies, a Puerto Rican of consid- erable beauty, overheard Mariela carrying on about the high prices of the blouses and walked over, asking in Spanish how she might help. That started their mother on how the two "chicks" in her company—Margarita, sixty-three, and Maria, fifty-nine—were but two of her fourteen daughters. And she went on, asking the saleslady, "And did you know that my son is Montgomery O'Brien, the movie actor?" And although the salesgirl had never heard of him, she nodded and listened to Mariela go on and on about the boy, her movie-star son, "the image of his father." Then she related the solitude of her widowhood, eventually working around to the premise that a widow's life, even given a wonderful family, was lonely and difficult and that, at the very least, Bloomingdale's should give her a special widow's discount, and the salesgirl as a Puerto Rican should appreciate the trials of her generation of Spanish-speaking immigrants and think about what her own life would be like in old age. Such was her persistence, her conviction, and the you-should-have-a-special-respect-for-your-elders charm that the salesgirl finally asked her, "Which blouses do you want?" and then proceeded to mark down the already discounted prices, later saying to Margarita, "That's some mother you've got there."

*

But lately it was more difficult for Mariela to get around—long journeys in an automobile often made her carsick, and just sitting in a car wreaked havoc with her aging, arthritic bones—so difficult that Margarita counted it among the happier miracles of life that she and her mother and Gloria back in 1964 had made a most special and (for her mother) epic trip.

With the Italian Saints

THAT YEAR, for Mariela's eightieth birthday, the family had chipped in to send their mother to the European country of her choice, so that she could see something more of the world. They thought she would naturally choose Spain, the land of her ancestors—and Margarita urged it—but Mariela Montez, expressing a rare political opinion, had no desire to set foot in

Franco's Spain and instead chose the country of Italy and its grand and illustrious capital, Rome. (She wanted to go for Holy Week, but only if she could see the Pope.)

(Happy then, their mother began to speak about a book she had once owned as a child, *En la ciudad de Dios*, a copy of which was still sitting in the drawer of a dresser that belonged to her mother and father in the house on Victoriana de Avila Street, where Isabel still remained with her husband.)

Arranging air fare to Rome and lodgings in that city through a travel agency, and getting their mother a new passport, they prevailed on Violeta's husband, the good Reverend Farrell, to seek out the Catholic Archbishop of Baltimore, with whom he was friendly, to arrange a special papal audience. And with all this accomplished, Mariela, with Margarita and Gloria, who had never been anywhere except to California, bid farewell to their sisters who were seeing them off at the airport and made their way to Rome and a little *pensione* in Trastevere called Il Paradiso. Its tiled halls were covered with late-nineteenth-century renderings of scenes out of Dante's poem, the ladies, gleeful but a little exhausted, sharing a large room that looked out onto a central courtyard.

Although they were enchanted by the city, it was hard for their mother to walk too long, for they were correct in their assessment that she was quite nearly beyond the age of travel, as she got tired easily and sometimes suffered from an arthritic condition in her joints. Still, Mariela reveled in the place. Wearing a bright flowery dress and a large hat—the very hat that Margarita bought her during her travels in Spain—she admired the marketplaces, as they reminded her of Cuba, and revered the beauty and cheerful spirit of the people. And, my God, the food and the cheap prices simply astounded her, the lady stuffing herself with bread, pasta, fish, and veal, as if she had not eaten a meal in years, and pronouncing again and again, "*¡Caramba!* This is better than anything I've ever tasted, even in New York."

And drinking wine, too! She adored the sweet and serene beauty of sitting at a table in the Piazza Santa Maria in Trastevere, watching the children playing soccer by the fountain, the bells clanging and sparrows flitting through the air, the sweet scent of springtime wisteria growing stronger and more compelling to Mariela with each sip, until, hearing some music out of a bar doorway, she would begin to sway in her chair and sing along, eyes wide, declaring, "The muse is coming to me." And soon she would take out a pencil and paper from her purse and scribble down one of her verses.

They'd walk back in the early afternoon, and while their mother contentedly napped, Gloria and Margarita would step out to get a coffee and more or less pass the time as they would in New York. Or when they spoke on the telephone, their conversations in those days centering on Gloria's growing disenchantment with her beau Arnold from Macy's, who not only still lived with his demanding mother but had begun to act more and more like a child in her presence, so that the nature of their bedtime romps, usually on weekend afternoons when Maria, Olga, and Jacqueline were out of the apartment, had lost much of its appeal for her. She wanted a man, and not a child, in bed. And while they were "intimate," as she told Margarita countless times, the great excitement of being overwhelmed by the pure physicality of a real man so diminished that she bedded him now primarily out of a sense of duty.

"And for another thing," she said to Margarita, "he is so afraid of his mother that not once in ten years has he brought me to his home in Canarsie. It confuses me, because I feel grateful to him—you know he's always been good to me—but some days when we meet for lunch I want to tell him it's all over, because soon I'll be too old to find myself another man."

"Then get rid of him. You're still pretty."

"Yes, I suppose I should."

But no matter how often they discussed it, she continued with Arnold.

As they walked along the streets of the Eternal City, the sight of a man necking with his woman would make Gloria sigh, but Margarita could not tell if it was because she wanted love or because she was feeling nostalgic for Arnold. He had wanted to join them on the trip, promising Gloria to tell his mother finally that he would take a vacation without her. Every year, whenever Gloria and Arnold made plans to go off to some romantic place for vacation, like most lovers, the plans always fell through and Arnold would spend two weeks with his mother at a resort hotel in Atlantic City. This so angered Gloria that she refused to bring him along. Besides, a little naughty, she entertained the idea of having a romance with one of those elegant Italian men who seemed to be everywhere.

(This did not happen, although on more than one occasion they'd experienced the mixed pleasure of feeling a man's hand taking hold of their still shapely bottoms.)

With their mother in tow, they made like happy tourists, visiting the Roman Forum ("Ay, if only your father was here to see this place," Mariela would cry), the catacombs on the Via Appia Antica, many churches, with one trip out to Tivoli and the fountains of the Villa d'Este. And during Holy Week, they heard Mass on Holy Thursday, Good Friday, and on Easter Sunday celebrated by the Supreme Pontiff himself, Pope Paul VI. Twice their mother nearly fainted. As they waited among the worshippers in the Church of St. John the Lateran, the Pope, resplendent in white vestments and papal hat and followed by an entourage of cardinals, strode quickly into the nave, giving his blessings to all, not two yards from where Mariela and her daughters were standing. And they stood close enough to touch him during the Stations of the Cross, by the Colosseum.

The day after the Easter Sunday Mass in St. Peter's Square, they returned for Mariela's audience with the Pope in the Pauline Chapel, joining a group of about twenty other devout Catholics who through generous donations or connections could have this meeting arranged. There Mariela had waited, trembling, intoxicated by the scent of incense and candle wax and the prospect of having a few words with the Pope himself, for the attending Monsignor to lead her and the sisters into his most sacred presence. When it was their turn and they were being escorted toward His Eminence seated regally on a throne, Mariela, in the dark formal dress that she bought especially for the occasion, grasped the golden crucifix on a chain around her neck with one hand,

her elbows crooked into the arms of her daughters, as she repeated, "Ay, ay, ay," and *"Estoy temblando,* I'm trembling"—
so often that Margarita had whispered, "Mama, *tranquila, tranquila,* Calm yourself."

Kneeling before Paul VI, whose harsh and stern birdlike
appearance startled Margarita, each kissed his papal ring and
received his blessing. And then, directing himself to Mariela, he
said in Spanish—for the Pope is advised on these occasions as
to which language the pilgrims speak: "Welcome to the church
of St. Peter." And: "How may I assist in your spiritual quest?
Are you here for a special blessing?"

"Yes, Father, I am," she responded in a quivering voice.

"And for whom are these blessings?"

"For the soul of my dead husband," she answered. "And
the souls of my mother and father."

He nodded.

"And I have a troubled son, Your Holiness."

"And the nature of his troubles?"

"It is his heart. He suffers so in this life."

Nodding and taking a breath, he then asked, "And your
names?"

"Mariela Montez O'Brien, Your Excellency."

"Margarita."

"Gloria."

Then he made the sign of the cross over them and said, "I
bless you, Mariela, Margarita, and Gloria, in the name of the
Father, the Son and the Holy Spirit. And I will remember your
wishes in my morning Mass. Now go in peace."

And when Mariela struggled, getting up, the Pontiff extended his hand and gave her a little tug, and though her back
was aching and she cried "Ay, ay, ay," she felt as if she was
going to ascend at that very moment toward the marble, cloud-
ridden palaces of heaven.

*

Their mother had gotten to make that one journey, at least,
and she experienced much pleasure from it, but upon her return

she'd pronounced that she was happy to be back home. For weeks, all she could talk about was the Pope and his blessings, the good food, and how wonderful she thought the Italians were. She was most impressed, Margarita remembered, not by their beauty, but by the way they treated their children, with great love. As they were leaving the Rome airport, bags packed with newly purchased silk scarves, a few ceramic plates, and endless ashtrays, fans, and paperweights that they'd bought at the Vatican as presents for the family, they saw an impeccably dressed Italian man strolling toward a gate with a homely little girl who was eating a drippy ice-cream cone. Holding her by the hand, he would stop every so often and, kneeling down before her, remove from his jacket pocket a handkerchief to wipe her chin, and then he would tousle her bangs, which fell over her brow, and pull her close, giving her a sweet hug. He'd say, *"Mia preziosa, mia bella bambina,"* and *"Tesoro,"* exuding such a total love that it would one day most certainly transform her homeliness into beauty. Speaking of this, Mariela had concluded that *"ellos, los italianos, son santos*—those Italians are saints."

In the House, 1967–71

SINCE THAT TIME, Mariela's trips away from the house had been few. Mainly they'd go to town to see the doctor if she was not feeling well, or to a dentist if a tooth ached (though past eighty, she still had every one of her teeth). And they'd visit with the families of Irene and Patricia at their homes in nearby towns. Of course, they would go to church every Sunday and to confession on Wednesdays, Margarita sitting in a back pew, pleased that the journey to Rome had in some ways energized the old woman, who now appeared in town wearing not only her large gold crucifix on a chain with several other religious medals (of St. Anthony and St. Francis and St. Teresa of Avila) but also a pendant of carved ivory bearing the image of the Pope, and an Italian silk scarf around her neck.

Her mother would spend a long time in the confessional, confessing heaven knows what—for, if she sinned at all, they were venial sins, though she was a little vain, sometimes staring at herself in the mirror for half an hour at a time and, deciding that she was still beautiful, would joke on their way to town, "Maybe I'll find some old man to fall in love with me, what do you think?"

And sometimes she became irritable with the family. Often on the telephone in the evenings, she'd go on in exhaustive detail about the more or less ordinary events of her day, recounting, for example, what she and Margarita and Irene had had for lunch at a place like the Hunter's Lodge (*Comimos muy bien. Yo me comí un bistek con papas y una salsa muy sabrocita, y Margarita un pedacito de pollo con arroz y . . .*"), or conveying, scene by scene, a movie she had watched earlier on television, like *Doctor Zhivago* with Omar Sharif. One evening she told the whole movie to Maria, going on for an hour and twenty minutes, until even the ever-patient Maria cut her off, saying, "It's a beautiful story, but I have so many things to do. Now, Mama, I have to say goodbye. I will speak to you soon. Okay?"

Afterward Mariela decided that she had been insulted, and that Maria had changed, and that became a subject for her speculations. Sitting in the very chair where her father used to spend his evenings, and preparing her lessons for the next day, Margarita sighed.

"You know why Maria's changed?" Mariela said. "It's because she's never had her own family to look after, and that's made her selfish."

"Mama, you know that Maria is one of the most unselfish people in the world. When has she ever turned you down for anything?"

"Well, she shouldn't hang up on me."

"Yes, Mama, but you were going on and on about Omar Sharif."

"That doesn't change the fact that I'm her mother."

"Mama, don't think that way. Maria was probably a little

tired. You know that she and Olga and Jacqueline are always busy teaching and working."

"Yes, tired, *mi vida*. If she's tired now, then she should wait until she is my age. I'm never too tired to let my children know that I love them."

"Yes, Mama."

She nursed other peeves, too, especially toward Helen, who sometimes acted as if she was ashamed of her. For some months before, when she had made the difficult journey to New York to attend Helen's fifty-seventh birthday party in her Park Avenue apartment, Helen seemed quite disturbed that Mariela had shown up wearing her crucifix and medals and the Pope's pendant, and her first words to Mariela were "Oh, Mother, did you have to wear all that? These are very refined people here."

And although Helen had later apologized to her mother— for Margarita pulled her aside to correct her—Mariela passed the evening feeling slighted and still, months later, could not help talking about it.

"But, Mama, didn't Helen make up with you and take you around to meet all the famous people there?"

"Yes, but only because you made her."

"No, Mama, I didn't say anything else to her. Don't you remember, I was sitting most of the time with her son Dennis and with Gloria. And when Maria and the others came in, we were all by the piano, where the composer Cy Coleman was playing."

"Yes, yes, I remember, but she didn't speak to me all night."

"Mama, that's because when you have a drink—and I saw you drinking at least two glasses of champagne—you don't want to have anything to do with speaking English. *¿Recuerdas?*"

"So? What of it? I did everything I could to raise her correctly. I don't understand why she doesn't know how to speak Spanish, and I don't see how she can expect me to remember English at my age. Even your father, whose Spanish was all twisted up, at least he always tried. You know it—and Isabel and Maria and Olga and Jacqueline learned it as well and speak it the way they sing, like nightingales." She made a clicking sound with her mouth. "I don't see why the others didn't."

"Ay, Mama. Sometimes you're very harsh."

And her mother shrugged. "What of it, I've lived this long. And what do I care, as long as I know they all love me."

On certain evenings, the two were the image of felicity, Margarita tending to her schoolwork and reading in the parlor, novels mainly; her mother sitting nearby, scribbling one of her verses on a yellow pad which Margarita bought for her, or reading from a book—most often, as she got older, *Life on the Planet Mars*. But sometimes when her mother was restless and just wanted to talk and talk, Margarita would lose patience.

"Please, Mama, a little peace and quiet."

On one of those nights Mariela interpreted her daughter's longing for silence as some kind of censure, and, approaching her, said, "You're feeling sad, aren't you, my daughter?"

"No, Mama. I'm just reading."

"Oh, my darling, you can say that, but last night I couldn't sleep, thinking about the tragedy of your marriage with that fellow Lester."

"Mama, no."

"And I was thinking that you would have been happier if you'd stayed with him than to end up one day in this big and lonely house with me."

"Mama, you know that's not true. I'm not unhappy."

"Yes, yes, I know that you will say these things to make me feel peaceful, because you've always been a good daughter to me. But there are times when, in order to get along, one wants to forget the truth. Your father, for example, was a very, very good man, but did you know that for many years he always had a little bit too much to drink, nearly every day . . ."

"We knew that, Mama."

". . . And that every day I would kneel down before my bed, praying to God that He help the poor man, and to this day I thank God that, for all your father's sadness about life, he ended up being so fortunate. And sometimes, child, when I think of all our suffering, all the hours I spent here worrying about you, I always regret most that you let that good man Lester go."

"Mama, I didn't let him go. He was very bad to me."

"No, child, you say that now . . ."

"I've always told you so."

"No, child, you're saying that now because it brings you peace in your advancing years, and I know that you tell yourself that so you will forget all the good between you and what you lost."

"Mama, I think it's time for you to go to bed. I don't like it when you start up like this, and you know we'll just have a bad fight."

"But, child, it only upsets you because I'm speaking to you from my heart."

"No, Mama, you're telling me this because I am in a quiet mood and you want me to speak to you about everything in the world. And when I'm this way you think I'm ignoring you, when night after night we speak for hours, and all I want to do is to be tranquil in my house, and yet you always want to bring something up to agitate me."

Her mother, looking down, was shaking her head, and whispered, "If my mother were alive, God bless her soul, I would listen to her for years."

Margarita, taking hold of her hands, said, sighing, "Mama, Mama, look at me."

But her mother went on staring at the floor and a tear rolled from her eye.

"You know that Lester was bad to me," Margarita said to her. "That was nearly thirty years ago. Don't you remember that nice lady, Miss Covington?"

"Yes, the poor woman."

"And how Miss Covington would take us down to the Ladies' Society in town and how impressive she was in her womanly dignity?"

"Yes."

"Well, one day she told me never, never to take abuse from a man—and men can be very abusive toward our kind—and even though I nodded and said yes to her, I went on with that man, and do you know why? Because I looked at you and Poppy and I thought that marriage meant everything. And don't get me started talking about what he did to me. I've told you a hundred times, he was cruel."

At that, her mother looked up. "But didn't he take care of you?"

"Yes, but there are things you simply don't know about."

Her mother, composed, thought about it. "I don't know what the man did to you, but whatever it was, I don't believe it was truly part of his character. You were his wife, and as I've always told you, no matter how many times I felt like going back to Cuba in the days when your father changed, I really never once thought of leaving him. We had partaken of the sacrament of holy matrimony and, as you should know, that contract was not written just for the civil clerks of this earth, during this poor lifetime of ours, but for the clerks who preside over eternity."

Her mother's turn of phrase delighted Margarita, making her smile.

"As for your husband, who knows what the poor man was thinking during his abuses."

Then, "Don't forget," she added, "that you could never bear him a son."

With that, Margarita excused herself, heading up into the familiar and comforting surroundings of her old room. Waiting to hear her mother's troubled ascent up the stairway, she heard her opening her bedroom door and with a loud "Ay!" tumble down on the bed. She'd usually help her up the stairs and into bed, but after their conversation, she wanted her mother to know what it would be like to roam the halls without her. She listened to sighs and yawns and, through the space under the bedroom door, noticed the dimming of the light. Her mother slept in the same bed as she used to with her husband, and beside it was a lamp, which she turned off before laying her head on the pillow.

Satisfied that her mother was asleep, and feeling a little agitated, Margarita returned to the fine novel *Madame Bovary*, by Gustave Flaubert. She read for an hour and sleep started to come to her eyes. And with resignation, for she hated to leave the book, she turned off the light. But she could not sleep, thinking about her mother and all her years with Lester.

A flutter of emotions ran up through her rib cage as she remembered the first time Lester had brought her back from a speakeasy in the days when he would sit in a restaurant with her and, slipping his hand under her skirt and into the elastic material of her underdrawers, finger her and say, "Oh, my little gypsy." They then headed back to Cobbleton to their house—long since torn down—and they undressed down to their underclothes. He always loved to have her kneel on the bed, her rump raised high, the creases that her undergarments made against her flesh and the pubic hair that spilled out of the material exciting him. He would sometimes nip at those hairs, pulling one or two out with his teeth—she'd hardly felt more than the plucking of an eyebrow hair—and then, rubbing his erect member, as her father's book would put it, against her buttocks, he would pull the delicate cloth of her underwear down over her legs and make his way into her vagina. But one night, for whatever reason, he had wanted to probe her bottom, and while it had felt quite all right at first to Margarita, who squirmed and "ohhed" and opened her thighs wide, she could not anticipate the rough shove of Lester's thin but very long penis into her. When she cried—with pain—he stroked her hair and said, "My darling!" And when she, feeling a muddy discomfort, had said, "Let's wash ourselves and do it the normal way," he had thrust and thrust again, until, coming, his semen had balled up inside her.

"Let's not do this again," she said to Lester.

But he wanted to, again and again, though she never liked it.

*

Generally, however, mother and daughter got along tranquilly enough, Margarita ever patient, as she knew that soon, that year or a few years hence, her mother would be taking her leave of the world. And besides, the older woman seemed quite content to spend many a day off in the field, under a tree, writing. It had always been a subject of curiosity for Margarita that her mother kept her all-consuming work to herself, never leaving her notebooks around the house but hiding them at the end of the day somewhere in her closets. Over the years she'd heard snippets of the verse, her mother bursting with pride at a recent line and sometimes reciting a portion of one of her musings in Spanish to Maria or one of her other Spanish-speaking daughters. But she never handed her daughter the notebooks, guarding them as if they held the contents of some secret life which even her oldest and closest daughter could not see while she was still alive. And on the few occasions when Margarita had crept up behind her to take a look at the work over her mother's shoulder, the old woman clapped the notebook shut and said, "*Mi vida*, you'll have plenty of time to read them when I'm gone."

In addition, she seemed quite enchanted by the efforts of the American space program to put a man on the moon. Of all the items that would come on the evening news about the Vietnam War, the progress of the President's Great Society programs, or the occasional bit of information about Cuba, she seemed most fascinated by the NASA space launches. Whenever astronauts went into orbit around the earth, she would spend the evening out on the porch among the moths and fireflies, just looking up at the sky, as if she might see the orbiting craft. Perhaps she had been influenced by her book, *Life on the Planet Mars*, but she was certainly convinced that once the Americans landed on the moon they would find life, if not entire civilizations. She had, after all, come into the world before the invention of the airplane and television, and into her maturity at a time when it was not at all unusual to read in a newspaper articles with titles like "Men on the Moon, Will They Be Like Us?" More than that, though, Mariela Montez was convinced that God in making the universe with love in His heart would certainly allow that love to go everywhere. Looking up and daydreaming, she imagined that in those very great distances there were other places with flowery gardens along whose paths young lovers walked hand in hand—for what other point could there have been for El Señor to have such a large universe and to light the heavens with spectacular stars and to send comets like Halley's spinning across the sky, or to send meteorites shooting radiantly through the atmosphere, if not to remind us that His power and goodness have no limit?

Sometimes she would sit for hours just looking up at the moon. She prayed to God that she live long enough to learn what the astronauts would one day discover. (Certainly winged, nearly transparent angels, floating above the lunar surface.) Such diversions gave her much comfort and it was only occasionally that Mariela would feel her solitude. Every so often, after Sunday Mass, she and Margarita would go to the Catholic cemetery and she would stand before the Celtic cross that marked Nelson O'Brien's resting place to say a prayer and to leave some potted flowers, the woman sadly sighing as she walked along with Margarita past all the tombstones in that metropolis of the dead where Kate O'Brien also resided. Then they would head for the ice-cream parlor, now operated by the Friendly's chain, and she would devour a big breakfast of syrup-drenched waffles or, simply, an ice-cream sundae. And sometimes on a Sunday they would drive out to visit her daughter Irene and her family or Patricia, and before having a late-afternoon meal they would play canasta. Occasionally, they would all come over to the house on Abelmyer Road, and Irene would take over the kitchen, and Mariela would revel in the company of her grandchildren and great-grandchildren, the littlest ones playing in the halls of the house and bringing much joy to her heart.

Margarita's Love from Cuba

ONE DAY, a 1966 Chrysler pulled up to the house, and out of that automobile emerged the sturdy, thick, and gray-haired form of Luis Vasquez, the Cuban gentleman of whom Margarita had first become enamored in Spain years before. Back in the 1950s, Margarita and Luis would meet once a year on secret trips away from Cobbleton and Havana, in Miami Beach, holing up in a hotel room for a week at a time, where they'd frolic like young and indecent lovers. They'd made an agreement—"no involvement"—but each year they greeted each other with the same fervor, running into the other's arms and kissing endlessly with their first embrace. With shutters closed to the sunlight, Margarita could hardly wait to take off her dress and slip, Luis kissing and biting everything he could reach, Margarita blushing and laughing with joy. And when he'd lower his trousers, they would fall on the bed, devouring each other with the same adamancy as they'd known in Spain. Back in 1954, Margarita looked like Ava Gardner when she met Luis in Valencia. She was fifty-two years old at the time, he fifty-three or fifty-four and balding. They dined the first evening, talking, but the second night he stood gently kissing her against a park wall. Pressing close to her, against her feminine center, with the ardor of a much younger man, he muttered, *"Eres muy mujer."* Later they went to his high-priced hotel, El Palacio, and Margarita, who had not made love to anyone outside of her husband and a forlorn soldier during the war, so opened herself to Luis that night that they made love seven times—not counting when she took his filling penis into her mouth and made him come that way. Forget that her breasts had become pendulous and that in a little game they played she would sway them before his mouth and he would try to catch them with his lips.

They kept these annual appointments until the Cuban Revolution came along (in that troublesome country of her mother's birth), turning his life upside down. He had been the owner of a garage in Havana and the manager of a General Motors dealership, and when the government nationalized that business he found himself out of work. For two years Luis wrote her letters, asking for her love and for some basic amenities—and she sent them, toilet paper and cans of beef and shirts and trousers and underwear, aspirins and Alka-Seltzer, too. He was one of those Cubans who escaped by boat, arriving in the Florida Keys one dim night in 1964, and living in Miami for a time. But through old connections in America, he relocated in the town of New Elm, Connecticut, where General Motors had a parts manufacturing plant. Once he'd settled into his new life in Connecticut, Margarita would try to get away to see him. (During their first reunion, in 1965, Margarita removed her brassiere, and though she was old—sixty-three at the time—he kissed her on her un-sightly varicose veins and when she felt embarrassed, saying, "Ay, but I'm so ugly now," he continued to kiss her, saying, "No, no, my darling, you are still beautiful.")

Since then, they would see each other every few months or so, and because it was hard for Margarita to leave her mother in the house alone, Luis would drive into town and take a room in the Main Street Hotel or in one of the motels out in the countryside and Margarita, slipping away on the pretense of marking some papers in school, would head out, spending the days with Luis in bed. But by the evening's end she would come back to the house—a necessity that depressed them both, for she would miss the warmth of his body and the simple pleasant company of the man. So one day Margarita, tired of this kind of arrangement, told her mother that she was involved with a gentleman.

"That is a good thing, my daughter," Mariela had said. "And who is this gentleman?"

"The Cuban fellow, Luis, I once told you about."

"The one you were always sending packages to?"

"Yes, that's him."

"And it's an involvement?"

"Yes, Mama, I would say so."

"And at your age?"

"Yes, Mama."

"Is he good to you?"

"Oh, yes, Mama."

"Then invite him to the house."

When he arrived, dressed in a leisure suit, carrying flowers and a box of chocolates for Mariela, he sat in the parlor recounting to her mother the events of his recent life and his current circumstances. His family in Cuba wanted to leave and to that end he was trying to save money so they could get out via Spain, but he was still worried because he had reached the age of retirement and General Motors, though grateful to him for his many years of service in Cuba, was anxious to take him off its full-time payroll. He was stoic and a little bitter, but, just the same, tried to be as pleasant as he could—though the strain of his circumstances seemed apparent in the tiredness of his expression. "For some reason," he recounted, "I don't sleep very well in this country."

He visited them several more times that summer, and because he was so attentive to Mariela and very Cuban and sad, she always welcomed him into the house and did not mind when Margarita and Luis would go off for a drive, returning in the late afternoon before Luis would either drive back up to Connecticut or head for a motel. On one of those afternoons, Luis invited Mariela for a drive along the beautiful country roads, and after visiting with Irene, who was not feeling so well of late because of her worsening diabetes (the poor thing, loving sweets so much), they went to the hotel for dinner, and that evening, when Luis got up to use the rest room, Mariela had leaned over and said to her daughter, "And where is he going to be staying for the night?"

"I think here in the hotel."

And her mother surprised her: "Nonsense, I'll have nothing of that. He can come and stay with us in the house."

"Yes?"

"Why not, and for all I care, old lady that I am, he can stay with you in your room."

"Mama, have you been drinking too much wine?"

"And if I have? My darling daughter, even in my old age I haven't forgotten what happens between a man and a woman. Besides, you're not exactly a young girl whose life is going to be ruined by a little fun." And throwing up her hands and sipping a glass of hearty burgundy, she added, "When he comes back, you tell him that as far as I'm concerned he's part of the family."

*

In her bedroom later that night, among the dolls and books of her youth, Luis and Margarita pressed their aging bodies together, kissing very quietly, touching and trying not to sigh too loud, as they were aware, like anxious teenagers, that her mother's bedroom was three doors away, the house otherwise so quiet that all they could hear besides their own hushed breathing and moans was the tick-tock of a pendulum clock in the parlor, the chirping of cicadas in the fields, the occasional slapping shut of a barn door in the wind, and the skitter of mice in the ceiling boards. And while Luis tried to be as quiet as possible, when he entered Margarita, in the slow and dense immersion of his still lively sex inside her he had moaned and told her, "Oh, Margarita, you feel as moist and delicious as the first time we ever went to bed." And Luis, who found in the act of love a release from his worldly troubles, turned and twisted around inside her, shaking the bed and making the floors creak. Even though they shared a hundred and thirty-nine years of life between them, they were soon caught up in the revelries of mutual pleasure and affection, and their age seemed pointless. They were as frolicsome as young newlyweds, each trembling, each perspiring and loving the taste of the other's sweat and tongue and all the bodily caresses that filled the room at a certain moment with the muffled cries of love.

That night, Mariela was vaguely aware that some amorous mischief was taking place down the hall. She had been reading some of her writing when at one in the morning she heard a cry of pleasure. Of course she knew what they were doing in Margarita's bedroom, and that was fine—what did she care? There was something about Luis's suffering that reminded her of the sufferings of her own father, and perhaps because of that, she found herself blessing their union, for in her ripe age, and despite the crucifix she always wore around her neck, she had no objections to those simple moments of earthly happiness that were a salve to the pains and troubles of this world.

*

Eighty-seven years old and delighted, Mariela Montez spent a morning dressing in a white gown, too large now for her withered body. She was to pose in the downstairs parlor of her house in Cobbleton for her photographer son, who had come in from California, tanned and fit and happy—there were rumors that he was again in love—and although she noticed that he now walked with a slight limp, he was ever attentive and courteous.

Margarita threw a party for her mother. The Chanteuses arrived in Cobbleton with Gloria; then came Irene, Patricia, and their families; Sarah from Philadelphia with her husband; Violeta and her saintly spouse and their children; Veronica alone; Marta and Carmen and their husbands. They all converged on the house to wish their mother another happy birthday.

Only Helen and her husband—off on a tour of the South of France—and Isabel, still in Cuba, were unable to attend.

Much activity around her—peals of laughter—and the old woman, who'd let her hair go white, sitting down among them.

She only spoke in Spanish now—her faculty for the English language having slipped away from her. That was unfortunate. At times she could barely discern what Irene was saying when she'd call out to her grandchildren, "Now be still. Your great-grandmother doesn't have all the time in the world to wait for you to get settled." And Mariela would say in response, "Soon I'll have all the time there is!"—few understanding her.

She would tickle the little ones' chins, saying, "Now comport yourself with respect for your elders," but in Spanish, and the children would look at her and smile, not knowing what she'd said. Sometimes just the activity, their scampering, their blowing of bubbles, would make her laugh, and getting up, she'd chase after them. She was so busy trying to catch the tots as they'd run by that she did not hear her son, Emilio, poised behind a large portrait camera, directing everyone to hold still. He had been saying, "Please, everyone, together please, and, Mama, please sit down."

And then he surprised her by calling out in a deep voice, "Mama, *siéntese!*" And, as if hearing a command from her father or from her husband, Mariela settled in a chair whose arms were as knobbed and grainy as her own.

*

She'd lived to see the splendid August landing of the American astronauts on the moon some few years before. The event, which found her sitting before the television with a thick-beaded rosary in her hand, had left her transfixed. The cratered surface of the moon, with its bleak valleys and pointy mountains, the nearly somnambulist movement of the astronauts, the camera following them, had led her to believe that around the next corner they would soon come across some splendid city. Waiting for that moment, she kept the television, with its live broadcasts from the moon, on every night, and she was disappointed when no great discovery of civilizations was made. Finally, past midnight and feeling drowsy, she would turn the set off and, with the help of Margarita, go up the stairs to her room.

She imagined, on one of those nights, that a splendid crystal vehicle had drifted down like a soap bubble, nearly weightless, in the yard and that from this glowing craft emerged ethereal creatures. In her dream the men resembled the movie actor Rudolph Valentino, each dressed in a flowing, nearly transparent Roman-style gown, and the ladies of this species, in their similar garb, resembled Rita Hayworth. Floating through the walls like ghosts, they occupied Mariela's room. They seemed so real that her heart's beat became erratic and she thought she would have a heart attack. But one of these gentle and benevolent beings, a man gallant in the Old World sense, bowed before Mariela, making a request: "Queen Isabela of our planet, Mars, wishes the pleasure of your company."

And because Mariela had nothing better to do, she accompanied these beings into their craft; that is, she blinked and found herself looking out the window at countless stars. When she saw the planet Saturn she swore that she could reach out and chip off a piece of its porcelain rim. Then someone said to her, "We know you're very old, but that doesn't matter to us. We bless you with all the love of the Lord." And after coming down through an atmosphere of sunlight, brilliant clouds, and a horizon of palaces about which floated winged beings like butterflies, Mariela Montez found herself being led to the surface of the red planet.

Soon she was dressed in a silvery robe and escorted into the company of Isabela, the queen of that planet. Beautiful and regal, a diamond-and-sapphire crown on her head, her hands covered with rings, she wore a long, flowing gown. Isabela said to her, "Welcome to the planet of happiness."

There was a grand feast going on—banquet tables covered

with food and a savory aroma in the air, with attendants carrying great flasks of wine, and so much confusion, with so many of these ethereal citizens blowing kisses and cheering her as she walked along the great hall that it suddenly dawned on Mariela that the banquet was in her honor.

Mariela asked a courtier, "Do I curtsy before Her Majesty?" and the courtier had whispered, "Yes."

So Mariela curtsied, and the great Queen said, "I've brought you here to confer on you a medal of honor."

"Your Highness," she asked, "why is this honor being granted?"

The Queen laughed. "Because of all the life you have brought into the world." And after consulting with one of her magistrates, she added, "Because of your beautiful, beautiful poetry. Would you honor Our Presence with a recitation?"

"Oh, yes, with much pleasure."

And searching through the pocket of her nightgown, into which, hours before, she slipped a verse she had written in the kitchen, she began to read a poem called "*Mariposita*," or "Butterfly," which fell delightfully on the ears of her listeners.

The Queen said, "Well done," and then taking a scepter, she laid it on the old woman's shoulder.

"And I say to thee, ye who believe in me, one day you will be in Paradise."

But Christ had once said that, and His words on the Queen's lips startled Mariela.

She awakened, thinking such a dream the intrusion of fantasy into the last days of an elderly woman's life.

Her Final Days, 1972

OF ALL HER DAUGHTERS, it was Margarita who most closely observed her mother in the pasture of old age, where she reigned over a meadow of memory, scattering emotions before her. In those last months, she'd reminded her children that she'd spent a third of her life bringing them into the world, that she was the mother of their sleep, their tears, their doubts. If Margarita and Gloria once boarded a jet to Rome, if they had toured the Roman Forum, dined in the trattorias of the old Jewish quarter, if they kissed the hand of the Pope, it was because she had given them life. If Maria, Olga, and Jacqueline concertized in Monte Carlo, or entertained at a private party aboard a luxury liner for the Count of Avignon, or dined on some Parisian terrace, or had croissants and Swiss marmalades for breakfast, it was owed to her. It was their mother who had given them the planets, the sun, the star-hazed night; it was she who made Halley's comet appear in 1910, who had given them the opportunity to weep with sadness over the death of Rudolph Valentino in 1926, she who presented them with the glory of a meadow on a lovely spring day. They owed her their very lives, the Cuban woman whom they sometimes tolerated, and loved very much until the end.

When she lapsed into her final days (in 1972) with a cancer, Margarita arranged for all her daughters and her son to come to visit her. (Even Isabel made the journey from Cuba, remaining in Cobbleton for a month, sitting each and every day at her mother's bedside, but in the end heading reluctantly back to Cuba and her husband.)

All her children came to pay their respects and she opened her eyes to see them. Just lifting her hand to touch the cheek of her son, Emilio, made her wonder why, with so much love in her life, she would now lose it forever. And though she had made her confession and received the sacrament of extreme unction, she opened her eyes one evening and, focusing them on the crucifix on the wall in front of her, saw it turning into the devil, and just then she was stricken with a loss of faith. She became impossible, swearing that the sisters had put her away in a home, fanning away bad spirits, and crying out with terror as she made acquaintance with death.

"Nothing, nothing will come of this," she repeated so often that even Margarita, thrusting herself on her mother, whispered, "It's not like that, Mama"—her mother, turning her head one way and the other, saying, "It is so!"

But after three days of torment, the devil, who had put such doubts in her heart, was chased from her bedroom by an angel with a flaming sword, and the light of heaven returned to her life.

In those last moments, she was surrounded by her children, and though she was a little delirious, saying, "I can see Jesus and your father and my mother and father and my sisters waiting for me at the gates of heaven," she was grateful for their presence.

Emilio, her only son, kissed her and held her hands, for she cried, "Oh, hold me," and then in a moment Mariela Montez, experiencing some of the same sensations that had come over her while giving birth, felt the soul slipping out of her body into another world.

A New Life

WITH HER MOTHER GONE, Margarita took it upon herself to put the house in Cobbleton up for sale and spent her days going through its rooms, making decisions as to how she would distribute certain keepsakes, which clothes were to be thrown away and which were to be packed and given to charity, which chairs and tables and cabinets were to be turned over to an antiques dealer and which they, the family, would keep for themselves. Helen wanted one of the cabinets that stood in their mother and father's bedroom, which resembled a high German altar, with spirals and knobs. The other sisters would choose smaller, less cumbersome items, like old tin boxes, painted jars, framed photographs, mirrors, and crucifixes, but Margarita chose for herself the porch rocking chair that her mother sat on for those many years and the mirror that hung in her bedroom.

Emilio, of course, would get his father's old camera, the one with which he had traveled to Cuba around the turn of the century. He would put it in his studio window in Los Angeles and later bring it to New York.

Margarita felt odd, cleaning out her mother's and father's

closets, which over the years had taken on the aromatic scent of firewood, camphor, and perfume, for each piece of her parents' clothing was redolent of their spirit. And although she packed most of these items into boxes for charity, she could not help setting aside some thing that she would forever identify with them: her father's derby, one of her mother's ribbon-brimmed hats; her father's watch with its cameo of Kate O'Brien, which she had not remembered for years; his pipe; his photography manual, which she would send to Emilio; and that other book which always made her laugh, *A Gentleman's Guide to Love.* Then her mother's hand mirror and her books (*En la ciudad de Dios, La vida en el planeta marte,* and her Spanish Bible). What surprised her was the amount of memorabilia kept in a black trunk—envelopes marked with her sisters' names that held first teeth and locks of hair, as well as old rosaries, prayer and communion cards, hair ribbons, school report cards, newspaper clippings from the Cobbleton *Chronicle* (among them, birth announcements, obituaries—one dating back to 1897 for Katherine O'Brien, another for her father—and wedding announcements from here and there, among them her own to Lester Thompson in 1925). And there were parcels of letters, mainly from Cuba. And in their father's shed there were boxes of photographs, many of which seemed to her to have some historical value, as they went back to his days in the Spanish-American War, and his photographs of the family over the years, which she would distribute equally among them all.

Her greatest discovery—in a hatbox in the closet—were her mother's notebooks. She laughed when she found the note her mother had left, in the minuscule and unsteady handwriting of her last days:

My dearest Margarita, I know that you will one day find these little verses and writings of mine and they are yours to keep. When you read them, remember that your mother never had much schooling, but that she always tried very hard. Don't be harsh with them—for they were good company to me during

*my life, and as you read them, remember, God willing, that I
will be watching you from Paradise.*
   Love, Mama

Carrying them down into the parlor, she opened a bottle of
wine and poured herself a glass, and then sat by the very window,
brilliant with light, where her mother would often compose her
verses, and she began to read.

Page after page was filled with pleasant musings and poems,
many about an imagined afterlife:

> *I want to be transported to a place where I will hear the hymn
> of sleeping birds, where streams flow with musical waters, and
> where I will find majestic trees in whose boughs I will hide my
> soul.*

And sometimes sad, unfinished pieces:

> *I am surrounded by life and yet feel alone, with open hands
> begging . . .*

On some pages there were simple observations that harkened
back to the days when the house was filled with children:

> *Margarita spends too much time in front of the mirror, but
> then, at her age, so did I.*
>   *Today Maria started to cry because she wanted an expen-
> sive dress from town and Poppy would not buy it for her.*
>   *Irene is too fat, but food makes her happy as a mouse.*
>   *Poor Gloria, the other day she found a dying bird in the
> snow and tried to warm the creature by the fireplace, and
> when the poor shivering thing died in her hands, she cried and
> put it in a tin box and buried it in the field.*
>   *I am worried because Violeta has too much of an eye for
> men—but I am praying to God that she will preserve her vir-
> ginity for marriage.*

> *My husband was drunk today, but I said nothing to him,*
> *the man works so hard . . .*

Then this, among many others, in an old ledger-style book,
dating back to 1902–3:

> *I don't know very much about my husband's life with his poor*
> *sister, Caterina. But in a dream I believe I saw her. She was*
> *standing in the hall outside our bedroom, a beautiful woman*
> *with long, curly red hair, but with much sadness in her eyes,*
> *for she had left this world and knew it. She was wearing a*
> *white dress that fell to the floor, with frilled butterfly sleeves . . .*
> *How lovely she seemed and yet so sad. I knew that she meant*
> *me no harm, that she was just lonely. And because I was not*
> *afraid, I moved toward her, and she said to me, smiling, "I am*
> *happy that my brother has found so good a woman," and that*
> *was all. And then she passed back into the shadows. I thanked*
> *her the next day by walking to the cemetery, where I placed*
> *some flowers on her grave, the poor woman.*

Reading late into the night, she found narratives, among
them one that filled nearly half a notebook, called "The Birth of
My Daughter Margarita at Sea," dating back to 1902, and this,
written sometime during the past several years, which she had
titled "Our Love," a brief passage that she had tried to cross out
but that was still legible:

> *My dear husband: Although you are not here, I woke this*
> *morning remembering the day, so long ago, that we set out on*
> *our honeymoon. My papa and mama and the others had seen*
> *us off as we made our way east to that little house by the sea.*
> *Do you remember how the world looked that day, my love? In*
> *the fields everywhere were wildflowers and we were so happy*
> *that we would stop the carriage, picking so many that they*
> *were heavy and sweet-scented in my arms—but I held them*
> *close to my breast because they were the blossoms of our love;*
> *and I remembered that they were our companions on that day*

*when we finally entered the house by the sea and that we were
both so nervous that you closed the shutters because the sun
was too bright, and perhaps out of humility and respect for me,
because even though we had kissed the night before, in my
moodiness I had not allowed you to go any further. And yet
thinking about your sadness that night I remembered how you
slept in your evening clothes, and how you had pressed against
me, sighing, and how the touch of your body against mine left
sweat between my virgin's thighs. But that next day I was as
prepared and ready as a young bride could be, and in the half
light of the room, we both began to undress and for the first
time we touched each other with our nakedness. Do you remember, my husband, how I passed my hand from your lips
and down to your chest and below, feeling much surprise, for I
had never touched a man before? I remember closing my eyes
and taking a deep breath because your flesh was long and hot
—and do you remember then that I did not care if we could
see each other and I opened the shutters and the room filled
with light and the flowers burned with color? Then we fell on
the bed kissing and my breasts began to swell from your kisses,
and because you were so shy and respectful of me, I began to
play a game, examining your masculinity like a doctor—until
you could not control yourself and you opened me up with a
thrust that left a flower of my blood on the sheet, and while at
first I cried in your arms, when you pulled away from me I
wanted you back inside me, and to show you I touched myself
there and rolled my fingers around my femininity until I was
very wide and then you came back into me, and instead of
crying I felt as happy as a young bride could feel. I was thinking about that this morning, my love; and so I send you these
thoughts—the thoughts of* una viejita *who spends her days
thinking about you and awaiting our reunion in Paradise.*

Margarita, blushing, cried out: "Mama!"

Her Own New Life

SOME MONTHS LATER, when much had been cleared away, a young newlywed couple, out to start their lives together, met with Margarita a second time and decided to buy the house for some twenty thousand dollars. A few other prospective buyers, whom Margarita did not particularly like, also came by, and for a time Irene and her husband considered moving in, but in the end they decided to remain in their happy home. So, seventy years old and retired from high school, Margarita passed one sad afternoon moving through the rooms of that house, remembering the happy past she and the family shared there. Her own new life was to begin now. Luis, her Cuban love, had driven down with a U-haul to bring Margarita and her possessions to his rented house in the town of New Elm, Connecticut.

These were days of new love for the oldest of the sisters. In Margarita, Luis would always find refuge from the troubles of his life and he treated her with the purest affection. Over the years he'd managed to bring some members of his family out of Cuba—a younger brother and his wife and children, now settled in Miami—and while they were working and would be able to help bring other relations to the States, Luis, ever concerned and a little bitter, kept toiling all the more toward that end. Retired from General Motors, he'd gotten himself a part-time job at one of the local garages, its owner a Cuban who had come to the States in the 1950s. Luis would show up at the garage five days a week, and on the weekends, instead of relaxing, he'd moonlight as a mechanic at the local Greyhound depot. He was rarely at home except in the evenings and was often so exhausted that, after eating his dinner, he would sit in front of the television watching old Hollywood movies until he began to fall asleep and then Margarita would help him off with his clothes and into bed, where suddenly, after an hour or so, despite his exhaustion, his eyes would pop open, his head filled with worries for his family and with the strangeness of his new life, which he never really liked.

He would open Margarita's gown, smothering her with his body. He was still virile enough that these sessions of love would last for a long time, and after they'd both been satisfied, he would feel his tiredness again and drift off, sleeping for another twenty minutes before his eyes would pop open again and he would plant more kisses on her body. Then he usually remained awake, staring at the ceiling light and sighing.

As he got up for work, putting on his blue service-station coveralls, Margarita would prepare a breakfast of eggs, bacon and sausage, and fried potatoes, and while watching him eat, she would speak cheerfully about the prospects for their future. Now that they were finally together, in their waning years, it was time for them to enjoy life. "Luis, my love, why don't we go back to Spain for a little vacation?"

"Yes, yes, but what will I do for money? It doesn't come out of the air."

"I have money, Luis. Poppy left us all with money" (each of his children, after Mariela's death, received seventeen thousand dollars). "And I've got my Social Security and the pension from the high school, and I can always go back to work."

"Margarita, you're not a young girl anymore."

"No? When I'm with you, I feel very young."

"That's not how the world works, my love."

"But I would pay for you—please let's do something—we have to do something before you get too pent up with your worries."

"We'll see, my darling."

And wearily, after breakfast, he'd kiss her on the forehead and make his way out of the house, a lunch box tucked under his arm.

*

Though the political situation in Cuba had taken over more and more of his life, to Margarita the fate of the island seemed most distant. But for Luis it always loomed as a most pressing issue. Watching the evening news reports that sometimes spoke admiringly of the "socialist experiment" to the south, he would brood about how Castro had taken in the "Eastern Establishment liberals." He was unable to understand why the American soldiers stationed in Guantánamo, a base the Americans procured from Cuba in the first days of the Cuban republic—so that the Americans could intercede in Cuban affairs if necessary, as per the Platt Amendment—did not simply spill over into the surrounding country, retaking Cuba for the principles of freedom. That's why he cursed the Vietnam War, even though the Americans were fighting against the Communists—why, if they had only put half their efforts into Cuba, he and Margarita would be sitting on the terrace of his house in La Regla, sipping daiquiris, he'd say.

His Cuban friends and their wives were much the same way, coming to the house on Sundays, when he took the afternoon off, for a joyous meal, which, however, too often for Margarita's taste, turned into a series of heated arguments about "what can be done," voices raised in the kitchen, and by the evening's end, poor Luis tied up in knots. And it surprised her, for the suave, kindly, and genteel man she first met in Spain in her younger days had changed.

She felt a great sympathy for him. She loved him, but heaven help her if, for example, she happened to mention her sister Isabel's calmness about the situation. Isabel remained in the house in Santiago, living humbly but comfortably enough with her husband, and while she harbored no great love for the new Cuba, her daily life, spent mainly in her house, by her husband's side, looking after the man—with his arteries layered with fat— had never really changed. And while in letters Isabel lamented the long separation from her wonderful family in America, and sometimes alluded to the discomforts of rationing and the intrusiveness of her neighbors—she and her husband always believed that everyone was being watched—she never talked about leaving, as long as her husband was alive. She did, however, miss her children. Her daughter had long ago married and moved to Havana, and from there, after the revolution, to San Juan, Puerto

Rico, where her husband worked for a bank. One son, an engineer, went to work in Chile, and the second boy, a lawyer, was now living with his own family in Ft. Lauderdale. (On her way back to Cuba after their mother's funeral, Isabel stopped off to visit him and to see her grandchildren, and she was quite pleased with his affluence and with the serenity and love of his family, a life she saw as happy.)

It did not help that Luis, who'd once lorded over several hundred workers, spent hours alongside a fellow he did not like, whom he referred to as *"un negro americano."* The dispatcher at the Greyhound depot was an elderly, good-natured black man with whom he got along well enough, but one of the other mechanics, a fellow named Calvin, seemed too free-spirited for Luis's taste. He'd turn up at work with a conk hairdo, loved to tune in the blues station on the radio, and seemed quite happy-go-lucky, a posture that struck Luis as indolent. (And on their occasional trips to visit with the sisters in New York, mainly during holidays, he was always astounded by what he perceived as the arrogance of New York blacks, who, in his eyes, were well off and did not know what suffering was really like.) A single moment of disrespect—Calvin always made him angry by calling him Ace—"My name is Mr. Vasquez!"—would set him off, and he would come home and complain for hours about the humiliation of his days.

So many things made him angry that Margarita would take him aside and say, "Luis, why are you always working yourself into such a state? It's not worth it. People are the way they are, and there is really nothing we can do about it. If you don't like that job, then leave it. I'll take care of us. Otherwise, you'll end up having a heart attack, and I don't want that for you, my love."

In his absence she kept busy. She read, and passed hours with a Spanish-language dictionary, translating the poems from her mother's notebooks, which she read a half dozen times, and made copies in English for the sisters who never learned her mother's language, so they would know a little more about their mother's heart. And after a time she went to the local high school and, speaking of her experience as a Spanish teacher in Cobbleton, got herself a few hours of work tutoring kids at the school, and spent her Saturdays conducting a special class in English for children who were the sons and daughters of recent Spanish-speaking immigrants from all over: Cubans, Mexicans, Colombians, Dominicans—work, she'd recall, that filled her heart with special sweetness and pride. In Cobbleton, most of her students had been the sons and daughters of American farmers and factory and railroad workers, but these kids, fresh from their respective countries, not only invoked her own mother's experience but reminded her of her own childhood, when the music of her mother's language was lost in the daily buzz of English. For several years, that had made her feel a certain confusion, for there were few others like herself then. And there they would sit, attentive and respectful—a new bloom of a generation that she took much pleasure in helping. (And because so many of them were poor, she turned the end of these classes into something of a weekly party, so they would have something to look forward to besides their studies, Miss Montez, as she called herself, bringing in sandwiches and soda and cookies, and, in the season of Christmas, presents—board games and books and, for the poorest of the poor, a new sweater or scarf to protect them from the wintry cold.)

In the evenings, while waiting for Luis, she would sometimes read their simply written compositions about their countries, all so beautiful, even Cuba, in the memory of children. But what was Cuba, she would ask of herself, but a conduit to some pleasant memories, a language, for she was an American. She'd imagine what Cuba must have meant to the others in her family. For Isabel, of course, it was her first true love, and for Maria, Olga, and Jacqueline, it was one of their sources, these women having spent more time in places like London and Paris than in Cuba. For Helen, it was as far away as China, for, apart from a visit in the fifties to a special meeting of advertisers at the Havana Yacht Club, it had existed mainly as a sum of phrases uttered by her mother—a crocodile-shaped land on the map, sometimes alluded to, because of the revolution, in newspapers and on television. What could Cuba mean to her other sisters? For Irene, she thought it definitely boiled down to the delicious cuisine, for she loved fried *plátanos* and could make a good roast pork. To Sarah and her husband, Rafael, in Philadelphia, who'd raised their daughters to be good citizens, or to Patricia, with her folksy husband out in Pennsylvania, or to Veronica in Illinois—her accent in English having gotten twangy over the years—what could it have been but a detail from their parents' lives? And what of the others? To Marta and Carmen in Anaheim; Violeta, reverent in Baltimore; and Gloria, with her Macy's job in New York? A source of pride, distant and far removed, perhaps—that was all.

But then she thought of her former movie-actor brother, Emilio, out in Los Angeles. What was it that he, then forty-seven years old, told her in the days after their mother died?

"I'll learn some of that Spanish, one way or the other."

Walking a line that placed the emotional above the political, Margarita supported Luis, for all his troubles. Still, the sweet idyll of their lives together seemed to have passed. Reluctantly, she began to regard him with caution and distance; it was hard to be around him when he was poisoning himself with bitterness. One evening, she suggested that they drive over to Hartford, where there was a Cuban psychiatrist, from whom he might seek counsel. But that only made him angrier.

"You think I'm crazy, don't you? But you don't know what I'm feeling, like I have nothing? You're Cuban, but only half Cuban by blood, and even though that's better than not being Cuban at all, you don't know what it's like for me. So I would thank you to leave me alone with my thoughts, because right now they are keeping this crazy bird alive."

During the winters of their years together, they liked to go to the movies and then drive over to Hartford to a restaurant run by Cubans, where they would have a great feast, gorging themselves and drinking wine and laughing with the owners, who were a sturdy and cheerful lot. But with time he simply preferred to stay home, fed up with the snow and the life of that New England town, the only events of interest to him being boxing matches and phone calls to family and friends in Florida, the sameness of the Cuban situation making him more tense with each passing day. She would caress him and say, "My sweet darling, if I could change everything for you, I would." And that would mean something to him, because for a moment he would seem calmer, and they would retire like young lovers to bed.

She devised other strategies. One day, while driving to town to buy groceries, she noticed a new shop next to the drugstore, the Peace and Love Herbal Emporium, whose owners were hippies. She went in, finding them most amusing and gentle, and she liked the sweet incense that filled their shop and the harmonious Nepalese chimes that tinkled musically whenever the door opened. In their eyes, it seemed to her, was an impassioned serenity, as if they were perpetually looking up into the sky on a beautiful spring day. Examining their shelves filled with bins of organic grains, cereals, and nuts, she turned to a rack of books on Yogic treatment and spiritual healing, and peered at the labels of apothecary jars filled with herbs and roots, which the gentle owner said were good for a soothing, soul-cleansing bath.

And so Margarita bought some tea and a pound of an herb mixture that seemed to consist of flower buds, seedlings, and butterfly wings.

That night, when Luis came home from work, she set about to calm him. She made him a cup of orange-flavored tea with a teaspoon of honey and three ounces of rum, and she drew him a hot bath into which she poured the herbal concoction. Skeptical but amused, Luis lowered himself into the tub and found that the waters indeed seemed soothing. He liked the scent of the herbs. "Reminds me of the market in Havana," he said. Dressed in a robe, she knelt on a cushion before the tub and with a sea sponge began to wipe his body; after a while, he leaned back and closed his eyes, his tension leaving him. And mischievous still, she began to caress him until his penis, engorged and livid, rose up out of the water, and in a moment he was out of the tub, dripping water, a portion of his aged, still virile anatomy bobbing in the air.

In the bedroom of that house, they made love for the first time in months, and in the peacefulness of their embrace, they laughed and recounted memories of passion in Spain, in Miami, in Cobbleton. Snow was falling, and it seemed that his physical release calmed him. He told her that night, "Maybe I have gotten too worked up about things, but today was a good day for me, I was able to send some money to my brother in Miami. But perhaps what we should do now, my love, is look again to the future, maybe go to Spain for a little vacation in the spring. You know, Andalusia is the most beautiful in May."

"You want to?"

"Yes."

When he fell asleep, she rested her head against the fleecy white hair of his chest, listening to his heartbeat. Now and then she caressed him, and then sleep came to her, too. But when she awakened in the middle of the night, she again laid her head on his chest, and instead of that loud heartbeat, there was the odd silence of a body in complete and, perhaps, eternal repose.

In Her Regal Old Age, 1987

IN THE YEARS BEFORE she entered her regal old age, Margarita Montez O'Brien liked so much to work with the children of the town that, after Luis's death, she rented another house and remained in New Elm, Connecticut. For twelve years she worked as a Spanish tutor and a teacher of English, until the school board decided that Margarita, well into her eighties, was too old to continue. Then, in 1987, she found a new profession, spending her days in the public-minded and solitary work of a senior-citizen librarian. Her hair had turned white, but she dyed it black. Her breasts seemed pouty with stretch marks, and one day she noticed for the first time in her life, while standing naked before her bedroom mirror, the faint tremor of her breathing diaphragm, so thin was the surface of her translucent skin.

But sometimes she liked to think that she was quite young still—a delusion, she would later tell herself over a glass of wine or while having the dreams of the very old. She'd sit before a

vanity that dated back to her marriage, stroking with a cherry-
wood, black-bristled brush the hair which fell down past her
shoulders, and with her head held at a certain angle, skin
stretched tight, the lines of facial antiquity lifted, she resembled
for a moment the Margarita of her youth.

During her visit to Cuba in 1932, her grandmother Doña
Maria had seemed to her, a young woman, as old as the moon
itself—and yet at that time her grandmother couldn't have been
more than seventy-five. And here was Margarita, past eighty, in
spritely good health, though her hands sometimes shook. Her
alertness would startle her when the sight of a sparrow alighting
on a fence or a beautiful piece of music, say Bach or Mozart, or
something upbeat from the easy-listening station on the radio
still seemed so new. In fact, each of her days was spent navigating
through her feelings of permanence in this world, as she had
lived so long that it seemed as if the threads of life would hold
forever. Her doctor, to whom she made twice-yearly visits, would
examine her and declare, "You have the health of a much
younger woman," and she, having what she considered the powdery recesses of her interior, would usually blush. She could not
imagine taking leave of the world, though she knew it was inevitable; but when she considered this, she found it impossible
to think the outcome dark, her childhood dreams of angelic flight
striking her as a very great possibility.

Still, she did not allow this conviction to interfere with the
daily maintenance of her health. Three times a week she would
drive her station wagon into the center of town and make her
way with sweatpants, sweatshirt, and sneakers to the Seniors
Fitness Center, as it was called, for a half hour of aerobic exercise,
modified, of course, for the older folks, who stretched and bent
to Perry Como and the golden arrangements of Liberace. Afterward she might walk into the local Agway, lingering by the
counter where some years before she had purchased one of her
favorite books, *The Audubon Society Guide to the Butterflies of
the Northeastern United States*, which had inspired her to observe
more closely the leopard-winged fritillaries and monarchs that
fluttered among the blossoms which she, with visored cap or

brilliant, oversized sun hat, would plant in the early spring. And at the market, the big A & P off Route 9 just outside of town, she'd make her way with her shopping cart down the aisles, ever conscious of the diet that *Prevention* magazine recommended, filling her cart with lean and healthful cuts of meat and fillets of fish and chicken, and clear plastic bags of the most salutary vegetables—zucchini, lentils, carrots, and squash, among many others. She had stopped smoking twenty-two years before, except for an occasional puff if she happened to be around one of her less health-conscious sisters, and she did not drink more than two glasses of Premiat Cabernet Sauvignon a day—her favorite brand, a good bargain, too, at $4.25 a bottle—which would ease her into a lovely sleep, the sleep of bitterly cold New England winters, her body snug under the warm covers.

Sometimes she would climb the stairs to her bedroom laughing, a little tipsy but still able to maneuver those stairs, a nearly invisible band of pinkish light skirting the corners of the rooms, and the wine taking the edge off her two greatest fears—loneliness and boredom. She would sometimes sit at a table in a small sewing room just off to the right of the landing, writing letters and telephoning the family. She had thirteen sisters, one brother, and eighteen nieces and nephews who had themselves brought thirty-one children into the world. Her telephone bills would include calls to New York, Illinois, Florida, California, Maryland, and Pennsylvania—her usual inquiries about the lives, health, and happiness of the family.

Being the oldest, she wanted to make sure that communication among them never dwindled, as she knew happened in many a family. And at times of crisis it was Margarita who would fly out to help. She did so back in 1978 when Veronica divorced her husband, out in Illinois, for, despite his age and his basically good heart, he had continued his philanderings over the years with one younger girl or another, finally shattering her resolve to keep the marriage together. (When she arrived, finding her younger sister in a bad way, gloomy and frightened of the future, Margarita said to her, "Do not be afraid, because you'll never be alone. You can always come stay with me.") And she went out to Anaheim in 1982 when Marta's husband died, and Marta, in a most sorrowful state, repeated again and again, "My life feels as if it is over." That was when Margarita, knowing what such pain meant, left the house and returned an hour later with three tickets to Hawaii, and she, Marta, and Carmen spent a week there, sitting under umbrellas, sipping piña coladas through bent straws, taking the sun, and watching the Pacific and the young people frolicking in its waters. On their way back they stopped to see their brother, Emilio, photographer of the stars, in Los Angeles. That visit ended with Marta's arms wrapped around her older sister, and the younger sister, feeling sad, yet not as sad as she'd felt a few weeks before, saying, "My God, Margarita, you're so good to me." And Margarita said, "That's because I love you."

The following year, there had been Jacqueline's open-heart surgery, when the prospect of death entered the apartment on West End Avenue and the union known as the fourteen sisters seemed endangered. One afternoon, during a casual recital in the salon of their apartment, Jacqueline, resplendent in a velvet dress, happy with music for most of her life, and delicate as a flower, had simply collapsed, sighing, her violin dropping from her hands. Always in the best of health, Jacqueline, seventy-five and quite content with the sisterly life, had not seen a doctor in nearly thirty years. Her condition, a hospital physician said, required immediate surgery. Olga, her twin, maddened and feeling chest pangs of her own, made the call to Margarita in Connecticut, and she rushed down that very evening to console Maria and Olga and Gloria, joining them in their vigil of prayer (for they were all religious).

The surgery was a success, and after six months or so, Jacqueline rejoined her sisters, Maria and Olga, in rehearsals, the apartment once again filled with the sonorous music for which, to a wide circle of cultured friends, it was much renowned. But, that crisis past, Jacqueline reassessed the meaning of love, and though she had been content for many years with the constancy of her life, she underwent a spiritual crisis. She suddenly wanted, after a lifetime of virginity—so the sisters thought—to know the physical pleasures of love.

During one of their after-dinner recitals, a quite handsome

singer of twenty-five, Ramón, a Spaniard from Málaga who took voice lessons from Maria, dreamily stared, and stared, and stared at Jacqueline as she played her violin. And later this young man pursued her, finding her, frail and uncertain, by the punch bowl, and he said to her in his Castilian Spanish, "Miss O'Brien, I cannot begin to describe the feelings in my heart when I look at you," and he kissed her hand. "There can be nothing better in life than a dedication to beauty."

Then they sat off in a corner talking until very late that night.

The next morning, with her hair tightly curled under a barrette and wearing much 1920s jewelry—it was early summer— Jacqueline left the apartment. Down below, the Spaniard waited for her, behind the wheel of a rented car, and soon they were driving north along the Hudson, making their way to Bear Mountain Park. There, during a picnic, the young man took Jacqueline into his arms, kissing her. That night she did not return home, the couple taking a room together in the lodge, a scandalous event.

No one in the family would ever know if they went to bed together, but for about three months Jacqueline and this fellow kept constant company, and although both Maria and Olga betrayed their cynicism as to his motives, Jacqueline fell into the habit of referring to Ramón as "my young man." Her revelry, however, gave strength to Jacqueline, and for that the sisters were grateful, though they were happy when the affair ended. On a stroll along Sullivan Street, after having dinner in an Italian restaurant, the Chanteuses saw Ramón on a street corner, necking furiously with a brunette. That ended the love affair, and Jacqueline, with a crisscross of scars up the middle of her chest, between the breasts which he might have kissed—the sisters did not know—never saw him again. With an embarrassed air, but a glint of mischief in her eyes, she rejoined the humble and unromantic life of their sisterly household.

And there was her sister Helen, suffering from what Margarita would call upper-class idleness. When her son, Craig, came back from Vietnam with half his right hand blown off, he began to depend on his parents, retiring to the family house in

Newport. Helen Montez O'Brien Anderson, a doting mother, worried that her son would turn out badly. But long since then, the young man, now nearly forty, had gotten out into the world, marrying a girl from Boston and studying law at Harvard (he had gone to Yale before he saw service in Vietnam), and although he suffered from bad nightmares, his union produced a young and healthy son, Craig Jr.

By that time, Helen, ever beautiful, ever elegant, her social life spent among the very best of high society, was addicted to tranquillizers, the intake of which ordered her days. With her children gone from the apartment and her husband busy in his work—he was of retirement age but owned an advertising agency and was then coordinating a campaign for a nationwide hamburger chain—she would spend nearly every afternoon looking over her old photographs and the advertisements in which she once appeared, and appraising herself in the mirror, feeling despair, for it had struck her, at the age of seventy-five, that she was getting older.

As youthful as Helen looked—for she would always have a young face and was still quite beautiful—her hours were so empty that she found herself longing for the days when she lived in Cobbleton with her sisters. She had other interludes, when she would swear it was 1957 and she would wake up thinking that at three-thirty she would pick up the kids from school, taking her son Craig to French lessons at four, and her boy Dennis over to the piano teacher on Central Park West. (That son Dennis, a lover of music, in adulthood would open a record store in Boston, specializing in classical music.) She had a car and driver then and would usually spend the time between lessons walking along Madison Avenue in the Seventies, going into dress and jewelry shops, the car following her slowly on the street. By five-thirty, she would have picked the kids up and headed home. (She missed that. Now she swam in a sea of Valium, whose effects she enhanced with two glasses of late-afternoon wine. On one of those afternoons, bored and a little angry about her life, she fired her maid and butler, and when her Spanish Institute teacher arrived for their 5 p.m. lessons—for she, too, after so many years wanted to learn Spanish—Helen, naked behind the door, told him to go home, saying, "You will be paid, in any case." Afterward, while urinating in the bathroom, her eyes on a signed Picasso print on the wall, she decided that her husband married her because of her importance as an ornament, and in a fit she stormed through the rooms of the apartment, pulling off every painting and framed photograph from the walls, throwing them to the floor. (She spared the Picasso print in the bathroom and a lovely Florentine portrait by Piero di Cosimo in the hall.) Then, the apartment wrecked, she drank a quart of gin. At eight that evening, her husband found her sprawled naked on the eighteenth-century Persian rug in the parlor. (Her hair was still blond, for she dyed it, but as she lay on the floor, her pubic hair, between her legs, was curled and gray.) At three-thirty in the morning, her husband telephoned Margarita in Connecticut in despair.

"She won't speak to anyone," he said. "Would you please come down?"

So Margarita took the train into Manhattan the next day, and shortly appeared before her younger sister, saying, "Helen, why are you doing this?"

And in that room crowded with the Chanteuses and Gloria, she opened her eyes and answered, "Because no one loves me."

"But we all love you, you must know that."

"Then prove it."

Margarita then imagined that if she were a man she would slip into bed with her—was that what she meant?—but she simply leaned over and gave her sister a kiss on the forehead and spent the hours of that day, and many others, trying to console her.

*

By then, sister Patricia had moved to a psychic community called Lilydale in Upstate New York, her husband having died many years before and her kids now on their own. (Her older son, Henry, ran the farm on which they lived. Her other son, Harris, was in the United States Navy, and Clara had married a businessman and lived in Houston, Texas.) For many years, Patricia, having her visions of spirits and her intuitions about the ordinary events of life, subscribed to a spiritist newsletter, and in that newsletter she often read about Lilydale, a community for spiritists. When her good husband died, she moved there, renting a gothic house which overlooked the town's small lake and put in her window a sign that read: "Fortunes told, Futures divined." There was nothing lucrative about the business; in the peak season of July perhaps ten people a day would come to her, seeing their future for five dollars each.

After she moved there in 1977, her most illustrious customer had been a soft-spoken Southern President whose political future she sadly divined. A rock star, performing in Buffalo, also visited, and her prediction that his next recording would be a number-one hit propelled her name into the newspapers. In 1982, she even received a phone call from a man claiming to be the current President of the United States—but she doubted that it was so. And yet her reputation as a psychic had grown: by the time she was seventy-five, in 1989, radio and television stations around the country would call and ask her about the future. She did many interviews, particularly after the CBS network aired a piece on her (in which she foretold the collapse of the Soviet Empire "in the next few years or so," and the death of Fidel Castro in 1995, in retirement in Mexico, from cancer). "This elderly and plain lady," the CBS commentator said, "may be ordinary-looking, but it wouldn't surprise us at all if Patty, as she likes to call herself, really holds the keys to the future. From Lilydale, New York, this is Rod Owen." Her minor-celebrity status, even at its peak, had not made much difference in terms of business. Though she could really read and see the most in-ward manifestations of personality and destiny in her clients' hearts, she relied upon symbolic interpretations of their lives. To a young man whose fiancée was sitting in the next room, she said: "I see you standing before a ladder and you do not know whether you will go up or down." She said this even when she knew he would die in a car collision a year later. To a pregnant woman, she said, "You will have a beautiful son," though she saw him with a pistol, robbing a store in the future.

She saw many people in those days—most just wanted to know that their lives would turn out okay—but though she could see their future, she came to prefer vague interpretations. She saw men riding on horses, nails being hammered into walls, a man—or woman—standing before a door, deciding whether he or she should open it. That's what Patricia, the ninth-born of the fourteen sisters, would say, knowing a sorrowful truth but refusing to reveal it.

*

Margarita was eighty-seven when she visited her younger sister in Lilydale. They had a good time, as sisters will, the two driving around and visiting antique shops and the local sights. While Patricia sat divining the future for a customer, Margarita would read a book.

On one of those evenings, Margarita, curious and playful, asked her sister, "And what do you see for yourself?"

"I know the exact day when I will leave this world."

"Not soon!"

"No."

"And for me, what do you see?"

Taking Margarita's hands, her thumbs pressed into her pulse of life, she had said: "You are going to live to be unbelievably old."

*

In those years she got to spend some time with her sister Isabel—not in Cuba, however, but in her nephew's house in Ft. Lauderdale, to where Isabel moved in 1980, the year of the Mariel harbor exodus. Isabel had always told the family that she would remain in Cuba to her dying days, but her husband's death in 1979 left her alone in the house on Victoriana de Avila Street, and after months of solitude and many a day when she thought she would lose her mind from loneliness, she found herself packing a single bag and, leaving the house to an old friend, made her way west to Havana, where she joined the throngs Mr. Castro was unleashing on America. Within a week she found herself at sea on an overcrowded, dangerously listing cabin cruiser which the Cubans of Miami piloted, along with many other boats, to rescue the Cubans of Mariel. In a matter of weeks she became one of those Cubans who at an advanced age abandoned what in fact had become her adopted country, joining her lawyer son and his family in a new life. Of course, she was welcomed by the family. At her house in Ft. Lauderdale she would receive visits from the sisters, Margarita among them, and Isabel would on occasion travel north to see the family in New York and Margarita in New Elm. They would spend many a tranquil day together, often in silence, for they had loved each other for so many years that, like an old couple, they could sit out on Margarita's sun porch without saying a word, until one of them would break the silence with a sigh and a sentence like, "*Dios mío*, do you realize that Mama would have been nearly a hundred years old if she were still alive?" Or: "Sister, do you remember when that nice fellow García used to turn up at the house in Cobbleton with his packages of plantains from New York, back in the days when there were no plantains to be found in the entire state of Pennsylvania?"

"I do."

It was Isabel's good fortune to come back home to a new America. Why, Ft. Lauderdale and Miami were packed with Cubans, and New York had long become a Latinized city. Margarita and Isabel could drive over to the A & P and find, in the produce section, green and ripe plantains, and over in the frozen-food section, packages of frozen *yuca*—even in New Elm.

*

And Gloria, in 1983, ended up marrying, at the age of sixty, her Macy's beau, Arnold, after so many years. As long as his mother was alive, Arnold could never work up the nerve to leave that woman, but when she died, Gloria told him, "It's now or never," and within a few months of his mother's death, the couple went off to City Hall, a nervous, frightened Arnold making his vows with Gloria in the company of the Chanteuses, Margarita, and a few friends from the department store. At long last, they made a vacation trip together—down to Bermuda—and on their return they set out to find their own apartment, though Arnold wanted to keep his place in Canarsie. For the first time in her life with Arnold, she stepped into that apartment and wanted nothing to do with it—his mother's presence everywhere, an old lady's scent, the very atmosphere so thick with her influence that for weeks Gloria dreamed about the woman's dresses drifting out of the closet and wrapping themselves around her, suffocating her the way his mother had suffocated him. She told him, "I would rather go live with my sisters than stay here." And she most nearly left him over it. "But the rent is so cheap" was one of his first arguments. The other: "All this seems to be happening so quickly."

"Quickly! I've been waiting forever, and you say it's happening quickly?"

She was so adamant that Arnold finally agreed to take another, more comfortable, well-lit apartment a few blocks south of where the Chanteuses lived. Arnold should have been happy in their new life, for they could frolic in bed and do exactly as they pleased, but he would head back to Canarsie after work, on the pretense of clearing out things, to spend the evenings listening to his mother's old Benny Goodman records, and he would work himself into such a state that he would be unable to move. On each of these nights, he would come back with shopping bags filled with his mother's records and with the little bric-a-brac that she used to decorate her apartment with—porcelain hounds and glass animals and photograph albums of Arnold and his mother posed in the park and out at Atlantic City, and her favorite cushions and dishware and coffee mugs, and some of the linens from their cluttered closets, among many other things. He brought home so many of his mother's possessions that the new apartment became gloomy with her presence.

Arnold began to reveal his nocturnal proclivities—remember that before their marriage Gloria had not slept a single night with the man. He tended to sigh and wake up in the middle of the night, a lost expression on his face. Devastated, he would sit in the living room by the window in the dark, as if he felt ashamed to sleep beside his new wife, and he would remain there until Gloria got up and brought him back to bed. This went on for months, until Gloria, on the verge of walking out, called her oldest sister, Margarita, in New Elm, pouring her heart out and relating the oddness of her marital circumstances.

Listening attentively, Margarita said, "Oh, my darling sister, you must be strong. You cannot allow your timidity to overwhelm you. Arnold is a good man—you realize that. Only remember that he has just lost his mother, and, like all mothers, she was a powerful woman. Remember how we all dreamed about Mama after she died, when her spirit was very strong."

"Yes?"

"What you must do, *mi vida*, will be difficult. He must get rid of the apartment in Canarsie, even if it only costs sixty-three dollars a month. And you cannot allow him to bring any more of her things into your home. If he objects, you must be prepared to leave him, because if it goes on in this way, he'll just get worse and worse. Do you understand?"

"Yes, sister."

"And do not be afraid, because you will always have your family."

That very evening, with Arnold out of the apartment, Gloria resolved to stand up to him, a necessity that made her feel nervous, as she loved the man and did not want to lose him. But when he came home later that night, she was already in bed and dreaming. She'd never met his mother, and knew her only from photographs; yet she dreamed that Arnold's mother was sitting in the living room, and when she got up, she saw his mother's ghost as a young and pretty woman in a dotted 1930s dress, hitching up a young boy's trousers and covering his face with kisses, and that woman, noticing Gloria's presence, looked up and said, "He was the love of my life." And that was all, for she then felt the weight of Arnold's body on the bed beside her, and waking, she told him about the dream and he told her that he had been having many dreams about his mother but that lately her presence was becoming fainter and fainter in those dreams.

That night, while going through her effects in Canarsie, he'd felt such gloom that he'd told himself, "This has got to stop."

And with the resolve of a new husband living in this world, Arnold said: "Listen, I know it's time to move on."

And he left the shadows of mourning and not only promised Gloria that he would get rid of the Canarsie apartment but pledged himself to the rejuvenation of their flagging love.

My God, How the World Had Changed

IN THOSE DAYS, Margarita Montez O'Brien liked to pass her time reading magazine articles about the advances of women in the world and was most pleased to see reports of their progress. Women were coming forward, making more money, getting better jobs. Divorce was up—she knew that. She would read long arguments about abortion—a great subject of national debate when she was nearly ninety—and quite simply thought the debate foolish. Life was beautiful, and it might be said that a soul was spontaneously generated at the moment when the male sperm fertilized the female ovum. But she doubted very much that the politicians could even conceive of a soul, few, in her opinion, having souls of their own. The body and soul moving through life, their felicity, was what counted, and as far as she was concerned, there were too many lost souls in the world. She had come to believe in destiny, not cruelty, and certainly not in the murder of unborn children, but she knew that many, many children came into the world despite the benevolence of the Lord, to live out miserable lives.

Religious, she would tell herself that God had inspired the decisions that a woman took to—and she hated the word—abort a child.

And if compassion was the guiding spirit behind those marchers protesting the existence of abortion clinics, such as she would see on television, why were they not out protesting the destitution of the poor and hungry, who, in recent years, were everywhere? And much worse off than she had ever observed during the Depression—for those hoboes always seemed to have some inkling of hope for the future, she thought, a sense that things would get better. (In New York, while walking down Broadway to see a show in 1933, Maxwell Anderson's *Both Your Houses*, she would see gentlemen, dressed in suits and ties, selling pencils or apples on every corner, fellows who would ask the more prosperous for a line on a job. And during a stroll through Central Park's Sheep Meadow she'd seen a shantytown of makeshift crate and burlap and cardboard dwellings, and many unfortunates living there, but there were also soup kitchens in every church, in every Salvation Army storefront, and the Red Cross would set up a tent near Columbus Circle, among other locations, to look after the poor. Hooverville shantytowns were everywhere—she would see them in the countryside—but those poor, she would tell herself, did have hope.)

Look at Veronica, who ended up marrying a "hobo," now a prosperous man in Illinois, if no longer her husband.

On a recent trip to visit her sisters in New York, she had watched a man staring at a beautiful girl walking down Broadway near Seventy-eighth Street, her body quivery in tight clothes, and the man shouting, "I can't take it anymore!" And as he undid his trousers Margarita and Maria both thought he was exposing himself to masturbate an ardent erection (Maria had looked away), but the man crouched down with his underwear around his ankles and relieved himself in the middle of that crowded thoroughfare. And it seemed that she could not walk ten feet along a street without having some beggar ask her for change (she always gave). In her more pensive moments, it would occur to her that cities like New York were quite akin to the English cities of the Industrial Revolution, the sweatshop-filled, corrupt, waif-ridden London that Charles Dickens, whom she much admired, had written about. Where was the compassion for these people, bereft of any confidence about life?

Speaking of Charles Dickens, she once expressed a rare criticism of her sister Irene back in 1985, during a Christmas visit. Irene and her husband had brought three children into the world, two boys and a girl, and they in turn married and brought eight more into this life. At the time of Margarita's visit, they were all gathered in the house and greeted their Aunt Margarita with much love. And one night, after a grand meal, they sat down before the television to watch *A Christmas Carol* starring Alastair Sim. They had all cried over poor Tiny Tim's plight and been outraged over Ebenezer Scrooge's unwillingness to help, and, later, delighted when Scrooge, having experienced the visitation of three spirits, changed, becoming the most benevolent of men, they cried again. Then Irene, sniffling still, watched another program in which President Reagan had announced, for the sake of the country, further cutbacks in social programs, which Irene and her husband applauded.

"Irene," Margarita asked, "how can you be so sorrowful about Tiny Tim, in a movie, and then accept what this President is telling everyone? He is Scrooge at his worst, and yet you sit there nodding in agreement. Really, I'm surprised at you."

And Irene, who loved Margarita very much and who could not recall a single argument with her, countered: "Are you saying, sister, that the world is the same now as it was back then, and that we, the common people of this country, should pretend that we're all so rich that we can take care of everyone? Back then, at the time of the story, poor people like Tiny Tim didn't ask a penny of anyone, while now all the people who don't want to work ask for everything. It's not the same. As Mama used to say, sister, 'If you work in this country, you can have anything you want!' "

And she turned to her husband, waiting for his nod.

"Furthermore," she added, "that was just a movie. And even though I don't know very much about Charles Dickens, I bet if he were alive today he would not be going around giving his money away. He was rich, and rich people are cheap, as you know, sister, and the point of that story, which makes everybody so sad, is that it would be a much nicer world if rich people weren't so stingy, but that's no reason for people like us to have to pay. All the President said is that things have gotten to the point where charity and giving all our tax money away doesn't change a single thing. You think I wouldn't give money to help a poor little boy like Tiny Tim? I would. But do you think that I would if Tiny Tim turned out to be a fake? That's what he's saying, there are too many fake Tiny Tims running around, and it's about time we took stock of that."

"Oh, sister," Margarita said, shaking her head. "Oh, sister."

In the Library

SHE WOULD ALWAYS THINK about the children at the library, children in the thick of a new life, boys in striped turtlenecks and football sweaters, girls in neat, creaseless dresses, with their countless questions about the world, lying about on the carpeting and on cushions as she would read aloud to them.

She took this job on a volunteer basis in 1987, four days a week, her hours ten to six. It was a peaceful place, filled with the radiance of sunlight in the spring, a refuge from the cold in the winters. And there were books everywhere. When the library was empty, she would pass the time reading, her taste leaning toward history and biography, especially about women. She was particularly fond of Lytton Strachey, his *Elizabeth and Essex*, *Queen Victoria*, and *Eminent Victorians* among her favorites. But she also read with great pleasure the heartbreaking *Mary, Queen of Scots* by Antonia Fraser, and the lives of many others, Virginia Woolf, the poor thing, and Emily Dickinson, Amelia Earhart, and Madame Curie. Sometimes she would linger by the classical section, which existed because a retired professor of archaeology from one of the nearby Connecticut colleges bequeathed to the New Elm library his dog-eared editions of Martial, Seneca, and Plutarch—his many-volume *Lives of Noble Romans* taking up a shelf unto themselves—books that with their cradle-to-grave narratives always left her with the impression of having drifted through time. In the summer, locking up the library and walking on the street toward her car, Margarita experienced moments when she would look off into the brilliant sunlight and see in the elongating shadows of people in the distance the intimations of human life in a place like ancient Rome, or, for that matter, like Cuba, where her mother was born.

Tending to paperwork and returns, or sometimes reading, she looked forward to the arrival of the tots, little children left in the care of the elegant elderly lady. With her slackened and drooping neck and her heavily veined hands, she may sometimes have frightened them, or perhaps she suggested to them an ancient queen or an enchantress or a witch, though a good one, with kindly eyes, who could, with the wave of a wand, turn straw into gold, or awaken from a deep sleep of a hundred years the subject of a spell. She must have seemed beyond this world, though she wasn't, walking in some field of their imagination and biding her time among the angels and the flowers.

When they left with their mothers, she would search the shelves for books to read to them the next day: Dr. Seuss and Maurice Sendak, and *Little Nemo in Slumberland*, *The Little Prince*, *Charlotte's Web*, and *Babar*, among so many others. But her favorite was Lewis Carroll's *Alice's Adventures in Wonderland*.

That book always fascinated her, perhaps because it was one of the first stories she had ever read, or simply because it brought back her memories of those days so long ago when she was a young pupil, with an Irish father and a Cuban mother, at Miss Peterson's school in their town of Cobbleton, Pennsylvania.

There was a day Margarita would always think about. It was mid-morning in Miss Peterson's school, the fall of 1910, and she, eight years old, was up in front of the room, before the teacher's desk, nervously facing her classmates. The children were taking turns reading selections from their favorite books. Of course, the children were cruel, for as soon as Margarita, one of "those girls from up the road," said, in a halting manner, "I'm going to read from *Alice in Wonderland*," that wondrous book in her hand, some of her classmates laughed. And her face turned red and she began to feel weak in the knees and wanted to run away: but that was not Margarita Montez O'Brien.

Wanting to do her classmates one better, she'd put aside the book and started again: "I'm going to read from *Alice in Wonderland*, but I'm not going to use the book."

Having committed the first chapter, "Down the Rabbit Hole," to memory, she recited it without a pause. In her early confusion with language, she drew some laughter with her mispronunciation of certain words—mangling, for example, "curtseying," which she confused with "courteousling," or saying "thoomp! thoomp!" for "thump! thump!" and tripping over others. But as her recitation continued for what to a child was an epic length of time, ten minutes or so, she began to impress even the brattier and unkinder of her classmates. They quieted down and applauded her, along with the rest. Miss Peterson gave her a little box of gum-backed golden stars—most children received only one star—and an apple, telling her, "This is for being such an intelligent little girl." That afternoon she walked home with a row of stars stuck triumphantly on her pensive and delighted brow. She had devoured the apple.

Blessed Are the Children

ONE AFTERNOON A WEEK she tried to teach the children Spanish, if they were so inclined, and another she set aside for the young children of New Elm who spoke only Spanish, reading stories first in English and then in translation. Grateful mothers were always bringing her gifts and inviting her into their homes, "the poor old woman" always in their thoughts.

Her favorite season was Christmas. She would teach the children to cut out silhouettes for a mural, something she had learned from her mother's friend the butler García many years before, and she presided over the children's decoration of the tree with homemade or store-bought ornaments, these gatherings of boys and girls reminiscent of Christmases in the house of her youth. And it pleased her that the children of New Elm were for the most part happy, though every so often there would be a child hopelessly entangled in the problems of his home.

Of Margarita's kids, there was one boy, a runny-nosed, nervous child of seven or eight, Billy, who already possessed an air of disappointment about life. His mother would leave him in the library a few times a week, to get rid of him for the day, usually because she had gotten up too late and didn't want to put herself through the embarrassment of taking him to school. "Now, you sit there and learn something," she'd tell him. And to Margarita: "I'll pick him up before closing." Then, his mother gone, he would sit quietly in the children's room, waiting for the elderly librarian to bring him candy (she did) and to call him over by her desk, where she would read him a story or try to show him how to cut out a silhouette, the boy working aimlessly until he started to shred the paper.

The poor child; she knew that something terrible was happening to him—what, she could not say. But she did know that his mother was out of work, on welfare, and that when she came back to get him around closing time, she was often drunk.

Thinking about those days, she would recall two occasions around Christmas when the boy's mother did not return. The first time—it was late November—she had waited until seven, and then, uncertain about what to do, she called the sheriff's office, where the kid, trembling and crying, ended up spending the night on a cot. The next morning, unable to imagine how anyone could leave a child alone, she called the Social Services department of the town, asking that they look into the boy's life, but they said that with the hard economic times and cutbacks and such, they were short-staffed, and besides, the boy's mother was within her legal rights as long as there was no evidence of physical abuse. "Yes," Margarita replied. "But I can see by the way the boy carries himself, and by his sad expression, that he's not being cared for properly. Something should be done, don't you think?"

And Miss Jenkins, the Social Services representative, sympathetic but a little jaded, answered, "Yes, but what?"

On the second occasion, a week before Christmas, a heavy snow was falling over New Elm and Margarita, with the boy by her side, waited in the library again until seven, but that time, instead of taking him to the sheriff's office, and after many unanswered calls to the boy's mother, she decided to bring him home with her, ordering in some Chinese food and letting him sit in front of the television to watch an old movie, *It's a Wonderful*

Life. Then she scooted him into the shower and put fresh sheets
and warm blankets on her living-room sofabed, and later, wishing him the best in life, she bid this somber boy a good night.

She was telling herself, Blessed are the children of this world,
and slipping into a sweet 1920s you-will-live-forever sleep, when
she heard the crash of a porcelain lamp in the living room; then
the breaking of glass. When she went into the room, she found
the boy tearing to pieces one of her favorite photographs of herself
and Maria, from the 1940s. Compassion was a great rule of hers,
and so, without anger, she asked him why he pushed that lamp
off the table and why with a single swipe of his hand he had sent
many framed photographs flying to the floor. And because he
told her, "I'm afraid of the dark," she spent the next few hours
sitting in a rocking chair beside the sofabed, the boy asleep and
her own thoughts drifting.

It was around three in the morning when the police arrived,
with the boy's mother, drunk and agitated and shouting about
how some old bag had kidnapped her baby. The officers, sympathetic to Margarita, tried to calm the boy's mother down, and
in the end, after the mother had threatened to prosecute Margarita for the abduction of a minor, and the poor child had been
taken away in the sheriff's car, into the oblivion of his future—
his mother repeating, "Goddamnit, boy, don't you know I love
you!"—the deputy made it a point to tell the librarian, "Listen,
I see this kind of thing all the time. She's drunk and she'll cool
off by tomorrow, and for another, I don't think there's anyone
who would fault you for your kindness. But for your own good,
in the future I would keep my nose out of other people's business.
Now good night, Miss O'Brien, and Merry Christmas."

*

(On the other hand, she would remember another incident
involving the folding sofabed, when one of Helen's grandsons,
a boy of about seventeen, traveling to New York from his first
year in college in Massachusetts, stopped by New Elm to visit
his nice Great-aunt Margarita. He called her from a service station on the highway, asking if he could spend the night. "Of
course, my dear Edward. Of course, you can." But when he

showed up at her door, he was in the company of a girlfriend whose presence surprised her. "Is it okay if we sack out together?" he'd asked.

"Yes," she said. "But do be quiet."

Bed noises kept her alert that night, and in the morning, when she was accustomed to the happy chirping of birds and the distant hum of a bread or newspaper vehicle on the quiet streets, she had gone downstairs to the kitchen and heard distinctively sexual sounds. Standing in the hallway, she had the impression that if she walked straight down the hall another five or six feet and peered into the living room she would catch these children in some act of unbecoming behavior. But she cleared her throat and closed the kitchen door with a slam, so they would know she was there. And then, in her determination not to meddle, she took a long shower.)

*

In those days, she organized some of her mother's better poems into a kind of chapbook, finding a Hartford vanity publisher to put them together in a volume of some hundred pages, her mother's poetry appearing in the original Spanish on one page and on the next translated (as best as she could manage) by Margarita. Three hundred copies of this book, which she'd titled *Happiness Consumes Me, As If in a Song*, by Mariela Montez O'Brien, were printed, and one Christmas, late in her life, Margarita had the pleasure of opening a UPS package of these books, the ink smelling good and the tidy print making each book look like the work of a consummate professional. She had one good friend in the town of New Elm, a Puerto Rican woman named Lupe whom she'd met at the senior citizens' aerobic class in town, a sprightly and rambunctious woman in her early seventies, plump and given to wearing too-tight clothes. As she unwrapped the package and withdrew the first book, she decided to give the first copy to her friend—Margarita writing on the title page, "*From Margarita (and her mother, Mariela), with love and felicitations for my friend Lupe.*"

She mailed a copy of the book to each member of the family.

In California, Emilio received it and sat out on the patio of his house reading it carefully, his eyes darting between the Spanish, which he could still barely understand, and the translations on the opposite page. His mother's soul, it seemed to him, was filled with love: religious and mystical, and ever aware of the niceties of life. He was happy, by God, so happy that he wanted a drink, under whose influence he would better appreciate and imagine her presence, but he resisted. In the living room of his house— it was 1988 or 1989—were the thirty-eight-year-old woman (he was in his sixties then) and her little daughter who had moved in with him. A happy story: In the way that the family's history seemed to repeat itself, Emilio Montez O'Brien, former movie star, and photographer in the mold of his father, had been sitting in his shop one afternoon, waiting for clients, the way his father had so many years before in Cuba. He would leave most portraits to a staff of assistants, but when this woman walked in with her daughter, Emilio happened to be there.

"And what is your name?"

"Diana Rebolt."

"And what do you do?"

"Well, I used to be in the business. But I've got my daughter, see. It's her eighth birthday, and I thought—"

"Yes?"

"—that I would bring her in."

"And?" he said, playing with the lens.

"Here we are."

"Well, very good, very good, indeed."

Emilio took their portrait and the next day he delivered the photographs to her house, near Newport Beach. After so many years of being complacent about the opposite sex, dates here and there, he felt delighted by her.

"You seem very familiar to me," she had said to him. "Haven't I seen you somewhere before?"

"If you watch bad movies on TV, you have."

And he stayed all afternoon, telling her about his film career—his greatest performances, he said, coming in the long-forgotten Father Byrne pictures. (One night he'd noticed that his first Father Byrne film was going to be played on the nostalgia channel, and he called her. She watched him as a handsome and noble priest, and decided he was good, and at midnight she called him back, saying, "You were wonderful.")

He dated her for a year, and as he grew attached to the little girl, it was not long before Emilio, happy in his old age, asked them to move into his bungalow, and when they did, a powerful domestic bliss came over him.

*

Margarita tried to place her father's more historical photographs with universities. Certainly, they were of historic value, at the very least. In her spare time she wrote letters to many a university and college, the letters of response saying that, while the copies of the photographs were generally "most interesting," the Spanish-American War was "much tilled" territory.

No, thank you, they said, the oldest daughter of Nelson O'Brien lowering her head.

Her Prospects for Marriage

''WHY IS IT THAT you don't get married again?" her friend Lupe used to ask Margarita. "Don't forget that you're young, so what if you're ninety, you still look like a young chick. And let's face it, old age can be a terrible time for a woman to be without a man. Who knows? Maybe the fellow would be amusing, and you'd have someone to go to the movies with, do things like that. You know, Margarita, I'm not going to be around to keep you company forever. Why not think about it? I'm sure there are plenty of widowers out there who would love to be with a beautiful woman like you."

Lupe to Margarita, in 1992.

*

She was sometimes tempted to wear a short skirt, like the young girls at the local mall, or a loop-ringed zippered skirt, and once, strikingly out of fashion, she put on a pair of go-go boots and fishnet stockings, which she used mainly to disguise her varicose veins. But one look into the mirror made her feel so undignified that from that day on she decided to accept the simple elegance of her old age, wearing senior-cut dresses and flowery blouses.

*

When Luis died those many years before, she told herself that another love affair was out of the question—even if Lupe, ever exuberant, advocated a late-life love ("Look, that handsome old man is staring at you"). Besides, she had relished her own free time. Being the oldest of the fourteen sisters, she wanted to become a bon-vivant duchess of the Old World, one of those high-born ladies about whom she had read (with envy) since childhood, finding comfort and enlivening her own daily routine with the memories of her trips to Spain and Italy. At the same time, a sadness would come over her as she realized that there was not too much time left in her life.

Resigned to the steady unfolding of her days, she made one more trip, at the age of eighty-eight, which to her mind was going to be epic and revealing, a trip to Ireland, the land of her father. But by then she'd started to have trouble getting around and, despite the nimbleness of her mind, decided to depend on a tour. What she wanted was to travel over with one of her sisters, Maria perhaps, or with her brother, Emilio. She called him to suggest this, but her brother at the time was deeply in love and preoccupied with his new romance—thank God—and he turned her down. And Maria, with engagements here and there, said, "Let's wait a few months."

So she signed on with a tour, and as her plane arrived over Shannon, in the west of Ireland, descending toward the marshy flatlands, she told herself, as if approaching a sacred altar, that she would kiss the ground. But when the airplane landed, she emerged into a terminal that resembled a shopping mall, the tour guide waving a green flag: "Now stick with me, will you."

After an hour to shop in the airport stores, they were led onto a bus.

Bunratty Castle and Limerick were their first two stops, and then they made their way into the interior, past Tipperary, into the midlands. As the tour bus drove them along the countryside with its many bogs and streams and canals, pastures and farm-lands, Margarita, looking out through the window, daydreamed about her father's life many years before, the sight of a young man on the road, cap pulled low over his brow, inspiring in her a vision of her father as a young man, and she nearly cried. On their third day out, toward dusk, with heavy clouds hanging low in the sky and a storm imminent, they came to an inn, its walls musky and old, in the town of Kilbeggan, where they settled for the night. A few troubadours sang to the group before their meal, and though she hardly ate her food, a steaming plate of stew, she allowed herself the pleasure of drinking three mugs of Irish ale, which put her in a happy and relaxed state of mind. Later she retired to a room that she shared with sweet Mary Dolan, from Boston, and although the thunderclaps and heavy downpour and flashes of lightning lasted through the night, Margarita—or Meg, as her father sometimes called her—settled peacefully into her bed.

Tucked under a blanket, warm and comfortable, Margarita closed her eyes, every so often opening them, as if she would see on the wall a message from her father that would tell her just what she should be feeling on her visit to the land of his birth. She liked the Irish people, linking them to the Spaniards, for they and the Irish had raided and interbred with each other for centuries. She liked the openness of their faces, but she did not like Mary Dolan's snoring. She liked the fact that the Irish were in her blood and reflected in her blue eyes, still so clear after so many years. She waited that night, as she would on all the other nights of her trip, to feel the spirit of Ireland flow into her.

However, she'd had a sweet dream in which she saw her father. He was sitting in the corner of the room, old and tired-looking, in a derby and bow tie and stiff waistcoat, scraping a piece of wood against the mud-caked exteriors of his boot. Now and then he would look over at her and smile, his crooked teeth showing. And while she thought him part of a dream, when he whispered "Meggy" and then smiled again, that had been enough to make her get up in the middle of the night and, at eighty-eight years of age, ask, "Poppy, where have you been?"

And he told her, "Purgatory."

"Is it terrible?"

"Well," he said, "it rains fire constantly. And there are fierce animals to be wary of. They'll bite off your limbs if you're not careful. And you always have a terrible thirst. And one more thing, you can't take photographs. Yet you don't mind it at all, the way you do on earth, because you know that one day you'll be leaving for a better place."

"Then what are you doing here?"

And like a character in an old superstitious tale, he told her, "I'm here because you're dreaming about me. Your love has brought me to you."

"Poppy, I do love you, I always will."

And she blinked and, just like that, he faded away.

It had been a wishful dream, for she did not recall telling him, while he was alive, how much she loved him, during the many years of his life.

No unusual incidents after that. The storm faded by mid-morning. For eight more days, on the bus touring the rest of Ireland—down around the Ring of Kerry to Glengarriff, over the treacherous Connor Pass, and around the beautiful West Cork area and back—she continued to dream about her father. And again and again, while gazing out the bus window, her partner for the trip, Mary Dolan, sitting beside her, found herself feeling a certain emotion. For all the Irish beer mugs, all the T-shirts and sweatshirts with Celtic-lettered "Ireland" logos, for all the Blarney Stone key rings and St. Patrick's medallions that she would buy as souvenirs for the children of the family, and for all the times she had felt some satisfaction overhearing Gaelic (wondering if her father knew that language), she could not look on a simple scene—a young man passing on the road with his daughter, a woman beating a rug in her yard, a farmer shep-

herding his sheep, a country priest walking with his hound—
without thinking of her father, and his early life, Irish, the mys-
teries which separated them.

With Lupe

SOMETIMES SHE'D GET dressed up and with her friend Lupe
go off to the local college to attend lectures, readings, and the
occasional cocktail party. She made friends at these gatherings,
one of whom was a certain Professor Perkins, a retired linguist,
who could drift effortlessly from Castilian Spanish to Catalan,
French, Italian, or Latin. They'd have dinner together, from time
to time, Lupe coming along, the drift of their conversation elud-
ing her. Mainly they'd talk about the past, say about Roman
times, and how, for example, one could fly to Italy, take a train
out of Rome, toward Brindisi, and have lunch and drink Chianti
in Sulmona, where the poet Ovid had lived. And there were the
parties, much crowded with professors and intellectuals, some
unhappy and some ecstatic about their lives, that would enchant
Margarita but bore Lupe, everyone behaving cordially and some,
drunk with wine, eventually pouring their hearts and minds out.
She'd remember one conversation about Cuba, in which a certain
professor, a bohemian-looking fellow named Malcolm Ives, went
on and on about the glories of the revolution. He tended to
describe the Cubans who'd left the island as socially irrespon-
sible, cowardly, and rigidly opposed to the "noble experiment,"
as he called it. (On one of those occasions, the erudite Professor
Perkins, overhearing the conversation, joined them, observing
that a nineteenth-century slogan among the Cubans of the *in-
dependista* movement had been "*Siempre fidelísim*" or "Forever
faithful," adding that it was now "*Siempre Fidel.*")

Although Margarita had some interest in what was going on
in Cuba—because of how it had affected Isabel and Luis—she
was split in her opinions and could never really believe that the
changes over which Mr. Castro presided were for the good. She
found it nearly impossible to let go of the version of Cuba that

she constructed out of her mother's memory and the few brief
(and now) distant glimpses she had nurtured over the years, so
it came down to a simple emotion, a wish that people not be
hurt. And at those parties she would learn about the books of
Latin America—the novels of García Márquez, Manuel Puig,
Cabrera Infante, and José Lezama Lima, among many others,
that she might read.

And her good friend Lupe? She would endure those evenings
and signal their end by yawning and by patting her lips as if she
were an Indian out of the movies.

In New York, Late in Her Life

DURING HER VISITS with her sisters in New York, she sometimes caught the eye of an elderly man while strolling in a museum with Helen or shopping in Bloomingdale's (which her
mother, the humble Cuban immigrant, had liked in her later
years, when she blossomed after the death of her husband), but
she found it a little cheap to strike up an acquaintance, at her
age, with a stranger.

(That did not stop her, some evenings, from resting her body
in the tub and daydreaming about the days when a man would
possess her and she would feel a certain terror and elation.)

She'd travel to New York mainly to see the family—nothing
more complicated than that—and was always happy, after the
heavy schedule of visits and dinners and arguments and laughs
and moments of complete boredom, to get back home.

When she stayed with Helen on Park Avenue, things were
better. She'd have her own bedroom and Helen, always out to
impress her oldest sister, would treat her to operas and Broadway
shows. Afterward they would come back to her quiet and roomy
apartment, its walls covered with gilt-framed paintings from
nineteenth-century England ("Those days of the fox hunt, how
I envy the men who lived in that time," she'd once heard Helen's
husband say), the furniture thin-legged and impeccable. The
evenings would end in the quietude of the pantry, where they

would sit having coffee and Hungarian pastries, and Helen, happily entranced with her sister's companionship, would overcome her troubles.

She'd remember one night when Helen's husband was away on a business trip and she accompanied Helen into her bedroom. It was a long walk from the living room, down two hallways and through many french doors, past countless fireplaces and pleasantly arranged chintz furniture, on and on, to the great bedroom, with its many-curtained windows, which looked out on a garden fitted with timers so as to light up the evenings like the sun. They spent the night together, Margarita hugging her and feeling for the solitude of her sister and Helen desperate for the days of the past, saying, "Sister, can you remember how noisy our house used to be?"

An Even Better Love

IT WAS NOT unusual for gentlemen of retirement age to come into the New Elm library and, after browsing in the general-science or biography sections, to appear before her desk and, books in hand, sheepishly ask Margarita, "Would you care to accompany me to a movie?" Though she was often flattered, she had gotten into the habit of saying, "No, thank you." That she lived alone did not bother her. She sometimes missed her sisters' companionship, but she had come to covet the silvery light and quietness of her days as preparation for the new life to come.

But one afternoon at the age of ninety she was surprised to look up from her desk and see a tall, white-haired, blue-eyed gentleman, a rugged-looking fellow in work shirt and blue jeans, with eyes so clear and so intelligent that for a moment she felt smitten, as the magazines of her youth would call the feeling. He was a younger man, about eighty-five, with such a serenity about him that she thought he might be a retired minister. In his eyes she saw an intimation of powerful experiences—of a life long and well lived.

Blushing, she asked him, "Is there something I can get for you?" and the man said, in a deep voice, "I'm looking for a book on aviation, for my great-grandson, a boy of about eight. And a book on archaeology for myself."

"Aviation and archaeology?"

"The book on archaeology is for me; lately it's become an interest of mine."

"Well, let's see."

She got up from her desk, her hair in a bun, on her mouth a light peach-colored lipstick, a little rouge on her cheeks. In a black dress, pencil in hand, she led the gentleman into the general-interest section, finding, as he wanted, an oversized book on the history of aviation and another entitled *Famous Excavations*. As she pulled them from the shelf, she was aware that this man, like her brother, towered over her, and her heart fluttered, for she felt, or remembered, what women of her age thought of as a very distant urge.

"Now, sir, do you have a card here?"

"No, ma'am. I, uh, just took a house over on Hartford Road."

"With your family?"

"Well, no, I'm alone, but one of my kids lives here. He runs a little air-shuttle business over at the New Elm airfield."

"He's a pilot?"

"Yes, ma'am. I taught him myself."

"How interesting."

"It was." Then he added, "I flew planes for the Air Force for twenty years and then worked as a pilot for Pan Am for another twenty. I flew all around the world."

"You're a lucky man."

"I suppose I am."

And he smiled with such pearly teeth (false? his own? she could not tell) that she blushed again.

"Anyway, my name is Leslie Howard."

"Like the actor?"

"Yes, I've had to live with that coincidence most of my adult life."

And then, books in hand, and just as a group of schoolchildren came in through the door—she was to read to them that afternoon from a book that explained how, in prehistoric times, flowers had gotten their colors—he shyly lumbered out.

*

She did not see him again for two weeks, but every morning the possibility that Mr. Howard would come by the library had inspired Margarita to spend more than her usual time at her vanity table. She'd wear her string of Majorcan pearls and her big, pretty loop earrings, and she'd walk back and forth before a mirror to make sure that her dress hung properly on her body. Each time the library door opened, she would feel a rush of expectation, then disappointment. But he walked in one day to return the books, and they fell to talking. Widowed for eight years, of late he had been feeling a little more lonesome than usual.

"I was lying in bed, trying to figure it all out, ma'am. Then I realized that I was thinking about you. I wanted to go to the movies one night, and after sitting through the thing—it was a film called *Indecent Exposure*, a detective story—I asked myself why was I at that movie by myself when I could have gone with you. So, now, I figured there's another movie playing in the triplex that I want to see, and I was wondering if you would be at all interested in joining me for the seven-forty-five show. Maybe we could have some dinner before. I don't know—whatever's okay with you."

"If you wouldn't mind, I'll say yes."

*

Mr. Howard was not a bookish man, though his imagination was solidly ambitious. At his age, he was interested in seeing some of the wonders of the world, like the pyramids of Egypt. He liked books with solid facts, books about car engines, or carpentry, which he would take out. And yet he regarded Margarita's packed bookshelves with respect. "Maybe in another life," he would say, "I'll get the chance to read all this kind of stuff." He was healthy, strapping, and did not have the air of

impending death that hovered over so many of the elderly gentlemen she would encounter in the library and at the senior citizens'
club. Nor did he seem the kind of introspective fellow who would
obsessively contemplate his mortality. He'd flown bombers over
the Pacific during the Second World War, and ever gentle with
Margarita, he would hold doors open for her and never walked
too quickly for her steady but slower pace as they'd stroll through
town. He impressed her with his strength, his can-do attitude
about things. He'd come to the house if she needed something
repaired—a loose cabinet door, a light fixture in the hall—and
when the flowers started to bloom and Margarita would get out
sun hat and gardening tools, he would help her dig a flower bed.
He'd drive over to the Agway and buy her more seeds than she
would need, and bird food for her feeders—for he was aware
that the presence of robins and blue jays and flitting sparrows
brought her joy. And though he never had that much to say, he
was a good listener. That Margarita had a Cuban mother interested him. For six years, on and off, he had piloted Pan Am
flights out of New York to Havana and had spent many a layover
in that city. And he pleased her by saying, in his slightly twangy
voice—he was born in Georgia and to that day owned two soy-
bean farms—"I kind of liked the Cubans."

They'd been seeing each other for five months—but only
Lupe knew about it—when after lunch on the sun porch one
summer day in 1992, he took her by the hands and said, "I think,
Margarita, that you have the kindest eyes I have ever seen."

"That's what I thought when I saw you." And she looked
down at her hands. "But what do we do?"

"I don't know, sometimes I just think that, well, maybe—"
And then he leaned forward and gave her a long, deep kiss, and
though she had begun to tremble, she said to him, "Come along,
my love, and let's go to bed."

She had not seen a naked man for many years and she had
never seen such masculinity in any man in her entire life. Like
the rest of his body, his sex was quite long and solid—and though
it took her a long time to arouse him, for he was old and her
sagging body had seen better days, she found herself feeling the

ancient pride of a woman satisfying her man. With kisses and
caresses and the wisdom of her years, Margarita commenced to
bring about in her lover a vitality that would have put many
another man, regardless of age or romantic impulse, to shame.

*

And then on another day he asked her to marry him, and
she said yes. That same day, he'd driven her over to the New
Elm airport, where he and his son, Russell, were planning to
take up their airplane, a Beechcraft Bonanza. Margarita's sole
experience in a small craft went back some seventy years (with
that handsome aviator from another age), but she said yes to
their invitation.

They were high up in a cloudless sky, Mr. Howard at the
controls, the plane soaring over the crisscross terrain, lilting toward the sun, then serenely drifting, the patches of farm and the
highways and railroad tracks and rivers flowing down below, the
tilting edge of the world in the distance—Margarita breathless.
They had been flying for about a half hour, Mr. Howard's son
in a rear cockpit seat, when his father, looking out over the
horizon, asked Margarita, "Are you okay?" And even though her
stomach had filled with wax and feathers, she had nodded, swallowing, the same way she had many years before, when she had
gone flying with the handsome man from heaven. And then the
low-key Mr. Howard surprised her once again. "Do you want to
try flying this bird?"

"Not on your life."

"Oh, come on, it's easy."

And relinquishing the controls, he said, "Now, to keep the
craft level, you just hold the control steady. To bring the plane
down, you press the controls down ever so slightly, and to bring
it level, or to climb, you just tip it back toward yourself ever so
slightly, without too much effort. You understand, my dear. It's
a Zenny kind of thing." She nodded. And just like that, with the
simple touch of her hand, Margarita Montez O'Brien, in the
ninety-first year of her life, pulled the control toward herself, ever
so slightly, and within a few minutes the plane climbed some

five hundred feet. Mr. Howard, his hand atop hers, gently pushed, and the plane leveled off. Then for a few minutes the plane drifted through the cloudless, unturbulent sky and Margarita laughed, for late in life she seemed to be experiencing yet another moment of unexpected earthly pleasure.

Retirement

NEARLY TWO YEARS LATER, Mr. Howard was out in the yard of their house in New Elm, tinkering with a car engine, work which left him most content, especially on a nice spring day. And Margarita, following her usual routine, had prepared, with some sadness, to make her way out to the library, for it was going to be her last day as a volunteer. It was 1994 and arthritis had been giving her some trouble of late. It seemed that in a very short time, three or four months after she returned from visiting the pyramids of Egypt with her husband (a fascinating trip, but too hot—at Abu Simbel, where it was 120 degrees, she had fainted from the heat), her age had finally caught up with her. Her joints ached, and while she could still get around—with some difficulty, for she had to use a cane and take medications—and could still, on occasion, enjoy love's embrace with her husband, the tasks of the day had become, quite simply, so much more of a chore that, with regret, she had tendered her resignation at the library.

She considered herself a positive thinker and gloried in her independence, but certain events had saddened her. Professor Perkins, and Lupe, and Sarah's husband had died. And there had been news from Irene's husband that her diabetes was worse, that the poor woman who loved her sweets had taken to a wheelchair. On the other hand, down in Florida, Isabel was still going strong, her days spent mainly in her son's house in Ft. Lauderdale, punctuated by strolls along the beach and the occasional visit or phone call from her children and grandchildren. Patricia, in her spiritist's trade, was living out a happy retirement in Lilydale, making occasional consultations with beings from other worlds, and Maria and Olga and Jacqueline, who still held occasional salons, had become more inseparable than ever. They were either in their apartment together or would make careful forays into the museums, concert halls, and restaurants of the city, their apartment, like a museum itself, cluttered with photographs and scores and souvenirs from the days of their youth, those ladies now retired. Retired was what all the sisters were, living off savings and Social Security with humbleness like Gloria and her husband, and Veronica, who'd never remarried and spent her days as a church volunteer, or like Marta and Carmen, now both widowed and living together again in Anaheim. Or gloriously retired like Helen and her husband, with their occasional jaunts to London to catch the West End theater shows, having left the chaos of New York for the good yachty life of Newport, where she passed her days forever taking lessons (in French and Spanish, which she had never really learned) and attending the social season.

Even her beloved brother, Emilio, had retired, selling his business and taking a house with his woman, Diana, and her daughter, Jill, in Santa Monica, where he devoted his days to their life together. (Sometimes he'd be quite amused when one of his old movies turned up on television, pointing out to Jill, "That's me, in my youth," his own head filled with memories of Cobbleton and women, Italy and Alaska, Errol Flynn and the trappings of Hollywood, which he had escaped.) And he was happy. Margarita remembered the day, some months after she returned from Egypt, when Emilio had visited her. He and Diana and their daughter were on their way to Italy, and he thought to stop off to see her, because she was very old and he'd noticed a slight fatigue about her whenever they'd speak on the telephone. He'd just come by for a few hours in the morning, as they were to board a six-thirty flight out of Kennedy for Rome, and after lunch, he could not resist posing her in her back yard, finding her elegant and still quite beautiful.

Sometimes what made Margarita sad was the feeling that she would never see Emilio or any of her sisters again. She knew that it would be difficult for them to have another reunion, as they did, quite felicitously, at her marriage to Mr. Howard two years before.

On an autumn day, the wedding was held not in New Elm but back in Cobbleton—for Margarita, in the logic of her years, and thinking about her mother and father, wanted the ceremony to occur near their mortal remains. And besides, she felt a nostalgia for the places of her youth, and her intended had not minded at all.

The day before the wedding, she and Leslie had gone driving around, and their route took them to her family's former property. As they approached, she had been delighted to find her brother, Emilio, standing by the white picket fence with his friend from California and her daughter. She called out, "Brother!" And they had embraced. It was then that Emilio met his future brother-in-law, the two tall men shaking hands, and Margarita for the first time met the new love of her brother's life, the woman who'd given him so much happiness.

"We were on our way to the hotel," Emilio had told her—he'd rented a car in Philadelphia. "I wanted to show Diana the house where we lived."

"It's the same for me. I wanted Leslie to see it, too."

And there she stood, looking out into the yard, the trees more splendid and full than ever, the back of the field stretching into the beautiful distance, for the trees everywhere were turning. And looking around, she told Mr. Howard, "When I was a little girl, there used to be this fellow with a great beard and bent-brimmed hat who would come with his horses and wagon, a nice, religious man, a Mennonite farmer. He used to stop when I played here and say, 'Isn't it a nice day? And do you know why?' he'd ask me. 'Because it's the work of the Lord,' he'd answer." And she began to feel how life had continued ever vivid around them, God brilliant everywhere, and the many years of her life, their sweetness and their moments of unhappiness, overwhelmed her, and she lost her composure and began to cry, Mr. Howard holding her close, repeating, "Now, now, my dear."

And she said, "I was just thinking how kindly that man was

to me, for he always gave me a piece of sugar or a hard candy, and those simple sweets, melting on my tongue, made me almost unbearably happy."

"Well, there'll be more of those sweets," Mr. Howard had said.

She laughed. "I feel as giddy as a young bride."

As they were standing there, a woman had opened the door. She was wearing a simple housedress and an apron, and behind her followed three children, a toddler crawling out into the world, and two teenage boys. Walking toward them, Margarita remembered the young couple to whom she had sold the house. And there were introductions, the woman inviting Margarita and her company to walk about in the yard and come into the house for some coffee if they liked. Soon Margarita and Emilio were at the edge of the property, looking over the hills in silence.

"It was beautiful, wasn't it?" her brother had said.

*

Her sisters traveled to Cobbleton from all over. Marta and Carmen and her husband, and Veronica, in from California and Illinois, stayed with the hospitable Irene, the rest of the family commandeering the rooms of the Main Street Hotel and a nearby Holiday Inn (the one just off the big K mart on Route 27, outside of town). The evening before the wedding, the families had congregated in the Main Street Hotel dining room, tables covered with bright crystal and flowers, the wine and champagne flowing.

It had been so long since they had all been together that their initial reunion left the sisters weeping with affection, each delighted that after so many years they were all still very much alive. Seated at a long table, the fourteen sisters chatted and laughed and had exerted such a strong female influence that the utensils and glassware started to clatter and shake. (It was actually the rumble of an ore-filled many-car train passing through town, but the champagne and her imagination had induced this thought in Margarita.) Maria was seated between Olga and Jacqueline, and Isabel, in from Florida with her son, sat beside them, and then there was Helen and her husband, then Sarah and hers, while opposite sat Patricia and Veronica and the ever-plump Irene with her man. Then the righteous presence of Violeta's minister husband, and Violeta herself. Toward the end of the table, Marta and Carmen and her husband, and Gloria with Arnold. Margarita sat toward the front, her friend Lupe beside her, her future husband, Mr. Howard, opposite with his son and his wife.

At the end of the table sat Emilio, the man of the Montez O'Brien family, presiding over the toasts. As he stood up to raise a glass of wine, towering over the table in his handsomeness and elegance, he said: "To our bridegroom, Mr. Howard, and his family, and to our precious Margarita. All happiness to them forever."

The clink of glasses, much applause, and the next day a hail of rice.

*

"I'll see you later," she told her husband. "I should be back by five."

In the library that day, she sat at her desk, tending to the last of her duties. For a teenage girl who had to write a high-school term paper on a great romance of history, she had recommended Lytton Strachey's *Elizabeth and Essex.* (How vivid that Queen, in her velvet beaded gowns, had always seemed to be.) And when two other teenagers had come around looking for books on birth control and abortion, she counseled them in their choices, thinking, My God, how the world has changed! Then a woman of middle age had come by, looking for a bestseller to read, and though not all those books were to her taste, Margarita recommended the latest Tom Clancy novel, which, she said, was "quite popular with our readers." Later, after three, the children came in, and as they gathered around her, she explained how dinosaurs had once roamed the earth. Then it was very quiet, the light through the window serene.

In her desk drawer she had a copy of a publication entitled *Woman's World: The Magazine of the Middle West,* an issue dated September 1923. Her sweet husband had picked it up for her at

an antique shop, saying, "I thought you might get a kick out of
this."

Her hands trembling as she turned the pages, she had felt,
all the same, delighted by the articles and stories, which reminded
her of her youth. She read "Wayside Tales—sketches of real
people—taken from life's highways," and "The Postman's
Whistle—a messenger of sunshine and good cheer," then "A
special little poem for our very special subscribers":

> *September sunshine, warm and low,*
> *On all the hills is lying.*
> *But through the fields and pastures go*
> *The vagrant breezes, sighing.*
>
> *The butterflies flit aimlessly*
> *Above the short, green clover.*
> *The squirrel with his glancing eye*
> *Has searched the woodland over . . .*

(Oh, Mother, Margarita had thought, remembering how
Mariela would sit and write her verses, remembering also how
during their glorious trip to see the Pope they had sat in a garden
atrium and Mariela had commented on how vivid the flowers of
Rome were. Tiny sparrows would bound every now and then,
and there would come a swirl of butterflies, rising in their elation
for life. Then an old priest, more than eighty years old, had come
along, meditating, rosary beads dangling behind his back, and
he had stopped and nodded and then continued walking, and
his serenity had inspired her mother to quickly write a poem.)

There were advertisements for Buster Brown hosiery and
Montgomery Ward & Co. catalogues and for cross-stitch embroidery linen cloths.

A picture of a Happy Home—a couple and their child, comfortable and content in the parlor of their house. Then another
article, advising how a young woman of moderate means might
sew her own "dainty underthings" ". . . Hemstitch two-inch
nainsook band onto dimity, making one-inch band when finished

on nightgown, ¾ inch bands on other articles. Mitre all corners . . ." Then a cooking tip: "Before baking potatoes let them stand in hot water for at least fifteen minutes. They will bake in half the time—Mrs. C.A.F., Ind."

And there was Sadie Le Sueur's Needlework Page for Mothers, and an advertisement for Grape-Nuts cereal. Then Sunday Dinner Menus for September (an ideal meal consisting of "Fresh corn soup, chicken Croquettes, Mashed Potatoes, Mashed White Turnips, Sweet Pickled Pears, Date Muffins, Tomato Salad, Cucumber Dressing, Chocolate Walnut Pudding, Cream Sauce, Coffee").

What women were once expected to go through! she had thought, laughing.

The mayor of New Elm and the New Elm Friends of the Library had given her a plaque attesting to her fine service, and a $200 gift certificate for the local bookstore, which she had not yet used. These items she packed into her purse, and locking the library door behind her, she made her way back out into the world and home.

In Her Idle Moments

DURING MANY a future evening in the years after her retirement, she could not recall how long she had been with her second husband, or many of the events in the recent lives of her family. Now and then someone would telephone or an envelope would arrive with a note and perhaps some photographs of new great-grandnieces or nephews, life going on. She was not even sure whether her husband was in the house watching some sports event or out in the yard working, or whether he was in the house at all. She did not often leave her bed, and because of her headaches, she would have lapses of memory. She knew that she had her books, and in distant places, so gloriously alive, her family.

On these nights, she'd wait for her husband to come to bed and would sigh because she did not hear his heavy, steady footsteps on the stairs. She was never quite aware of the year—but she'd notice that she had a nurse—thank God, a Puerto Rican woman—dressed in white, who would wash her with a sponge and bring her meals and cups of water with tablets, and with whom she would speak Spanish. There were evenings when she would think that the nurse was Lupe or Isabel or Maria and the confusion over her identity would annoy her, and wanting nothing to do with such confusions, she would content herself instead with her books. She could still read, and even though certain ideas seemed overly complex to her (one night she had confused the word Ireland with "ironing" and Cuba with Cubism and, trying to fathom its exact meaning, with "cover"), she clung to that habit of reading, as if for dear life. But such confusions sometimes bothered her, so that this elegant lady called out perhaps once too often to the nurse, asking her the meaning of a word.

("Cuba, that was where your mother was born.")

She often prayed and liked to open the pages of the Spanish Bible that her mother had given her in 1925, its inscription heartening: "For the jewel of my dreams."

In the Late Hours of the Night

ON THOSE EVENINGS when she was feeling particularly well, she'd ask her nurse, whose name was Anna-Maria, to bring her the parcel of her mother's notebooks kept in a cabinet drawer in her bedroom, and the nurse, sighing, would carry them to her once again, as she often did, and the oldest of the fourteen sisters would pass the hours before she fell asleep turning the pages of those notebooks, which she would hold in her trembling hands, her pretty eyes squinting, as she read over her mother's poetry and those longer passages that always pleased her.

*

She got into the habit of reading one passage again and again, the evocation of an early and happy event from another

age, which lifted Margarita out of herself, so that in the late
hours of the night she floated back like a moth through time, a
powdery winged creature, heart filled with love, flitting through
her beloved mother's description of her journey to America many
years before.

1902

FOR THREE DAYS the young newlyweds, an Irishman and his
pregnant Cuban bride, had been on a ship out of Havana headed
for New York, the couple staying in a cramped compartment in
the second-class section, near the fiery boiler room on the lower
deck. At first, as the ship made its way northward through the
Windward Passages, the weather was fine, and although the
rocking of the choppy windswept sea had made for some discomfort, they would often pass the daylight hours on the upper
deck, in the first-class section, taking the air—as the ship's kindly
captain, a German fellow who knew of the wife's pregnancy, had
allowed them access. On that deck the men were very properly
dressed in flat black brimmed hats or bowlers, white frock coats
and striped summer suits, and stood by the railings, watching the
sea for the occasional school of dolphin and whale churning the
surface. They would check their vest pocket watches for the time,
read old newspapers, step aside politely for women, and consult
with the captain about the conditions of sea and sky. And the
ladies with parasols and rump-raising dresses seemed touched
by the sunniness and quiet demeanor of the wife, that diminutive
but pretty woman whom the Irishman always referred to as "my
Cuban beauty."

Those mornings would find the husband, Nelson O'Brien,
a handsome and sturdy young man, cordially greeting their fellow
passengers and playing the affable and hopeful Irish chum, respectfully doffing his hat and never interrupting while hearing a
piece of advice, despite the sad feelings buried deep inside his
heart.

He'd carry a ledger book around with him and keep himself

busy filling its pages with English phrases for his Cuban bride, Mariela Montez, to learn. He'd hug it close to his breast, protecting it as if it were the key to their future, for in those days he was intent on preparing his wife for their sojourn in the Pennsylvania countryside, where he owned a house and land.

Pulling out the ledger and turning to a page in which he had jotted down some phrases, Nelson would say to Mariela in English, "And how are you today?" ("Fine, thank you.") "How lovely you are!" ("Oh, thank you.") And "Are you hungry?" ("Yes, thank you.") And he would go on and on, and Mariela, Margarita's mother, would look off into the sky and, with her pensive brow creasing, stare straight into the sun, imagining angels around it.

His fellow passengers noticed this friendly young man and his pregnant wife, the "darkish one," who would join him on the deck, timid in her movements among the passengers, and while she did not say very much, quite content to look about and smile, or to lean back in her chair, eyes closed, holding him by the elbow, she seemed very much in love. Under her plain dress, her pregnant belly seemed big as the moon, and although the unsteadiness of the journey must have been hard on her, she was of a cheerful disposition. They never seemed to speak, except when he would look up a few phrases in that ledger book, pronouncing them in his Irish brogue, but she was always content, humming and singing little songs. And they noticed Nelson like a grand tutor reciting to his wife a litany of useful phrases to which she would listen like a diligent student. "From here on in, I'd like you to speak English, understand? For your own good."

She would nod, as she always did, as if she understood.

But it did not often work out that way, because very few of the Americans on board spoke much Spanish and Nelson, always a gentleman around his wife, took to translating the polite exchanges in spite of what he'd told her, speaking in Spanish and often gesturing to Mariela with his hands, his voice loud as if she were a deaf-mute. And indeed, to some of the passengers, she had behaved so, especially to the haughtier types, who tended to whisper behind fans whenever she and Nelson came up on deck together, speculating as to why this uncouth Irishman and this mute Cuban woman were traveling to New York—the comment "The trash remain with trash" from the unkinder souls.

They had gracefully endured that attitude—for Mariela, a series of disapproving glances and haughty surveillance—and when his young bride would lower her head with shame or sadness or doubt, he would pull her close. When he did so, she would feel heartened by his concern for her and would try to give him a kiss, but he would stroke the back of her head and say, "Not here, in public." And yet she would continue to press her lips against his, and even though people were watching, he would begin to kiss her with pecking and timid kisses and say in Spanish, "My darling, I will take care of you." And those simple words would restore her.

*

At night, while Nelson went to join the other men to smoke cigars in the bar, Mariela would remain below in her bunk, singing and floating on a ship in her own sea of life. Gazing out the porthole, she'd daydream about the hallways and shafts of moonlight that shimmered in the depths, and she would feel so touched and happy that she would take out of her suitcase a concert harmonica that a laundress had once given her, to play cheerful, jaunty *zarzuelas* and *contradonzones*, the music of her childhood. She'd play for hours, and the music would sometimes carry up onto the deck, and now and then a sailor or a passenger would rap on her slightly open door to pay a compliment, or, as in the case of Mr. Myers, a ruined banker, to tell her to shut up. She enjoyed the praise, but mainly played because she did not have much else to do. Dreading the inevitable confinement of that compartment and those trips down the corridor to the narrow toilet, which she tried to avoid, she played to keep her mind off the discomfort of the journey. Suffocated by the stale engine oil and tobacco-saturated air (and always the perfume of that toilet), she'd make do until her husband, Nelson, *el irlandes*, came back below to rest beside her: whatever his true nature, she thought him a good man, but even so she could only guess at what he was saying in his lilting, hope-laced English, which she did not mind listening to and was reluctantly learning, as this was a big improvement over the sternness of her father's demanding voice.

In their compartment she would play with the curls of his reddish-blond hair, fondle him under his shirt, sigh, kiss his face, and then put his hand on her belly so that he could feel the child, the man always kindly but oblivious, she felt, to the inner workings of her heart.

When they'd married in Cuba, after a year's courtship, Mariela did everything she could to further her young husband's vaguely defined ambitions. She, too, would sit around with a dictionary and for many hours they would grapple, grunt, and laugh over the most basic of messages, his brogue further confusing her ear. She rewarded him with kisses and her exuberant and fecund company in bed, and only when the pregnancy was well along did they refrain, as love had become their most common language. And while she comported herself as a demure, passive spirit, she knew what the moments of intense heat inside her body meant, and that even when she thought men useless and none too bright—just look what they had done with the world—she enjoyed his lovemaking, invited his caresses, and explored his body with the unabashed and mischievous curiosity of a child.

At evening's end, Nelson would find her waiting in their berth and always gave her a kiss. Then they'd strip down to their undergarments and pass the night holding one another, he asleep and she cherishing the life within her.

*

Holding her belly and feeling the movement of her daughter one night, she had slipped off into a dream about her father, who since childhood had loomed in her mind as a tempestuous force of nature, represented in fantasies and dreams by shadows, electric shocks, lightning, fire, and tropical storms. Thinking of him, she remembered an afternoon when she was a little girl and a storm had filled the sky and the acacia tree quivered and the rain beat down on their house and patio with such force that the ceiling began to sag and all the flowers in their garden collapsed in mangled piles of stem and blossom on the ground. She had felt enchanted by the first rain, and while the family hid inside their house, she decided to enjoy it, running out the door and turning in circles as little children do, oblivious to the terror. In those days, her father, Don Emilio, had more patience with her, and when he had stood at the doorway and ordered her to come inside, she ran from their patio into the yard, headed for the cobblestone road in front of their house, wanting to play. He had called to her through the pouring rain—his voice muted as if through a mask—but she continued to spin, willing her father, in a clean white suit, to come out after her, to show his love. He waved her inside, clapped his hands, and finally charged out into the powerful downpour, grabbing her roughly by the wrist, and with the fiercest and most unforgiving expression on his face dragged her toward the house. Once inside, his little girl now in tears, he could only speak about how the storm carries stupid children away and that she was lucky that he loved her enough to come after her, and that she should learn to be like the other good girls on the street, obedient and respectful of their fathers, which was why he slapped her hands until they were as red as plums. So now, in the logic that pervades dreams, she found herself on this uneasy morning, to her own consternation, suffering from what was called in those days "feminine weakness." The future she had planned for herself with an Irishman who would take her far away to live in a different country seemed most bleak. And with these feelings came not only the memory of the day when her father had dragged her back from the storm but the storm itself, swirling through the room and battering her with such force that the imaginary rains drenched her bed, left her cheeks sore and chilled, and rolled her over on her side. With her hands covering her belly, she was overwhelmed with fear that the rising water would swamp the room and her baby would drown.

*

That did not happen, but on the fourth morning of their journey—the sea was rough, the sky gray with clouds and thready blackness—while her husband, Nelson, was dallying by the rail waiting for her, his head filled with thoughts of the future and with contemplations of the flat and endless sea (on which this ship was nothing more than a jagged-edged shadow of smoke stacks and bow and stern), their baby, the first of the fourteen sisters, had started to kick away in her womb. He had been on the upper deck when Mariela had awakened from her sleep. That morning she climbed the stairs, the thought that she had made a mistake by linking her future with her Irish husband's weighing heavily on her. Deckside, the winds were fierce, but she had joined him, Mariela thinking about their differences. (He was dismayed by the vastness of the water, while she reveled in its possibilities. Behemoths, mermaids, and underwater kingdoms proliferated there. She was not bored. She was eager to see what the days would bring. She was neither admiring of nor frightened by the frock-coated men on the ship, though she averted her eyes when passing them. She thought that whatever awaited her was going to be satisfying.)

*

On the day of the storm he was glad to see Mariela, and their breakfast together cheered her. But while they were eating a meal of buttered biscuits and deeply sweetened coffee, the skies darkened and high white-crested waves began to break against the ship. And, with that, a purser now marched along the deck with a megaphone, urging the passengers to remain inside.

Nelson, her husband, did not drink too much in those days, but he left Mariela in the company of a kindly Englishwoman, went to the bar, and, exhilarated by the storm, joined in the barroom camaraderie, the men throwing back drinks and talking about their prospects for an unexpected adventure. He was sipping Irish whiskey when the ship abruptly listed to one side, so that glasses, utensils, and plates flew off the tables, cane chairs toppled to the floor, and many a passenger went stumbling, some falling, like drunks. He was sipping whiskey again, and feeling quite amused, when the walls, battered by the wind, gave out thumping sounds and the bells of an ornate grandfather clock began to clang as if the ship were on fire or, sailing the seas, had just reached the furious waters at the edge of the world.

While the men remained at the bar, the women huddled in the dining room. Mariela, pale and queasy with what she thought was seasickness, sighed and the Englishwoman, beside her on a couch, held her, dabbing a handkerchief on Mariela's sweaty brow. The Englishwoman could not speak Spanish, but she would ask Mariela, "Are you all right?" And the kindness in the woman's eyes compelled Mariela Montez, despite her pain, to nod.

The sky was very dark, as all life might end, but after much listing, the ship had regained its bearings. All the same, a new crisis unfolded: two sailors carried a third, dripping with water and blood, into the dining room from the deck and laid him out on a table. He was a stocky middle-aged man with a hooked nose and he was gasping with pain. A few minutes before, a powerful gust had caught him on deck and sent him flying back into an anchor cable, snapping his spine. Shortly, the ship's doctor arrived to examine him and administer injections. And it was then, just as they were carrying the poor man on a stretcher to the infirmary, that Mariela began to feel she would burst and went into labor.

Soon enough Mariela, contorted and crying (and for the next ten hours pushing, weeping, sweating, and sighing), found herself in an infirmary bed awaiting a new life, while the sailor, resting on another bed not a yard away from her, awaited death. She would remember seeing the kindly Englishwoman and the doctor standing over her, and remember that her husband, Nelson O'Brien, passed the night traipsing between the upper and lower decks and that every fifteen minutes or so he would peer into the room and ask the doctor, "How is my wife?" And that he, who was sometimes a squeamish fellow, would take hold of her right hand and say in Spanish, his breath tinged with whiskey, "I'm here."

Years later she would weep, thinking of that time—for some of the ink of her notebooks seemed washed with tears—and she'd write that at two in the morning the hum of the winds died down and that, during the tedium of her labor, she would try to reach over and touch the injured sailor's hand, which dangled off his bed. For much of the night he was unconscious, but sometimes he'd cry out in pain, his head, pock-skinned and ruddy, as round as the moon (and "tormented as a lonely star"). Sometimes he tried to speak to her or the doctor, but what he said she did not know.

Recalling the moment he died, with a gasp—a bubble seeping with saliva and blood on his lips—Mariela had written, "I would have done anything to save him."

But life went on its way. Not an hour after the doctor had covered the man with a sheet, a torment came over her. In those moments while she was sighing, heaving, vomiting as if something had to get out, a fierce and powerful being with a claim on life—a daughter, Margarita—came into the world— Margarita Montez O'Brien, who, with trembling hands, would inherit everything around her and become the oldest of fourteen sisters and a son.

*

In some other place, an elderly Irish gentleman stands before an old camera with a folding bellows-type canopy, and he tries, for the life of him, to focus exactly on his subject, extending and retracting the lens, and he becomes quite happy when, looking out over a field, he manages to focus on a springtime rose.